OBSIDIAN PUMA

BY ZOE SAADIA

OBSIDIAN PUMA

The Aztec Chronicles, Book 1

ZOE SAADIA

For more information about this book, the author and her work, visit
www.zoesaadia.com

ISBN-13: 978-1520478678

AUTHOR'S NOTE

"Obsidian Puma" is historical fiction and some of the characters and adventures in this book are imaginary, while some are historical and well documented in the accounts concerning this time period and place.

The history of that region is presented as accurately and as reliably as possible, to the best of the author's ability, and although no work of this scope can be free of error, an earnest effort was made to reflect the history and the traditional way of life of the peoples residing in those areas.

I would also like to apologize before the descendants of the mentioned nations for giving various traits and behaviors to the well known historical characters (such as Ahuitzotl, Axayacatl, Moquihuixtli, and others), sometimes putting them into fictional situations for the sake of the story. The main events of this series are well documented and could be verified by simple research.

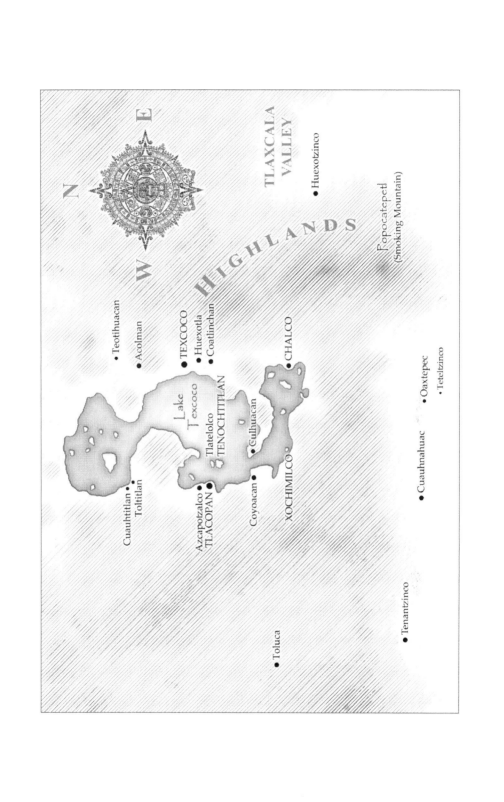

N
E
W

Teotihuacan
Acolman

TEXCOCO
Huexotla
Coatlinchan

CHALCO

HIGHLANDS

Lake Texcoco

Tlatelolco
TENOCHTITLAN

Culhuacan

Cuauhtitlan
Toltitlan

Azcapotzalco
TLACOPAN

Coyoacan

XOCHIMILCO

TLAXCALA VALLEY

Huexotzinco

Popocatepetl
(Smoking Mountain)

Cuauhnahuac

Oaxtepec

Teteltzinco

Tenantzinco

Toluca

CHAPTER 1

Tenochtitlan,
1473 AD

The ball bounced against the sloping wall, missing one of its marks by a mere fraction. Grinding his teeth, Necalli lunged toward it, throwing himself in the direction of the ricocheting rubber, knowing he had no chance. It hit the ground with a loud thud, bouncing lightly, indifferent to his team's looming defeat.

"Bring it here."

The commanding voice of Yaotzin, the veteran warrior responsible for today's training, rang with the utmost contempt. Not bothering to take the ball with his hands, as the trainer or the Master of the Game was allowed to do, the old warrior motioned curtly, indicating his wish to receive it as a throw. His unprotected-by-leather hip greeted the rubber missile readily, bouncing it off several times before using an elbow to send the ball toward the farther side of the wall, causing it to fly in an impressive arc, as though shot from a dart-thrower. It missed the mark by another fraction; still, all the boys held their breath, awed by so much expertise and skill.

"Here, on the court, the ball is your enemy," the teacher went on, not needing to gesture in order to send several students rushing to retrieve the discussed object. "You can't best it as long as you fear it, as long as you try to keep yourself from harm. No matter how hurtful the collision with it or your fellow players can be, no matter what it requires of you to prevent the ball from meeting the ground, you do whatever it takes, and much more than that. You do not think of yourself." The piercing eyes moved from face to face, penetrating, not letting their gazes escape. "If you must slide upon the dirt to insert yourself between the ball and the earth in order to prevent the forbidden contact, you do just that." This time, the fierce glare singled out Necalli, glimmering with the frostiness of the midwinter moon. "What should you have done that you didn't?"

To clear his throat or lick his lips was not an option. "I should have reacted faster, should not have taken my eyes off the ball."

The contempt in his interrogator's gaze deepened. "Did you look elsewhere?"

"No, I didn't." He needed to swallow, his throat as dry as cracks in an ancient pyramid wall, threatening to harm his ability to speak. "I should have taken into account that it might not hit the mark, should have positioned myself closer and been ready."

That came out surprisingly well. The teacher's lips, which were nothing but an invisible line until now, reappeared to enliven the stern mask. Weak with relief, Necalli watched the harsh eyes return to the rest of his fellow pupils.

"You have to treat this court as a battlefield. Your eyes should always assess and reassess the situation, the lay of the land and its current condition – is it dry, wet, bumpy, well flattened? The mood of your fellow players and your rivals as well – are they hopeful, fearful, full of enough fighting spirit, lacking in it? And all the while, you do not lose the sight of the ball and its possible next destination. You take it all into account, and you are always, always ready to change your tactics accordingly, to readjust your plans, like on the battlefield."

The flinty glare encircled his audience, half twenty pupils in all, the last class of the day. No young boys among those, and no training priests either. Only sons of nobles and a few gifted commoners who, upon reaching the age of fourteen and if having shown outstanding abilities, were chosen to attend *calmecac*, this exclusive school of the Royal Enclosure; very few of those. The rest of the city youth, a multitude of commoners and even some slaves, were sent to their local neighborhoods' *telpochcalli*-schools upon reaching their fifteen summer, learning crafts and regular warriors' skills. *Calmecac* groomed future leaders, elite warriors, and politicians – and priests.

"Back in positions!" The shout echoed between the sloping walls, sending the boys scattering. "Remember, you never fear the ball. If you fear it, you lose. No halfhearted attempt will help you to best your rubber enemy, no irresolute commitment. It can hurt you, but you are not to be concerned with any of this. Only then will you best it and make it do what you want."

Up on the tribunes normally reserved for the watching nobility when a true game was played, a few younger students – mere children but of the royal family – clung to the stone parapet, watching with unconcealed curiosity. And so did Axolin, sporting his bandaged ankle, exempted from this sort of lesson, however temporary, pleased with himself. A lucky frog-eater. When sure that the stern veteran wasn't looking at anything but the ball he was preparing to hurl flying into their midst, Necalli sent the youth a fleeting grin and an unmistakable gesture of his upper arm, the rudest motion of them all. The guffawing that washed the upper tribune was distant but unmistakable too. The royal children must have appreciated his vulgar gesturing.

"Pay attention!"

The ball was bouncing off the wall again, nowhere near his location. Still, he rushed toward it, mainly to prevent the teacher from getting angrier with him than he already was. Of all afternoons, today he didn't want to earn disciplining that would warrant his staying in school for this particular evening. Patli had promised that the temple near the wharves and the old causeway – not truly a causeway but more of a bridge leading to the neighboring island-city, a relatively short earthwork – would be well worth their attention, and as much as he distrusted that *telpochcalli* boy, the commoner from the slums of Tenochtitlan near these same wharves, maybe to be admitted to their *calmecac* because of some outstanding abilities, there was no doubt that he would kill for the opportunity to explore the underground tunnel of a strange temple, even though they didn't even know to whom it was dedicated. Or at least the commoner boy didn't tell. Still, a temple was a temple and to roam its secret passages was the opportunity of a lifetime, not to be missed.

"Necalli!"

The yell of his friend from the tribunes made him look up in time to see the ball descending like a bird of prey, aiming to reach him, out of all people. Catching his breath, Necalli disregarded the impulse to leap away from its path, clenching his teeth, preparing for the hurtful contact, tilting his body in hopes of making his upper arm meet the onslaught. Surprisingly, it worked. As painful as it was, his elbow did send the ball back into the air for Acoatl, the best player of the school, to catch it comfortably on his hip, launching it toward the nearest mark on the sloping wall. One more point for their team of five.

Unimpressed, the teacher regarded Necalli with a dour frown. His previous state of dreaming was apparently not missed, even though he did exactly as he had been told; confronted the ball when it might have been easier to avoid it. How frustrating! He ground his teeth, his arm hurting, but not like his pride did. The old school master had something against him today, damn it.

A glance up at the tribunes told him that Axolin was amusing himself with a conversation involving one of the royal offspring, a ten-summers-old brother of Tenochtitlan's Emperor, no more and no less. Even now, three summers later, the election of their new Emperor was still the talk of the city, the elevation of a young man when many eligible members of the royal family were there and available, ready to occupy the dearly coveted reed-woven throne. The old Head Adviser, the legendary Tlacaelel, wished it to be so, unwilling to take the burden of the reign himself once again, naming young Axayacatl, the grandson of the deceased Emperor Moctezuma Ilhuicamina, instead, even though everyone knew who made Tenochtitlan into what it was through the last four decades, since the fall of the Tepanec Capital; still, the doughty old man Tlacaelel kept away from the actual title, remaining to serve as the Head Adviser three emperors in a row.

Shaking his head, Necalli got rid of irrelevant musings, concentrating on the ball. No, he would not earn additional chores that would make him remain in school instead of enjoying his well-deserved free afternoon. Not today!

"But did you keep getting old Yaotzin mad, brother."

Axolin was the first to greet him at the end of the game, hopping down the sloping tribunes with the happy vigor of one who didn't have to run and sweat since the high noon, his limp unnoticeable, barely there. However, he did bother to close the distance before speaking, making sure that the back of the leaving school master was well away from hearing range, already reaching the far end of the court. Exempt from the game and more vigorous weaponry training for the time being, Axolin still didn't fancy sharp tongue-lashing or even detention for the evening; cleaning schoolrooms or bringing in firewood was not his idea of a good time.

"Are you going to huddle up here until it gets dark?"

Necalli just grunted in response. Perching on the low wall, he inspected his injuries, incensed. Everyone made mistakes, especially while running around the ball court, trying to prevent the heavy rubber from touching the ground while not allowed to use one's hands or feet. It was a difficult challenge and not such a pleasant pastime, even though there were boys who dreamed of nothing but being allowed to join the official games on some bright, lucky, benevolent day. Why they would wish to be slammed and pushed and hit all the time, either by the desired ball or by their fellow players, Necalli didn't know. The ballgame was not such a joy, besides the recognition it brought to the most famous of its players, those who represented Tenochtitlan against other city-states or just large towns, either partners in the famous Triple Alliance or the subjected provinces and their humbled but still very much alive and kicking nobility and ball players. Oh yes, the heroes of the ball court were sought after by the prettiest of women and the highest of nobility alike.

Making a face, he snorted, watching the grazed skin of his left upper arm. It bled but only a little, as did the other scratches and bruises, a mandatory thing on such afternoons. It was so much better to run around, fencing with training swords or shooting spears from *atlatls*, taking down faraway targets. If only they were allowed to shoot a real bow! Or at least to see one close up. Patli boasted that a boy from his uncle's workshop came from the lands where even little children ran around carrying their bows as though they were mere daggers. He was an uncouth villager from the far south with a spectacular name: ItzMiztli, Obsidian Puma.

"Are you going to sulk and fume until it gets dark? Old Yaotzin went hard on you, but it wasn't that bad, and he said nothing about staying in school in the afternoon."

Axolin was not about to let him be, beaming with wellbeing, his hair glittering, oiled and gathered in an intricate bun – a halfhearted imitation of the Eagle Warriors' hairdo. What an annoying piece of discarded tortilla! Necalli fought the urge to stick his elbow into his friend's temptingly unprotected ribs.

"He just pointed out what I did wrong. He wanted to make sure I understood."

The tall boy's laughter shook the sunlit enclosure. "And this is why you are sulking up here, hiding from others, glowing like a thunderstorm cloud, ready to burst?"

"Shut up!" Jumping down the cracking stones, Necalli scowled, embarrassed by the realization that even his closest friend could see through him so easily. What if the others managed to do this as well? "I didn't care for that one's reprimands. It was stupid of me to miss the ball that first time. It could be intercepted." Finding no better object than the lower slab of the stone wall, he kicked at it, making sure his sandaled foot did not connect with the crumbling plaster too forcefully. He had enough injuries as it was. "Don't you want to be invited to play in the real game when our time comes?"

"Of course." Axolin made a face. "But the way you played today, brother, you will be lucky to be invited to watch." This time, it was the tall boy's turn to snort thoughtfully. "Acoatl plays better than anyone in school. He'll be invited, mark my words."

"Acoatl sucks in all the rest. Even a pitiful training sword looks like a stupid stick when he uses it, and he can't write two glyphs together."

"But he hits the ball like no one else does."

"Who cares!"

"I'll be playing as good as Acoatl, even better." This time, it came from the boy, the royal offspring, who had apparently tagged after Axolin, feeling entitled after being graced with a conversation. Emperor's brother or not, this one was nothing but a pitiful *pilli*, a child as yet.

Necalli snorted. "We'll see about that. For now, that ball would squash you flat and make a puddle out of you if it lands upon you."

The boy's face took the color of a moonless night. He was called Ahuitzotl, Necalli remembered, such an exotic name. "Not like it almost squashed you when you were busy dreaming while they played."

A sharp *pilli*. Necalli made a face at him.

"Not bad!" As expected, Axolin felt magnanimous enough to appreciate a critique that was not directed at him. "He got you there, brother, he did!"

"Shut up." He rolled his eyes toward their royal company, knowing that annoying ten-summers-old *pilli* or not, one didn't goad imperial brothers. "Run along, cub. Join the next game and make us win. Or better yet, go straight ahead for the imperial games. You'll make our Tenochtitlan team invincible."

"You are nothing but a stupid vomit-eater, good-for-nothing drinker of excrements out of public pits!" cried out the boy before turning around and bolting toward the next low wall, leaping up it with an admirable agility, scaling it with true skill. Ahuitzotl, the Spiny Water Monster, reflected Necalli, a mystical creature from the Great Lake's waters that people feared and revered in the same breath. The way that one climbed more suited a cat-like creature. They should have called him Aocelotl, a Water Jaguar.

"Since when do you make friends with stupid children?" he demanded of Axolin, who, in the meantime, found it fitting to succumb to another fit of laughter. "They are such a nuisance, those stupid cubs, running between your feet, getting in the way. Thinking the world of themselves because they came from the Palace and were admitted to school the moment they stopped wetting themselves. Disgusting!"

"But he got you going, brother." Finally over his hearty spell of mirth, Axolin shrugged, still grinning. "I was bored, and he is a nice *pilli*, not pompous like the rest of them, and not stupid either." Another shrug. "I wish they'd let me out of the stupid bandage. It's boring to be out of everything, and my stinking ankle isn't hurting that bad."

"It stinks well enough. Or maybe it's the rest of you." Avoiding the hit of the elbow that was directed into his ribs with true zeal, he measured the lengthening shadows that were stretching across the perfectly swept ground. After the actual ball game, the court needed much attention, but their pitiful messing around it left the vast square looking almost untouched. "Patli said to meet him around that old temple near the old causeway. He said that today it'll be deserted for certain."

This made Axolin lose some of his breezy aplomb. "We can't!"

"Yes, we can." Frowning, Necalli glanced around once again, reassured by their obvious lack of company. Even their fellow *calmecac* students had scattered away, huddling in quiet corners like they did, inspecting their injuries or loitering with no particular purpose. No one was in a hurry to rush back to school, only a short walk across the court and beyond the two smaller pyramids and the temple their school was adjacent to. No one was in a hurry to return to the trap full of more chores and demands. "Old Yaotzin said nothing about punishments or additional duties, or lessons, or anything. He scampered off quite hastily himself, come to think of it."

"Still, you can't go back to school, then run all the way to the old causeway, tour an underground temple, and count on getting back in time. They won't miss our absence at the midnight rites. Fancy getting in trouble for real?"

"We may make it if we hurry. Also, if we start straight away from here." Chewing his lower lip, Necalli pondered their possibilities. "They said nothing about any more lessons, and we brought a lot of firewood in this morning, so they won't be anxious to send us out again, not this time of the day." He glanced at the sun, pleased to see it hurrying toward the western side of the distant Palace's wall, certain now. "We can do without detouring through school. They won't notice."

Axolin was scowling, his hands making a mess out of his

make-believe topknot. "They'll go down hard on us if they notice. That commoner friend of yours and his schemes! Are you sure he can be trusted?"

Smoothing his loincloth, trying to make it look presentable despite its violent brushes with the dust of the accursed court, Necalli just shrugged.

"If he isn't, then he is in for a good beating, that one. So don't worry on that score. You'll get your chance at revenge." Grimacing, he inspected his sandals, not an impressive sight with all the dust covering the wittily adorned leather. "He isn't a friend of mine. It's just that he is full of ideas, not as stupid or as uneducated as his *telpochcalli* classmates. Those *telpochcalli* boys are such stupid bores."

"Not when there are too many of them and too little of us." Chuckling, Axolin followed, falling into Necalli's stride easily, as always the best of company. It was difficult to imagine that they hadn't met until two summers ago, admitted to the prestigious Royal Enclosure's school at the customary age of twelve, the children of minor nobility, as opposed to the *pilli*s of the royal family. He shook his head, remembering that scampering-away Ahuitzotl.

"Stupid frog-eaters; that's the only way they can get anywhere against us." His snort shook the air, full of confidence and scorn, and it pleased him, the sound of it. They were nothing, those commoner schools' boys, trained to fight sometimes, yes, but only as regular warriors, replaceable, lacking in true valor or skill. "But Patli is not after fights. If he gets admitted to our *calmecac*, he'll be trained as a priest, that one. And, I don't know, he knows his way around some places."

CHAPTER 2

There was no point in trying to wipe the sweat off his face, even if his hands had been free to do that. Which they weren't. Clutching the accursed straw, its edge sticking out of the clay brazier, crowned with a typical clay tip and its other unadorned edge keeping his mouth busy, Miztli paid as little heed to the scorching heat as he could, accustomed to its assaulting attention by now. It washed over his face and his body in a powerful surge, incessant but familiar, a part of his daily routine.

With the crack of every dawn, he would be here, in this smallish room stocked with braziers, making several fires and then maintaining them all day long, blowing into each clay bucket to make its inside heat go up to impossible heights, enough to melt the precious mix of copper and gold, or sometimes other substances, to turn into a beautifully dangerous flow of glowing colors and shapes. Old Tlaquitoc, the renowned metalworker and the owner of the workshop, would deign to peek in every now and then, hurrying away when he wasn't needed in this hot, airless, smothering space, to wield his annealing hammer or jangle the rest of his intricate tools, leaving his apprentice to bathe in the lake of sweat.

Like *temazcalli*, the blissful steam baths, reflected Miztli gloomily, but without their comfortable benches and bundled twigs to rub the sweat off one's body, to relax and enjoy the wonderful sensation of floating and at peace. Quite to the contrary. Posing next to the burning brazier he was responsible for, armed with an assortment of reed straws with their special clay tips, he needed his entire concentration unless he wished to be burned badly. His predecessor, the boy who had served in this workshop before, still invaded his employer's conversations, mainly when safety matters were discussed, usually when Miztli did something glaringly careless or stupid.

There was no room for mistakes in this trade, his benefactor would repeat over and over. With the sort of the fire they maintained and the sort of the metallic liquid they dealt with, one single mistake could cost a person his life or, at least, his ability to live properly. Still, there were times when he didn't care one way or another, not heedful of the warning of his employer, or rather, slaver. There was a limit to a person's ability to crouch next to the blazing braziers, blowing to make them rage fiercer. One couldn't do it all day long for many days in a row.

The other workers, both sons of the owner and one disinterested nephew named Patli, did other things, hammered and scraped to refine the half-ready products, worked with blades and ceramic ladles on the less delicate ornaments, rushed around with bee-wax and pottery, *learned the trade*. While all he, Miztli, did was to slave in the melting room, tending the fire and not letting it go down in the insanely high heat, allowed to pour melted goods into various clay and stone utensils sometimes, starting his day earlier than anyone and finishing way after the others were well away at the main house or wherever, loitering and having a good time. He wasn't a son or a nephew or any other sort of a family member, but his father wanted him to learn how to work the precious metals and not only how to extract those from the earth, and so here he was, living in misery for more than three moons, blowing into the fire to make it rage fiercer. Some learning!

Grimly, he blinked the sweat away from his eyelids, watching the greenish powder that he was made to scrape from a solid piece of copper earlier in the day, in the blissful coolness of the outer room. There was another pile of powdered stone poured to mix in the pot this time, not gold but a duller-looking mineral. It created better results, a stronger metal that was easier to work with, sturdier but more flexible at the same time. Like magic. It was a beautiful sight, those simmering liquids of various colors, a pretty show to watch. In the beginning, it thrilled him to no end, the ability to turn something solid into a workable flow to be shaped to one's desire; any form, any size, a jewel or a brick, or just an impossibly thin sheet of metallic wonder to create detailed reliefs for noble establishments upon their request. These days, it bored him to death.

The outer screen screeched, announcing newcomers, quite a few of them, judging by the voices and the draft that managed to sneak in through the cracks in the inner screen. Miztli ground his teeth and let his fingers crush the straw he worked with. To throw the remnants of his tool into the raging fire made him feel better. In less than a heartbeat, it was consumed, ceasing to exist – one moment there, the other gone.

Twisting his lips contemptuously, he reached for another pipe, a whole pile of those, reed straws being as plentiful as the mud upon the shores of the Great Lake, but old Tlaquitoc would grimace all the same, scolding his apprentice for carelessness and lack of concentration. If only there was a way to feed this entire establishment to the fire.

The draft made his work momentarily easier, igniting the flames in both braziers, as the screen shielding the entrance to his backroom moved, letting a thin surge of the fresher air in.

"*Niltze!*" Instead of the squat, wide-shouldered figure of his stocky employer, the lithe form of Chantli slipped in, thousand-folds more welcome. "Still working on that copper from the morning pile?"

Pleased to notice her moving into the corner of his eye, Miztli smiled with the free side of his mouth, nodding ever so slightly. When busy with such fiercely raging flames, one could take his attention off of it up to a very small limit.

"Father left for the baths just now." Curious as always, she came as close as the blistering heat allowed her, peeking into the sizzling pot from a relatively safe distance. "Just copper powder this time?"

He nodded again, then, unable to fight the temptation, took the pipe out of his mouth, backing away and into a safer zone before turning to face her. Such a refreshing sight, all pliancy and grace, with her smile always beaming, coming straight from her nicely tilted eyes, never away from them; a glaring change from the rest of this household.

"Father said you are to finish with this brazier, pour it all into those things," she waved at a load of smallish ceramic vessels, "then not to melt any more powder or whatever is in there for you to melt." Her smile widened and turned mischievous. "After the baths, he is heading for the Central Plaza and maybe even the Royal Enclosure itself. They sent a servant to summon him there. Maybe he'll be allowed into the Palace. How about that?"

He didn't care one way or another. "He wants me to put the fires off for good?"

The vigorous nod made her braids jump delightfully high. "He told me to tell you this."

He wanted to jump as high as her braids did. "Are you sure?"

"Oh yes." Her laughter trilled in the smoldering air. "It'll be nice to have a whole afternoon without baking in this room, eh? Maybe you can sneak into the house and try to charm Mother into treating you with some fresh tamales. You never make it in time for the evening meals to enjoy them warm and fresh." Her face shone at him, its excitement unconcealed. "And if you want to know, I'm now to run to the house and make Mother let me dress as prettily as I can, in the best of my clothes. Want to know why?"

He didn't care much about that either. "Why?"

She hesitated, poised on one foot, the other in the air, vacillating, ready to run away and into the pleasant coolness of the outside. "I'm to accompany Father. He wishes to take me along."

"Into the Palace?"

"Oh yes!" Another sway of her braids, and she was gone, bestowing on him one more of her glorious beams. He listened to the voices from the outside rooms, praying that no one else would come in to ruin her good news with new chores and demands. Old Tlaquitoc's sons could do that, easily too, the annoying pieces of rotten meat that they were.

"Aren't you done yet?"

Just as the glowing of the brazier's embers was back, achieved by much puffing that left him dizzy from the effort, the lanky form of Patli, the coming-and-going nephew, blocked the opening in the screen that Chantli forgot to shut.

Hovering in the doorway, clearly unwilling to step into the savage heat, the skinny youth squinted like he always did. There was no need to stop one's activities in order to confirm that assumption. Attending the local *telpochcalli* school, the spoiled brat had it unfairly easy, exempted from most of the workshop duties, already noticed by his teachers for his brilliant memory, his writing and reading abilities that they didn't bother to teach in the commoners' school – Patli couldn't stop complaining about that, himself prone to poring over long, folded bark sheets deep into the nights – he kept safely away from the melting braziers, further than even both the owner's grownup sons liked or appreciated. A lucky frog-eater.

This time, Miztli didn't bother to take the straw out of his mouth, making his point at being busy, greatly preoccupied. He might have been new to this trade and in a position not much better than a recently bought slave – not a relative to enjoy privileged life like some nephews did – still, he owed his obedience to the owner of the workshop and his sons. There was a limit to his patience with anyone fancying giving him orders. The spoiled lanky schoolboy was not the one feeding him or letting him sleep in the workshop in order not to do it out there in the streets.

"Old Tequitoc just went out and away, all the way to the Central Plaza, agog with excitement," related the youth. "The priests of Quetzalcoatl's main temple sent for him, no more and no less. Which means an easy evening for you, village boy. After this one, you can put your braziers off, they say."

Surprised with so much chattiness from the youth who barely noticed his very existence before, Miztli sneaked a reluctant glance, unwilling to let this one know that the news was no news to him.

"On whose say-so?" he grunted, moving the straw to the side of his mouth.

The unwelcome visitor shrugged, non-committal, yet he could

feel the squinting eyes studying him openly, narrowing either against the fumes or from concentration. Grunting inside, Miztli returned his attention to the contents of the blistering pot. It glittered dully, grayish in coloring, not prettily greenish like the pieces he was made to grind into the easy-to-melt dust. Liquefied, yes, but not perfectly smooth, not yet, with harder congregations still there, floating near the container's bottom. Thanks all the great deities it wasn't one of the larger ceramic pots, or he would have to stay here until dusk, additional chores or not.

"How old are you?" His unasked-for company was still there, watching but offering no help.

"Fourteen summers," he muttered, holding his breath against the sizzling wave while leaning to examine the contents of the pot as closely as he dared. The blazing wave was vicious, warning him to keep away.

"Just pour it into the molds and be done with this mess." From his safe observation point, the spoiled *telpochcalli* brat could offer plenty of advice. Miztli swallowed various rude responses that were hovering on the tip of his tongue. This Patli was not as important or as well developed as both grim, dangerously muscled sons of the owner; still, he was older than he and part of this family.

"It needs to be melted completely," he said in the end, picking up the pipe, resigned to the necessity of basking in the inhuman heat for some more.

Offering nothing vocal in the way of response, Patli leaned against the plaster of the doorway, grimacing with a measure of impatience. As though it was his copper goods he was waiting for, an eager customer, reflected Miztli, hard put not to snort despite his mouth being occupied by the annoying straw yet again.

For some time, the silence held. Above the cracking of the angry fire, they could hear the voices from the main room of quite a few people talking. The owner was back, distributing instructions, brimming with excitement about the temple orders. Nobility, most surely; with plenty of demands and enough cocoa beans to make them all slave deep into the nights, the village apprentice more than anyone, of course. Oh, but why was Father so determined, so set on sending him to this huge, unfriendly capital, to learn something he could have learned back at home? Admittedly, the people of their village did not make intricate jewelry and ornamented sheets of various metals. Yet they were the ones to extract the precious greenish pieces of various shapes and sizes out of the secretive Tonantzin, Our Mother Earth, for the city artisans to melt and fashion into beautiful things. There were plenty of mines all around his village, plenty of beautiful stones and precious metals to extract.

"Where are you from?" The question hung in the air, echoing his thoughts.

Bending to examine the contents of the blistering pot once again – but for the prospect of an early release, he wouldn't have bothered to put his face into the hurtful fumes until more certain about the outcome of the prospective examination – he found no excuses to ignore the question with no pipes occupying his mouth.

"Teteltzinco, near Oaxtepec."

The searing extract was turning satisfactorily fluid. Miztli glanced at the doorway, half hoping that the owner would come in to check on the activities. He wasn't always allowed to attempt the more intricate parts of the trade, like pouring the precious liquid into its molded casts, even if those were nothing but regular bars for later reheating or reuse. However, if old Tlaquitoc was as busy with his impending trip to the Palace or a temple as Chantli or the lazing-around nephew maintained…

He forced his eyes back to the glimmering pot, wishing that the curiosity-consumed *telpochcalli* boy would scatter away, turn around and leave, disappear into the thin air for all he cared. But what if he didn't manage to lift the heavy pot neatly enough, to handle it properly, or, gods forbid, what if he made it fall, spilling the precious liquid? The pincers felt cumbersome in his hands, not comfortable or handy. He tried to make it look like easy work, clutching the unvarnished handles for dear life, their coated edges made to fasten around the base of the pot, locking it in its firm grip.

To his endless relief, he managed to lift the heavy container after only a second try, ridiculously pleased with himself. Hands trembling with the effort, he struggled to keep his cargo well balanced, knowing that had he dropped it, the melted copper would be all over the floor, ruining it, and his future along the way.

The simple-looking ceramic molds Chantli had brought arranged close by in neat rows, he still felt as though forced to walk an entire length of Tenochtitlan's causeway to reach it. Then another eternity, to bend his cargo carefully, pouring the glowing flow into one shallow pot after another, all those familiar forms. When not forced to sweat here, he was made to slave long evenings shaping those breakable forms out of raw clay, by tens and sometimes by hundreds, creating popularly shaped circles for rings and earrings, only to break their molds one by one after the precious metallic jewelry it helped to create cooled and needed to be liberated. The copper-gold mixed adornments were the last call of Tenochtitlan's fashion, or so the local metalworkers claimed, frantic to expand their workshops in order to stand the growing demands. This was how he, Miztli, came to be accepted here, curse those Great Capital's nobles' fondness of shiny jewelry into the lowest level of the Underworld, and then somewhere lower.

"Have you been to brawls?" The loitering nephew was still there, watching with glaring lack of appreciation.

"What?" Dumping the empty container back on top of the glowing brazier, Miztli struggled to catch his breath, the radiant vividness and the sizzling heat still there, warning to keep away. It took the brazier long to cool down into a possibility of cleaning it.

"Where you come from, have you been involved in fights and such things?"

He blinked the sweat away, accustomed to its accumulating in his eyebrows but still annoyed. "Why do you ask that?"

The dawdling youth made a face. "I'm just curious." Then the angular shoulders lifted in a shrug. "If you say you are not scared easily and can fight if need be, I'll take you along."

"Where to?" Catching his breath at long last, Miztli wiped his brow, fighting the urge to lean against something and wait for his strength to return to him. His arms felt wobbly, unpleasantly weightless, their trembling noticeable, or so he feared.

"Go and talk to Acatlo or his younger brother Ome, if they are still around. Ask them to let you go away for a little while. There is no reason why they wouldn't agree. Those things don't need you to help them into cooling down, do they? They can do it all by themselves."

"Why don't you ask Acatlo yourself?"

He didn't relish the prospect of approaching either of the grim, dangerously high-tempered sons of the owner. So far, both hadn't deigned to notice his very existence unless the need to perform one of the many unpleasant tasks of the trade presented itself, thousands of small errands. Old Tlaquitoc was stern and not very approachable, keeping his distance while using his apprentice as a cheaply bought slave; still, he wasn't as harsh and unfriendly as his sons were, above using physical violence, not even an occasional slap. Something that his oldest offspring Acatlo felt was necessary, at least when his demands were not met or understood promptly.

"Me? What does any of it have to do with me? I can go wherever I want to as of now. You are the one who will stay to bake here in all this heat, buried between the braziers, unless permitted to go out."

Grinding his teeth, Miztli admitted the truth of this statement. He was the prisoner here, not the smug *telpochcalli* boy. "You wanted me to come somewhere," he muttered, not sounding too convincing. "It was your idea."

"Yes, but I don't need you to come. I just suggested it." The youth made a face, relating it all in one single grimace. "And I'm not yet sure that I will let you join me at all. I've yet to see if your company is worth it. You are just a boy. I thought you were older."

"I'm old enough!" cried out Miztli, offended. This one was barely one summer older, and just who did he think he was to lord it over him like that? If forced to fight, he would take this one easily, the skinny forest mouse that he was. "I can fight and I was in brawls, and I can take *telpochcalli* boys if they fight fair, one on one and not all of them together." The memory of his single experience of roaming Tenochtitlan's streets all alone wasn't uplifting. Apparently, there were some neighborhoods near the wharves and behind the marketplace one was wise to avoid altogether.

The squinting eyes were measuring him again. "Then come," said the youth finally, seemingly impressed but not enough to treat him with more respect than curtly tossed orders. But he had had enough of those since arriving in the magnificent island capital! "We'll find Acatlo or Ome on our way and I'll ask them for you, maybe." The thin lips were twisting in an annoyingly overbearing manner again. "But you will owe me for this, a big favor too. Here," a square cloth flew at him, thrown with barely enough force to reach him in order to catch it comfortably, "wipe your face and hands and come. We haven't much time and you do look no better than a slave from one of the villages. The *calmecac* boys will run away in disgust."

What *calmecac* boys? he wondered, concentrating on something that had nothing to do with the helplessness of his anger. The stupid nephew was not his master or superior and it would be a pleasure to give him a black eye at the very least. However, if he did this, he would be in trouble, and the prospect of touring that huge capital as opposed to being stuck in the airless backroom, either slaving or kicking his heels, was alluring to say the least. To run these unknown alleys, accompanied by a boy who knew his way around; oh, but for this, he could put up with some patronizing. Well, at least for the duration of this one tempting afternoon.

CHAPTER 3

Chantli was hard put not to stare. The splendor of the temple was like nothing she had seen before, not even close. Those towering walls, a celebration of colors and ornaments upon the smoothest of plasters, the whole wall as slick as a brick of shiny copper sheet from Father's workshop after he had hammered it and heated it and then hammered it again for many rounds and tries. The temples in their part of the city weren't shabby or unworthy, not in her private opinion; still, those looked like cane-and-reed houses of the lowest of commoners compared to this wonder.

"The ornaments will be required in great quantity," the man in a dark garment was saying, strolling ahead of Father and the rest of their party, ten men in all, minor priests and a few others, the temple's servants or officials, was Chantli's wild guess. "Our house of worship and the adjacent facilities will require the entire amount by the time of the Mountains Celebration. However, it should be delivered at least a market interval earlier." The proud head turned abruptly, presenting Chantli with its eagle-like profile and the rich mane of elaborately knotted hair.

Shivering, she moved away, huddling next to the magnificent statue of the Beautiful Serpent, Quetzalcoatl, sometimes called Feathered Serpent as well, even though those were no stone feathers adorning his sleek grandiose body but ears of maize – feather-like looking, indeed – as appropriate for the deity responsible for something as important as creation of life in this current World of the Fifth Sun. It felt safer to be shielded by such a benevolent deity. Quetzalcoatl was a merciful god, even though it wasn't his temple they had let into this time.

"My workshop can guarantee timely delivery of these goods, oh Honorable Teohuatzin. In the exact amount you demand and more than this, if you wish it to be so." Her father stumbled over his words, his speech pouring out eagerly, almost frantically, in an atypical manner for a person who always talked with deliberate slowness, even when in the middle of his rare spells of rage. Oh, but did he sound eager and overwhelmed! Chantli held her breath, slightly disappointed. Father was a respectable citizen and their neighborhood was no shabby slum. A member of Tenochtitlan's artisan guild, he held a prestigious enough position among his neighbors and peers, other metal, wood, feather, and stone workers, all those well-off craftsmen who could afford to run a workshop of their own; his ways always somber, dignified, putting him slightly above his chattering, shrilling peers. She always thought that he was too good for his surroundings. Well, now it felt the other way around, and it was a disquieting feeling.

The man in the dark cloak pursed his lips in too obvious a fashion, his bushy eyebrows climbing slightly, not aiming to reach the pulled-away hairline. "My assistants will prepare list of items. Make your promises after you look at it, tradesman." The last word came outright contemptuous, not pronounced or stressed, but there. Was there something wrong with being a trader, a whole class above craftsmen and artisans?

The servants, clearly minor priestly officials who came to Father's workshop to summon them here, drifted closer, probably wishing to hear without being too obvious about it. Chantli breathed with relief and stayed where she was, huddling yet closer to the mighty deity's statue. It was so beautiful and somehow reassuring, as high as two men who would have to stand on the shoulders of one another, and so wonderfully detailed, the ornaments upon the thick serpent's body beckoning with their glossiness, inviting to touch. Shyly, she did just that, enjoying the smoothness of the stone and the light bulges of the glittering metal beneath her fingers, such a familiar sensation, a good one.

"You can't touch Revered Quetzalcoatl just like that!"

The words made her flinch, her heart pounding in a wild

tempo. Spoken in a high childish voice, they still caused her to leap away quite a few steps. Blinking, she stared at the boy, taking in the way he stood, straight-backed and preachy, younger than she, obviously, but very sure of himself, at home in this place. His eyes were large and nicely spaced in the broadness of his face, their challenging defiance fitting. It was as though he dared her to argue with him, to tell him to be off, ready to fight for his right to be here and say what he said. For some reason, it reassured her.

"Who are you to tell me that?" she demanded, making sure her voice did not rise above loud whispering. The people who had brought them here might be back, dragging her off the precious statue, backing the little brat on his claims.

His chin rose yet higher, even though it was anything but lowered before. "And who are you to sneak into the temple of our *calmecac*? You sneaked here, you did!" he called out, triumphant, then hurried to lower his voice as well, shooting a furtive glance around. Was he guilty of the same transgression he accused her of? she wondered.

"I didn't sneak here," she stated with as much dignity as she could muster. "My father was invited to meet the important priest and he brought me along, because this is what he wanted to do."

It came out well, with enough nerve and aplomb. She tossed her head as high as he did, a stupid boy of barely her youngest brother's age, although wearing a prettily decorated cloak and sandals adorned with glittering stones. Why would his parents bother to clothe him in all this splendor?

His eyes measured her with an unconcealed curiosity, his forehead furrowing with what looked like thousand creases. "He brought you here because he wants them to accept you in our school's temple," he announced in the end, solemn and matter-of-fact now, his lips pursed importantly.

"Accept me to do what?" she asked, puzzled. The voices were drawing away, even those belonging to her escorts. Father and his important converser were heading toward the plastered columns of the other side, she surmised, a quick glance confirming her assumption. To draw the list of the mentioned items?

"To serve your time in the temple, you silly." The boy made a face, looking funny in his half amused irritation. "All girls do that." Another contemplative grimace. "How old are you?"

"Fourteen," she said. "I have seen fourteen summers and some moons. More than you, surely!" It was too tempting to put him in his place. He was so sure of himself, that snotty temple boy.

As expected, he reared like a turkey surprised into confrontation, all feathers and aggression and rage. There were plenty such birds roaming near the wharves, grown there for the nobility to have their meals fresh and tasty. The rest of Tenochtitlan did with an occasionally imported meat hunted in the mainland, but mainly with the foodstuff fished near the shores of the Great Lake.

"I have seen enough summers," he cried out, finding his tongue at long last. "I've been to *calmecac* for many, many moons. More than you can count!"

Good for you, she thought, pleased with herself, but a glance at the backs of her previous escorts made her worried. They slowed their step and seemed to be vacillating, undecided as to their next move. Of Father and the important priest, there was no sight.

"They are coming back," she observed without thinking, suddenly worried. Would they scold her for picking arguments with local boys or for touching the statue, for that matter? The little turkey could tell on her, couldn't he?

To her surprise, he reacted by grabbing her arm. "Here!" His pull was strong, surprisingly forceful, not violent but convincing in its earnestness, signaling the urgency of his sudden decision.

Startled a little, she complied, diving behind the statue, catching sight of a small opening hiding behind it, dusty but not frightening or unfriendly. The corridor it presented reminded her of certain marketplace allies, walled areas between warehouses that she wasn't allowed to sneak along, the places she wouldn't have discovered but for Patli and his unquenched thirst for everything unknown and new. Not a native of Tenochtitlan, he had come to live with them upon the death of his family somewhere out there beyond the northern shores of the Great Lake, in the town called Coacalco, where reportedly Toltec people still lived, not far away from Teotihuacan, the City of Gods. Did it make Patli into a noble Toltec? Was that why Father insisted on treating him as a special family member and not just a nephew he barely knew before? Patli certainly wasn't forced to work as hard in the workshop, neither as both her older half-brothers, nor as the new apprentice, that nice village boy with the impressive name ItzMiztli, Obsidian Puma, from the opposite, southern side of the Great Lake. Out of the two, she liked the southern boy better, uncouth villager or not. If it were up to her, she would have sent him to school and let him have plenty of free time. But Patli was not that bad either.

"It'll bring us back to *calmecac*," whispered her companion, leading their way in the narrowing passage. "Straight away into the room with weapons and shields."

That made her stop her progress, abruptly at that. "I can't enter *calmecac*!"

"Oh." Halting his step in his turn, he pondered her words, comically undecided. "There is another opening out here. It leads outside, beneath the temple's staircase."

"I can't go outside just like that too," she insisted, feeling silly about this entire argument. "I have to go back in. They'll be looking for me." Still hesitating, she peered at him through the semidarkness. "You sneaked out of school, didn't you?"

He shrugged, not looking worried.

"Why did you do that?"

Another lift of his shoulders came as no surprise. "I do that all the time," he said, as though that explained it all, clearly pleased with himself.

"Why do you have to creep around like that? Can't you just go out? My brothers came home to eat meals every evening when they were at school."

"Every evening?" The face he made was predictable by now. "Why would they?"

"I don't know," she said, shrugging. "Maybe the food at home is better."

"They have tasty food in *calmecac*," he stated, raising his eyebrows high, again annoyingly smug, making her wish to put him back in his place. "The boys from the city have to prepare their meals, of course, so maybe it isn't that tasty. But they do have slaves to cook for us, and it tastes good. Just like in the Palace."

"Like in the Palace?" She didn't try to hold her laughter in, the derisiveness of it. "As though you would know what they eat in the Palace." As he began puffing up again, glowing with indignation, she laughed yet harder. "Also, my brothers' school was not far away from home. It's just behind the second marketplace main alley, near the square with the pool. They didn't have to go far to reach those meals. Maybe if they were here in your *calmecac*, they would have thought twice before setting out to run all over the city for the taste of my mother's tortillas and porridge."

This time, his eyes turned round with astonishment. "They weren't in *calmecac*? They were in the *commoners'* school?" Even his voice peaked, squeaking with pure shock.

"So what..." she began, but the voices coming from the shimmering rectangle they had left behind cut her short. The silhouettes of the people seemed to hover there, clearly visible but not moving, not stepping into the corridor.

"Has the Revered One gone to the Palace already?" someone inquired in a calm, measured voice.

"Oh yes, it's been some time since he left." Another man spoke more hurriedly, in a rush. "But Tecpan Teohuatzin is still here, talking to that commoner, the craftsman. Out there, behind the altar, in one of the inner rooms."

"What craftsman?" asked the first man, sounding interested now. "The stone-worker? The weapon-maker?"

"You wish!" said a new voice, trembling with a measure of mirth. "He brought here that metal worker, the one who does copper sheets. They say this one can keep up with big orders and his guild vouched for him."

"Copper-worker? Do we have such things in the city?"

"Apparently."

"What do they have in mind? Redecoration of the temple?"

"Maybe."

The boy's hands were tugging at her arm again, pulling it

firmly, with great resolve. He was a forceful beast, that one, with too much willpower. Hesitating, but only a little, as their silhouettes were blocking the light entirely now, not moving in their direction but as though about to do that, she let him lead her on, toward the opposite source of light.

"They would do better ordering goods together with the Palace." Oh yes, that voice definitely began moving along the corridor. Freeing her arm from her companion's grip, she hastened her step, anxious to keep up now. How embarrassing it would be to get caught eavesdropping on the priests of the important temple near the Royal Enclosure. Oh mighty deities!

"The Palace doesn't order ornaments or jewelry these days. With our warlike ruler, they keep mostly the weapon-makers busy. And when not those, then the stone-workers and other crafting commoners. Those neighborhoods by the wharves are exploding with workshops these days, overflowing with activity and stench, full of boorish villagers running around, as though belonging in Tenochtitlan's slums."

"Commoners!" echoed another voice, not sounding caring but probably just being polite. "But we do need all this weaponry. Especially now, with even our closest of neighbors across Tlatelolco causeway looking as though they are entertaining silly ideas."

"Tlatelolco will not make trouble," stated the agitated man firmly. "They will go on sending warriors to participate in our campaigns. There is nothing unreasonable in our Emperor's demands, the whining of his spoiled royal sister notwithstanding. She is just seeking attention, that one."

"Our Emperor is young and impatient. He doesn't phrase his requests wisely, and he does take his sister's complaints to heart. Not to mention his mother, who still holds enough influence over her wild brood of sons."

"Here," breathed the boy, diving into yet another dark opening, allaying Chantli's growing concern.

"Yes, the Emperor wasn't wise to demand explanations from the ruler of an independent city-state like Tlatelolco, neighboring island or not. It's not his business how Moquihuixtli treats his wives and in what order he visits them. Not now that his expedition in the west faltered..." The voices were drawing away, muffled, resonating against the plastered walls.

"Those expeditions didn't falter. They just didn't bring the expected results."

The breeze of the outside was a blessing, bursting upon them in the most welcome of manners. She blinked against the strong afternoon light that slid under the huge polished staircase as though unrestrained. The boy was scowling by her side, studying the ground around their feet, very put out.

"What's wrong? Can't you go back to your *calmecac* from some other entrance?"

"Yes, I can," he said, glancing at her from under his brow, puzzled.

"Then why are you making faces?"

"I'm not!" The argumentative beast was back, not missed in the least.

"Yes, you are." She grinned at him, actually liking the fierce little thing a great deal. Not like her younger brother, a boy of exactly the same age, but more like that apprentice from Father's workshop, the village boy, even though this one was not in the position to offer arguments. "And anyway, you said I can go back into the temple from here. Do you know of a better way? Another corridor, maybe? I don't want to mount this staircase, not in front of everyone." He seemed as though set on arguing, no matter what the subject, so she replaced her grin with a halfhearted scowl, still in the best of moods, like always when outside. "You were the one to drag me out here, remember?"

He pondered it for another heartbeat. "There are no other side entrances, but you can go in where we came from. When the priests leave."

"Will they do that soon?" She remembered ascending the previous larger and rounder temple's stairs, awed beyond reason. Yet somehow, with this boy by her side, the sensation of amazement and fright retreated, giving way to curiosity – thanks to this one, oh yes, but she wasn't about to let him know that – still, the glances of occasional passersby made her uneasy, singling her out, and not in a good way. They were so well dressed, these people, all clad in colorful cotton and glittering jewelry, their sandals a celebration of luster and spark, like her companion's merrily glittering shoes, their straps wide, climbing high around his the heel, adorned with pieces of turquoise connecting to the decorated bands surrounding his ankles, making those look like a part of the fancy wear. Her own sandals were simple pieces of leather tying the protective maguey-woven sole to her foot, not entirely fitting as her feet kept growing along with her body, but still in a reasonable condition mainly because she rarely wore them at all. Which reflected on the state of her actual feet, she realized, embarrassed.

"My brother is not impatient or impulsive," the boy was saying, paying no attention to the state of her clothing apparently. "And he is wise, very wise. He is the best Emperor our *altepetl* ever saw!"

She processed his words carefully. They didn't make sense. Perturbed by her own mounting predicament, she glanced at the temple's wall again.

"He warred in that valley beyond the western highlands and he beat their warriors and took prisoners and his victories were great!" Her companion still carried on, oblivious of anything else it seemed. "He brought plenty of slaves and warriors to sacrifice."

"Who?" she asked absently.

"Axayacatl. He is the greatest warrior and leader."

"The Emperor?"

"Yes!" That came out triumphantly, as though proving his point.

"What has that to do with anything?" He was truly too funny, that one, puffing up again. Did he do anything besides argue?

"They said he was impatient and not wise."

"Oh, the people in the temple?"

"Yes!" Another emphatic statement.

She tried to remember what they said. "The Emperor *is* young. They said he has seen barely twenty summers."

"Twenty one! And it isn't young."

"Yes, it is."

"No, it isn't."

She laughed in his face, unconcerned. "You are the funniest boy I ever met. Do you do anything besides pick fights with everyone?"

He thought her question over, glowering.

"Do you have any friends?"

This brought the aggressive turkey back. "By twenties," he declared. "By many twenties!"

"But not in *calmecac*," she said shrewdly, knowing the signs. He was lonely, this boy, hungry for company, but too proud to admit that. Just like the village boy. It was difficult to make the villager talk in more than short sentences too, even though she didn't have much chance to develop any sort of conversation with him working day and night, never out of the melting room.

The boy in front of her frowned, but this time not angrily. "I have friends in *calmecac*, yes. But…" His teeth were making a mess out of his lower lip. "It's just that the city boys are not of my age. They can go out on afternoons, right after the lessons. But we are not allowed to do that."

"Why not? Because you are too young?" She pondered his words over. "Why did they put you in school before you are fourteen?"

He shrugged. "Because that's what they do. My brothers were in *calmecac* too, when they were of the same age. And my other half-brothers and cousins are here. Everyone!"

"And the city boys?" she asked, mainly to keep him talking, sensing his need to do that. It was boring back in the temple, and he was a nice boy. Also, who were those city boys?

"No!" he cried out, bringing his arms up, as though trying to ward off the unreasonableness of her suggestion. "They come to *calmecac* later. When they are twelve or more. They are not noble enough." He nodded thoughtfully, as though agreeing with himself. "Not like me and my brothers and cousins."

Not offended by his snobbery, she made a face. "Not noble, but free to run around and have a good time." His face fell again and she felt bad for this jab. "Do you know where they went?"

As on cue, his eyes lit with renewed enthusiasm. "Yes, I do! I overheard them and they were so silly that they never noticed. That boy from old Yaotzin's class, he played ball so badly today. He is no good at all. He just thinks that he is the best would-be warrior ever." Suddenly, his eyes fixed on her, filling with surprising mischief, even anticipation. "Do you know where the old causeway is?"

"The one that leads to Tlatelolco? Of course. It's not far away from the wharves, behind the marketplace plaza and all the way down the canal. They grow turkeys there. And dogs. You can't miss *that* smell."

He nodded eagerly. "They went to sneak into some underground temple there."

"Where? Near that Tlatelolco causeway?"

"Yes." His eyes shone with triumph. "That's where they went. They said there is an old temple there or something. They said it has a tunnel. Necalli, this conceited good-for-nothing, said he has some commoner *telpochcalli* boy to show them this thing."

For a wild moment, she thought to ask if it was Patli, this 'commoner telpochcalli boy.' That would fit the description perfectly, with Patli, street rodent that he was, sniffing around mysterious places, knowing the city's pathways and alleys better than the locals.

A glance at the brilliance of the outside light made her worried again. Father would be coming back from the inner rooms of this temple soon, and he would be mighty upset with her going out on her own, consulting no one, not waiting, even though he said nothing to that effect. No exact words demanding that she stick around or trail behind. Actually, when he had told her to run into the house and change to her very best clothes, even to put her sandals on – an unheard-of demand – he didn't explain why she was required to do this, he who would sometimes talk to her at length, usually through this or that cozy evening, after an especially tiring day. He would tell her stories and she would listen, enthralled. But this time, he just told her to come along, and now here she was, stuck in the middle of the uncomfortably noble crowd, all cotton and jewelry, sticking out like a torch in midnight, stared at and with no way back into the relative privacy of the temple. They won't let her in just like that, that much was obvious.

"If you know where it is," the boy was saying, tugging at her arm once again, unceremoniously at that, "maybe we could go there now, follow them, see this thing for ourselves."

"No, we can't. Well, I can't." But as she said that, she knew that the temptation was great, difficult to battle. He claimed knowledge of a mysterious place in the part of the city she thought she knew well enough. It would be amusing to prove him silly, this haughty, argumentative beast. As for a chance to discover some secret temple with a tunnel she didn't know a thing about – oh, but that would give her such an edge over Patli, something to flaunt, something to tell him and maybe, only maybe, if he behaved, to take him there. That boy boasted too much knowledge over all sorts of strange places since joining *telpochcalli*, and he made her jealous. Well, just a little bit. In the beginning, it was she who had shown him everywhere. He had never been to a city as large as Tenochtitlan, not even half as large. He even admitted that himself.

"Maybe another time," she offered, not wishing to disappoint her current company. He was a cute little thing, after all. "How about that?"

"When?"

"I don't know. If they take me to serve in this temple like you said, maybe we'll meet all the time."

"Not all the time," he corrected her gravely. "We are not brought to the temple that often. But," his eyes lit again, "I can sneak here whenever I like. Also, the girls take classes in our *calmecac* as well. All those cousins of mine, they have a classroom of their own." He shrugged. "Maybe they'll let you join those."

She pondered it over. "Like girls who attend *telpochcalli*?"

"No, not like the commoners!" He snickered, amused by the very thought. "But some gifted commoner boys get admitted to our school, so maybe the girls are too. Are you gifted?"

"I don't know," she said, again wondering about his talk and his clothing. Could he truly belong to the royal family, that one? She never spoke to a person nobler than the traders' children, never meeting an offspring of the warriors' class, let alone someone belonging to the royal family. "Do you truly live in the Palace?"

He nodded absently, again sinking into his gloomy thoughts, his forehead furrowing direfully. "My brother is not too young or too impatient, and my sister is not a spoiled brat. These men had no right to talk about them in such a way, stinking temple servants that they are. Honorable Teohuatzin isn't this way, I know he isn't! He is loyal to the Emperor, truly loyal."

"I don't believe that our Emperor is your brother!" But as she said that, she knew that it might be true after all. He was certainly too richly dressed, his sandals especially – so many beautifully polished pieces of turquoise stones – and he kept getting offended on behalf of this same badmouthed ruler, time after time. It could not be just wild mischief on his part. "And who is that sister of yours?" she demanded before he had time to start arguing, protesting his family ties. His forehead was creasing in painfully familiar fashion, boding no good for her patience with him.

"My sister was given to Moquihuixtli, that good-for-nothing scum, the would-be great emperor of Tlatelolco. She is supposed to be his Chief Wife, of course, but she complains that she isn't." He shrugged. "My mother keeps talking about that. She wants my brother to interfere."

"Your brother the Emperor?"

"Yes." He made a face. "My brother says that he won't be running around, solving his sister's marital problems."

Against her will, Chantli snickered. "Wise man."

His chuckle rang with matching mischief. "That's what my father says too." Then he glanced at the small opening they had emerged from before. "I think they are gone. You can go back in now." A heartbeat of hesitation. "I'll go with you halfway."

"Thank you!" She felt like hugging him. Maybe she'd manage to get back without trouble after all, with them not noticing her absence. "What's your name anyway?"

"Ahuitzotl."

"The Water Monster?" she repeated, amused and taken aback at the same time. "What kind of name is that?"

"The Water Thorny One," he corrected her gravely, not amused in the least. "The mysterious creature out of our Great Lake, yes. When I was born, my calendar suggested that, the most outstanding name of them all."

For good measure, she made a face at him. "We'll see about that. See how brave you would be if meeting those things for real one day."

As he grimaced back, curiously not offended, his tongue stuck out far, daring her to return measure for measure.

CHAPTER 4

The corridor stretched ahead, more of a tunnel, a passageway, invisible in the darkness, but there. It greeted them with its musky odor, rancid and dank. It was easier to pay the smell little attention when the soft afternoon light was still on their side, but now, with the last of the sunrays dissolving behind their backs, it assaulted their nostrils viciously, as though warning not to proceed.

Pressing his lips tight, Necalli pushed on, stepping with care upon the slippery floor, his hands groping the damp stones of the walls, thrusting so close that he didn't need to stretch his arms in order to reach their support. He felt his warriors-like lock – but he would have to retie it before they got out, before anyone saw him imitating the warriors in such an unlawful way – brushing against the wetness of the ceiling stones. Were they closer now than before, the walls and the ceiling? He shuddered and fought the impulse to rush back toward the friendliness of the light.

"Are you sure it leads anywhere?" he whispered as loudly as he dared, annoyed with the necessity to trail after their guide. Usually he would be the one in the lead, especially when a visit to places they should not be at was involved.

No answer came from the moldy depths. He hastened his step, annoyed with the presence of another boy, a barefoot commoner from the worst of Tenochtitlan's slums, someone Patli, their stupid *telpochcalli* accomplice, bothered to bring along for reasons unknown. When introduced to the soot-smeared newcomer with no sandals, Necalli didn't even bother to listen to his name or the explained connection – an apprentice at the workshop or something. Still, the commoner trudged along, breathing with an irritating ease as opposed to Axolin's rasping, which was beginning to wear on Necalli's nerves. If only he had thought of bringing along a torch. Not that he knew where to get such thing, aside from trying to steal one from their sleeping quarters at school.

"It's getting narrower." Axolin's thundering whisper startled him into stopping for good, his heart pounding.

The commoner boy bumped into them both, surprised by the sudden halt. Using his shoulder, Necalli shoved him aside.

"Watch it!" He heard the sharpness of his exclamation bouncing against the stony walls, echoing eerily, exaggeratedly loud. Drawing a deep breath to calm his nerves didn't help. The air was so moldy, repulsively damp. "We'll go on for a little longer. If it keeps getting narrower, we'll turn back." He hated the sound and the urgency of his whispering. It had a clear ring of panic to it. "Where in the name of every Underworld creature is Patli?" That came out better. Growing angry always helped.

"Still here in the tunnel, obviously." The commoner volunteered his comment readily, as though asked for his opinion, annoyingly in control as opposed to the wariness he had displayed outside, when they had walked toward the causeway and behind the wharves, clearly ready to fight or bolt away or do both. He didn't speak a word back then. "Where would he go but forward?"

"Shut up!" For good measure, Necalli pushed the unasked-for adviser with his shoulder again, not violently but firmly, relaying a message. "We go on, catch up with the stupid *telpochcalli* boy. This tunnel can't be that long. It has to end soon, or it'll dive right into the lake."

"It could be leading under the lake's waters." Not getting the message or not impressed by it, the workshop boy didn't move, standing his ground, irritatingly not intimidated, or maybe hiding his uneasiness well. "There are tunnels that long and longer, and if there is a bit of land anywhere around –"

"And you would know all about it." Contemplating his next move – to discipline the pushy commoner with something violent like a punch or to let the insolence go unanswered? – Necalli turned to go. "Come, Axolin. Don't fall behind. If it doesn't end in another hundred heartbeats, we turn back. But it'll bring us somewhere before that happens. I know it will. And it will not be the bottom of the lake," he added testily, pushing their unwanted company in a deliberate manner.

A muttered sentence in a tongue he did not understand sounded vicious and obscene. He rolled his eyes and cursed as colorfully, this time meaning Patli as well. The *telpochcalli* boy was the one to initiate this adventure, discovering this tunnel and diving into it with such eagerness he didn't even bother to wait for the rest of them to catch up. Tucked in the courtyard of a smallish abandoned temple, it might lead them to a treasure hidden somewhere there underneath. This was Patli's claim, not such a baseless, farfetched assumption.

Even though not a native of Tenochtitlan – just like this barefoot commoner, come to think of it – that boy was like a city rodent, not noble in his bearing, even though his Nahuatl sounded like that of the Acolhua people from the eastern shores of the Great Lake, where aristocratic Texcoco, the capital of the Acolhua and the equal partner of Tenochtitlan in the invincible Triple Alliance, stood aloof and somewhat apart, not conquering as lavishly but not humbling itself either. Just towering there, sporting pretty pyramids and lavish libraries, looking down their long aristocratic noses, indulging in arts and poetry and engineering feats, participating but only in important campaigns, with promised rich picking. Or so Father would say, remembered Necalli, reflecting on the same sense of resentment shared by the entire island-capital, or so it seemed.

Still Patli's accent was noble and some said that this boy had already been interviewed by the *calmecac* authorities, maybe even by Tecpan Teohuatzin personally, the high priest from the round Quetzalcoatl's temple, among whose responsibilities was the task of supervising the noble school, if not running it. There were a few such boys, admitted to the exclusive establishment for their outstanding abilities; gifted, most promising youths from various commoner *telpochcalli* that dotted every city's district. Oh yes, those who showed exceptional talent combined with enough diligence or promise were examined by the educational institution of the Royal Enclosure, the one that produced future leaders, governors, great priests, and great warriors. Tenochtitlan's nobles weren't snobs. Or so the people of the highest nobility claimed.

Resuming his walk, Necalli snorted into the moldy darkness. Born into a noble family himself, with his mother being an offspring of one of Tenochtitlan's most influential elders of their district, he never forgot something his older siblings did not care to remember or face. His father, while being a great warrior and a prominent former leader, had not always been one of the nobles. Far from it! When close to thirty summers earlier Tenochtitlan was fighting for its life, resisting the oppression of the evil Tepanec Empire, Necalli's father, then just a young warrior, had distinguished himself mightily in the battles around the western side of the Great Lake, before and after Azcapotzalco, the mighty Tepanec Capital, fell. Performing feats of courage, undaunted and unafraid, he had earned the notice of his superiors, promoted into minor leaders' ranks and then eventually taken into the presence of the Emperor himself upon his return to the city. Taking of more than two captives did this, always the surest way to earn the respect of not only the rulers, but of the deities to whom those captives were to be sacrificed. Outstanding bravery was to be rewarded, lavishly at that, with gifts and titles, and even some lands to rule, the sign of a person becoming one of the nobility. A good turn for a brave warrior; and for his offspring as well. He, Necalli, could have been born into a commoner family, trader or maybe a craftsman, mighty deities forbid such a possibility.

Sensing both boys pressing close behind, he pushed the thoughts of his father away, never ashamed by this man's less noble origins like both his older sisters were. Stupid fowls. The bravery on the battlefield was the only worthy trait. Oh, but to be as lucky as this great man was, to distinguish himself as early and as decisively!

The gust of something that felt like a movement sent his heart to a wild start, his muscles going rigid, stiffening with fright. One heartbeat, then another still saw him gaping into the dank blackness, unable to move. Had he imagined it? No wind should be coursing through such tunnel-like corridor, having no place to originate at, unless at its exit, but then the darkness wouldn't have been so blank, so oppressive, with a little light seeping in, the last of the pre-dusk illumination. Unless the passageway led deeper into the earth, toward a room full of treasures, like Patli claimed.

"Did you hear it?" The familiar, Acolhua-accented whisper should have reassured him; instead, it made him bump his nape against the moldy stone.

"Where in the name of the Underworld have you been?" he demanded, having heard no footsteps approaching them from the direction they were heading toward. His own words came out rasping, unsteady, shamefully weak. He clenched his teeth tight. "I heard nothing."

A shrug of his companion did not need to be visible to relay the typical offhanded indifference. "We better keep quiet."

"I –"

Another movement, that of a clearly raised hand, made him pause in spite of himself. What if that one knew what he was talking about? He was certainly more at home here, closer to the slums of the commoners than to the well-to-do neighborhoods around the Central Plaza, having never sneaked anywhere underground before.

"What now?" He managed to let out that question in the form of a grudging whisper.

Another shrug could be guessed, moving the darkness ever so slightly. "There is a room there, but it leads nowhere." The ensuing pause had a begrudging quality to it. "We should have brought a light."

"Yes, we should have," growled Necalli, forgetting to keep quiet. Just who did this one think he was, to imply that it was his fault for not bringing the torch.

"No torch would have worked for you here." This came from the workshop boy, again in an annoyingly firm voice, with no panicked or otherwise agitated tones to it.

"And why-ever not?" Patli's voice rang with a poisonous condescension, clearly as put out with the insolence of the pushy commoner, reflected Necalli, briefly amused.

"Not enough air to make it work well." Apparently, it was the workshop boy's turn to shrug, another clearly felt gesture. "You need either a shorter tunnel or more openings to let the air in."

Taken aback by so much displayed knowledge, they stared for a heartbeat. Then Axolin moved jerkily. "We should go back," he breathed, his voice barely heard, strained and trembling. "There is nothing here anyway."

"There is something in there. I know there is!" Over his previous indignation, Patli shifted his weight from one foot to another. "That room leads somewhere. If we could just see it properly –"

"Well, we can't." He felt the moldy walls closing on him, moving to press from all sides, to squash him or trap him or do other dreadful things. But they shouldn't have sneaked into that temple and this tunnel at the first place. Axolin was right. He didn't want to enter it at all. "So let's just –"

Another breath of invisible air enveloped them, more distinct than before but as untouchable. It was as though something moved the suffocating darkness, something that didn't wish them to be here. Necalli felt his heart sliding down his stomach, to stay still and maybe die there. There was something out there, something bad!

"Did you hear it?" breathed Axolin, aghast.

A new movement nearly shoved him into the damp stones; however, this one belonged to an earthly creature. The barefoot apprentice pushed his way through, heading toward the darkness in question, not afraid in the least, his steps rustling with decisiveness, sure of themselves. For another heartbeat, they remained staring.

"Where did he go?" whispered Axolin.

Necalli bit his lower lip savagely. "Only the lowlifes of the Underworld know."

"Miztli, wait!" Patli's voice rang with strangled urgency. "Where are you going?"

"To check that room of yours." The nonchalant answer reached them from further away, muffled but there. "There must be an opening in there. That's why the air here is moving. Don't you smell the stench of the lake?"

Necalli's heart was back, fluttering near his throat now, still out of tempo. He clenched his teeth tight, ashamed.

"Come." To signal them into following made him feel better, still in control. "Are you just a bunch of cowardly women?"

Even Axolin's steps rang firmer after that chastening. Necalli hastened his step, liking the upward tilt the floor was taking. Maybe it would lead them out after all, without the need to retrace their steps back into the suffocating darkness.

The walls narrowed some more, then retreated with startling suddenness. Now he could smell the heavy odor, oh yes. The lake was somewhere there, splashing above their heads, maybe. Was the workshop commoner correct about the final end of this tunnel? Necalli reached out to trace the moldy stones. There were chests there, piled one upon another, wooden cases judging by the feel of it, slippery but whole. He slid his fingers along the uneven surface.

"What are those?"

"Try to open one." Patli's whisper came from another corner. "It's difficult to lift these things. If only –"

"Yes, yes, the light, I know," snorted Necalli, then felt his heart cascading down his stomach once again as something brushed against his leg, something mangy and hairy, scurrying away hurriedly.

He didn't have time to reflect on any of it. In the next fraction of a heartbeat, he felt himself bouncing off the opposite wall, not such a long leap in this crammed, overloaded space, crashing into more wooden objects, making them scatter in a dim thud, hitting his limbs, trying to foul his moves. Panicked, he kicked them away, but the wooden obstacles were everywhere, making him fight for his balance, struggling to stay upright. Oh, but he had to escape, both this strangling closeness and the terrible darkness, and the creatures inhabiting it!

"Necalli!" He could hear Patli's voice, anxious, rising to strident tones. "Necalli, what happened? Where are you?"

To draw a deep breath didn't help. The air was so stale, full of the musky lake's odor. The clatter of something heavy being pulled over the dusty stones made him think of the creatures living under the earth again. Something hairy!

"I'm here," he breathed, pleased with his ability to utter these words in a reasonably comprehensible voice. "Just stumbled over this stupid pile." Oh, but sometimes the darkness was a mercy.

He could hear Axolin uttering a funny yelp before hurling himself somewhere, judging by the crashing noise.

"Don't panic, you silly woman. Those are just rats."

But now, he could hear even Patli jumping onto his feet with an indecent haste. "Where? Where? Did you see one?"

"I felt it," he said, pleased with himself for being now the calmest of the three. "How could I see it?"

As though answering his words, a sliver of light flickered from somewhere above, drowned in the explosion of grating and screeching. A fairly large slab was moving above their heads, Necalli's instincts informed him, pushing him to leap backwards, again hitting too many obstacles on his way. The others were huddled close by, pressing with their angular limbs and sharp elbows. He paid them no attention, the sliver of light growing along with the screeching, allowing his eyes to pick up the form of the commoner boy, balancing on top of a cumbersome crane, hovering on his tiptoes, pushing one of the rectangular slabs at the upper part of the wall with both hands, making it rasp. In the hesitant dusky light, he looked grotesque, a silhouette with no definite form, a creature out of the Underworld stories.

For another heartbeat, Necalli kept staring, then, shamed, leapt up the same wooden chest, causing it and its human cargo to waver precariously, clutching to the wall he was now assaulting for support. The disharmonious stridency stopped.

"Careful!" hissed the boy, but as Necalli reached for the edges of the removable slab, he pursed his lips and said nothing, resuming his pushing efforts, his teeth locked around his lower lip in an uncompromising grip. Oh, but this slab *was* heavy. Necalli felt his fingers sliding, tearing against the sharp edges, protesting the need to find another crevice, to press it again. The help of his companion was a blessing. How did this one manage to move it in the first place?

"Does it lead outside?" he groaned, causing the stone to screech another width of a finger. It brought in more light, but not like from the outside, unless he was mistaken and it was dusk already. "It doesn't look..."

"It's another... another corridor," gasped the boy, clearly as out of breath and exhausted. "But with an exit... out there..."

Not relishing the idea of trudging along another tunnel, Necalli said nothing, pausing in his efforts to examine his bleeding fingers. "How do you know?"

The commoner was examining his palms as closely, clearly welcoming the respite. "There are always openings in such tunnels. Who would make a room like that, fill it with goods, and make no additional entrance?"

That made Necalli glance at their uninvited company with renewed interest, while the others came closer, crowding the base of their makeshift dais, drawing to the source of the light like early flowers, encouraged. "How do you know all this?"

The boy shrugged, peering at the opening they had just created, biting his lips again. "We can squeeze through that," he muttered, contemplative.

The strong odor coming from their new prospective route wasn't encouraging. Not an outright rot, it made Necalli think of spoiled food, of foul-smelling piles the marketplace slaves came to clean after the vendors finished their business for the day. Not a pleasant aroma.

He frowned against the shimmering gloom. "Yes, we'll squeeze through it, but only if you say it's a short walk. Not like that one." He jerked his head downwards, indicating the room that looked even creepier now, illuminated in such a gloomy way. A mess of chests and piles, spears, *atlatls*, other sorts of dart throwers, roughly carved clubs aplenty. But this place was a treasure of weaponry!

"It's shorter. Or there would be no light." Again the annoying apprentice was being smart. Necalli squashed him with a direful glance.

"Come up here." He motioned at the others, feeling leader-like and back in control. A very nice feeling he missed through the tedious time spent underground. "One by one. Axolin, you first."

The commoner boy waited for no orders, grabbing the edges of another slab and pulling himself up, sliding into the breach with the agility of a monkey. Or a marketplace rat, a likelier comparison.

"Go after him." He helped Axolin up by a halfhearted push, then watched Patli manage a cumbersome climb of his own.

A last glance at the mildewed room made him shiver. What a place to spend one's time at and in the darkness. Now he could hear the rats scurrying behind the heaped weapons, and maybe other sorts of heavier creatures. They made his scant body hair rise.

They didn't wait for him up there, not even Axolin. Grinding his teeth, he pulled himself up, pleased with the ease his arms held his weight, the grace with which his body completed the exercise, like a jaguar and not climbing monkeys, the slum boys, using all their limbs to get up. Oh yes, he was going to be a great warrior.

Hesitating, he played with the idea of pulling the stone back, concealing the signs of their trespassing; however, the rustling below intensified, joined with a different even if distant shuffle. Was someone coming, following them through the tunnel they had just left? In another heartbeat, he was pushing on, his heart again out of tempo. Just to reach safety, to escape the closeness and the stench!

"Why didn't you wait, you stupid half-wits?" he hissed, reaching them near the murky rectangle, crowding the longed-for opening, relieved. "Were you too eager to catch up with your barefoot, naked new leader, the one who can scurry through tunnels like the marketplace rat that he is?"

The workshop boy wasn't around to enjoy being put in his place, surely already out and away, but the rest of his companions quailed, visibly shamed.

"We did wait for you," protested Axolin. "We waited for you here. It's a really short walk, this other tunnel, and we didn't go out but waited."

"Oh yes, how touching!" He pushed his way past them, noting that the *telpochcalli* boy seemed curiously subdued. Or maybe just deep in thought.

The smell of the lake assaulted his nostrils the moment he emerged into the twilight of the outside, the spicy odor of fish and seaweed. The water was everywhere, licking the gravel, washing it with small waves. Above their heads, beams of greasy wood created a sort of a roof, obstructing the last of the light, more of the wooden planks blocking the rest of the view.

"Where in the name of the…" Necalli tried to make his head work. The massive construction with its sloping earthworks – was that the old causeway? But if so, what were they doing underneath it?

"It's that thing that leads to that other city, no?" The workshop boy appeared from behind the swaying reeds, spooking some waterfowl on his way.

"What thing?" asked Necalli, ridiculously relieved. The commoner knew his way around strange places more than even Patli did, that much was obvious. Still, it was unseemly for him to rely on a half-naked foreigner with no shoes. "Where have you been?"

"I think if we climb it, we won't have to swim our way back." Ignoring the question, the boy frowned thoughtfully, chewing his lower lip. "If we help each other, we can manage. It's too steep and too slippery, but we can make a rope, maybe. Out of our clothes." The squinted eyes scanned the greasy planks again. "If we tie together all your cloaks –"

"Stop talking nonsense!" Fed up with this flood of ridiculous musings, Necalli scowled. "What's behind the bushes?"

"More water."

He blew the air through his nostrils. "So we did go some way under the lake."

"Yes, in its shallow parts," agreed his converser, not noting the rhetorical nature of the question.

"What are you, an engineer?" demanded Necalli, impressed against his will once again.

The boy snickered. "You can't dig under the water where it's deep. You don't have to be an engineer to know that."

"I know!" He drew a deep breath, motioning the others who appeared out of the dusty opening like hesitant rodents, blinking against the dim light. "But what you know about tunnels and such is not something commoners with no sandals would know. Where did you come from?"

The boy studied his muddied feet, clearly pondering. "Teteltzinco," he said in the end, somewhat reluctantly. "It's in the south. Beyond Lake Chalco and all that."

"Oh, those pitiful losers!" Only a decade ago, the old Emperor, Moctezuma Ilhuicamina, the fifth Tenochtitlan's ruler, put the insolent dwellers of the southern Lake Chalco firmly in their place, following a tradition of warfare that went back generations. The Chalcoans gave trouble for many decades, not only to Tenochtitlan but to the previous rulers of the Great Lake's Valley, the vile Tepanecs as well, something that only the great fifth Mexica ruler put a stop to, once and for all. Good for him. "The Chalcoans are done for now."

"I'm not a Chalcoan," protested the boy hotly, his forehead furrowing with too many creases. "We are far from that lake, far beyond. Our villages were not conquered by Tenochtitlan. Only those near Cuauhnahuac. We came to join of our own free will!"

What a passionate speech. Necalli couldn't help smirking. "Your will is a nice thing, but it's not like they could decide not to join. Or to pay no tribute, for that matter. No one says 'no' to Tenochtitlan. Not even naked villagers who know their way under the earth."

A burning glare was his answer. He paid it no attention, uncomfortably aware that he liked this uninvited new companion of theirs better than Patli.

"What are you doing here in Tenochtitlan? Wherever did Patli unearth you?"

"He works in my uncle's workshop," volunteered the telpochcalli boy readily, too readily, as though not trusting his commoner protégé to handle the sudden interrogation well.

"Doing what?"

"Melting copper." This came from the working boy again, as

expected. Oh yes, this one had his share of pride, not a typical peasant from a forsaken village out there in the south, splashing in his muddy non-floating fields.

"In underground tunnels?" This time, it was Axolin, over his fright of the ominous tunnel and back to his cheerfully needling self.

"What?"

"How did you learn to find your way under the earth?" clarified Necalli, out of patience but still curious. "Not by melting copper."

The boy's face brightened with a surprisingly wide grin. "It's lying under the ground, all this copper and other things for melting. Before it gets to the braziers and your pretty jewelry, it has to be picked from under the earth, tunnels and all."

"And that's what you did back home? Oh, that explains things."

A rumbling noise coming from further down the lakeside caught their attention. The beams above their heads shuddered ever so slightly. Necalli frowned, watching the weak rays of light that managed to sneak into their spontaneous hideaway. Even on such a short causeway – not truly a causeway but a sort of a passageway, as Tlatelolco stood so nearby the two cities were sometimes regarded as though sharing one huge island instead of two close by ones – the bridges would be lifted only when the sun was about to commence its night's journey through the Underworld, not a long time from now, surely.

"We have to hurry," he said, suddenly worried, not relishing the idea of wading along the Great Lake's shores in the darkness, or even just semi-darkness. "Unless you can think of a way of getting us up there without ruining our clothing for good."

No one mistook his address as meaning anyone but their copper-melting company, their eyes darting in the same direction, wondering and expectant.

The boy shifted from one muddied foot to another, clearly uneasy under so much undue attention. "We need to make a rope," he muttered, shrugging. "Tie a noose in its end and try to make it cling to one of the bulges up there. That'll make the climb easier."

"And how about more realistic solutions?" inquired Axolin, ridiculously polite, bordering on offensive.

The commoner shot his mocker another of his fiercely burning glares.

"Then the way of the reeds it is," declared Necalli, in no mood for more arguing. It was getting dark and no person in his right mind would wish to wander the lake waters after the light went off, unless wishing to end his life in its bottom, dead and missing one's eyes, nails, or teeth, all eaten up by the ferocious *ahuitzotls* lurking in these waters, greedy for these parts of the human beings alone. Shivering at the very thought, he pushed his way past them, not liking how the nearest cluster of reeds rustled, as though warning them not to proceed.

"It can't be deep enough to make one need to swim," he went on, needing the encouragement of their words as much as they did, but not about to admit to his fear. And to think that they had encountered someone bearing this very name only this afternoon, may the annoying royal offspring fall into the lake, straight into the claws of his namesake and the mercy of their teeth! "And even if it is, it'll be only a short swim. We are still close to that shore of the temple with the tunnel; it's as sure as the sunlight." Which was retreating with unsettling haste, now merely a flickering gray, spreading equally whether shadowed by massive construction or not.

"I can't swim," murmured Patli, hastening his step and so catching up with Necalli and ahead of the other two. "I do it really badly."

"You won't have to. It's just a shallow swamp here."

"But what if we do?"

Shrugging, Necalli side-glanced his companion, impressed by the blank face and the matter-of-fact tone. Some boys that he knew would be whimpering now, begging to stop and find another solution. "We'll manage to get to the shore without letting you drown."

"The reeds will help." The copper-melting boy was again commenting without being asked to, not appropriately respectful of his noble company. "He can always clutch to those."

"Of course," tossed Necalli tersely, angry with himself for not thinking of such additional means of reassurance. "But it won't get to us swimming, and it is not our main concern anyway."

For a heartbeat, they proceeded in silence, with the swishing of driest of reeds being the only immediate sound, the clamor of the shore with the warehouses and the workshops dotting it aplenty, like the more distant hum of the lake and the lively activity all around it, nothing but a background, not on their side.

"What are you afraid of?" asked the workshop boy after a while, when the plopping of their sandals disappeared, swallowed by the muddy water, now splashing around their thighs, jumping there in no gradual way.

"As though you don't know." Axolin's snort seeped through the deepening darkness, having lost its lightly amused or mocking quality again. "Don't play it dumber than an average villager, will you?"

"I'm not playing it dumb, you stupid lump of rotten meat!" There was evidently a limit to the foreigner's burning glares as an answer to insults. "You are the one looking dumb, back in the tunnel and here on the –"

"Miztli!" cried out Patli, not foreigner enough himself not to understand the implication of yelling at the noble *calmecac* pupil while being nothing but a dirty apprentice in the workshop of this or that city slum; let alone something as insulting as name calling and worse.

But the copper-melting commoner had had enough. While Axolin's eyes widened with shock, then narrowed with red-hot fury, as he launched sideways, aiming to reach his offender in one leap – not a possible feat while being stuck hip-deep in the mud – the workshop boy didn't retreat, planting his legs wider while bringing his arms up and forward, ready to withstand the attack, if not to mount one. Necalli felt nothing save amusement. It would have been different if the naked villager flared at him, of course. However as of now, they had simply no time for this foolishness, and Axolin's twisted face and blazing eyes promised no good. With his light temper and nice disposition, when goaded, Axolin tended to lose any grain of good sense, blinded with fury, turning as unreasonable as they come.

"Stop it," he said, reaching out in order to grab his friend's arm, not liking the way it shot toward the girdle, as though aiming for the dagger attached to it, the prerogative of a *calmecac* student who was old enough to be allowed to join classes concerning actual warfare, and not only the theoretical side of it. Axolin was the best in some of it, throwing knives with enviable accuracy, besting even his older fellow students.

The interfering hand caused the charging youth to sway but did not deter him from his course. In another heartbeat, he was upon his offender, lashing out with both hands, not burdened by flashing obsidian, none of this. Still, Necalli pushed forward, set on inserting himself between the two antagonists, his blood boiling with rage of his own. How stupid it was to start fighting when deep in the mud of the lake's shore and just as the darkness was about to fall, the surest way to make every dangerous creature aware of their uninvited, unwarranted presence.

"Stop it!" he barked, this time quite loudly, his shout overcoming the clamor their stupid thrashing around was making. His fist missing its target by a mere fraction, Axolin had another one planted upon his rival's high cheekbone quite neatly, drawing away again with a clear intention to return, even though his own ribs sustained quite an assault in the form of an opposing flurry of landing fists, which were of admirable size and firmness, only expected in the working commoners, of course. The warriors were superior while fighting with weapons, which worried Necalli to a degree. Not as much as the possible upsetting of their side in the muddy waters, though.

"Are you out of your stupid mind?" Grabbing his friend's arm more forcefully, which now was wrapped around the working boy's neck with firm determination, disregarding the similar state of affairs on the other side, he used his entire weight in order to pry his friend loose, if only a little. "Stop that, both of you, you stupid half wits. Get away from each other."

Using his shoulder as a wedge, he pushed them so hard, they both went down and into the water, and he had a hard time maintaining his own balance from the suddenness of it.

"You stupid –"

And then it happened. He had never seen it, not from close proximity and not from afar, but the stories were there, told and retold by all sorts of people, usually at nights, the boys huddling together, scaring each other. The fishermen from the city and the villages had first-hand accounts to report, and there were books depicting the creature, serious books, priests' calendars and such, drawn by eyewitnesses, those who saw it and managed to get away, not many, usually just witnesses, not the direct objects of the monster's attack.

In the gathering darkness, it was difficult to see, so his senses informed him before his terrified eyes did. Both boys were still spluttering, struggling to get to their feet before the other did, still eager to attack, oblivious to anything else, but the slick body of maybe half of his size was sliding alongside, the pointed ears and head, the spiky fur, and the tail, huge and as black as the gathering night.

Numbed with terror, he watched it circling, nimble and deadly, meaning harm. The tail, it would be using its tail now, he knew, blinking to make his mind work. It would grab them one by one with its tail, wrapping its human-like fingers of this same lethal limb around them in order to pull them under.

Patli's scream tore him from his stupefied staring, brought the sounds back in force, crumbling down his stomach, making it turn violently, as though he was about to get sick. The others stopped thrashing and were jumping away too, waving their arms in a ridiculous manner. The slick silhouette was darting every which way, like the shadow of the Underworld, which it might very well have been. No one knew from where *ahuitzotls* originated.

The next thing he knew, the workshop boy uttered a funny yelp, falling backwards in a strange fashion, head first, or rather his neck, as a person would dive when trying to do it backwards, a bizarre picture. His limbs were thrashing wildly, but his head, half under the water and half out, was stretched out weirdly, wrapped in a blur of slick limbs, while Axolin, living up to his name of a Water Lizard, joined the melee quite fearlessly, beating at the strangling paws, trying to pry them off.

The realization that brought Necalli's frozen body back to life with a start, made him hurl himself into the raging fight with little consideration, his hands claws, grabbing the flailing hands, pulling hard. For a heartbeat, it felt like a lost struggle, then the workshop boy was back, gasping for air, gurgling desperately. Of the creature there was no sign.

Blinking in confusion, his instincts still screaming danger, not letting the sense of victory prevail, he tried to unlock his grip on the elbow he was clutching for dear life before, then again felt rather than saw the movement, this time much closer, the slick fur brushing against his side, making him shudder in revulsion, frozen yet again against any better judgment. *The tail with the human hand, where was it?* His mind kept wondering, desperate to locate the source of danger. The creature would attack with its best-fitting feature, like he did with the workshop boy, like it did in every story and tale.

Axolin was beating at the water around them, his knife out and ready. About time! The workshop boy managed to regain his balance along with an upright position, apparently not hurt too badly. But of course! *Ahuitzotls* were reported to drag their prey down, into their caves at the bottom of the lake, to drown them and only then begin feasting. They weren't fighters but ambushers. So maybe they could keep each other safe, not to let the creature drag them below, just like with the foreigner boy.

"Axolin, keep close, don't let –" Surprised to hear his own voice doling out orders, or any reasonable sounds at all, he felt the push and had to fight for his balance as the water splashed yet again. The next thing he knew, something heavy was clinging to his arm, hanging there like a dead weight, making his struggle to stay upright more difficult. No pain, just the weight, the fierceness of the clasp.

Disoriented, he tried to push it away, shooting his hands up, both of them. A futile attempt. Something was fastened around his arm, crushing it in its savage grip. It made him stagger and the scream that tore from his lips had a frightening sound, yet the strong hands were pulling him back, steadying, supporting, and after more thrashing around – he couldn't tell if it was Axolin or the working boy – the weight wasn't there anymore. Only the pain remained, that tearing, bone-crushing agony. To pull his arm up and out of the water apparently wasn't a good idea. It doubled the pain, or maybe even tripled it. Like the dots of the glyphs they were made to multiply in school, the dots and the bars, the pain spiraled in no orderly way.

"Is it dead?" the commoner boy was asking, his voice coming in waves, not very steady.

"Don't know, no, I think not... well, maybe... maybe it got hurt, I think..." Axolin was stammering as badly, in a way that would make Necalli laugh and make ridiculous imitations, he knew. But for the pain, and the fear, and that stupid ringing in his ears, he might have thought of commenting on that. As it was, he let the hands of the workshop boy direct him back out of the reeds and into the stretch of land they had just managed to leave, wondering briefly what sense it made to go back, unless willing to enter the tunnels once again. Not such a bad idea, come to think of it. The suffocating closeness was twenty times more preferable to the dark water inhabited by monsters.

CHAPTER 5

The necessity to crawl back into the oppressive darkness, pressed by the crude, revoltingly damp slabs of stones from all over did not make him cringe or even hesitate. Unlike these spoiled city boys, he had been around underground caves and tunnels since he could walk straight or close enough to this time. Father never missed the opportunity to bring his sons along on the less dangerous missions of mining, to learn the family's trade, and to have a good time as well. It was never boring with Father, never unpleasant despite the hard work of excavating hard pieces of copper and other precious materials hidden in colorful or dully grayish stones, of separating them from each other.

Oh, but how he missed Father!

Fiercely sometimes, fighting the urge to run away and back home every dawn of waking up in this towering island-monster, so huge and so busy, imposing, humbling, unfriendly, brimming with foreigners but despising them all, the uncouth savages from the various conquered lands, the lands they themselves bothered to go out and conquer. So what did they expect? Still, here was Father, succumbing to this same idea the other conquered or wisely joined towns and villages did, going themselves or sending their promising children to the mighty Capital in hopes of a better future.

Some future indeed, he thought bitterly; a wonderful opportunity to spend one's time between raging braziers all day long, working into exhaustion, receiving nothing but humiliating ordering about. Even though compared to those whom Patli called '*calmecac* boys,' the people of the workshop were not so haughty or violent after all.

Rolling his eyes, he slipped through the crack they had left while fleeing the stupid first tunnel, hanging on his hands, seeking the support of the wooden planks, finding none. Bewildered, he let go, his hands trembling, refusing to support his weight any longer. It wasn't high anyway. Still, the throbbing in the back of his head interrupted his concentration, made him wish to feel it out again, for the tenth or maybe twentieth time since escaping the accursed lake. Was the stiffness there all dried mud, a result of his thrashing about in the lake, or had the monster's teeth sunk into his flesh after all? The mere memory made him shudder violently, in unstoppable tremors. That terrible creature, so frightening and vicious, set on having him dragged under the surface, set on devouring him, oh mighty deities.

His fingers reached into a small pouch tied to his loincloth, still there, reassuring, giving him strength. The smoothness of the polished obsidian did this, his knowledge of the talisman. Oh, but it kept him safe today, this dark, glassy, beautiful puma, carved and fashioned out of solid obsidian, given to him upon his tenth birthday but made on the day he was born, while Mother was struggling to bring him to this world, like all women did, engaging in a long strenuous battle. They said it took her days to do that and that she almost died, and all the while Father was working on the obsidian puma, carving it lovingly, pledging to various deities, begging for help. Unlike jade or turquoise, granite or malachite, obsidian was no material to fashion figurines or jewelry out of – too brittle, too easily chipped or fragmented. Yet Father had worked stubbornly, praying and carving, asking for guidance and help of powerful deities, producing this wonder in time to greet his newborn last son, a strong healthy baby, miraculously undamaged by the difficult delivery. They had told and retold him the story several times, and he had his share of unauthorized peeking at the obsidian wonder, marveling at the wonderfully detailed, majestic, glossy creature, as dark as a moonless night and as powerful; his namesake – ItzMiztli, Obsidian Puma. Oh, but the wonderful talisman made it easier to go through the days in the melting room. It made the longing for home bearable. He never let it out of his reach.

Clutching the glassy smoothness tightly between his fingers, he looked around, probing with his senses, listening intently. Even the lake's monsters were powerless against his talisman; still, what a vicious creature it was! They hadn't dared to even talk about what happened. Spilling pell-mell into the relative safety of their previous hideaway under the earthworks and beams, they busied themselves with the bleeding arm of the *calmecac* boy, the one who was distributing orders before. He was having a hard time with it, clenching it with his good arm, all swollen and bleeding, torn in quite a few places. It was easy to hear the grinding of this one's teeth, the way he must have clenched them against the pain.

The sensible thing to do was to dive back into the tunnel, run its length as fast as they could, back to the normalcy of the city and help. However, sensibility was not the strong side of the *calmecac* boys, apparently, whatever this *calmecac* thing was. Both the wounded and his annoyingly violent, haughty friend refused to even contemplate the idea. In the end, it came to Patli volunteering his, Miztli's, services, to rush back using the tunnel and get that rope he was suggesting to make out of their precious clothing in the first place, climb the earthworks, and walk back home leisurely, taking their time. An unnecessarily intricate plan, but apparently, their fancy cloaks were too important, more than the bleeding arm of their would-be leader. So the tunnel it was for him, not such a difficult challenge. He was no city boy afraid of stone walls and some musky air.

His landing was smooth with no crushing crates greeting him with their sharp hurting edges; still, it made his battered body protest. But he had collected too many bruises on this stupid adventure aside from his aching head! How was he to explain those to old Tlaquitoc if asked? Or to Acatlo, the elder of the sons, such a grim, demanding person. It was hard enough to face him this afternoon, asking permission to go out, explaining that nothing was left to do in the workshop in the absence of its owner. The annoying man made such skeptical faces. But for Patli's intervention, this boy's quick seemingly lighthearted reasoning, he would have been refused, most surely. But then, maybe it would have been for the better.

The darkness enveloped him, pitch-black as opposed to the simmering lightness of the outside, with nothing to illuminate the closeness of the cramped space. It was eerily quiet, and it made his nerves prickle. Something was wrong. What?

He tried to probe with his senses, remembering Father's words. When underground, one should be capable of finding one's way without the light. Sometimes mines would crumble, on account of occasional earth's tremors, or when they were dug without proper care or planning. Then a good miner would have to find his way out, having his limbs and his senses at his disposal, but little else. The tunnels were never deep enough to trap a person for good, but if panicked, a man was done for, Father would repeat over and over. So the first thing was not to panic, not to lose one's lucid thinking to frantic running or thrashing about.

Holding his breath, he listened carefully, reaching out with his hands, moving slowly, and feeling out the obstacles. The crates seemed to be still there, and the towering piles made of clubs and the spear-throwing devices. But where was this chest he had dragged in order to climb the opening? This crude construction of plants that left his palms full of splinters which were still there, the least of his worries.

Then it hit him. The chest! It was back in its place, or anywhere; *it wasn't under the opening where they had left it.* Otherwise, he would not have to jump. His heart was again making wild leaps, trying to sneak out through his throat. Breathlessly, he listened, desperate. Who or what moved that chest? And where was he, or it, now?

From the direction where his senses informed him was the tunnel that brought them here, came nothing but silence. Not absolute enveloping silence like before, he noticed now. Some noises were reaching his ears – faint rustling, the scurrying of tiny feet. Rats? Underground creatures? A mysterious beast of the lake? It must have been lurking up there, directly above this tunnel, come to think of it. Oh mighty deities!

The urge to scramble back, to claw his way up the wall and

charge through the gaping opening welled, but he forced his limbs into stillness, willing his mind to think it all through. That panic Father was talking about, he must not succumb to it. Maybe he should still try to brave the tunnel. The narrowness of it was oppressive but promising. No beast larger than a fox would be able to squeeze through some of its turns, to chase him and corner and this time devour him for good. The beast of the lake was larger than that.

The memory of the slimy, revoltingly muddy, foul-smelling limbs wrapped around his head, biting and pulling, smearing his face with scratches and worse, made him nearly lose his painfully gained sense of control, washing his whole body with a wave of patent dread. But it was grabbing him with everything it had – *more than four limbs?* – determined to pull him down, determined to devour him on the way or after reaching its lair. *Still out there, lying in wait.* Could it escape the water and burrow its way down here? But he had to get out of here, he had to!

Groping the slanting stones, he staggered onto his only possible route of escape, determined to put as much distance between himself and the whole accursed place until the pressing walls began to retreat, enabling a more straight-backed posture. There he managed to force his legs into a calmer pace, not succumbing to the urge of running in a neck-breaking speed, the most unwise of the courses. Broken limbs would not help him escape any faster. Neither would it help the others, who counted on his coming back with a rope, stranded on their piece of flattened land, surrounded by water teeming with monsters. Did they expect him to bring along more substantial help? But of what sort? He had no friends in this cold and aloof *altepetl*, no relatives. A bare-foot villager, a foreigner; a commoner, as they claimed. Well, who knew that the sandals were not an unnecessarily expensive wear but a way to prove one's worthiness? But how did this Necalli boy keep carrying on about it, the conceited piece of meat, he and his friend. And yet they were the ones to come to his rescue, to fight the water monster and pull him, Miztli, out of the beast's clutches. They could have bolted away or stood and screamed like Patli did, but they didn't. How very strange.

The ground was tilting upwards, as he remembered it should, and he let out a held breath, then caught it again. The voices! Very muffled, they reached him, drifting from his left, an impossible direction as the tunnel spread behind and ahead, not sideways. Freezing, he listened, picking up a faint scratching, as though something dragged over the wall he was pressed against.

The silence returned, to be interrupted shortly. This time, it was a muted bang that made him jump away and straight into the dampness of the opposite wall, not a distance at all. Above the wild pounding of his heart, he heard the voices again, unmistakable this time. People were talking somewhere behind the surrounding stones, working as well, dragging things. The images of another room full of weaponry or other sorts of treasures filled his mind's eye. Despite his fear, he brushed his palms against the wall in question, feeling it out. If he dared, he would have knocked on it, trying to hear its quality. Was it hollow in parts? That would explain the noises.

Silently, he crept on, his ears pricked up, fear forgotten. People were easier to deal with, to talk to or run away from. They were not bloodthirsty beasts. Sure enough, a tiny draft told him that another opening was gaping discreetly to his left. Maybe those people would be willing to help. They might have ropes and other useful tools. Were they searching for copper here, under the lake's shore? It seemed to be a strange place to extract it, as usually precious metals were to be found in mountains and hills.

Still unsure of himself, he headed toward the draft, sensing another opening, hesitating, then diving into it, determined. The faint flickering at its far edge led him on, warm and inviting.

"Careful with this thing!" cried out a voice, so near it made him freeze dead in his tracks. Another thud like the one that caught his attention on the other side of the wall shook the moldy air. "If it breaks, you pay from your share. I'll make sure to tell them that."

His heart was again thundering too loudly, threatening to give away his presence.

"You just try to do that," hissed the second voice, positively shaking. "You filthy piece of excrement, I'll make sure you will never be able to walk straight again."

Two panicked steps brought Miztli back to the relative safety of the previous corridor.

"You try to do that yourself," snickered the first voice, unimpressed. "Empty promises, brother. You can't best me and you won't be able to carry on with your canoe-loads if you keep messing things up."

The darkness came to life with more grating upon the heavily damp stones.

"I'm not messing anything up. That other opening under the causeway; it wasn't me who left it open."

"Who then?"

To his relief, the voices began drawing away, leaving him holding his breath, his back covered with sweat, heart still fluttering. They were talking about the stone he had removed and left open, weren't they? They were the ones to discover it and move the crate away. And what if they were still lingering there when he rushed to jump in without thinking?

"They pay us to put the clubs there without making the entire Tenochtitlan aware of it, you stupid frog-eater."

"I wasn't the one to leave that passage open!" protested the second man, his cry echoing between the narrow walls. "I wasn't there since we arrived."

"Then who was there to move that stone aside and peek in? Curious fishermen? Oh, you are laughable, brother, you are! And the highborn Tlatelolcan scum won't be pleased, that much I promise you."

For some time, he didn't dare to let out a held breath, then, as the voices died away for good, he ventured to turn around, anxious to grope his way back without being detected. No, these people wouldn't be offering any help, that much was obvious. They would rather harm the intruders instead.

A new draft of air swept over his bare back, bringing along the strong scent of burning torch, all this cheap oil. Whirling around, his incredulous gaze took in a silhouette, standing rock-still, staring at him.

For a heartbeat, nothing happened. The torch flickered weakly, giving barely any light. In its poor illumination, the man's face looked like a skull, with two dark round holes for eyes and the gaping mouth to match. Miztli felt his heart coming to a total halt. Yet, as the man lurched forward, as though not clear about his own intentions, whether to grab the intruder or just strike him with his torch, his heart came back to life with a start. Desperate not to let his assailant block his only route of escape, he literally threw himself toward the corridor to his right, his only aim – the safety of the darkness in there, no flickering dots in the original corridor and no stinking musk of the smoking torch.

The man guessed his intention, waving his beacon as though it was a weapon itself, thrusting its glow onto his path, the narrowness of the corridor on his side. It drew a prettily glowing line, shimmering weakly but still scorching hot. A familiar feeling.

He didn't hesitate, not even for a heartbeat. This flame was no vicious blaze from his red-hot braziers, not even close. Pushing it away with both hands, he barely felt any burning sensation. In the next heartbeat, the feeble flare was flickering, fluttering upon the floor, defeated.

He didn't stay to watch it die. As though all the creatures of the Underworld were after him, he charged into the blissful darkness, praying that he remembered the way.

CHAPTER 6

The moment her oldest brother came back, taking their mother's attention away, Chantli bolted for the outside, relieved beyond measure. There were only so many activities one could take on a given day and this particular afternoon was full to bursting already. She needed time – time to think, time to understand, to absorb the imminent change. However, with Mother fussing about the possible expense of new clothes, shoes, and other accessories that would have to be purchased, and on such a short notice, it was plain impossible to concentrate, so her brother's usually annoying chattering and complaints – what a self-centered lump of meat he was, the precious first-born, the prospective successor – came just in time.

Jumping over the twisted rows of vegetables adorning their tiny patio, just a strip of dusty earth, really, with no border to separate it from the greenery of their neighbors, nothing like the patios one could glimpse in the neighborhoods beyond the marketplace and toward the Central Plaza, Chantli hastened her step, not willing to be detected and probably called back. There were evening chores that still needed to be attended, with Mother not being happy if left to deal with the washing of the cooking facilities or rearranging the inner rooms for the nighttime by padding them with plenty of *petate*-mats all by herself. Still, there were times when a person needed the opportunity to think things over.

Oh, that towering bright, beautiful temple; so high, so imposing, so polished and refined. Would she manage to enter it without making some terrible blunder? Would she manage to go through one single day without committing twenty mistakes along the way? They were so sure of themselves, these dwellers of the Royal Enclosure, so confident, so cultured. How could she spend one single heartbeat there without sticking out like a torch in the night, without making them angry with her? And why didn't Father tell her beforehand? He could have, at least, hinted. When he ordered her to dress her best and accompany him to the Great Pyramid's precinct, he could have let her know about any of it, relay what was at stake. Then she would have behaved better, wouldn't have followed that boy into his dubious secret passages, for one. But were they angry with her sweeping through the main entrance, as though nothing happened, and just as they were coming back. Oh mighty deities, but Father even looked as though he might strike her, he who rarely slapped even his sons. And that scary man, the priest of that temple, the most important one. When Father made her face this dark-clothed statue of a person, she had been positively terrified, way beyond words or actions. Such a tall, aloof, freezing presence, eyeing her through his squinting eyes with a certain amount of interest, as though she had been an insect that he had yet to decide its usefulness – to squish it out of the way or to boil it in the cooking pot? Like the delicious crispy *chapulin*, the grasshoppers, prepared in a special way, the snack the children of their neighborhood cherished above any other.

Hesitating over the dusty pathway leading toward the nearby workshop of the feather-maker and his family house, she tried not to let her misgivings gnaw and make her lose the last of her confidence. Didn't she expect to be sent to school anyway? She had seen fourteen summers; she was of age. Their local *telpochcalli* had a vast ground-floor room dedicated to girls and their lessons, the female children of traders and craftsmen, those who wished to improve their daughters' skills and, most of all, their marital eligibility. Even so, the school was reported to be fun. She was looking forward to it, to attend the classes with several of her girl friends, to see what it was all about. However, now?

Oh mighty deities, but how was she to make her way beyond the Great Plaza every morning, such a long walk, to enter that scary temple or the sprawling cluster of buildings behind it that her unexpected companion was talking about; to spend her days alone and out of place, challenged with unfamiliar things. Would she manage? And would she be required to sleep there, like that boy from the temple? In *telpochcalli*, only boys slept, but who knew what the rules were in the imperial snobbish *calmecac*? Would she be as unhappy there as that boy, sneaking away the moment she could? Somehow, she suspected it would be exactly the case. Oh mighty deities!

Shaking her head, she remembered their conversation, the shared adventure of sneaking through that corridor, eavesdropping on the gossiping priests. He was such a rascal, a funny type that one couldn't but wish to like and put in his place at the same time, a strange combination. He claimed to be one of the royal house, that his brother was Tenochtitlan's Emperor, even though she had her doubts about that. An offspring of the royal family? No! One didn't meet such legendary persons out there on the streets. Even though it happened near the Royal Enclosure, come to think of it. Still, this boy must have been making it up, taking her for a silly commoner who wouldn't know better. How surprised he was with her claim that her brothers went to the 'commoners school' – that was how he put it, the haughty little beast. As though he was any better, even though of course his clothes were terribly expensive, his cloak elaborately decorated, and his sandals the most glittering wear she had ever seen. It was difficult to see the leather under the sparkle of pretty stones.

"Chantli!"

The apparition, a form caked with mud and splattered with streaks of earth alternating with patches of dust in an elaborate manner, like a war paint, with a messed up loincloth and a disheveled hair to match, fell upon her as she hesitated under the torch fastened on the wall of Father's workshop, uncertain of her destination now that it was already dark. Deep in thought, she didn't notice anyone nearing, and now her heart pumped madly, trying to jump out of her chest. What an annoyance!

"What's wrong with you?" Wide-eyed, she stared at the workshop boy, recognizing the familiar features but barely, all mud and scratches and maybe even some blood.

"Nothing," he panted, obviously having a hard time catching his breath.

Taking in the wildness of his appearance and, more importantly, the atypical way his eyes darted, looking furtive and afraid, she stepped closer, curious now, even perturbed. "Where have you been?"

"Nowhere." He was still gasping, doubled over, evidently putting it all in the attempt to catch his breath, his palms planted against his muscled upper legs, supporting, in a way.

In the few moons he had been living in the workshop, she never saw him either that drained or that agitated; or so neglected, for that matter. Half-naked villager from the gods-forsaken south or not, he did bother to wash his face every morning, arranging his uncut hair in a neat bun. There was no way to work in his blazing prison otherwise without chancing burning one's hair and the rest of one's body along the way. Also, she remembered, he was very meticulous about going to the nearest shore for a thorough wash up at the end of each day, even for just a quick dip. He wasn't invited to visit local *temazcalli* baths along with their family and other respectable people of the neighborhood. Still, he always looked satisfactorily neat when outside of the melting room, yet now he presented the image of the wildest of the barbarians from beyond the eastern highlands, or the way Tenochtitlan people would imagine those people.

"Were you allowed to leave the workshop?" she inquired, somewhat at a loss as to how to proceed.

He nodded readily, his breath stabilizing. "Yes, yes. Acatlo told me I can go. He agreed when Patli asked." Straightening up, he peered at her, uncertain once again. "Did he say something? Is your father back already?"

She just nodded. "We came back not long ago. Father is eating. Or maybe he went to the workshop again. If you go now, he might be there."

He shook his head violently, looking as though about to take a step back. "He is in the workshop?"

"Yes, why wouldn't he be? He is always working after the

evening meal. Do you know him so little?" Deciding to see the funny side of it, the safest of courses, always when something puzzling was involved, Chantli grinned. "I don't think he is mad with you being out or something. Maybe he didn't even notice. Out there in the Royal Enclosure, he was certainly busy with more important things than wild boys getting into trouble." A shrug seemed to be in order. "You can sneak back into the workshop the moment he is gone. He won't stay there for long, not this evening. He has things to think over and prepare." Her own predicament surfaced, serving to dampen her mood once again. But what would she do out there in the *calmecac* temple? What would they make her learn or perform?

"But I need…" Suddenly, his eyes widened and he peered at her with renewed interest, all expectancy and hope. "Can you… maybe… would you?"

"What?" It was funny, the way he gazed at her, like a child determined to ask but afraid at the same time. "You don't make much sense."

"Would you go in there and fetch a rope?" He frowned painfully, eyes boring into her, gauging her reactions.

"A rope?" she repeated, stupefied.

"Yes. Something long, durable; a good rope. He has those things. In the chest with the smaller tools, by the inner doorway. There are plenty of ropes there, not long enough, maybe, but we can tie them together. Two pieces." He was talking in a rush now, or rather, thinking aloud. "That should be enough."

She eyed him with growing uneasiness. "You don't make any sense, Miztli."

The ring of his name seemed to bring him back to reality. His frown deepened. "You won't tell him about what I asked? Your father or your brothers."

"No…" She measured him with a pointed glance. "But you will have to tell me what you need this rope for." Pursing her lips, she narrowed her eyes against his scowl. "Then I will help you and won't tell a word, I promise."

His forehead looked like a wrinkled blanket, furrowed by too many creases. "I can't."

"Yes, you can. You need my help."

Another painfully undecided scrutiny. "You promise not to tell?"

"Yes!" She felt the excitement tickling in her hands and feet. What secret did he harbor?

Dubiously, he glanced at the surrounding darkness, as though afraid that the dancing shadows the oiled torch was casting would give his secret away. "Patli and two other boys, they are stuck under the causeway. You know, this thing with bridges and beams."

"Under the causeway?" she cried out, then pressed her palms to her mouth, muffling the rest of the cry. "Which one?"

"The one that is near here."

"The Tlatelolco causeway?"

He just nodded, glancing around again.

"How did they get there?"

He rolled his eyes in a telling grimace. "It's a long story. I'll tell you later, some of it, I promise, but now I need to hurry. They are stuck there, and that *calmecac* boy, he is bleeding. His arm is in bad shape. And also, these people from the tunnels, they may try and look for us and trace our way straight away to where they are now. Or here, for that matter. I don't know if they followed me here." The sudden flood of his words stopped, mainly for lack of air, or so she suspected. "I need to return there and fast!"

She gave up trying to comprehend his fragmented phrases and words. "I'll get you that rope. Wait for me here."

"Bring two," he called after her, but she just nodded and hastened her step, her elation welling. Maybe Mother would not notice her absence if she was busy with either of her complaining stepsons or with anything, really. Oh mighty deities, please let her remain too busy. For this was one adventure she wasn't about to miss out on. Trust Patli to get his new friends in trouble. Oh yes, her cousin had a nose for places and experiences and an unquenchable thirst for risky adventures. And if the apprentice village boy was allowed to join, then so was she. Especially now that her freedom to run about was going to end, abruptly at that.

Father wasn't in the workshop at all and she breathed with

relief, her sense of urgency prevailing, making her rush through the chests, frantic. What if he came back and asked her for the purpose of all this poring around? Ropes, oh yes, he kept the maguey woven ropes, the sturdiest of them all, the very best quality. Enough to pull someone up the causeway? She didn't know the answer to that, but that boy Miztli seemed like someone who would know. Oh, how lucky it was that Father had every possible tool or accessory close at hand, even accessories he rarely used. For good measure, she grabbed a few coiled bundles before bolting toward the outside, in a rush now.

Miztli's silhouette was hovering next to the doorway, apparently unable to wait patiently at the place she had left him.

"Did you get it?"

"Yes." She waved her loot before his face but took her hand away quickly as he reached for it. "Let us go."

"You can't," he gasped, staring at her and not trying to resume the attempts to recapture her goods.

"Yes, I can," she repeated firmly, turning to go. "Are you coming or not?"

After a heartbeat of silence, his footsteps caught up with her. "Your father will be furious."

"He won't even know. We'll be back quickly."

"And what if we aren't?"

"Why? Tlatelolco causeway is such a short walk from here, and it's not yet dangerous. It's not the dead of the night. Everyone is still out and about."

He shrugged and said nothing, walking beside her silently, surprisingly light-footed for the strong broad boy that he was, fit for carrying his heavy loads, spending his time lifting massive ceramic pots and blazing braziers. Oh, but how Father kept reflecting on the usefulness of his new apprentice, boasting of his strength and endurance! Not every boy who had been admitted to work here lasted for longer than a market interval. Even her brothers found every excuse to avoid spending time in the braziers' room, not to mention Patli, the crafty troublemaker.

"Tell me what happened. Why do you look – and smell! – like someone who got dragged all over the lake's bottom and worse?

What's Patli got you into?"

He shrugged again, then looked around, openly troubled. "Is this the way to that causeway? We didn't walk through here before."

"It's the better way," she said, lifting her own shoulders with pretended indifference, thrilled with the feeling of proving herself better than them yet again. "Patli doesn't know all the alleys around this part of the city. But I do."

He looked impressed.

"Patli is just boasting around, but he came to Tenochtitlan not long before you. So if he lords it over you, any of it, tell him to go and jump into the lake."

This time, he giggled. "He won't do it unless pushed. Not with the scary things that swim in your lake."

"What things?"

But his brief outburst of merriment was gone. "I don't know. Something scary."

"Where?" The quietness of his voice made her aware of the surrounding darkness, despite the moon and the passersby's torches, flickering helpfully, lighting some of their way.

"Under that causeway. In the reeds."

"How do you know?"

"We... we ran into it. Out there, in the reeds." It was difficult to hear his words now, the way he was muttering, as though afraid to say it aloud. "It was terrible and... and vicious. Bloodthirsty. It wanted to eat us or drown us. Or do both."

She willed her legs into keeping their pace, because he didn't seem as if he was about to slow down or stop for good, despite his hair-raising stories. "It attacked you?"

"Yes! It jumped on me and it tried to pull me down. We were fighting with that *calmecac* boy. He is so annoying and stupid! But then, then this thing, it was grabbing my head. From behind. Clutching it with twenty hands or more, pulling me under the water. It was terrible."

The frantic flow of words stopped as suddenly as it burst out, as though drained. She didn't care. What he said was too terrifying to keep on listening. For a heartbeat, a silence prevailed, interrupted by the hum of people around the wharves and down the lakeshore. In the nearest alley, someone was playing a flute quite unskillfully, blowing in a mess of tunes.

"How did you get away?" she whispered, barely recognizing her own voice, such a pitifully weak sound. "If it was… if it was an *ahuitzotl*, then you were supposed to… supposed to…"

It was easy to feel his shudder. "What's an *ahuitzotl*?"

She halted for good. "What do you mean?"

In the strengthening moonlight, his frown was clearly visible, a deep scowl. "I don't know. You say… that thing… what is it, this spiny-water-something?"

"You don't know?"

"No."

Shaking her head, she resumed her walk, mainly to get away from the disharmonious flute that grew louder, desperate to succeed. "You are a strange one. How can you not know what *ahuitzotl* is? Even foreigners should know that."

He grunted something angry in response.

"The Water Spiny One is very dangerous," she said when the warehouses retreated, leaving them with the strong odor of fish and the view of the causeway, just a dark mass stretching in the glittering water, ending at the wharves of Tlatelolco, a desolate line glimmering with occasional light, not difficult to see. The other island was only a short distance away. The foreigners often presumed that both islands were one entity of two independent cities. "If you met it and came out alive, you are a very lucky person, you and your friends."

"What does it do?" he asked, hastening his step, clearly relieved to reach their destination at last.

"It pulls you under the water, makes you drown. Then it eats your eyes out and your teeth. And your fingernails too." Pleased with the effect, as he was gaping at her with an open dread now, she nodded in order to reinforce her claims. "It has an arm on its tail, which of course is long and huge, and it uses it to pull people under most effectively." To talk like that and in such close proximity to the water felt wrong. She curbed her urge to frighten him some more. "So if you truly ran into this creature, you are very lucky to be alive now and talking about it."

"Can it climb out of the water?" Again, he was walking too fast, making it difficult to keep up with him.

"No, I don't think it can."

"Still, we need to get them out of there in a hurry," he muttered, hastening his step into a near run.

Out of breath, she made it a point not to complain. Even though without her help he couldn't have reached the causeway so fast, running all the way or not, there was no need to give him cause to regret bringing her along.

"Do you think it was *ahuitzotl* and not something –"

A group of slim silhouettes sprang into their view, emerging from the darkness of the courtyard belonging to the old temple, now just a cluster of abandoned buildings. Gripping their torches, they moved decidedly, glancing around, curiously on guard. Nothing out of the ordinary, with this area abounding with smugglers and worse, she reflected, shrugging off the tiny splash of worry. At this time of the evening, they were still safe. It was… The suddenness with which his palm locked around her upper arm startled her, made her sway. She struggled to break free, but he pulled her on and into a nearby pathway, narrow and stinking, full of fish and its entrails, the leftovers from the activities of the day.

"What are you…"

"Keep quiet," he was hissing, pressing her arm tightly, even painfully. "Don't…"

Not accustomed to being treated in such manner, she pulled away sharply, ready to hit him or rake him with her nails if he tried to grab her again. "How dare you!"

The torches of the men were upon them, following, attracted by the noise probably. She didn't care. Just who did he think he was to treat her in this way? The uncouth foreigner, the stupid half-naked villager!

The stench of the cheap oil reinforced the natural foulness of the small alley's odor. She glared at him, welcoming this unexpected source of illumination. "Who do you think you are to do this?"

He didn't bother to answer, staring past her, at the intruders with torches, as tense as a metal string that was coiled too tightly, about to recoil; those copper strings Father used to produce for the woven bells. Puzzled, she glanced back. The men were four in all, thin and sinewy, wearing loincloths, their girdles outlined by the dancing shadows, surely stocked with knives and other cutting devices. Smugglers!

"Is that the whelp?" one of them cried out, thrusting his dripping beacon so close it made her eyes water.

For a wild moment, she thought he was going to grab them with the arm still burdened by the burning stick, or maybe strike them with it. Then the boy launched forward with the agility of a snake, and not the cat-like creature he was named after, striking fast with one arm, knocking the torch down. In another heartbeat, she felt herself being pulled again, more decisively than before, yet this time, she didn't resist. Panting, she ran after him, letting him pull her into one alley, then another, trusting his instincts rather than her knowledge of the area this time. He certainly knew what he was doing.

CHAPTER 7

The rope was good, made out of maguey and fastened with many strings. Necalli tried to pay no attention to his throbbing arm, which curiously troubled him less than immediately after being dragged onto the firm land. The gashes in it were still bleeding, but slowly, not vigorously, and there was a measure of consolation in it. It was torn badly enough, wasn't it? Still, it didn't seem as though he was about to bleed to death.

He shuddered again, remembering the dreadful encounter. How vicious the creature was, how strong. Attacking them with such relentlessness, not about to give up and go away. It was set on having them all for its meal, their eyes and their teeth, and their fingernails. Oh mighty deities!

"Just hold on to this thing with all you have. Don't let it go. Can you manage?" Axolin's voice brought him back to the rope he was clutching, and the reality of the damp humming darkness, the sound of the waves murmuring softly, too near to reassure. "You go up first."

He nodded briefly, clutching his lower lip between his teeth. Under different circumstances, he would have insisted on seeing the other two off before he went, like a good leader should. However, now he was too exhausted and numb with continuous pain; too scared, truth be told. Could the water monster climb up shorelines for a stroll around the dry land, or rather, for a good hunt? This question and many others of the sort had kept circling in his head through the endless waiting, while the darkness grew deeper and their fears mushroomed accordingly, with the workshop boy not coming back, the worthless piece of commoner meat that he was.

Why did they trust him in the first place, that little pile of excrement from some stupid foreign village? Why didn't Axolin or even Patli go? They could have, couldn't they? Or maybe even he himself, the torn arm or not. He could climb back into the stupid tunnel, make his way in the darkness until he found its far edge. How many additional corridors could be down there anyway? And yet, no one found enough courage to return to the accursed passageway under the lake, no one but the barefoot commoner who fought quite bravely back there in the reeds, leaping to his, Necalli's, aid along with Axolin when Patli wouldn't.

Every time he remembered, he would glare at the *telpochcalli* boy, even though the thunderbolts his eyes shot seemed to be wasted in the thickening darkness. Then the fear would return, triggered by the dreaded question. Could the monstrous *ahuitzotl* come back, swim after the scent of their blood or their fear, climb this pitifully small piece of land, attack them again, now only three youths; scared, exhausted, and wounded? What a thought.

"Are you coming?" This came from the dark mass of the earthwork, somewhere above their heads, a loud whispering. "Hurry up."

Necalli clutched the rope with both hands, disregarding the pain and the renewed trickling, the blood seeping out, oozing slowly, making the unseemly dread return.

"You go after me," he said hurriedly, addressing Axolin. "Let the *telpochcalli* boy be the last, the useless piece of cowardly meat that he is."

"I'm not a coward," protested Patli with little spirit or conviction.

Necalli readjusted his grip on the rope. "Shut up." The urge to tell this one what he thought about him and his kind welled, but he pushed it away, ashamed to admit that he might be lingering now on purpose, postponing the challenge of the climb. The slanting side of the earthwork's foundation was disgustingly slippery, reeking of rot, jabbing with its multitude of sharp edges, pieces of rock and sharp gravel, and whatever else it was built of.

But to have both functioning arms!

He clenched his teeth against the groan as the first pull had him hanging in the air, catching his breath, gathering energy for the next one. Another agonized heartbeat saw him clinging to the revolting surface, grateful for its existence now, pressing against it.

The rope shuddered and even though he knew that the workshop boy must be having a hard time trying not to let it slip, taking his, Necalli's, entire weight on the strength of his arms maybe, he still didn't find enough power to go on. Just another moment of respite. His wounded arm pumped with pain, each wave fiercer than the other, and he just couldn't make it attempt the next feat of bravery, not yet.

As the rope shuddered more violently and then actually began sliding, he was just about to push on, feeling his hands slipping anyway, afraid he would go plummeting down and after such a desperate effort. Busy fighting to keep himself glued to their only means of escape, he felt himself being yanked upwards, his limbs hitting the uneven surface of the wall, his mind in a jumble. The next thing he knew, he was tugged again, this time by his shoulders, jerked unceremoniously, pushed over the low barrier and onto the flattened ground, gasping with pain, the flattened stones jutting against his limbs, but not as badly as the ones of the outer wall, not as vicious and mean.

"Are you good?" In the silvery glimmer of the moon that poured its light generously here, unrestricted by the shadow of the massive earthwork, the workshop boy's face looked as though he had been preparing to go into a battle, with a strange sort of pattern covering his features, from the dark of numerous scratches to the dull gray of the splattered mud, his hair sticking out in a ridiculous manner.

Unable not to, Necalli snickered. "You should see yourself now, working boy. A crazy sight."

Unexpectedly, his rescuer grinned, his teeth flashing in the darkness. "You should see yourself, *calmecac* boy. Not such a pretty sight either." Another light chortle. "Feeling any better?"

Necalli considered this thoughtfully. "No, but it's good to be up here and away from there."

"I bet." Then the grin disappeared. "Let go of the rope. They are waiting for it too."

"Oh." He sat up, then took in their additional company. A wary silhouette adorned with two braids and some hair sticking out around it, standing there apprehensively, clearly not just a curious passerby judging by the assertiveness of her pose, all eyes and expectation. The bundle she clutched seemed to contain ropes or cloths or both. "Who are you?"

The girl said nothing, staying at a safe distance, studying him with the unconcealed curiosity of a person who has stumbled over a rare animal. It irritated him, this open scrutiny, inappropriate in a woman, whether a lady who wouldn't stare at a man no matter who he was out of mere decency, or a maid who wouldn't dare to look at the nobles directly out of pure humbleness if nothing else. Just who did this fowl think she was?

Giving her a look that he hoped relayed everything he thought about her presumptuousness, he pulled himself up resolutely, struggling onto his feet, painfully aware of the gracelessness with which he did this. But for the damn arm. The pain was again more bearable now that he didn't need to hang on to it, but he didn't care for his limb's obvious swollenness and the trickling blood, both pronounced more clearly in the helpful illumination of the moon, with no room for mistake or illusion.

The commoner boy was grinding his teeth, struggling against the rope that was jerking madly, dancing in his outstretched hands, threatening to pull him over the edge. It was obvious that Axolin, no climber under the best of circumstances, was having a hard time battling the embankment's wall. Necalli pushed his arm, along with the girl, out of his mind. To grab the edge of the rope with his good hand turned out to be surprisingly easy.

"The damn stupid wall," Axolin was gasping, dragged over the rough border stones, with both Necalli and the working boy having wasted the last of their strength, unable to summon enough enthusiasm to try to be gentle with their pull. "The stinking, rotting causeway!"

He could hear the girl's snicker, brief and muffled, but there.

"Now Patli." The workshop boy was already busy gliding the rope back down the edge. But did that one have an inexhaustible amount of dedication and determination! Necalli felt like leaving their cowardly *telpochcalli* accomplice to his own devices. Why was the working commoner bothering so much? It was not as though Patli did something for him, helped him in the lake while the monster attacked him, or even came to his aid when Axolin was trying to beat him into more humbleness. Then he remembered the connection. Oh yes, that one worked in Patli's father's or uncle's workshop, melting some stinking copper. Of course he could not slink back into his workplace without having the owner's relative along, hale and healthy.

"I'll help you," said the girl, coming closer in the meantime. She had a nice voice, quite melodious.

"Who is this?" whispered Axolin, picking himself up with as much artlessness as Necalli himself had displayed before. But was the climbing of the annoying water construction a stupid business!

Necalli just shrugged, watching the girl as she leaned over the slippery edge, doing so gracefully, with much skill. A marketplace fowl, undoubtedly, but an able one, a pleasant-looking sight. The occasional passersby, not many at this time of the evening, slowed their steps, some stopping to gawk, others just glancing, exchanging mirthful comments.

Pursing his lips, Necalli pushed forward, inserting himself between these two and next to the commoner boy, grabbing the edge of the rope once again. Lowborn fowl that this girl must be, he still couldn't let her do a man's work.

"We better hurry," he whispered, motioning with his head at the crowding people. "Before the authorities come and start asking questions."

The boy by his side shuddered. "Or the smugglers from the tunnel," he murmured, doubling his efforts, yanking at the rope hard.

"What smugglers?"

"The men…" Shaking his head in order to get rid of the wild tendrils that were fluttering in front of his face, muddied and insistent, he went on gasping. "In that tunnel… there were men…

They almost caught me, and then outside, out there by the wharves..."

Patli, apparently lighter than the impressively muscled Axolin, slipped onto the ground like a fish pulled into a fisherman's canoe. Amused, Necalli watched him fluttering by their feet, trying to catch his breath, or maybe to contain the pain. He remembered how it felt to be hauled over the spiky wall. Nothing pleasant, even though it was better than their battle with the lake's monster.

"Thank you," the *telpochcalli* boy was mumbling, addressing him in particular, glancing at Axolin, paying no attention to his peer from the workshop.

"Thank him," said Necalli curtly, suddenly incensed. "Your friend did more than anyone to drag you out of this mess."

An awkward silence prevailed. Even the people around halted their conversations, apparently enjoying the unfolding show.

"Let us be off."

"But you are bleeding." This time it was the girl, watching him through a puzzled frown.

"Not that badly," he said, ridiculously pleased with the opportunity to display his bravery, disregarding the wound among other flesh matters. The *calmecac* teachers, whether veterans or priests, always harped on that, the warrior's mandatory ability to be above physical pain or any other such concern. He scowled at the watching commoners. "The entertainment is over." Most of their audience stared back, unabashed. The dwellers of the poorest districts were always this way, and here, near Tlatelolco causeway, there was the best representation of those. "Let us go."

The workshop boy responded to this last command with surprising alacrity for the one previously set in his own way of doing things. Pressing against the edge of the embankment so closely he chanced falling back into the water or the meager piece of land they went to such pains in order to escape, he slipped alongside it, aiming to disappear back into the city and fast, or so it seemed. Necalli made a face. This one was a strange bird, but trustworthy, with a fair share of courage and good thinking. A surprise.

"What took you so long?" he asked quietly, edging their copper-melting company away from the rest of them, pleased to see that the boy got the hint, falling into his, Necalli's, step quite naturally, a few paces ahead of the others. "Did you run into trouble? What's with the girl?" A quick glance at their followers informed him that the pretty fowl was hurrying alongside Patli now, talking to him in a breathless rush. "Where did you dig this thing from?"

"Chantli?" The boy shot him a puzzled glance. "She is the daughter of old Tlaquitoc. She got the rope."

"Who is this old Tlaquitoc?"

"The craftsman, the metal-worker. The owner of the workshop."

"Oh." He side-glanced his companion again, taking in the broadness of the youth's shoulders and the sturdiness of his legs and arms, displaying scratches and bruises aplenty, some obviously not the fruit of their afternoon adventures. "Are you his slave?"

"No!" The boy reared in horror. "I'm no one's slave!"

"Relax," said Necalli, nudging his companion into resuming their walk with a swift thrust of his elbow, not hurtfully but firmly, his good arm supporting the wounded one. "You said 'owner,' and you look no better than a slave anyway. Also Patli, that worthless piece of cowardly meat, treats you like dirt. Not like a member of that workshop family or something."

The boy grunted something in response.

"What's your name, anyway?"

"ItzMiztli."

"Obsidian Puma? Not bad. Miztli will do, though."

"Of course. Everyone calls me that."

Shrugging in response, Necalli turned into the darker alley, glad to reach the mainland again. The worst of the reckless adventure was over and not too soon. Oh, but would the *calmecac* authorities be incensed with them coming back well after darkness. Even though the evening rites could be missed out on safely from time to time, if one didn't do it too often and didn't have the bad luck of popping into the temple's priests' mind while still missing.

"So, where you came from, that's all you people do, crawling tunnels and mines?"

"Some of us, yes." Even though away from the causeway and the attention of the curious crowds, the boy remained as tense as an overstretched maguey string, shooting narrowed glances around, evidently ready to bolt away. "My father works in the mountains. They bring green pieces of copper and other things to melt. Canoe-loads of those. They send them to *altepetls* like Tenochtitlan, for the people like old Tlaquitoc, to mix with silver and gold, or sometimes other substances, to melt and then work into beautiful things. The craftsmen work on those."

"Do they have to dig tunnels like the one under the causeway?"

"Sometimes."

"What do you think was there? Did you see anything interesting on your way back?"

Another furtive glance around. "Those weapons we saw in that room with the opening, there are plenty more in other corridors."

"What corridors? Are there more tunnels in there?" The web of narrow pathways began to haunt him. Were they going to find their way out and into more respectable neighborhoods?

"Oh yes. Plenty." The deep-set eyes rested on him, narrow, brimming with tension. "At least two more, and people running all over them, like underground rats, carrying chests from that other city, beyond the causeway."

"Tlatelolco?"

"Yes."

"You saw all this on your way back?" A new alley looked promising, lined by cane-and-reed shacks, but broader, suggesting that it might lead them to more acceptable places. From the colorful walls of the marketplace, it was not such a long way back to school and not so unfamiliar.

"Well, yes." The boy shrugged and returned to eye their surroundings, more on guard now that people were hurrying past or just strolling, his gaze scanning them alertly, narrowed against the generous illumination of the moon. "They had torches and it was easy to spy on them, as they were busy carrying things and talking and getting angry at each other. But then..." He grimaced painfully. "Well, then one surprised me from behind and I had to bolt away. Too far, too fast." He shrugged again, but this time, the pursed lips were twisting into a crooked sort of a grin. "That man with the torch was no runner."

"But he did try to chase you?"

"Yes."

Axolin's hurried footsteps caught up with them before the tall boy materialized by their side, evidently not interested in the company of the *telpochcalli* pupil and a pretty but dubious marketplace fowl. "Where are we?"

The workshop boy returned to watch the road ahead quite abruptly.

Necalli made a face. "I wish I knew." Pretending indifference seemed like the best of courses when lost and about to get in trouble with school authorities. "In the end, we'll get somewhere."

Axolin's snort rolled down the unimpressive row of would-be houses, ruffling their shaky walls like the gusts of wind that kept whipping all around. "We need to be back in school before all the stars are out and shining. Old Yaotzin will piss hot water if we don't appear at the temple in time. And you need to have your arm bandaged before that. Maybe it needs to be seen by a healer." His eyes shot toward the commoner. "Don't you know of a good way to reach the marketplace and fast?"

"No, I don't," drawled Miztli-boy, scowling with the challenge of a cornered animal, in the way he did through this entire evening, come to think of it, reflected Necalli. A puma indeed, obsidian or not. What a spectacular name for a foreigner from this or that gods-forsaken village.

"Useless piece of commoner dirt," related Axolin, back to the lack of patience he displayed in the tunnel or while wading in the reeds of the lake.

"Not like some stinking no-good piece of excrement," retorted the boy promptly, clearly not averse to resuming the fighting stopped by the water monster, inconsiderately at that.

Rolling his eyes, Necalli pushed himself between the two antagonists, incensed and amused at the same time.

"Stop it, you stupid ugly male turkeys, both of you. It's not the time." Axolin looked unimpressed, so he pushed his friend away, using his shoulder. "Miztli is no useless commoner, so stop calling him names. If you want to beat someone, go for Patli. He is as useless as they come." Slowing his step, he looked back, gesturing at the *telpochcalli* boy to catch up. This one was dragging unhurriedly, still plaguing the girl with his stories, looking clumsy and out of place beside the efficiency and the grace of her stride. Despite the modestly long, simply embroidered maguey skirt, it was easy to imagine the length of her legs or the grace of their sway. She *was* a pretty thing. "Patli, move your stupid behind. We need to find our way back to the city and fast."

Patli was glancing whichever way, set on not meeting his eyes apparently. Necalli snorted.

"It is not such a long way from here to the marketplace main square," offered the girl, meeting his gaze with no misgivings as opposed to her contemptible family member. "You need to stick to the workshops areas and then turn by the Tlaloc's temple next to the colorful wall of the marketplace and follow the roads there."

Against his will, he watched her, liking the way her eyes glimmered with earnest simplicity, answering his gaze openly, with a glaring lack of modesty, which now, for some reason pleased him, appeared like a natural thing. She was no shrill marketplace fowl, this one. Anything but.

"We don't know all those roads, behind the workshops or wherever." The thought occurred to him, pleasant and full of possibilities. "Can you show us the way?"

She frowned thoughtfully, but this time, Patli came to life all at once. "Who do you think she is, a market girl?" he demanded, regaining his past self-assurance or some of it, lost so entirely since the event in the lake. "Chantli is a respectable girl, not your commoner fowls you talk about day and night!"

"Shut up," growled Necalli, aware of the awkwardness in this situation and more incensed by it. Just who did this stupid piece of slimy meat think he was, to presume lecturing him on commoner fowls or anyone else, for that matter? And in front of her! "Swallow your tongue behind your teeth and keep it there before I make you do that."

But now it was Axolin's turn to take sides, and of the commoner part of their party as well. "Stop yelling at him. He talked sense. He can take us back to *calmecac*. Why bother the girl?"

"Because that's what I want to do," grunted Necalli, feeling at an acute disadvantage, worse with every uttered word.

"Nice of you to want things." The damn Axolin was enjoying it. He glared at his friend, contemplating putting his teeth out of use before doing this to Patli.

"It's too dark and too far." This time it was the girl's voice, delightfully calm and husky, with no undercurrents to mar it and make it sound as stupid as they did. "I have to run home and hope that Mother didn't notice. Miztli can take me, while Patli will take you both to your school. You have to go back to your *telpochcalli* anyway."

"Your father may want to see me before I go," muttered Patli, his lips pursed tight, eyes glowing eerily, challenging but wary, the regular expression.

She brushed his protests aside with sweet assertiveness. "I'll make excuses, keep Father busy. He won't notice your absence."

"He probably already noticed. And your absence too."

This served to dampen her radiance, and to renew Necalli's spell of anger. But did the slimy piece of work Patli enjoy rubbing her face into the trouble she might have gotten herself into.

"We'll take you home, then go back to our school," he declared firmly, taking the lead. "Which way is it?"

The glow of her face was back, even if partly. "This way." She waved in the direction they had just left, non-committal. "Behind the warehouses and the workshops. Where the feather-workers sell their craft."

"And what about your arm, you gallant warrior?" reminded Axolin, smirking again with no shame. "What if it falls off for good while you are busy doing silly things?"

"Shut up."

Oh, but he didn't need his friend's needling, not now, but the girl stepped forward at once, grabbing the limb in question with little ceremony. "Let me see."

For a heartbeat, he felt like snatching his hand away, startled by her lack of manners again. Then the warmth of her touch made him reconsider. Such a strange sensation, like jumping into cold water through the midwinter celebrations, invigorating and unsettling at the same time. He held his breath.

"It looks like a bite," she declared, pulling him into the moonlit patch of the road. "Something big, with large teeth."

"It was," confirmed Patli when no one else would.

"*Ahuitzotl*?" she breathed, dropping his hand as though it was poisoned, taking the thrilling sensation away. Her eyes leapt at none other than the workshop boy, who kept remarkably quiet, picking no fights with Axolin. One good turn.

They all nodded silently.

"Then you must visit Tlaloc's temple! You must consult one of the *tlaloque*, the priests. They are the only ones who can deal with *ahuitzotl* and its deeds."

Her eyes, nicely large and well spaced, now wide-open, peered at him anxiously, eager to convince, but the agitation did not suit her, spoiling the exquisiteness of her delicate features. He didn't care. Her words cascaded down his spine like sharp pebbles, hurting physically, sending his mind into panicked fits, like back in the lake. But of course! How silly he was, disregarding this matter as unimportant, trying to push it out of his mind. It was no simple rat or dog that bit him. No, he could not get away by putting on ointment and hoping the wound would heal soon enough without rotting into bad things.

"I... yes, well yes, I'll do it. Of course." To admit that some silly girl from a workshop knew better than he, a *calmecac* student instructed in the ways of the deities as much as in history, mathematics, and martial matters, hurt. "I know I should consult one of the *tlaloque*. I was going to."

"Tlaloc's temple is on your way to the Plaza," she offered briskly, missing the undercurrents again. Her eyebrows knitting in a thoughtful frown, her gaze brushed past Patli. "It'll be just on your way."

"Yes," muttered the skinny youth, his lack of enthusiasm on display.

Axolin shifted impatiently, his wide forehead adorned with too many creases as well. "Then we should go. No point in talking on and on in this gods-forsaken alley, is there?" His narrowed eyes brushed past the workshop boy. "He should come with us, though. He got bitten too."

The girl's gasp tore the silence that momentarily prevailed, with no one, not even that same Miztli boy, offering anything else in response.

"I didn't get bitten," muttered the commoner in the end.

Axolin's face was settling into a familiar mask. "Yes, you did. If you bother to feel your stupid head, you'll find plenty of blood there. One can see it from the distance of a ball court. It's not all mud, you can be sure of that."

The boy flashed Axolin a quick glance that heralded the coming of another violent exchange.

Necalli exhaled loudly. "Come, let us go. You too, Miztli-boy. Better come with us. Let the priests do their work. They are good at those things."

"And what about her? Who'll be taking her home?" demanded Patli, suddenly the role model of responsibility.

Necalli shot him a morose glance. "Is your father's workshop far from here?"

It was unseemly to let her find her way home all alone, unescorted and unprotected at such a dubious part of the evening. And yet, they needed to detour through the marketplace and this Tlaloc temple. There could be no doubt about the necessity to do so, and its location was promising, conveniently away from school, with a fairly high chance for their teachers not to learn anything about anything.

Also, speaking of school, the *calmecac* authorities' rage might reach a boiling point if they didn't hurry. After missing the evening rites and if still not around, he knew, their superiors' ability to resist the urge of making example out of them would plummet lower with every passing heartbeat. And, oh, but was their exclusive aristocratic school famous for harshness of its punishments. Against his will, he shuddered.

The girl tossed her head high, making her disheveled braids jump. "Maybe I should come with you. I want to see how they do it, the *tlaloque*, how they deal with such things. And anyway, you won't manage to find that temple as fast or as easy without me." Another challenging toss, the flash of the large eyes. "Are you coming?"

CHAPTER 8

Are you coming, indeed. Where had he heard that before?

Miztli couldn't help but smirk, watching the *calmecac* boy – not such a bad person after all – staring at her back, wide-eyed. Oh yes, Chantli turned out to be a force of nature. Even now, she was already drawing away, so very determined. In the corner of his vision, he saw Patli rolling his eyes, shrugging with acceptance. That one knew her more than everyone, of course.

Miztli tried to pay no attention to the heavy pounding in his head, the exhaustion creeping up his limbs, welling with every step. But he shouldn't be coming with them, scary monsters and their bites or not. He was so tired, and old Tlaquitoc might notice his absence and start asking questions, or worse yet, get angry, not letting him explain, should a good explanation occur to him. What to tell?

"Let us go." Necalli, their self-appointed leader, was again spewing brisk orders, taking the lead, apparently already over his initial startle. "We haven't got all night to wander about."

"Don't we?" The other *calmecac* boy, a rotten piece of meat, that one, made a face that could rival depictions of deities on old scrolls, not a pretty sight. "It actually does look as though we are about to wander the whole night, with our company getting stranger and our trouble with school authorities graver."

"Shut up," was the anticipated response. "Where is that temple exactly?" This was addressed to Patli, who seemed to try to fold into himself, hiding inside his hunched shoulders. If Chantli got caught wandering the night in this way, or worse yet, got in trouble on account of it, the spoiled youth wouldn't fare well, favorite nephew or not.

"It should be on the nearest side of the marketplace, where the food alleys and the healers are."

"Yes, don't you remember?" contributed the annoying one called Axolin, hastening his step, clearly not put out with being offered to shut up. "That's where Acoatl stole the tortillas during the midwinter celebrations. It was just behind the temple, in that smelly food alley."

His friend burst out laughing. "I remember that!" he gasped, doubling over while holding his injured arm in the grip of his other hand. "He was running so fast, and then he just tripped. Oh mighty deities, that was a scene worth watching."

"You were stealing from sellers of food?" inquired Chantli, slowing down while turning to face them. "Why would you do this?"

The *calmecac* boys smirked happily.

"It wasn't us, me or Axolin. It was another boy."

"From your *calmecac*?"

"Of course. Can't imagine this one anywhere but in *calmecac*. Acoatl is the snottiest noble, related to the royal family and ever so proud of it, as though he was the Emperor himself, or the next one in line."

Axolin chuckled loudly. "Like you wouldn't."

"No, not me. And certainly not like that. They think themselves better than reverent deities, those royal relatives. Yuck!"

He could hear Chantli giggling softly. "They are not that bad, not all of them."

But what did she mean by that? Miztli tried to see her better through the blinding agony of his headache. But he truly should not drag along with this bunch. They weren't acting reasonably now, Chantli more than anyone, and she seemed such a levelheaded girl before. What had gotten into her?

"You can't possibly know royal family members," the *calmecac* boy Necalli was saying, apparently as startled with her statement and the unreasonableness of it all.

"You may be surprised," she chortled, very pleased with herself.

Puzzled, Miztli tried to make out her expression in the darkness.

"Who do you know, then?" demanded Necalli, challenging. That one was changing too fast, not always for the best; one moment snapping and cursing, the other all patience and good will, less snobbish or violent than his companion, but not by much. Well, this island-city's nobles were such a pain. Back in his native village, one rarely saw any aristocracy and never from up close. The farmers worked the land belonging to Tenochtitlan nobility or dug up its treasures in the mountains that also had to do with the huge island capital, but the tribute collectors located in Oaxtepec or faraway Taxco were the only ones to appear every now and then, collecting what was due. The owners of the land didn't bother.

"Ahuitzotl?"

The loud exclamation tore him from his bittersweet memories, from the pictures his mind was panting too vividly – the dusty pathways and the simple one-story adobe houses with endless rows of edible goods grown all around, those tasty treats, fruits and vegetables. Even the mines looked like a better place to spend one's time at than this clamoring, unfriendly monster of a city.

"Oh yes," he heard Chantli crooning happily, bursting with aplomb. "That boy. He is nice and chatty and fun to run around with. He showed me some interesting places that I bet you didn't even know exist." The purr in her voice was impossible to miss now. "Right around your noble school it was."

"Why would the snotty little beast do that?" cried out both their *calmecac* companions in unison, their eyes as narrow as slits, ridiculously alike, like a pair of twins.

"I don't know. Maybe he thought it was better to run around with me than with his snotty *calmecac* friends."

"He is no friend of ours. He is a conceited little nothing." This time it was Necalli, all bursting with indignation.

But the second boy's eyes sparkled again with already familiar taunting mischief. "He is not. He just pissed you off when he talked about the ball game in which you played badly. That's all. He is a passable little thing, not as snotty as the royal family offspring go."

"Oh please!"

"Yes, he is a good boy," contributed Chantli, paying no attention to their once-again skeptical glances. "He told me that his sister with the pretty name Noble Jade Doll was given to the Tlatelolco ruler, whatever his name is, and that he has been treating her badly."

"Moquihuixtli." Patli, skulking in the shadows, his shoulders still folded unhappily, stirred to life wearily.

"What?"

"The Tlatelolco ruler, he is called Moquihuixtli."

"Yes, we know that, you brilliant history teacher," muttered Necalli, beginning to walk again, setting their step, aiming to reach a broader alley but pausing to examine his arm in the generous moonlight that was pouring here unrestrained. Curious, Miztli leaned to see better, forced either to stop or to detour, the youth's broad figure blocking his way. What if his head looked no better? Involuntarily, he reached for it, his fingers encountering nothing but the stiffness of the matted hair. Bother this! At least one could see one's arm.

Necalli was again muttering curses. "The damn thing hurts like the Underworld passage."

"It's not bleeding anymore."

"Yes, working boy. But it still hurts, and the healers will be busy making it bleed again, you can be sure of that."

"Why would they?"

"To wash the bad things out of it."

Chantli was pushing her way in. "Let me see." Touching in her usual earnestness, she bent until her thick braids were falling over the mangled limb, blocking it from its only source of illumination. She tossed those backwards again and again, in a nicely impatient gesture. "It doesn't look so bad. The swollenness is almost gone."

Her patient seemed to be fascinated with her gestures more than he was with his injured limb. *What's the point?* wondered Miztli, irritated beyond reason. Why did they crowd this stupid alley instead of going to their various homes and be done with it? If eager to reach this or that Tlaloc's temple, why did they keep stopping to gossip about things that had nothing to do with their current predicament? He contemplated turning around and leaving, either openly or by sneaking away. But then, of course, old Tlaquitoc would demand to know where he had been wandering the entire afternoon and evening, and if questioned about Chantli or Patli, what would he tell? What could he?

As though echoing his thoughts, Axolin snorted. "You are no healer and no priest, pretty girl. And I tell you all that we either go on looking for that temple wherever it is in a hurry or we go back to *calmecac*. I don't fancy any more punishments than I am already due, not for silly gossiping in a dubious alley." Snorting against the united front of two indignant faces, he turned around resolutely, beginning to walk again. "That business with the Emperor's sister and that stupid Tlatelolco ruler is no secret. Everyone knows that she was making plenty of fuss, plaguing our glorious ruler with messengers aplenty, begging for attention. No news this thing."

Chantli waved her free hand in the air. "Ahuitzotl says that it will bring war between Tenochtitlan and Tlatelolco, if that Moquihuixtli doesn't start treating his sister well."

"He doesn't treat her badly. She is a spoiled piece of work, that one. Haughty and impossible to please, just like her revered mother. My uncle says so and he would know, with all this dining at the royal chambers."

"That's not what Ahuitzotl says," insisted Chantli, ridiculously offended, walking beside her new admirer, oblivious of anything else. Both he and Patli could not have existed at all at this point, reflected Miztli, not caring even a little bit. The stupidest moment of this day was when he went to plead with the annoying Acatlo, asking for permission to go with Patli, the most foolish, absurd impulse of them all. What had he been thinking? Even Chantli, always the nicest and the most reasonable of this *altepetl's* dwellers, lost some of these much admired qualities, turning as unreasonable as they come. It was embarrassing, the way she kept pushing herself in the midst of their ventures and conversations, like a boy and not a girl of an advanced enough age, bragging about some dubious contacts she somehow made with some snotty children of the royal house. As though it was realistic or even possible. It was easy to see how embarrassed Patli felt since the moment she had imposed her presence on them. Everyone but the *calmecac* boy Necalli wished she was now safely home and busy with womanly things.

"Ahuitzotl is nothing but a coyote cub with his mother's milk still smeared around his mouth," this same Necalli was protesting, hurrying to keep up with both her and his friend, clutching his bad arm with the good one. Not a whiny type. Miztli shook his head grudgingly.

Patli drew closer, not an especially welcome presence. "When we reach that temple, I'll take Chantli home. We can't wait there for ages. Her mother will be furious as it is."

Miztli just shrugged, not inclined to talk, not with this one.

"You'll find the way back, won't you? It's not difficult if you keep to the main alley and then the warehouses." The sloping shoulders lifted sharply, somewhat defensively. "She can't keep running around, at night and in the company of boys. You shouldn't have brought her along. It's against every custom. Even a villager like you should have known better."

Miztli felt the air escaping his lungs all at once. Oh the cowardly piece of dirt!

"Leave me alone," he growled, not caring for proper address, not anymore. "Shut up and leave me alone!"

Back in the workshop, it was different, with him being in the position not much higher than a servant, the lowest status in contrast to this entire family, excepting one female slave that kept the workshop and the house clean and supplied with goods. And yet, after today, he could not defer to this excuse of a youth, cowardly rat that he turned out to be. They were not in old Tlaquitoc's workshop now and he didn't have to take insults from this one. Even the *calmecac* boys treated him with more respect, especially that leader-like Necalli.

Patli straightened dangerously, his eyes taking a darker shade. Taller if not broader, he didn't look insignificant despite his lack of wideness and the usually slouching posture. "Don't you dare to talk to me like that," he began, then noticed the others staring at them, stopping their royal family gossip. "Who do you think you are –"

But Miztli had had enough. "Leave me alone, you stupid filth eater. Keep your stupid muttering to yourself!" Clenching his fists, he drew himself straighter, preparing for the attack, not about to be caught off guard like back in the lake with that annoying Axolin. They didn't take talking back well, those rats of the huge city. Good for them. He wasn't about to take offense for things he was not responsible for, or anything else, for that matter.

However, *telpochcalli* boys appeared to be less proudly inclined than their *calmecac* peers. Eyes glowing dangerously, lips pressed into a very thin line, Patli hesitated for another heartbeat, glaring furiously, but making no effort to step closer or press his case otherwise.

"Shut up yourself, you aromatic piece of provincial excrement," he said finally, turning away. "Go back to your reeking coves and fields out there in that miserable valley with nothing but the stench of your fields to make one notice them at all."

"And you go back to your stinking wherever-you-came from," retorted Miztli, wishing he could pluck flowery curses with the ease the pampered piece of excrement did.

The *calmecac* boys roared with laughter, again reacting in unison, as expected. When they didn't quarrel, those two behaved remarkably alike. Yet Chantli did not join in their mirth.

"Stop talking nonsense, Patli," she admonished, her frown rivaling the darkness of the sky. "You are not such a perfect Tenochtitlan citizen yourself."

"Where I come from, one needn't boast your Great Capital's kinship," retorted her skinny cousin.

Necalli recovered from his fit of laughter with an evident effort. "But he does give pretty speeches, especially when pissed off. You have to give him that," he breathed, still guffawing. "Stop picking on the workshop boy, wherever you both came from. He is worth more than you when it comes to difficult situations, I can tell you that much." Still smirking, he motioned with his head. "Let's go."

"Yes, we should hurry," chimed in Chantli. "The temple is

truly not far from here." Her gaze brushed past him, holding a smile. "Come, Miztli. You must let the priests examine your head too."

He shrugged reluctantly.

"Yes, working boy." This time, it was Necalli, waving his hand without turning, beginning to walk briskly again. "Don't take heed of your snotty relative. He didn't mean a word of his pretty speech, and if he did, then he'll regret it." It came out good-naturedly, enough to make the other one snicker, but he saw Patli steering away, falling into their step safely behind Chantli.

Filthy rat, he thought, seething, resuming his walk mainly in order to do something.

"It's out there, behind the warehouses, before the walled areas."

The dark mass of long one-story buildings glared at them, not inviting or friendly, anything but. Behind those, the hum of the marketplace ensued, surprisingly lively for this time of the evening. Were people still selling and buying their things there? wondered Miztli, fascinated against his will. He had never been so far into the city. Not even on an occasional errand to the marketplace when something in the workshop was missing. The youngest of the owner's sons, a boy of barely ten summers, was lucky enough to receive such chores, or sometimes one of the older brothers. His own stance by the blazing braziers was, apparently, irreplaceable.

"Behind those things?" The *calmecac* boy dropped his voice to a loud whisper, still heard quite clearly despites the shouts and the clanking of pottery ensuing from behind the high crumbling wall.

"Yes." Chantli slowed her step, losing some of her good-natured forcefulness all of a sudden. "Over there, where the light is flickering. Behind this low fence."

"Some fence," muttered Axolin. "They invested in this wall, eh? I don't think they'll appreciate our trying to sneak in."

"We can see if the gate is open," suggested Chantli in a surprisingly small voice. "Maybe... if it is..."

"Well, it is or it isn't." Clearly arriving at the decision, Necalli gestured them to shut up. "Either way, it's about me and the working boy. So we will go and try to talk our way in. The rest of you stay outside. Or better yet, go back home."

"I'll go in with you two." As expected, Axolin was not about to abandon them, given permission to do so or not. "The priests may want to question me. I fought that thing together with you."

"And I –" began Chantli hotly, but this time, they all turned toward her.

"You are going home, and by the safest route possible. Patli will take you." The direfully squinted eyes rested on the resentful youth, gleaming with dark promise. "You take her home and you make sure she is safe before you scamper off to your *telpochcalli*. Even if it takes you half a night to do that. Otherwise, you better not show your face anywhere around Tenochtitlan at all."

"I was going to do that anyway!" cried out Patli, offended. For good measure, he took a step back. "She is my cousin. I wouldn't let her find her way back alone and at night."

"One never knows with your type," muttered Necalli, not pacified, squashing the *telpochcalli* boy with his glance. "And if she is not safe by midnight…"

"Don't talk about me as though I'm not there," protested Chantli, looking fierce and indeed very pretty in the light of the flickering torch. Her eyes glowered at them all, Patli included. "Unlike you all, I can find my way back!"

Miztli slipped around the temple's corner before they could see him rolling his eyes.

The torches glowed eerily in the gloomy semidarkness, the strong smell of copal overwhelming, overcoming the other stench, that heavy aroma typical to large temples. It made the clubs pounding inside his head redouble their efforts, his fingers rigid around the slickness of his obsidian talisman, going numb from the force by which they clutched the precious amulet. Oh, but he needed a gulp of a fresh air, at least one single gulp.

The *calmecac* boy was squirming on the stone floor, trying to withstand the treatment with his dignity still intact. Not a simple feat of endurance. The glowing coals did nothing to calm the swollen, inflamed, raw flesh. As it appeared, they did exactly the opposite.

"Would they stop torturing him already?" Axolin's voice shook as he leaned closer, pressing his palms together, fingers interwoven, his knuckles white.

Miztli shrugged helplessly, afraid to say a word, lest the priests would remember him and his head. Earlier, after being allowed to retell their tale, and while being hastened toward the altar, demanded to offer some of their own blood to the mighty Tlaloc, all three of them, given large maguey thorns to pierce their earlobes and bleed on the polished stone, his own head was examined as thoroughly as the arm of the bitten boy, resulting in a thorough washing with water and then liquid ointment that stung. No one said a word about the coal treatment back then.

Nauseated, he glanced at the darkness of the opening that was shimmering eerily behind the clouds of incense, swimming before his eyes. If he didn't manage to get there soon enough, he would vomit all over the stony floor, he knew. He wouldn't be able to hold it in for much longer. Not with the strangled groans of the *calmecac* boy.

"He is smearing things on his arm now," whispered Axolin, apparently set on reporting the events. "It's over. I think."

"It is?" It felt impolite to respond with nothing but shrugging. He forced his eyes to the crouching priests, one middle-aged and neatly robed, operating with cloths, bowls, and coals; the other young and simply dressed, occupied mainly with pinning their victim to the floor. An apprentice? Necalli was still struggling to break free but with less determination than before. How terribly painful it must be! Another priest, an elder clad in a black foul-smelling gown as opposed to the neat garments of the other two, was chanting, waving a smoking bowl, spreading clouds of copal. Miztli swallowed his nausea back, taking his eyes away.

"He won't manage to walk on his own, not after this." Axolin was clenching and unclenching his fists, his sandaled foot tapping an impatient refrain. "You'll have to help me bring him back to school."

"And how am I to find my way back afterwards?" He could not help glaring at his companion, his nausea forgotten.

"I don't know. You'll manage."

"Or maybe you'll manage."

His glare was returned redoubled. "Watch your tongue!"

He tried not to roll his eyes again. "Leave me alone."

"You are asking for a good beating."

"I don't care."

The younger priest was helping Necalli up, pulling him into a sitting position with little consideration. However, the *calmecac* boy seemed eager to cooperate. An encouraging revelation. They didn't dare move closer or try to offer their help.

"You will return to the temple of Revered Tlaloc tomorrow, with an offering of food or clothing," the older priest was saying, looking at no one in particular, busy collecting his tools. "And you will do it no later than midmorning."

"But…" began Axolin, then fell silent as promptly, quailing under the younger priest's gaze.

"We are not allowed to leave school before Father Sun is well on his way toward the other world." From his brighter spot upon the semidarkness of the floor, Necalli's voice came with surprising firmness considering his previous ordeal and his current unsteady stance. Crouching in a strange pose of someone caught in the act of getting up or maybe falling down, he evidently paused in his efforts, propped on his good arm, as though gathering his strength for proceeding with his attempt to gain an upright position. Miztli held his breath.

"You will be allowed when you tell your superiors of the adventure you got yourself into," said the older priest icily, evidently not appreciating being answered back. "The punishment you'll receive has nothing to do with your debt to Revered Tlaloc."

Biting his lips, their *calmecac* spokesman said nothing, returning to his struggle to get up unaided. But this one had his share of courage! Miztli fought his urge to come to the struggling youth's aid no longer.

Slipping along the damp stones, he crouched next to the wavering form, offering his own shoulder as a prop, noting that his gesture didn't go unappreciated. The alacrity with which it was grabbed, clutched in a crushing grip along with the weight of his companion that was suddenly upon him, told him that. A considerable weight. They evidently ate well out there in that mysterious *calmecac* school.

"Don't forget to let the priests examine your arm again," repeated the younger assistant, watching them with a measure of compassion. "When you go to the temple with your offerings, tell its priests of what happened. They still can give you much trouble, those wounds." A light frown. "You too, young man. Your head didn't get hurt as badly, but if it still aches by tomorrow or the day after, go to your local healers and ask for their help."

They mumbled their thanks, eager to escape the suffocating closeness now, stumbling toward the outside, spilling out and into the cool nightly air as though surfacing from under the water. What bliss!

"How do you feel?" asked Axolin in surprisingly small voice, supporting their wounded companion from the other side now, careful not to touch the bandaged limb.

"Lousy," was their laconic answer. "If you'll keep dragging me like that, I'll vomit all over you two."

They stopped in unison, too abruptly, wavering and fighting to keep their balance. The next thing they knew, their charge was on his knees, retching wildly, choking with the intensity of it. Fighting the own nausea, Miztli tried to remain supportive, not successful at his attempts to do so. It was difficult to hold on against his own need to retch, without the cumbersome position all three of them crouched in now, half lying, propped by their own limbs, battered and exhausted, in dire need of respite from it all.

"Let's just get away from here," groaned Axolin, struggling to drag his friend back to his feet. Done vomiting, Necalli was still spitting, cursing faintly, not eager to leave the support of the dusty ground. However, a few silhouettes drawing from the surrounding alleys, attracted by the noise probably, made them all strengthen in alert. Not the type one meets in the daytime. Miztli rushed to help Axolin along.

"What are you doing here, boys? Fighting?" One of the men spat upon the ground, having done with the greenish sprout he had been evidently chewing. "Wild rascals, eh?"

Two more darkly outlined forms burst into loud chuckling. Without the helpfulness of the temple's torch, it was difficult to see. Miztli felt their wounded companion redoubling his efforts to gain an upright position.

"We aren't fighting," Necalli said in a surprisingly clear voice, considering the wildness of his previous vomiting. "We are late for school. Need to run really fast to get there. It's out there, by the wharves." His good hand waved in the direction they had come from, non-committal.

"Your *telpochcalli* teachers will go hard on you, eh?" Another man snickered loudly, openly amused. "Wandering out here at night, oh my. Tomorrow you'll be slaving with no pause to catch your breath."

"How do you know?" interrupted another man, drawing closer as well. There was much clamor coming from that other alley, clattering pottery, indignant shouts, drunken laughter. Nothing good or respectable. Even Miztli could guess that. Men of his village would drink *pulque* on occasion, not in moderate amounts sometimes. Even Father did this, usually after the trips to the luxurious Oaxtepec or the tribute-collecting Taxco, bringing back payment for the fruits, vegetables, and metal.

"I've been to school, you stupid provincial," claimed the first man, growing indignant. "I'm not some uncouth villager like you."

"Shut up," suggested the newcomer, unperturbed. "If that's the best your Tenochtitlan schools can offer…" His hand swept in a casual half circle, indicating their general direction, but as he did so, another of his companions, a tall, sinewy man, stepped closer, leaning as though trying to see them better.

"Is it not…"

"Run when I tell you," whispered Necalli, breathing normally now, back to his leader-like inclinations. "And keep close together."

They offered no argument. Yet, still so close to the temple, even the riffraff of the nighttime marketplace knew better than to make trouble. A silhouette of the priestly garment appeared next to the crumbled stones of the entryway they had just left behind.

"Go away, *macehualli*," the authoritative voice commanded. "Don't crowd the mighty god's vicinity, let alone with spitting and cursing." A thundering pause. "You too, boys. Go the other way and don't linger. You've done enough mischief for today."

They waited for no additional invitation. Staggering, but only a little, they bolted for the merciful darkness of the pathway between two long wooden constructions, not caring if this new route took them any closer to their desirable destination, not at this point. Panting and gasping, they slowed their steps only when no noise but that of the distant lakeshore reached their ears, reinforced by the chirping of the night insects. The silvery light shone uninterrupted, illuminating the broader alley adorned by stone and adobe houses on both sides, each hiding behind the darkness of their patios.

"Think we are... are safe now..." rasped Necalli, leaning against a wide tree heavily, fighting for breath. "That was a bad thing, this alley. Not a place... to run around... at night." Shutting his eyes, he paused, drawing in the crisp air loudly. "Glad that priest had mercy on us. He didn't look that merciful back there in the temple."

"They were pissed at us for coming in out of the night with our wild tales, waving hurt limbs to prove our claims." Catching his breath along with a fair amount of cheerfulness, Axolin cackled between his gasps. "Think about it. They had to drop everything and get busy with all this chanting and special prayers, not to mention the thorns spent on our earlobes and the healing tools. You made them work, those lazy priests. Both of you." This time, a wink was directed at Miztli, colored by no memories of their previous conflicts. But this one forgot grudges fast!

"Well, that's their work," grunted Necalli, clearly refusing to see the funny side of the affair. "But to burn my arm with those coals? Oh man!" His face twisted fiercely, not a pretty sight. "I bet they could have used ointments and such but preferred to hurt in order to teach a lesson. I know how their minds work, priest-teachers or not."

Could it be? wondered Miztli, taken aback. But this would be such an unnecessary cruelty.

"They didn't treat my head with coals," he said, receiving a dark glance as an answer.

"Maybe they didn't think you needed a lesson," ventured Axolin, now definitely himself again, his wide lips twisting, eyes twinkling. "Maybe they still believe something can be made out of hopeless cases like him, but not out of wild commoners with no clothes and no better sense than to mingle with crazy *pillis* from the Royal Enclosure." The grin stretched wider, challenging their glares. "Or maybe they were afraid to set your pretty hair on fire. Your cuts and scratches were barely visible under this matted mess you have on your head."

"Shut up." This came from Necalli, still busy regaining his breath or dominating the pain and exhaustion, or both, his frown deep and troubled, yet his lips quivering, fighting a smile. Miztli tried to suppress a giggle of his own. But it was too funny, this whole thing; there could be no argument about that. In another heartbeat, they were doubling with laughter, trying to be quiet about it, failing miserably. The silent neighborhood wouldn't deal well with such fits of hysterical mirth; still, they couldn't help it. It was truly too wild and too funny, this entire evening and night.

"You should have seen yourself, twisting on that floor like a stepped-on snake," gasped Axolin, practically lying against the rough trunk, fighting to say his piece. "And you, workshop boy, gurgling there in the lake, popping up and down like a hairless puppy that fell over a fisherman's canoe."

"Shut... up," cried both Miztli and Necalli in unison, fighting for breath, staggering as though drunk on *pulque*, groping for support.

"Yes, yes, and your running here," went on their entertainer, encouraged by the reaction, pleased with himself, "like commoners drunk on *pulque*, like a canoe in storm waters."

More heartbeats passed amidst hysterical laughter. The dark patios paid them no attention, but for how long? Miztli fought the urge to slip along the rough unevenness of their support.

"Should have seen yourself," managed Necalli in the end. "Perching on that stair in the temple, like a spooked bird. Both of you. A pair of spooked birds."

That sent them back into uncontrollable fits again. In the end, they just panted, drained of strength but heartened, in the best of spirits, as though cleansed by the unseemly laughter.

"We'd better hurry back, all of us," said Necalli, adjusting his bandaged arm in the cradle of the good one. "To face infuriated superiors and all that." He shrugged, not looking worried. "Will that metal-crafting owner of yours get mad seeing you coming back in the middle of the night?"

Miztli felt himself sliding from the cloud of euphoria. "He is not my owner. I work for him, to learn the trade." He shrugged. "He may get mad, if he noticed. In the worst of cases, he'll throw me out and I'll go back home. The best solution as far as I'm concerned."

Both *calmecac* boys rolled their eyes. "The best solution? Won't your old man kill you for such a failure? His father and mine, and everyone else's, for that matter, would burst worse than the Smoking Mountain of the eastern mainland if we were thrown out of school. You would have to assemble us part by part after they were through with us. Not the 'best solution' at all."

He tried not to snicker at such an unattractively painted prospect. "My father won't be that mad. I think…" Or maybe he would. It cost plenty to send him here, plenty of negotiation and promised goods to make old Tlaquitoc accept a foreigner for an apprentice, plenty of promised good behavior. Would Father be disappointed? Oh, let it not happen that way!

"Well, don't make that old craftsman madder than he is with you now, workshop boy." Straightening up resolutely, Necalli drew a deep breath. "Not until we are through with that tunnel, eh? Stay around Tenochtitlan until we know more. It might get interesting, you know." A wink. "Tomorrow, we'll go there again. No, on the day after that, or the one after that. Tomorrow, we are sure to get stuck in the school, doing extra chores." He frowned. "If you can get away from your workshop, go there and sniff around, see what you can make out of this place. Don't go inside. Just sneak in the proximity of that old temple, see if there is something there, something interesting."

"If I can get away before it gets dark."

"If you find something, let us know."

"And how would he do that, you brilliant planner?" demanded Axolin, argumentative again. He clearly didn't like being bossed over, not by his friend. "Should he go up our school temple's stairs out there next to the ball-court and the round pyramid and demand to see us or send us word? I can just imagine this happening. They'll be falling all over themselves in their eagerness to do his bidding, our dignified priest-teachers and veteran warriors."

Necalli made a face. "He'll find a way. Won't you?" The friendly wink was impossible to resist. "If you are sneaking around there, be careful. These people who saw you in that tunnel might have gotten a good look. Even there by that Tlaloc temple it looked as though some of this marketplace scum was scrutinizing us a little too closely. Just before the priest started yelling at them."

The memory came back in force, making his stomach knot in a painful way. "They would have chased us if they wanted to get us."

"Maybe. Or maybe they were afraid of the priests." A one-sided shrug lifted a broad shoulder. "Anyway, be careful if you are going to sniff around and let us know right away." Another wink, now mischievous rather than friendly. "If no better way occurs to you, send the word through that pretty girl, the craftsman's daughter. She seems to be at ease around our school temple and all, eh? Running around with snotty royalty, just imagine that."

Before he could get offended on Chantli's behalf, Axolin grabbed his friend's good arm. "Come, come. Or you'll start talking any wilder than you do now. Old Yaotzin will beat all this silliness out of you, I promise you that. Unless we manage to sneak in like real quiet marketplace mice. Come, you crazy adventurer."

Watching their silhouettes melting in the darkness, Miztli stood for a little while, blinking in confusion. What wild pieces of crazy meat those *calmecac* boys were, wilder than any of his friends back in the village. The haughty nobles of the mighty capital? Well, the distant aristocrats strutting around Oaxtepec, coming to enjoy the cool air of the country, the crispiness of it, or so they were reported to claim, were nothing like that, surrounded by armies of slaves and bodyguards, impossible to get a closer look at even if one tried to do that, something the boys of their village never bothered with. Why would they? And yet, now he knew that those same unapproachable nobles were, indeed, crazily haughty, but not truly bad, not untrustworthy, not like the other citizens of the mighty capital turned out to be, all those craftsmen and metal or feather workers. How odd! People like Patli and old Tlaquitoc's sons, treating him with the utmost coldness, with so much condescending arrogance and chill, while those *calmecac* boys didn't do anything of the sort. Well, not to an unbearable degree, even that annoying Axolin.

Turning around, he shook his head. It was still pounding with pain and exhaustion, but not as badly as before. Or maybe it was his mood. And if he managed to sneak into the workshop without being noticed, then it might still come to nothing serious, this wild impossible evening, the first interesting night spent in the great city after three moons of loneliness, boredom, and desperate longing for home.

His fingers reached for the pouch, clenched around the familiar smoothness of his obsidian treasure, reassured by it like back in the temple. Then his attention snapped back to the present without an obvious cause. The bushes at the edge of the alley rustled with no breeze accompanying the movement.

His thoughts racing about, he pushed the unsettling feeling away, calculating his way hurriedly. These well-to-do neighborhoods looked nothing like the alleys surrounding the workshop, and the scent of the lake was not heavy here, barely reaching him. How far was he from his destination? And in what direction?

The silhouettes sprang into his view as he turned into a narrower pathway, the dark forms of two people. His heart came to a sudden halt, then threw itself wildly against his ribs, desperately. Were those the people whom the *calmecac* boy was warning him against? His instincts screamed danger. No robbers would try to harass a youth with nothing to offer but a dirty loincloth and little else.

Whirling around, he burst into a wild run, his instincts telling him that the direction of the wharves and the marketplace offered no shelter or sanctuary. The well-to-do neighborhoods! He should try to reach them or to run in the direction his companions disappeared such a short time ago.

Something swished and he didn't understand what made him stumble, shoving his face into the dusty stones of the paved road. Disoriented, he tried to push the stupid stones away, the buzz in his ears annoying, interfering with his ability to hear. The next thing he knew, someone's heavy body was upon him, making the struggle to get up more difficult.

He squirmed wildly, beyond panic, like back in the lake, but unlike the hostile water and the monsters inhabiting it, this time, there was no one to come to his aid, to help against the crushing weight. The last thing he felt was an explosion in the back of his head and then it was under the water, sinking into the suffocating darkness, helpless and terrified, hopelessly lost.

CHAPTER 9

The chance to sneak away came only when her brothers burst into the house, sweaty and soot-smeared, demanding their well deserved meal, complaining about the difficulty of their day, overrunning each other with the loudness of their grievances.

Despite her own mounting worry, Chantli couldn't help snickering. It was too funny how alike they looked, with their faces so dirty and their expressions mirroring each other in their indignant resentment, their lips just a thin line, barely there.

Father had been away through the most of the day, attending an important meeting, the gathering of his craftsmen guild and the other unions of the city. Even the influential Traders Guild would sometimes grace such gatherings with its haughty, all-important presence, a whole class above the rest of the respectable people of the city. Which left both her brothers to mind the workshop, to do all the work, even the less pleasant task of the actual melting. Oh, but did the need to maintain raging fires, blowing into clay-tipped straws, and maneuvering pots overflowing with liquid metal leave them bubbling with fury, as red-hot as the braziers, muttering about worthless pieces of dirt from the provinces. The amount of curses heaped on the head of the missing apprentice was staggering, so much frustration and rage! Every time Mother sent her into the workshop to try to be helpful in little things, she heard them cursing the village boy, promising to discipline him in ways that made her scant body hair rise. No, no one liked to do the melting, the task her brothers forgot how to do since that boy arrived here. Which served them right. On that score, she smirked unashamedly when sure that no one was looking her way.

Yet on another account, the account of the missing village boy, she was worried sick. Why didn't he come back yesterday, late at night or not? He was supposed to, wasn't he? He had nowhere to go, nowhere to sleep or eat, and he must have cherished his place at Father's workshop. He wouldn't just scamper away as her brothers suspected he did. He was not that sort of a person. But if not, what happened to him at that Tlaloc temple or on his way back? What made him not return?

Her worry mounting, she kept running into the workshop under every pretext, hoping to see him back, even if facing dire punishments. If he cared to retell their previous evening's adventures, she would have helped him by backing his story. Father wouldn't be thrilled to discover that she took a part in it, running around after darkness and in the company of boys; oh yes, Patli was right at pointing that out while swearing her to secrecy on their way back. Still, she resolved to tell some of it if it helped the village boy get out of trouble. He deserved that.

However, as the day dragged on, and her chores at the house were completed – plenty of weaving, her loom sporting an almost ready piece of an intricate pattern, then helping Mother with meals, sorting maize, grinding some of it, the chores their only slave usually did but not always, not on the busy days – she became worried for real. Something was wrong, something had happened, and the only way to find out was to ask Patli to find his *calmecac* friends, or better yet, to go with him and do the asking herself. They might know, or at least might try to find out Miztli's whereabouts. They seemed to be good boys, courteous and helpful, especially the one called Necalli, so handsome and full of great spirits. He would be glad to see her too, she knew, feeling her face beginning to burn worse than the melting room braziers, trying to cover these obvious signs of embarrassment. But she was silly for thinking these kinds of thoughts, wasn't she?

However, no one was there to watch her and her anxiousness. Patli was not yet back from his *telpochcalli*, maybe not allowed to leave on account of coming back to school so late last night. Which left her alone with her worries, with no one to turn to for help or, at least, to share her misgivings, while the shining sun deity kept rolling along the sky, leaving her with less and less hope of seeing the village boy return, with or without good excuses to keep him from punishments but still alive and not harmed. What had happened at the Tlaloc temple?

In the end, the moment she could sneak away without being too obvious about it, counting on Mother being preoccupied with two spoiled overgrown crybabies, Chantli didn't waste any time. Patli would be a great help, but she couldn't wait for him to come home. She had to do something!

Feeling strange in her best festive *huipil* pulled over her regular skirt hastily, she rushed along the busy alleys, her sandals' sturdy leather soles clacking pleasantly against the dusty cobblestones. It would be better if she could linger for long enough to take care of her hair, to arrange it nicely like on the day before. Would they let her near the huge towering temple or that precious noble school? Yesterday, she stuck out like a red tomato in a pile of green avocados, drawing dubious glances while huddling under the temple's stairs with that boy Ahuitzotl, even though she had been dressed in her very best clothes, her hair combed and arranged wittily, divided at the nape, then pulled up in the respectable manner of the well-to-do ladies, while now it was simply tied in two regular braids. A bother! Would they banish her before she'd have a chance of finding either of the boys?

The sun was still strong, blazing unmercifully, reflecting off the polished plaster of colorful walls. The stones of the Great Pyramid were so smooth, their colors slick and glittering, the buildings around it towering high. Slowing her step, she slipped into the narrow alley, attempting to circumvent the smaller pyramid until able to come out next to the round Quetzalcoatl's temple, and another lower pyramid as close to the stairs and the hidden entrance as possible. But for this boy Ahuitzotl to be there and waiting, like yesterday!

To her disappointment, her calculation was no good, bringing her back to the Central Plaza next to the wrong pyramid, the one belonging to Tezcatlipoca, judging by the symbol adorning the temple towering upon its top. The mighty deity of the night and the wind, patron of nobles and warriors but their punisher as well, the smoking mirror, the spirit of double meaning, the good and the bad of the darkness. Shuddering, she hastened her steps, only to nearly bump into an open litter that was progressing along the wide alley, turning into the vastness of the Plaza as she did.

Desperately, she tried to sway out of its way, the exclamation of the sturdy litter bearer she collided with ringing in her ears, gaining power. His elbow pushed her away with enough force, sending her crashing into the dusty stones, but the warriors who slowed their pace were the ones to leave her breathless with fright, the anger upon their faces, their open impatience.

"What in the name of the Underworld?" one of them cried out, towering above her, his brow wrinkled dourly, face the color of a thundercloud. "What's with the marketplace scum running all over the Plaza of the Royal Enclosure? Disgusting!"

The assaulted litter bearer muttered something, while the rest of his peers and the other warriors nodded vigorously in agreement.

"Where did you come from, girl? What are you seeking here?" The growling demand made Chantli go numb with fear. Such a bark! "Get up and stop staring. Answer the question!"

A sensible proposition. She tried to make her limbs work.

"Or better yet, run along, girl, and fast," offered another warrior, less foreboding than his peer, almost amused. "You have no business sneaking around noble places. Don't come near the Royal Enclosure again."

The beautiful woman upon the cushions of the open litter leaned forward, her forehead adorned with an exquisite sparkling diadem, the polished topaz reflecting the afternoon sun. "Do proceed," she said coldly, addressing the servants. "You can't stop every time you step on a marketplace rat."

The litter bearers turned away hastily, and the warriors stopped chuckling.

"Go away, girl," repeated the first man, pushing her with the tip of his sandal, as though afraid to mar it with an actual kick. "Run along and don't come back here, ever."

The assortment of bared and sandaled feet began drawing

away, enabling Chantli to breathe again. Her hands trembled too badly to help her in her frantic attempt to get up; still, she put it all into the effort to gain an upright position, so terribly clumsy, swaying as though she had been drunk on *pulque*, the spicy beverage that Father and other respectable people consumed rarely and only in the privacy of their homes.

"Are you well, girl?"

"Have you been hurt?"

Some of the passersby slowed their steps, peering at her with a genuine, good-natured concern, their expressions inquiring. One of the men caught her elbow as she swayed, helping her up deftly, with what looked like practiced skill. "Did the warriors hurt you?"

"N-no." She hated the way her voice shook, so badly it made her stutter. Their faces were swimming, blurring behind the welling tears. "I... I th-thank you. I'm g-good. I have to... have to..."

"Don't cry, little one." This time, it was a female voice, gentle and lilting, pleasant to the ear. "Here, let us dry those tears, eh?"

The touch of the soft cloth brushing against her face made Chantli feel better. "Thank you. I'm not... I didn't..."

"Here, here." The round homely face beamed at her with an encouraging smile, the woman's hand coarse but friendly, wiping the tears away. "Now run along, little one, and don't fail to move aside when the royalty's litter is nearing."

The others nodded with vigor, their faces open, studying her with curiosity, lacking in hostility or reproach. "It's difficult not to recognize the Emperor's mother's litter, eh? The symbols and the amount of the warriors alone..." One of the men, a construction worker or maybe an engineer, judging by the state of his short dusty cloak, shook his head. "Couldn't you see that, girl? Weren't you taught to use your eyes?"

"Yes," joined several enthusiastic voices, talking all at once. "You should look around more carefully."

"Unless not used to strolling in these surroundings," suggested someone. "Where did you come from?"

"Not from anywhere near," declared the man with the dusty

cloak, pleased with himself. "She is from out there, from the slums that have nothing to do with this part of the city. That warrior was right. She is better off keeping away from here. Do you hear that, girl?"

Numbly, Chantli nodded, wishing nothing more than to disappear from the surface of the earth, never to return. The home, the wharves, and the marketplace were a much friendlier place, familiar and good, not eager to hurt or humiliate her, to make her feel like the muddiest leftover off the old food stall.

"I have to... have to go back, yes," she muttered, suddenly anxious to escape their talk and attention. They were no better than the arrogant noblewoman and her violent escorts, thinking themselves worthier than her only because they were used to walking around the Great Plaza and the Royal Enclosure.

Her anger rose, giving her enough power to push her way through. They were still talking, offering advice or maybe just gossiping now, discussing her lack of knowledge or belonging. She didn't care. Tenochtitlan's slums? No, her neighborhood wasn't like those cane-and-reed clusters of houses next to the old causeway or the worst of the wharves. How dared they talk about her like that? Back home, behind the marketplace's district, she knew when to move away, of course, when litters or warriors escorting richly dressed ladies appeared. One was required to clear one's way in order to let those pass. Still, they wouldn't push people into the mud, unless challenged with rude answers. Not like the vile warriors and the disgustingly haughty noblewoman they carried. Was it truly the Emperor's mother up there in the palanquin? A filthy piece of rotten fish, that what she was.

Rushing along the crude low wall, she fought her tears, blinking violently, not about to let those blur her vision. If it happened, she might bump into yet another litter or procession, offered insults or condescending advice. But for something like that not to happen in the first place. She didn't come from the slums, she did not!

From behind the stony barrier, cries and shouting reached her along with the dim booms of a heavy object crashing against it, making a dull sound. A ball game? It was easy to recognize those particular noises. Not an official game with a multitude of watchers and a lot of pomp. She had been taken to such a game only a few moons ago, when Tenochtitlan's team competed against the visiting Texcoco, its players and its dignitaries, along with the entire population of the Great Lake that seemed to crowd every vacant space around the Great Plaza. But this time, it was probably just training or a local game.

Slowing her step, she hesitated, the temptation to peek in great, difficult to battle. The ballgames were a thrilling thing to watch, even when it was nothing but marketplace boys drawing an improvised field in the dust, tossing their cherished rubber, having no walls or marks to hit but the only rule not to let the ball touch the ground.

"Commoner girl!"

A high-pitched but somehow familiar cry made her jump, looking around frantically, seeking the source of it.

"Up here, you silly."

On the far edge of the crumbling stones, a small figure perched daintily, in a birdlike fashion, waving his hand, motioning with vigor. This time, she did not hesitate. The boy from the previous day, this same controversial Ahuitzotl, might have been a haughty thing in itself, but he wasn't spiteful or mean, and he was the only familiar face here, a friendly one.

"What are you doing here?" she shouted, shielding her face against the glow of the afternoon sun.

He motioned again, more impatiently this time. "Come here and stop yelling."

"You are yelling yourself," she retorted, following the invitation, the good feeling evaporating once again.

He didn't hurry to jump down, clearly enjoying his elevated position. "I'm not yelling. I was waving my hand. I was motioning you."

"And a big difference it makes." Again she shielded her eyes against the merciless light that was pouring straight into her eyes, hurting them. "Get down. I can't talk to you when you are up there."

He shifted with indecision. "I can't. I have to be in there."

Another heartbeat of hesitation. "We are not allowed to sneak away. Only to watch the training."

"But I need to talk to you, to ask you something," she pleaded, suddenly needing his company, the good feeling he brought after the despondency following the humiliating incident on the Plaza.

"What?" He was still towering up there, like an emperor judging in court, aloof and above it all.

"It doesn't matter." The tears were back, blurring her vision. Stumbling on the uneven pavement, she turned away, catching the bulging part of the wall in order to keep her balance. She had had enough falls for one afternoon, hadn't she?

"Wait." Behind her back, the cobblestones creaked, rustling under the quick shuffling of his sandaled feet. "Why are you crying?"

"I'm not," she said, turning her face away.

"Yes, you are." He broke into a quick sprint, darting ahead of her, blocking her way. "You are crying, you are! Why?"

"No reason." She tried to push past him, but he was quicker, darting to and fro, obstructing her passage. "Let me pass!"

"I won't."

The way he stood there made her wish to chuckle against her will, his legs spread wide as though preparing to withstand an attack, his shoulders hunched forward. He was a tall boy, almost the same height as she was, thin but not stringy, satisfactorily broad. Still, she could take him, she decided, if tricking him into an unexpected push, then breaking into a run. He could not possibly beat her on that. She was a good runner, better than some boys on the marketplace.

"Why are you laughing now?" he demanded, his eyebrows knitted in a puzzled line.

"Because you are a spoiled little brat," she told him, pleased with her power to make him angry. He *was* a spoiled little thing. "They don't say 'no' to you very often, do they?"

"They do!" he cried out, his darkening eyes shooting thunderbolts. "And you are nothing but a filthy commoner from the filthiest pit of excrement in the filthiest corner of the marketplace!"

The colorful detail of such an inventive expletive made her burst out laughing almost against her will. "Under the filthiest roof and with the filthiest floor and with the filthiest walls all around. You forgot that."

Now it was his turn to giggle, though reluctantly.

"Now tell me what you were doing up there on the wall of the royal ball court."

"Watching them training." His hand waved in the general direction of the shouting and thuds. "We are made to watch when the city boys are taken to train. Old Yaotzin, he always insists. Every boy in the school has to come, because he'll be training us soon too. He promised."

"Don't they let you run with the ball now? At least a little, when no one is playing?"

"No!" He reared away, staring at her as though she had just sprouted another head. "No one is allowed to touch the ball just like that. Only when you are training or participating in the game, and, even then, only the Master of the Game is allowed to hold it. You can't –"

"I know the rules of the ballgame!" she cut him off impatiently, not about to be lectured who could touch the ball and under what circumstances. She had seen plenty of boys running around with their rubber treasure, tossing it to each other, trying to take the hits with their elbows and thighs alone. She had tried to do that too, several times, admittedly with little success. "The boys all over the marketplace are playing this game. Only your *calmecac* teachers make a special event out of it." Before he could start puffing up again, preparing to give measure for measure – but couldn't he go through one single conversation without trying to prove his worth? – she rushed on, determined, remembering her initial reason for sniffing around this aristocratic Central Plaza. "The city boys that are playing now, those are the boys who learn in your *calmecac*? The older ones?"

He nodded sullenly, his lips pursed tight.

"And if I need to talk to one of them, how can I do that?"

"To talk to them?" He peered at her, wide-eyed, his previous grudge forgotten in this typical fashion of his, the trait she had noticed about him yesterday, the one that probably made him so likeable despite his snobbery and too easily igniting temper.

"Yes, to talk to them. You see," for a good measure, she looked around, pleased to notice no passersby, not in this narrow square, tucked between the wall of the ball court and the crumbling side of a smallish pyramid with its peeling off plaster and lack of typical ornaments, "it's very important. I need their help, help in finding someone."

His eyes were turning larger by the moment. "Who?"

"A boy. A boy who has been missing since last night. He had been with them, you see, so maybe they know what happened to him, what he was planning to do. He works in my father's workshop and he never is late or missing, but now he is. He hasn't been around all day."

A gust of chilly breeze made her shiver and tuck her festive *huipil* closer to her body. Or was it fear? Talking about Miztli's absence aloud made her realize how truly dire the situation was. Something bad happened to this boy; something terrible, maybe.

"Who were the boys who were with him?" Oh, but this one was a quick little thing, understanding the essence of the problem, arriving at the proper course of action. What if he could help her if the other two *calmecac* boys wouldn't?

"One of them was called Necalli. That was the name they used when addressing him all the time. He must have a spectacular full name."

"Necalli?" He reared again, eyes still huge and round but full of indignation now. "Necalli sneaked out of school last night?"

"Well, yes," she mumbled, suddenly recalling what this same mentioned Necalli told her about this boy Ahuitzotl, nothing complimentary or remotely nice. "I think he can help us...help us find Miztli. The missing boy, you see." Would he be telling on Necalli now, letting the school authorities know about his running around at night? Oh, what a mess!

"Necalli is the worst piece of rotten fish, the most stinking loathsome pompous part of human excrement!"

Again she found it difficult not to snicker at the pictorial vividness of his swearing. "He is not *that* bad."

"Yes, he is," insisted the royal boy, spreading his legs wide again, his favorite argumentative pose. It had been only two meetings, but she felt as though she had known him for summers, like her little brother, so predictable.

"Well, I need to talk to him and you are the only one who can make it happen." She wrinkled her nose, peering at him with a measure of mock pleading. "I need you to help me."

He was still pouting, undecided. "You don't need me to talk to him," he muttered in the end. "You can go and talk to him all by yourself." Still sulking, he motioned toward the wall and the clamor behind it. "He is out there, playing."

"Playing ball?" she called out, elated.

"What else would he play?"

She paid his glowering no attention. "But I can't just go in there, can I?"

He rolled his eyes. "You can't now, but when they stop playing, you can sneak in and talk to them. They are always lingering, trying not to go back to school." He snorted. "They are such lazy no-goods." A frown crossed his pleasantly broad features. "No, only Necalli is no-good and lazy. The other boy, Axolin, is fine."

"Oh, Axolin, yes." She remembered the other one; a saucy, easygoing boy. Not as handsome as his friend and not as impressive, but a nice person as well.

"Was he out there with your workshop family member too?"

She shrugged, not about to give him more information than she had until now. Enough that her loose tongue might have put Necalli in trouble. "My cousin isn't working in my father's workshop. He is learning in *telpochcalli*, and they might admit him to your *calmecac* in the end."

"But he is the one who went missing?"

"No, it's the other boy, the one who does work in the workshop."

He wrinkled his face in the funniest of fashions. "You are all strange."

She tried not to snap at him or to avoid rolling her eyes. "Will you help me to sneak in and talk to them? Please?"

He pouted for no more than another heartbeat. "Come." The motion of his head indicated the crumbling wall, his former favorite perch.

CHAPTER 10

Shielding his eyes, Necalli watched the ball pouncing toward the mark on the wall, missing it by a fraction, bouncing off and straight away toward the dusty ground. His muscles strained, as though he was the one to run all over the field for the entire afternoon. He followed it with his eyes, craving to be near, to insert himself between the ball and the dusty pavement, even at the price of hurtful rubbing one's back would sustain at such an exercise. Oh, but it was more painful to sit and observe, able to do nothing, he discovered. Such frustration!

Easing his shoulders, he watched the teacher motioning angrily, scolding the players nearest to the wall, Axolin among them. Against his will, he smirked, remembering the previous day. Back then, it was his turn to get scolded and yelled at and Axolin was smirking up here, passing his time chattering with silly children. Still, if offered, he would have switched places now. To merely watch was quite an ordeal. But for the stupid arm!

He glanced at the crude bandage, now sullied and stained after a whole day of school activities. He wasn't offered any reprimands on account of his wounded limb, besides the demand to sit up here on the tribunes while the others battled the ball. Old Yaotzin made a face, grunting uncomplimentary things, yet not even demanding to inspect the wound. A relief, as the sight of the half burned, half ripped gashes would bring questions and he had no good story to offer, nothing that wouldn't have challenged and inevitably get them caught in their web of lies. Luckily, this same arm in question was still slightly swollen, not badly but noticeably, convincingly, and that, together with bloody stains upon the crude leather, was what must have put the old veteran off the continued interrogation. Instead, he had been sent to the priests of the adjacent temple to have his arm examined and taken care of, then bidden to sit here and watch the game. A small comfort, but better than earning punishments. To be held over the steaming pot full of hot chili peppers, inhaling the hurtful stinging smoke they produced, was not his idea of a good time, even though at his advanced age, the punishment would be harsher surely. Younger pupils, like that annoying royal family *pilli* with the exotic name, would be liable for the joys of breathing in stinging peppers, which would only serve that one well, he decided.

As though answering his thoughts, this same irritating *pilli* sprang into his side view, making his way along one of the low walls and down it with the natural grace of a monkey, at home on the uncomfortably narrow edge. No water monster, this one. He shuddered at the mere memory, clutching his bandaged arm with the good one a little too tightly.

"What do you want?" he asked rudely as the boy landed beside him, perching on the peeling-off stones, ready to spring back to his feet. A restless piece of work.

"Nothing!" As expected, the stormy eyes and the direfully creased forehead were his answer.

"Then hop along."

If the glares could have killed, he would have been done for, he reflected, grimly amused. That boy was a force of nature, a haughty royal brat or not. Why did he make him wish to put him in his place time after time? Axolin got along with this particular *pilli* well enough, and it wasn't wise to antagonize royal family. This one's brother was Tenochtitlan's Emperor, and his mother and father both offspring of the previous mighty rulers.

"If you want to stay, sit quietly and watch the game."

"That's no game. They are just training."

"That's game enough for you." Rolling his eyes, he tried to will his irritation away. "Old Yaotzin will put you down there soon enough, to be squashed by the ball all around, but until then, that's the most game you can get."

"My brother will be playing with his nobles and warriors in a market interval from now and I'll be invited to watch." The boy tossed his head high, his short pointed nose facing the sky loftily, with a clear meaning. "That's more to see than your silly training."

"Good for you." He shrugged with as much indifference as he could muster, as though to be allowed to watch the Emperor challenging the best of his warriors for a ballgame was nothing out of the ordinary, an everyday occurrence. But to be allowed to witness something like that! "Careful that old Yaotzin doesn't hear you talking like that about his lessons. The smoking peppers are just the thing to better your afternoon."

"If you tell on me, I'll let him know all about your running away from school yesterday."

"You what?" Forgetting all about the Emperor and the nobles and the ball that once again kissed the ground, drawing a new outburst of reprimands and lecturing on the stern teacher's part, Necalli stared at his unwanted companion, speechless for the moment.

"I'll tell on you if you tell on me," was the laconic answer, the level eyes facing him, flinty and unafraid.

"If you dare as much as to let out a peep..." he began, then thought better of it. One didn't threaten to beat up imperial brothers. "Forget it, you little piece of dung. I wasn't going to tell on you speaking silly things, even if you do run around spreading stories about me. I don't care." He forced out a shrug, his limbs still stiff with fury. "Also, I didn't run away from school. I went out when we all were allowed to go out, to visit our families."

"But you didn't go to your family home," called out the boy, triumphant.

"That's none of your filthy interest, little turkey."

"The girl you were running around with told me all about it," went on the annoying whelp, unimpressed.

That brought him back to the unseemly staring. "Who?"

"The commoner girl."

"Chantli?" It surprised him that he did remember her name, having thought of her since yesterday, occasionally yes, but in a fragmented way. "Why would she be telling you any of it? And how do you know her at all?"

The victorious glow didn't dim. Oh, but the filthy thing was happy to have an upper hand, even if temporary, the little pest. "Because she was looking for you just now, that's why. She said that the boy you've been with is missing and she wanted you to help her finding him."

"Oh!" He tried to process this flood of information, from his puzzlement that the haughty royal offspring would know the workshop commoner girl and on such intimate terms, to the missing boy who needed his help in order to be found. What had Patli got himself into?

"Yes, and she is still out there, you know. I promised her to bring you out."

"What? Now?" The pieces of the puzzle kept falling together. Oh yes, she was bragging about her friendship with this same Ahuitzotl, wasn't she, claiming that he was a nice boy and that he told her plenty of gossip straight away from the Palace's halls. "Where is she?"

"Out there. I just told you." The satisfied glitter made him wish to strike the presumptuous little beast whatever the consequences. "You are slow."

"Don't push it!" He bit his lower lip, willing his thoughts into calmer directions. "I'll tell you what. Take me to her, but then make yourself scarce. Go back here and watch that Yaotzin doesn't look this way."

The boy sprang to his feet readily, as though pushed by the stones under his bottom. "Don't give me orders. I'll stay if I want to."

"No, you won't!" But the regular annoyance with the pushy brat didn't come. "Stop arguing and lead the way."

The renewed fighting for the ball drew their attention with its loudness and the lively shouting, offering possibilities. Half bent behind the cover of a stone parapet, they slipped alongside it, then leaped for the next cover of the old wall.

"I'm not climbing that," hissed Necalli when his companion leaped up the crumbling stone. "It will put us in a clearer spot than to yell to old Yaotzin outright."

"It'll take you ages to go around it." As expected, the little beast pushed his way up, not even bothering to turn his head for a reply.

Necalli eyed his bandaged arm, glad to channel his irritation toward it. His lack of climbing skills was not an issue, not now. Warriors didn't climb like monkeys, not Jaguar and not Eagle elite warriors.

"Wait for me there and tell her to do the same."

While slinking along the towering stones of another higher wall that separated the court from the Revered Tezcatlipoca's temple and pyramid, he thought about what had been said. So that pretty Chantli's cousin got himself in trouble, the cowardly piece of rotten fish that he turned out to be, and out of all people, she came to him, asking for help. The smile threatened to sneak out, unheeded and uninvited. She could have gone to her father, the workshop owner and Patli's uncle, couldn't she? Or she could have even asked for the help of the courageous apprentice, the barefoot villager with a spectacular name. Obsidian Puma, of all things! But this foreigner's father must have been hopeful while reading his son's calendar upon the day he was born. Was this why he sent the promising thing to Tenochtitlan, the Capital of the World? To slave in the workshop and be snubbed by everyone who felt like it, even this same annoying Patli – some glorious future!

Diving into the crevice between two adjacent walls and the blissful shadow it provided, he shook his head, elated for no reason. He couldn't possibly sneak away for the duration of another evening, not after the dressing down he and Axolin had to endure, first by the priest responsible for the evening rites they had missed, then by the veteran who came to teach morning lessons, having been told tales of their transgressions but in a light enough manner, as it seemed. They could have been disciplined more severely than by being made to work in the kitchen house when the others were out there practicing with *atlatls*. They had certainly gotten away lightly. Still, to push it by going missing again and on the very next evening was unwise. Nothing was said about the demand to stay in school this afternoon, but nothing was said to the contrary either.

She was easy to spot in the lively clamor of the afternoon alley, the simplicity of her plain, barely decorated dress and the loosely tied braids setting her apart, making her stand out in the busily walking noble crowds. Even the servants and the Royal Enclosure's slaves were dressed better, more richly, with more flair. And yet, somehow, she was the most pleasing sight, keeping his eyes glued to her along with some others, he noticed, pursing his lips while hastening his step. Ahuitzotl was there already, talking lively and waving his hands, reinforcing his words, a vigorous beast. It wouldn't be easy to get rid of this one, damn it.

Her face lit like a temple's hall through the days of great ceremonies as she turned to greet him, her smile one of the widest. It took his breath away, the radiance of it.

"*Niltze*," she shouted, not waiting for him to close the distance, waving both hands as she did.

He felt his grin spreading wide. "*Niltze*, Chantli."

"It's nice to see you in a better state. Refreshed. Not beaten up like last night." Her laughter trilled the air, pleasing Necalli's ear but leaving him uncomfortable. What was one to offer in response to this? She did have the manners of a boy, that one. "You should have seen him yesterday," she added, turning toward her royal company, still beaming. "Quite a sight."

Ahuitzotl just snorted, not interested in any of it. "Tell him about that boy, the one who is missing."

This time, Necalli didn't feel like shooing the annoying thing away. Maybe it was better to have someone who knew how to handle her. For the first time, he wondered how they came to know each other, the royal *pilli* and the workshop girl.

"Yes, tell me what happened."

"Oh." Her smile faded at once. "I, yes, I came here looking for you, because... You see, Miztli, he didn't return. Not through the night and not in the morning. He has been missing the whole day!"

"Miztli? You mean the workshop boy?" he asked, taken aback. "I thought it was Patli who got in trouble."

"No, no!" She shook her head vigorously, making her nicely thick braids jump. "Patli is at school. Well, I suppose that he is. He should be coming home for the evening meal soon, so we'll know." Her delicate eyebrows knitted worriedly. "You don't think anything happened to him, do you?"

"To Patli?" He couldn't help snorting disdainfully. "Nothing, not to that one. He is good and healthy, out and away from danger." A shrug seemed to be in order. "But tell me about the workshop boy. He didn't come back at night?"

"No." Her frown deepened, banishing the remnants of playful lightness. "He sleeps in the workshop, so I didn't know if he came back or not during the night. But in the morning, Father was very put out. He likes to start working early, with the break of dawn, and he expects the braziers to be lit by the time he comes in, and the tools arranged and ready. But this morning, not only were the braziers off, but even the firewood wasn't there, not gathered or brought in, as he does in the evenings. Well, obviously, as through the previous evening he was out there, with us, you see?" He liked the way her eyes clung to him, pleading for help, so huge and wide-open, delightfully trustful. Such pretty sight. "Father was so furious. Oh, I never saw him like that before. So I wished that Miztli would not appear just yet. Maybe later, after Father calmed down. But then," her shoulders lifted in a shrug, "then, when he didn't come back at all, I wished he would return, even if to get punished. Something bad must have happened to him. Something terrible, maybe. These people, you know, the ones that you thought were after you all…"

"Is he your father's slave?"

She shook her head. "Not formally, no. But I imagine Father does have a right to punish him, or at least to throw him out, and then he won't have a place to sleep even. And it's not his fault. Patli said it was his idea to go to that tunnel. He told me all about it on our way back."

"Patli should talk less and do more," muttered Necalli, in no forgiving mood whatsoever. But what might have happened to the workshop boy? He said that some of the smugglers from the tunnel saw him and went after him, yes, when on his way back from the terrible island of the monster, but how had those people tracked him afterwards, with all their wandering and the time spent at the temple? And why weren't they all attacked, if so? Didn't the smugglers know that they had been sniffing around? They must have left plenty of stupid marks. Or did the workshop boy go back there to take another look, instead of heading back home? He, Necalli, did suggest that he should do that, didn't he? And if so, it was his responsibility to try and find him, to help him out, maybe. That boy was too good to go down like that, either killed by the smugglers or beaten by the lowly copper-melting scum, Chantli's father. How to go about it and with his own troublesome situation at school? Even now, as they stood there, he was chancing being noticed as missing from the ball court. Damn it!

"Who was after you all?" Ahuitzotl's voice brought him back from his uneasy dilemmas, made him concentrate on both pair of eyes – hers prettily large and shaded by the thickest eyelashes he had ever seen, and the boy's, narrowed into slits, suspicious.

"It's not of your interest, *pilli*-boy –" he began, but Chantli's frown deepened again.

"Maybe Ahuitzotl could help us in this."

He rolled his eyes. "How?"

"I can be of help more than you are!" called out their royal company hotly. "I can help her and I want to!"

Chantli was eyeing him almost pleadingly. "He knows things. About Tlatelolco and the trouble it makes. It might be connected to what happened. Think about it. The weapons you saw, and the tunnel leading into the piece of land that can't be seen from the causeway but comfortable for reaching it by canoe. And Tlatelolco wharves are famous for their smugglers, eh? Everyone knows that."

"Who are these 'everyone'?" he grunted, not pleased with the shady knowledge she displayed, let alone her readiness to spill their dubious adventures in front of the royal brat busy pushing himself in. "I see Patli was busy retelling you our every step, stupid blabber that he is."

She shrugged, not offended. "He needed to talk. He looked

badly shaken. You have been through plenty of trouble. Just look at your arm!"

Her gaze shot toward the dirtied bandage, so openly concerned it mollified him, to a degree.

"It's good now. It'll be all right." Pursing his lips, he shrugged in his turn. "Out of all of us, nothing happened to your Patli, so he is the last one to complain. That Miztli villager sounds as though he is in trouble and he was the braver of the two, not like the cowardly *telpochcalli* boy." He shook his head, trying to get rid of his rage. "We must find him, yes. Maybe he is in that tunnel, caught or held prisoner or something."

Her small even teeth were making a mess out of her lower lip. "Will you go there and look?"

He nodded gravely, pleased with the way she gazed at him, all trust and expectation. It made him feel powerful. "Yes, I'll go there. We'll wait until they stop playing, get Axolin, and go to that tunnel right away." Warming to this idea, encouraged by that same nearly adoring gaze of hers, he narrowed his eyes, thinking hard. "A torch. This time, we'll need a torch, at least one such thing. To wander there in the darkness won't help." The memory of the furry creatures, rats and whatnot, made him shudder, but he brushed it aside, determined. "I must think of something."

"I know where to get a good torch," said the royal boy readily, without his usual challenging scowl. "A good torch, with the best quality cloths and oil."

"Where?"

"In the temple. I know where they store those things."

For the first time, he found himself eyeing this unasked-for company with a measure of interest and no disdain. "Can you get it for us?"

The boy nodded smugly, pleased with himself. "I'll bring it, maybe even two. But I carry it." The scowl was back, more challenging than ever. "I carry the torch, or I won't be getting you any."

"You are not coming with us!" cried out Necalli, taken aback by such a wild idea.

"Yes, I am." Spreading his legs wide, as though readying for the attempt to dislodge him or throw him away by force, the little beast glared at him, set on fighting for his rights. "She said I can be of help, and I want to help. And you can't stop me anyway. You can't tell me what to do!"

"If you ran away from school, the entire city would be on our heels before we so much as managed to reach that causeway. Are you insane? You are the Emperor's brother, for all the mighty deities' sake!"

"No one will be running after us. They won't even notice. I sneak away all the time!"

"He does," confirmed Chantli readily, taking the little brat's side. "Yesterday, we met out there, not even in the temple. He knows plenty of passageways and corridors. He is good at those things."

Necalli exhaled loudly, cornered by their united front, not appreciating the sensation. They were just a commoner girl and a little boy!

"You run away from school?"

"Oh yes. All the time!" That came out plain victorious. The boy's eyes sparkled. "And you do need this torch, and other things too. I can bring weapons as well. I know how to get into the room where they store training swords and spears."

"Another corridor, eh?" purred Chantli, conspiratorial and as though proud of her charge.

"Oh yes. Straight into the storage of weapons and shields."

"The training swords won't help us," grunted Necalli. "With no obsidian, they are nothing but clubs."

They both glared at him, clearly offended.

"Oh well, if you can get a torch and you promise that no one will be looking for you..." He scowled at the cheeky cub as direfully as he could. "Also that you will not be crying for your mother if we are attacked or something." He thrust his bandaged arm closer to the boy's face, noting with grudging admiration that the little beast did not take a step back. "See that thing? It looks ugly and it still hurts like the Underworld's middle levels. So if you are afraid of things like that, don't bother to follow, torches or not."

"I don't care," muttered the royal *pilli* stubbornly, now clearly fighting to stay where he was. "I'm not afraid of those things."

Hiding a grin, Necalli shook his head. "Then go and get the torches and maybe a training sword or two. Be as quick as you can. I'll get Axolin, and you..." He looked at Chantli, not trying to hide his smile, not this time. It was inappropriate to bring a girl on such an adventure, but it was good that she was coming, whatever the convention said. Maybe the commoner girls did behave differently. Not the serving maids in the noble houses like in his and his friends' families, all of them humble slaves, bought and paid for, and not like uncouth loudmouthed fowls from the wharves and the marketplace, but the true commoners, children of craftsmen and such. She was certainly most pleasant company, even if delightfully unpredictable.

"What?" Her eyebrows knitted again, this time in a question.

"Nothing. You better go back to your house, see if Patli is there. If so, bring him along, make him take you to that temple near the causeway and meet us there. If he isn't, then just come to the causeway and we'll find you there."

This time, she nodded readily, offering no argument, her smile as victorious as Ahuitzotl's. Was she afraid to be denied the participation too? The thought made him laugh.

"You." He turned back to the royal *pilli*. "Bring two torches if you can. They are preferable to the clubs, if you have to choose between the two."

Another eager nod made him wish to chuckle. But it was wild, this entire thing, the wildest and not even a little bit prudent, but he didn't mind. Not this time.

CHAPTER 11

The slivers of light were still there, painting the earthen floor into playful patterns, not in a hurry to dim, or better yet, to disappear for good. Miztli hated the sight of them.

To curl in the filthy corner, pretending that his ties were still intact, was challenging, stretching his nerves to their limits. The darkness, would it never come? Since the first light, since being dumped here, in this filth-covered rectangular building full of crates and cases aplenty, he had spent so much time pretending to be unconscious or asleep. Or drifting somewhere, anxious to draw as little attention as possible, to make his captors forget his very existence.

Which was not such a difficult task, as the people who entered this shed during the day did so rarely; busy, preoccupied types, in a hurry to fetch things and be gone. His ears informed him that there was much activity outside the roughly fixed planks, but this particular shed was not the center of it. Thanks all the deities, each and every one of them. After the terrible night, he knew that only his ability to bluff his way through might keep him alive; this and the willingness of the dusk to come faster.

Shifting to better his position, his limbs stiff and hurting, every single move, he remembered the night, shuddering badly against his will. Those people in the deserted alley, pouncing like jaguars from the shadows, lethal and vicious, set on capturing him. No simple robbers those, no marketplace types the *calmecac* boy Necalli warned him against. Terribly strong and determined, impossible to fight or escape. It was difficult to remember what occurred back in this alley, but the mere fragments were enough to make the terrible waves of panic return, to send his mind into the depths of uncontrollable fear. Not to mention what came next!

Grinding his teeth against the intensified shaking, he remembered coming around for the first time, climbing out of the pitch-black suffocating depths, opening his eyes to more darkness dotted with flickering lights. The stench of rancid wood and rotten fish attacked his nostrils, bringing his nausea to the point where it was beyond his power to hold it in, bursting out in an agonizing spasm, as though the clubs hammering inside his head or the claws tearing at his chest were not enough. He retched and retched, curled upon the wet gravel, terrified beyond reason, sensing the darkness groping, wishing to find him and drag him back under.

When finally able to breathe again, he felt nothing but relief, the ridiculous sensation of safety. The darkness could not snatch him, not anymore. However, the good feeling didn't last. In another heartbeat, rough hands pulled him over, or maybe kicked him onto his back, to stare at the dimly lit sky and the grotesque faces peering at him from above, dark holes for eyes and mouths, terrifying outlines, like in the worst of nightmares. A renewed wave of terror gave him the power to roll away, or to try to do that, an attempt frustrated quite easily by a vicious kick that brought him back where he was, to be studied thoughtfully for another heartbeat, then hauled to his feet violently, with much force.

"Bring him in and let Nexcoatl know," tossed a curt voice, digging into his elbow, pulling as though determined to tear it out. "Bring a torch too."

"Why don't we drop him into the lake and be done with him?" inquired another, calmer voice. "Why question the little piece of dirt? He knows nothing, that one. A barefoot commoner; what do you think he would know?"

"We'll see in a little while," insisted the first voice, his hurtful grip supporting, enabling Miztli to stay upright despite the terrible dizziness and the shudders. The nausea was back, assaulting his entire being with vicious strength.

His willpower dedicated to holding it in, he didn't resist the pull that directed him toward one of the darker shades, its low uneven shape somehow familiar, sparking a memory. Pushed through the narrow opening, he stumbled and was busy fighting for balance and against the unrelenting pull when the realization dawned, making his limbs lose their power again. *The temple with the tunnel!* Oh yes, the low half broken wall that they had passed by, with the *calmecac* boys asking Patli if he couldn't find a more presentable place to drag them into, a better looking temple than this ruin. Oh mighty deities, but they were back in the tunnel or heading there!

The struggle to free himself ensued with renewed desperation, resulting with him being kicked in rather than pushed through, sprawling on the stone floor, paralyzed with all-encompassing fear. The memory of the underground room with rats and the stakes of weaponry, the mysterious monster of the lake with terrible claws, the smugglers he had escaped on his way out earlier, the temple with priests and the marketplace riffraff; all mixing in his mind, united against him, managing to get him somehow.

He fought the attempt to drag him back up, struggling wildly, pushing and kicking, biting someone's fist that brushed past his mouth, frenetic with fear. Even when pinned to the stones too firmly to move a limb, he kept wriggling and twisting, desperate to break free, oblivious of reason, until the blow on the side of his head softened the reality, turned everything into a foggy mist-covered haze, not frightening but delightfully light, floating, reassuring. It was good to escape the nightmare at last.

Vaguely aware, disinterested but curious, just a little, he took in the movement of forms, hovering harmlessly, sometimes drawing nearer, accompanied with lights, sometimes just floating like he did. One such outburst of a smoking beacon resulted in his nausea coming back, the pleasant floating interrupted by unwelcomed bumps and jolts, as though the night air suddenly sprang obstacles like back on the ground.

In the end, the smell of the lake prevailed and the monotonous swaying, as though the wind picked its tempo. It nauseated him again, badly at that, the floating sensation not returning. Instead, the dread reappeared with redoubled strength. He was still in these people's hands, still at their mercy, but now back in the lake, in the realm of the underwater monster!

To try and straighten up didn't help. His face tucked against some fetid damp substance – a maguey bag, judging by its texture and smell – he didn't manage to move any of his limbs, his knees pressed against his chin, hands stuck behind his back, not reacting to his efforts to make them move. Even the option of taking a deep breath in order to fight the panic wasn't there, not with the revolting rag filling his nostrils with a rancid stench. Oh mighty deities!

In desperation, he pushed with his entire might, recoiling wildly, unable to hold his terror back. His feet hit something, a hard plank, then something softer and warmer. The boat lurched like a startled animal.

"Careful!" muttered someone, a voice in the darkness. The boat jerked again, its screeching filling the dampness of the night.

"The stupid whelp and the stupid beam," cried out another voice. "That canoe is too heavy."

A hand groped for his leg, caught it firmly in a painful grip. He tried to kick it away but in the crowdedness of the narrow vessel, all he managed was to rock it badly.

"I'll throw the whelp out. Help me!"

The paddle kept struggling against the water, lessening the lurching. "It's not deep enough here. Too near the causeway."

"It's deep enough. Also, the stupid cub is tied. What do you think he'll do, walk along the lake's bottom?"

"Well…"

The monotonous splashing paused, but not the rough swaying. He stopped struggling as well, the strange calm prevailing, making his head clear.

"Let the fish feed on him. Or maybe the Spiny One. They will thank us yet. How stupid it was to make us take all those things together with the wild cub. Do they think we have a war canoe here, with five men to row it along?"

He felt the hand pulling him hard, making the boat swivel again.

"Wait!" It was easier to talk without the filthy maguey stuck in his face. The lake's breeze was a blessing, refreshing, making his thoughts organize, calming the unseemly horror. "Wait, don't... don't throw me out. I... I know things, things your... your superiors would want to hear."

The pull lessened momentarily. With an inhuman effort, he forced his body to relax, to stop the struggle to break free.

"What are you blabbering about?" The rough fingers were still pulling, but with less determination. "What do you want to tell us, wild boy?"

"Things." He licked his lips, craving a gulp of water all of a sudden. But not the one from the lake's depths. "About Tlatelolco... and weapons..." He swallowed, trying to make his throat and not only his head work. Those smugglers back in the tunnel, the ones he spied on while hurrying to get the accursed rope, they talked about rich Tlatelolcan getting angry because of the damaged crate, didn't they? And then Chantli, bragging about running around with some royal *pilli* from the Palace, the one that kept making Necalli angry. She used names in her story, important names, didn't she? The Emperor's sister with a beautiful name ChalchiuhNenetzin, Noble Jade Doll, a spoiled brat according to the other *calmecac* boy, and then the ruler of Tlatelolco, the lady's husband, Moxqui-something...

"What do you know about the weapons back there?"

The rough hand pulled harder, frustrating his panicked attempts to resist, but as he unfolded into the semblance of an upright position, it pushed him to lean against the crudely carved side, making the boat career again. The man behind his back cursed.

"Why do you think your tales will be of interest to anyone, boy?"

He took a deep breath, this time enjoying the damp air, so much better than the stinking bottom of the boat. "I... I know who will want those weapons. And I..." He tried to make his head work, the calm still there, pleasantly reassuring, but not helping to think of a good reason to give these people, to talk them into keeping him alive until they reached firm land again. "I know

what our Emperor's sister... that other island's ruler's wife, that
is..."

This time, even the man with the paddle froze somewhere
behind his back.

"You do?" drawled the man in front of him, nothing but a dark
silhouette in the dimming moonlight. The dawn was not far away.

"Yes." He didn't dare to let his breath out, his relief spreading,
making his limbs weak and as though out of control, trembling.
"They would want to hear me out."

"They?" In the faint illumination of the fading moon, the man's
grin was eerily wide, transforming his face into a grotesque mask.
"And who are these 'they,' eh? Who are these important
Tlatelolcans? The Noble Jade Genitalia herself maybe, eh?"

Despite his terror and agony, he almost snickered,
remembering that the word *nenetl* meant not only 'doll' but the
intimate female private parts as well.

"I say drop the stupid foreigner into the lake and be done with
it," cried out the man with the paddle, not amused in the least.
"He is blabbering nonsense, and we were told to toss the damn
cub into the lake anyway. Come, man, we are late as it is."

"Throwing him over would take more time." There was a grin
in his captor's voice, the satisfied tone of a person who has
managed to snatch something good all for himself. "Our greedy
Tenochtitlan would-be empress is just the person to stick her
pretty nose into all this, eh? Think about it. And if we get to
implicate her, the Emperor would be pleased enough. Think with
your head, man, not with your back exit."

"I'm thinking with my head, you stupid lump of meat,"
protested the other one, striking the water with his paddle, angrily
at that. "And I say your greediness will be the end of you. That
boy knows too much, that is obvious, and you should get rid of
him instead of using him to let yourself into any of it. Throw him
over or I will do it!" The boat lurched again upon yet another
abrupt halting.

"No, you won't." The other man didn't seem worried, so Miztli
managed to force his body into relaxing as well. "Row or give me
the paddle. We still want to make it to the wharves without half of

Tlatelolco staring at us and our cargo."

The man with the paddle muttered something inaudible. And even now, half a day later and still not anywhere near being out of danger, he remembered the vastness of his relief, the immensity of it. They weren't going to kill him, to toss him into the monster's claws. He was going to reach firm land.

The sliver of light moved closer to the doorway, encouraging. He must have drifted off, sinking so deep in the terrible memories. Good! With nightfall, he would be able to sneak away, provided no one came to question him and check on his ties, or worse yet, to remove him somewhere. Oh mighty deities, don't let it happen. It was so hard to get rid of the ropes, good pieces of sturdy maguey, too good and too durable. It took him half a day of rubbing his back against a sturdy beam, working when no one was in or looking his way, those grim, sweat-and-mud covered people, carrying crates or enormous bags, paying him no attention. A small mercy. He wouldn't be able to summon enough patience to sit for half a day doing nothing, waiting to be questioned about things he didn't know. He would have done something stupid. Yet, as it was, the effort to untie his hands kept him busy and now he was about to sneak away the moment it became suitably dark, whatever the consequences. The danger of getting caught while running was no worse than the alternative of being questioned by whatever authorities these people served. If only he could move his hands more freely, if for no other reason than to return the feeling in them. Or to find his talisman, to hold the obsidian wonder and feed on its power. Oh, but why did he feel as though it wasn't there anymore? Terrified by the mere possibility, he shut his eyes.

The slivers of light weren't there anymore when he heard the voices, loud and nearing, speaking with unmistakable confidence. Not the people who kept coming in and out, the mere workers or slaves. He felt his heart coming to an abrupt halt.

The crude wooden screen shielding the doorway screeched, letting in the last of the light. The silhouettes poured in, blocking the view. He forced his eyes to remain steady, to count, his mind numb, refusing to offer advice. Back in the lake it was easier, facing a certain death, having nothing to lose, gambling with everything he had – death or postponement, a blissful delay, a chance – but now, oh, now he was too tired, too numb, too exhausted and dazed. What could he say to make them let him go? Nothing, nothing at all. There were no right words or information, no worthwhile offering to suggest. Maybe the *calmecac* boys could have offered their families' wealth, begged their captors to let their fathers know, to accept a ransom. Would these people agree had he had any means of payment to offer? Well, there was no way to prove that. Old Tlaquitoc wouldn't pay to free his disobedient apprentice. He would rather feel like punishing the missing worker himself had he managed to get away from these people last night, shoving his charge's face into a fire full of stinging smoke belonging to the roasting chili pepper. But would he pay to save his life if promised to be served as a slave until the debt was paid? The stingy man could have considered that. If only there was a way to let him know, to offer the bargain. Maybe through Chantli.

"Is this the cub?" The words ricocheted against the coarse walls as heavy as stones and as sharp as pieces of obsidian.

It made his heart stop for good, the obvious contempt, the cold hostility. He forced his eyes to look up, taking in the broadness of the towering man, the wideness of his features. His nose looked as though it had been smashed or maybe just shifted, moved aside.

"What do you have to tell me, boy?"

The veiled eyes didn't blink, studying him with the chilly interest of a predator facing an unworthy meal, a squeaking forest mouse instead of a plump rabbit or a healthy dog. Miztli tried to force his cracked lips into working, his mouth dry, tongue like a dead weight, swollen but useless, the sides of his throat clinging to each other. The thirst that was haunting him the whole day now became unbearable and just as he needed to talk, to say things.

"Well, will you talk or will they have to make you?" demanded the man, ominously calm, his voice gaining an unpleasant caressing quality.

"I... I'll tell you... the things..." It came out ridiculously strident, more of a rasp than normal speech, cut by the barking cough that he could not hold in, a grating ugly sound. He tried not to double over, anxious to keep his hands and their lack of ties away from his interrogator's attention, facing the man against the rocking bark, choking in merciless convulsions.

Through the veil of tears the cough brought, he could see his interrogator's eyes narrowing.

"Get him something to drink," he tossed curtly, half turning his head, making some of his followers scatter. The rest were bestowed with a contemptuous snort. "Can't you make this one look more presentable, eh? He'll die on us at any moment, choking and gagging. Is that the sight worthy of my eyes, eh, you lowly scum?"

The rest muttered, lowering their heads humbly, not prostrating themselves but looking as though they might. Over the worst of the cough, Miztli watched, fascinated against his will. As long as the man was busy getting angry at his captors, he wouldn't be busy making him talk. And maybe, just maybe…

"Let him drink, then clean him some." The broad back was upon them, drawing away together with the indifferent voice. "Bring him to me when he can talk without choking. Send someone and I will let you know where."

He didn't dare blink, watching the swaying cloak blocking the doorway yet again, its patterns pretty and bright, glittering with polished turquoise. The remaining men stirred, looking at each other.

"A haughty piece of rotten meat," one of them muttered through pressed lips.

"Well, you heard Honorable Teconal." This time, he recognized the voice easily. The man from the boat. Not the one who insisted on dumping him overboard. He breathed with relief. "Clean the boy some, give him something to drink. Water, then after the cleaning, pour him some *pulque*. This will give him enough strength to go through the questioning without collapsing once again." He could see the wide shoulders lifting in a shrug. "If his information will not displease our revered noble, that is. Otherwise, count that *pulque* as a spilled out beverage." The broad face moved closer, swam into his view. "On second thought, give him that *pulque* first, before the attempted washing. Then give him another cup, just before setting out. Maybe it'll help. Can't make Revered Teconal angrier than he is now, can we?" The narrowed eyes twinkled, one of them shutting momentarily, in a sort of a wink. "Hold on, wild boy. Try to do your best and you may live to see the next dawn." A slightly mocking grin joined the wink. "Our trade welcomes people with enough spirit and guts. And if combined with physical strength like yours..." Straightening up, the man shook his head. "Do your best and you may have a chance."

The rest of them followed yet another retreating back, leaving him blissfully alone, limp with relief. The aftershock of the confrontation dawned, making his entire body shake. He curled in a ball, trying to gather his senses. What could he say to that dangerously calm, richly dressed noble, so cold and menacing without saying one threatening word? And what if they would try to beat the truth out of him, what if they tried to find what he knew by torture? What then? Would he manage to convince them that the tidbits of the Tenochtitlan Royal Enclosure's gossip was all that he knew without being pressed to reveal his sources? He could not mention anyone; neither Chantli with her royal family boy carrying the name of the water monster, her source of information, nor Patli, nor their *calmecac* accomplices. If these people managed to track him down on the same evening they had become aware of his presence, then no one was safe from them, no one!

Shuddering, he looked at the doorway, now a mere outline, dim and opaque, pouring grayish light through the gaping entrance that no one bothered to close this time. Was it time? It was not suitably dark yet, and the people who were sent to bring water and *pulque* might be on their way back already. And yet, it was his chance now, his only chance.

Clinging to the wall he was leaning against for the entire day, he managed to claw his way into an upright position, his head reeling badly, threatening to make him fall. The doorway looked terribly far, a gray rectangle, promising safety. Just to reach it somehow.

Digging his fingers into the crevice of the nearby beam, he pulled himself up, then partly pushed, partly threw himself toward the next wall, clinging to it with his entire body, pleased with his success. Another such leap looked like a wild bet, so he dragged himself along the rough wooden planks, delighted at the touch of the light breeze reaching him through the cracks and the now-near doorway. So close.

Before he could grab another supportive beam, a shadow fell across the earthen floor, a faint outline, barely noticeable but there. His heart stopped, then threw itself wildly against his ribs. Somehow, he knew it was none of the men sent to bring him water or *pulque*. Also that the intruder was here for him, not for the goods stored in this place. The way he stared now, surprised but alerted, already on the move and pouncing, told him that.

He tried to dart away, swaying backwards and toward the safety of the other wall, but of course his attacker was faster, his hands strong and reeking of fish, one grabbing his shoulder, crushing it in a stony grip, the other pressing into his mouth with too much force, slamming his head against the choppy planks as though eager to crush it and be done with it.

In desperation, he bit the smothering hand, revolted by the salty taste of the coarse skin but determined, not about to get beaten again, kidnapped anew, or choked to death, for that matter. The rock-hard palm was squashing his nose as well, blocking most of the air from coming in or out.

Kicking with all his might, free to do so with the heavy body pinning him to the wall, which freed his legs from the necessity to support him, he sank all his teeth into the smothering hand, putting it all into another savage bite. A muffled groan was music to his ears, but as the bitten hand slipped, allowing the air back into his clogged nose, he felt the other one returning in an unmistakable fashion.

Not quick enough to move out of the heavy fist's path, he busied himself with another kick before the already familiar explosion brought the floating sensation back, as strangely reassuring as back in the temple. He didn't remember reaching the floor, but being dragged along it ruined some of the calming effect.

"What a wild beast, the stinking dung-eater," the muffled voice muttered, somehow familiar, shattering his sense of security once again, making him struggle against the floating sensation and the hands that were pulling him on as though he was a bag with provisions, not something one might be afraid to damage, to avoid multiple collisions with the obstacles dotting the earthen floor. *The man from the boat!* Oh mighty deities, but he did remember this voice, talking in between the paddle's splashing, insisting on throwing the prisoner into the lake, on letting him drown and have *ahuitzotls* feasting on his flesh. Oh mighty deities!

CHAPTER 12

Only when their flickering torch went off did it become truly frightening. Until then, she felt good enough, thrilled by the adventure, enchanted by it, not distressed by the pressing walls and their crumbling, dank, leaking stones. Well, not too badly. Not like the others, especially Patli and the other *calmecac* boy, whose fright was pronounced, proclaimed in their hunched shoulders and their lowered heads, the colorlessness of their pressed lips.

Necalli was busy leading, carrying their torch, with Ahuitzotl keeping very close, not out of fear, she suspected, but to prove his point. He didn't like the way his *calmecac* older peer took control of their precious cargo after managing to light it, working with two suitably flat stones, gaining enough sparks to achieve fire. They didn't think to bring a burning coal, those boys, and it made her smirk back behind the temple's yard when they were confronted with the problem, arguing about their plans and the details of those. Why would one carry a good sturdy stick wrapped in a cloth soaked in high-quality oil without thinking to bring the means to light it? Boys!

Back behind the small temple and later, while gathering enough courage to slink into its neglected patio and toward the tunnel, there was much argument running between the leader-like Necalli and none other than the young Ahuitzotl. Despite his unimpressive age, the boy was a match to his older peers, if in nothing else, then in his fierceness and determination to be heard and listened to, in his readiness to dive into verbal altercations and maybe even fights. Even the forceful, decisive Necalli couldn't override the royal *pilli* effectively, himself not averse to leaping into arguments when his decisions were dared to be doubted, with Axolin taking the younger boy's side, mainly to spite his friend, was Chantli's amused conclusion.

Well, they were still arguing in the neglected courtyard, when Patli had come back, apparently having sneaked into the temple itself in the meanwhile, not as useless or as cowardly as their *calmecac* self-appointed leader implied before, even though it had been difficult to convince this cousin of hers into joining the improvised rescue mission. It had taken her time to do that, time and some barely veiled threats, like being told on. Her father wouldn't be happy to hear about his nephew's previous day's adventures, she had claimed, withstanding the fierceness of his glare, afraid only that their argument would make them late for the meeting place, resulting in the boys going out on their own, not waiting for her. If she had known where this tunnel was, she wouldn't have bothered with Patli at all.

Still, her cousin turned out to be useful, efficient enough and not truly cowardly, she decided to her somewhat grudging sense of family pride. While they were busy arguing about their immediate destination or the identity of whom would be holding the torch and hence leading the way, Patli reappeared at the crumbling doorway, motioning them to come in, the urgency of his gesturing making them obey, their wariness and excitement soaring.

She remembered how the temple turned out to be not as threatening as they were afraid it would be, its half ruined walls letting enough light and air in, dispersing with the typical temple's smell. The altar was half-broken, sprouted with plenty of dry yellow grass, the dusty floor cracked, more earthen than paved by this point, easy to step on. It carried plenty of footsteps and other signs of activities, and that was what Patli was pointing at, beckoning them to come closer instead of just standing there, gaping.

"See this?" he whispered, as though afraid to be overheard. It made her glance up and all around. Oh yes, people were frequenting this abandoned temple. Why?

"The marks?" asked Necalli, lowering his voice if not to a whisper, then at least to a considerably lower tone. "The footsteps?"

Impatiently, Patli shook his head. "Yes, that too. But look here." The dust was all rumpled, exposing the cracked stones of the pavement, with darker spots littering it. "Someone has fallen here and then was held in place, maybe beaten, maybe restrained, fighting hard, probably. See this?" His finger outlined one of the darker spots. "That's blood."

They all shuddered, even Necalli, she noticed, herself frozen with a sudden wave of fear. But they shouldn't be here, in this place. One overheard stories of smugglers from both sides of the Tlatelolco causeway, their brutality and ruthlessness. And what if... She shuddered again, reading the question in both their *calmecac* companions' narrowing eyes.

"What makes you think it was the workshop boy?" drawled Necalli slowly, his hand already on the hilt of his knife, which was tied to his girdle in a showy manner.

Patli just shrugged. "Maybe it isn't him. But who knows? He wouldn't be missing if able to come back. He never dared to be absent for one single heartbeat, not even when everyone was still asleep, before dawn broke. My uncle made sure he understood his position in the workshop well."

These words made Chantli feel bad. Father was too harsh with that boy, oh yes. He did make him work as hard as a slave that was not intended for long use, didn't he?

"My father isn't that bad," she protested, feeling obliged because of their companions. "He demanded from Miztli what he demanded of my brothers as well. Hard work and all that."

Patli's lips twisted in an annoyingly condescending manner.

"Well, it doesn't matter now." Necalli's voice interrupted the developing argument in time. "We need to make sure it wasn't him bleeding on that floor." His eyes narrowed thoughtfully, measuring Patli with a new flicker of respect. "Can you see how long ago it happened? How old this blood is?"

The question had her cousin sinking to his knees, exploring the floor so closely he looked as though he was sniffing it. Did he?

Puzzled, she wondered where he acquired the ability of reading marks left upon the earth, that perfectly urban Patli. Did his previous life out there in the north, near the City of Gods, include hunting or any other fascinating activities like that? Slightly perturbed, she turned away, eyeing Ahuitzotl, who in the meantime had wandered off, bored with their worries and dilemmas, crouching next to the fractured pile of stones, studying something closely, all attention. They paid him no heed.

"It didn't happen now or close to this time," was Patli's final verdict. "Maybe in the morning."

"Or at night," drew out Axolin, his frown rivaling that of his friend, the light amusement and readily offered needling gone. "If he came back here, sniffing around, like *you* asked him to do," an accusing gaze shot at his *calmecac* companion, causing the latter to narrow his eyes in a challenging manner, "then he might have been attacked somewhere there in the tunnel or near it, then dragged here, maybe."

"For what purpose?" growled Necalli, his eyes two glittering slits, the nostrils of his eagle-like nose widening. "What would they do with him here?"

The other boy's scowl didn't waver. "Kill him, maybe. Or beat him up to get answers, then kill him."

"They could have done it back in the tunnel or anywhere!" exclaimed their accused leader, not caring to keep his voice low, not anymore. "And why have you decided it's him anyway? The smugglers can settle their differences here like anywhere, beating each other up or killing one another." This time, he did lower his voice, as though reminded of the possibility of these same criminals reappearing at the place they had evidently frequented. "There may be another explanation to the workshop boy's disappearance."

"Look at this pretty thing!" Ahuitzotl rushed back, glowing with excitement. Absently, they peeked into his outstretched palm, even Necalli, his eyes dark with anger, the handsomely defined cheekbones flashing red.

"What's that?"

In the last of the light, the object upon the boy's hand glowed darkly, its black head intercepted with greenish lines, spreading along the roughly outlined spine, so polished it shone.

"It's a jaguar," declared Ahuitzotl firmly. "Obsidian jaguar. See these fangs?" Proudly, he traced his finger along the carved cavities. "It's mine. I found it!"

Fascinated, Chantli fought the urge to reach for the precious object, its smoothness alluring, inviting to touch.

"It's beautiful," she muttered. "Why is it green and not only black?"

Then she heard Patli swallowing hard, leaning closer but keeping his distance, wary as though ready to leap away, as though afraid of this thing.

"It's no jaguar. It's a puma," he said, then drew a convulsive breath. "It's Miztli's talisman."

The silence that prevailed was deep, disturbingly empty. Chantli felt her fascination crashing down her stomach, shattering into twenty little pieces.

"How do you know?" asked Necalli quietly, atypically subdued. "I didn't see him wearing a talisman, any talisman, let alone something as precious as this. Save his loincloth, he was running around quite naked, with nothing to wear such a thing on."

"He didn't wear it." Gaze firm upon the floor, Patli shifted backwards, like someone wishing to stay away from the beautiful talisman and its dubious influence. "He kept it tied to his loincloth, in a sort of a bag." He shrugged. "I saw him take it out several times."

"Maybe he dropped it yesterday, on our way to the tunnel, or when he went back."

The loudness of Axolin's grunt shook the air. "Maybe we should look for him or his body, instead of playing here at being scouts, musing about amulets and such."

Chantli felt like shutting her ears against their terrible speculations, the images her mind painted too vivid, making her wish to scream and run away. Why would the village boy go back here all alone and at night? It didn't make sense, but Axolin said they asked him to do that.

"Why did you ask him to come here?" she whispered, pressing her palms to her mouth, hearing her own words coming out quite muffled.

Necalli's gaze refused to meet hers. "I didn't mean it that way," he muttered. "I said that he could sniff around today if he had time to do that." He shrugged. "Because we weren't likely to be let out of school, not after we had done. Even now..." Helplessly, his voice trailed off, then died away.

"He didn't have time to sniff around anywhere," she tossed, unable to control the suddenness of her anger. "He worked like a slave, as hard as no school boy would ever have to!"

He pursed his lips and said nothing.

"Are we going down that tunnel of yours or not?" demanded Ahuitzotl, matter-of-fact, practical, and uncaring. His fingers closed around the figurine, clutching it tightly. "Maybe that boy is held somewhere there. If he was dead and thrown around, we would have smelled it already."

Chantli found herself staring.

"Why would we..." began Necalli angrily, then paused, his eyes widening, eyebrow climbing up. "Well, yes, if he was killed here last night... and through the heat of the day... Good thinking!" He grinned at the smaller boy fleetingly, with grudging appreciation. "Yes, let's go down that tunnel and hope that he is in there and still alive, eh? Get that torch of yours ready." Full of his cheerful high spirits again, he motioned at them briefly. "Let us hurry."

However, wandering in the sultry dampness, with no breeze and no freshness, brought no results. It was exciting in the beginning to descend through the small opening, clutching to the slippery stones, diving into the unknown. She had done it competently enough, pleased with herself and the gaze of an open appreciation Necalli had shot at her, standing close by, the torch that he didn't let Ahuitzotl carry despite the boy's protests flickering weakly, dripping oil, his whole being watchful and ready to help should she find the exercise of climbing down difficult. A perfect warrior out of stories. It made her feel strange, more spirited and agitated, wishing to do wild things.

The tunnel did not stink as badly as the wharves after the fishermen were through with their catch. Not afraid of darkness or closed places, she walked it quite happily, keeping close to their torch-holding leader, sure of her step as opposed to some of the others. The awareness served to enhance her aplomb. Even Necalli seemed to be on edge, keeping their pace slow and careful, jittery enough to look like someone who would jump truly high if surprised from behind. None of them felt too good or too confident, save her and Ahuitzotl, both crowding their torch-bearing leader but for different reasons. The rest huddled behind, hurried and ill at ease.

The voices burst upon them just as they were preparing to retrace their steps, having reached the room brimming with clubs and spears, loaded with wooden chests, the room that apparently the boys had explored on their previous visit. It had an opening in the upper part of the crumbling wall, a slab of stone that did not fit perfectly, exposing a wide enough crack of brightness through which a much-welcomed breeze stole in, causing the flame of their torch to dance. The *calmecac* boys exchanged haunted glances and Patli lost the last of his coloring. That was the troublesome opening that had had them pitted against the vicious *ahuitzotl*, their frowns told her. This caused her to abandon the idea of climbing it altogether, remembering Necalli's arm and how it looked on the previous night. It was bandaged now, still noticeably swollen, exuding an unpleasant odor of ointments and maybe even burned flesh. Out of them all, only the namesake of the water monster didn't look afraid.

"We should climb through this thing and check all around," the younger boy declared, unbearably smug, his pose typically challenging, legs wide apart, chest trust forward, chin up. "What's the point of crawling under the ground if you don't check everywhere? Maybe that boy you are looking for has been thrown out there, in the reeds."

That speculation made them all go rigid with fear.

"If you are so efficient, you go out there and check," growled Necalli, his eyes nothing but dark slits in the grotesque outline of his face, with enhanced cheekbones and overly sharp angles.

"We'll wait for you here. You can take your time crawling between the reeds, getting friendly with real *ahuitzotls*."

For a heartbeat, no one said a word.

"It's too high to reach it like that."

"I'll drag one of the crates for your royal feet to step on." Necalli's smile flickered wickedly, exaggeratedly wide. "Will be too happy to oblige."

The smaller boy's face set into a stubborn mold. "Do that."

Necalli didn't make himself wait. Tossing the flickering torch into his friend's hand, he swept past them like a storm wind, grabbing the nearest chest – a wide, sturdy affair of wooden plants tied in an intricate manner – dragging the whole thing over the earthen floor with a visible effort, his face glittering with sweat.

"Here," he panted. "Hop up on that one and be gone!"

The younger boy hesitated, but only for a heartbeat. With matching agility and resolve, he leaped up the proposed prop, reaching for the narrow opening, attempting to grab its edge. It didn't go well, with him being too short, his fingers slipping, unable to get a good grip.

Speechless, Chantli stared for another heartbeat before rushing toward the same obstacle in question. "You can't let him go out like that," she cried out. "Not alone!"

In the dim flickering of the dancing torch, Necalli's face looked frighteningly fierce. "Oh yes, I can!"

But now Axolin came back to life as well. "Stop that! It's childish and plain stupid." The torch in his hands shook, seemingly as angered. "We either go up there all together or none of us is going!"

Another heartbeat of glaring ensued, but just as Necalli made an uncertain movement, as though about to push his friend or his unasked-for charge away, the faint thumping reached them, as though something heavy fell in the distance, or maybe a screen shut. Blinking, they listened, momentarily stunned. When more distant trampling followed the first one, joined by the muffled voices, unmistakable now, they let out their breaths at once.

"Put it out," breathed Necalli, snatching the fluttering torch from Axolin's hands. His sandaled feet made a quick work, stomping the weakly resisting flame out, casting them into a helpless darkness, enlivened only by the crack of the brighter blackness above their heads.

If not terrified before, Chantli felt the wave of most latent fear gripping her stomach, crushing it in a merciless ring, pressing viciously, squeezing her insides. It all happened too suddenly. Unable even to scream, she waved her hands, desperate to touch something, to get a grip, to make sure the world didn't go suddenly empty, leaving her here, under the earth, alone and abandoned.

In another heartbeat, a hand caught her upper arm, holding her firmly against her wild flailing. "Up, up, now!" hissed Necalli, pushing her upward and into his previously improvised prop along with the boy Ahuitzotl, another lively form, still struggling to clamber his way up. "Don't move!"

Calming suddenly, now that she realized that she wasn't forgotten here in the darkness, she felt him messing around, whispering urgently. In another heartbeat, the boy's warm presence beside her disappeared, hauled upward and away, blocking the dim brightness, climbing like a desperate monkey.

"Quick!"

Strong hands were already gripping her waist, lifting her up, pushing her in the direction the boy disappeared before. Obediently, she grabbed the slippery edge, the gust of fresh air encouraging, helping her pull with more spirit, to use the drive of his push. In no time, she was in another corridor, this one blissfully illuminated, out of the trap, gasping for breath, enveloped in the heavily scented aroma of the lake, so welcome and familiar, *so safe*.

In the dimness of the late dusk, she could see the boy Ahuitzotl perching closely, his pose that of a pouncing predator, peering into the opening they had just squeezed through, all eyes. The others were spilling out as well, Axolin and Patli, the latter clearly pushed up, judging by the abruptness in which he popped out.

"Where is Necalli?" she whispered loudly.

Axolin was hanging over the edge, chancing a fall back into the dank depths. "Necalli, quick!"

In response, their extinguished torch shot out, landing beside Ahuitzotl, as though directed at its former owner. Next came the club the royal family boy managed to smuggle out along with their only illumination, followed by Necalli's lithe frame. The distant sound of shuffling feet, more than one pair, made them freeze with fear, the faint flickering reinforcing what their ears were trying to tell them. Oh, but they had made it out in the nick of time.

Necalli shot out with the speed of a missile hurled from an *atlatl*, gesturing wildly as he broke into a run, motioning toward the end of the corridor and then the dark mass of the causeway above their heads. The rising voices beneath the earth reinforced his command. No one waited for another invitation.

Putting it all into the wild dash, afraid to trip in the deepening darkness, Chantli raced after their self-appointed leader, determined not to let him out of her sight wherever he was heading to. It felt safer by this boy's side. The rasping breath of the others assaulted her ears, especially that of the Palace's boy. That one rushed beside her, keeping close, typically determined, a courageous beast.

The breeze was refreshing, rustling in the thick reeds, murmuring dreamily, heavy with the lake's odor, offering shelter. As the shouts behind her back erupted louder, she leaped toward the swaying mass with no additional thought. The water was cool, pleasantly calm but for the surrounding darkness. Crouching in its shallow depths, she held her breath, taking in another bout of splashing, feeling the smaller boy huddling close by, waist-deep in the water, clearly uncomfortable but not daring to move. Troubled, she wondered where their *calmecac* companions and Patli were. Had they run on, knowing a better place to hide? She felt the cold sweat breaking, covering her back, making her shiver in the intensified breeze. The flickering light neared, dancing in the wind, quivering.

"It's Tepecocatzin's doing," rasped an angry voice not far away, muffled by the wind but clear. "All this spying around. It's that old scoundrel, trying to stick his nose in again."

The other man just grunted in response, poking his light here and there, judging by the fluttering of the weak flame. "Can't see anything with this thing. Are you sure there was someone in there?"

"Am I sure?" the other's voice grunted. "Didn't you smell the stench of the burning oil? Are you simple in the head?"

She could almost feel them, so close the man with the torch was. Holding her breath, she tried not to succumb to the panicked urge to run.

"Check under the causeway. If they didn't climb up it, they may still be around."

The torch danced away.

"When I lay my hands on the filthy intruder," cried out the voice with no light, drawing away as well, to the overpowering immensity of her relief. "He and his master will wish they had never been born, let alone stuck their noses into any of this." A heartbeat of pause. "And the meddling mealy-mouthed ChalchiuhNenetzin too! What a piece of work that worthless filthy *nenetl* is!"

She felt her nerves quivering like an overstretched copper string, the boy beside her just an inanimate form, barely breathing. However, at the last words, he stirred imperceptibly. Afraid to move as yet, she listened, the reeds rustling too loudly, as though trying to interfere. Where did these men go? Was there a place to hide further down the causeway? The boy moved again, shifting lightly, causing some of the reeds to murmur more urgently.

"Hush," she hissed, afraid that he might be intending to come out. "They are still here."

"I know that," he breathed, just a warm gust brushing past her cheek. Then a murmur containing a long, elaborately colorful expletive came. Chantli stifled a nervous giggle. But this boy was something else! "My sister is no filthy *nenetl*," he breathed in the end.

Before she could react to that claim, with an outburst of hysterical laugher, maybe, having understood the double meaning well enough, something that their angry pursuer clearly implied, a new outburst of splattering was upon them, the surrounding reeds rustling with a thundering quality now, bringing danger.

Leaping sideways and away, out of an instinct rather than as a conscious reaction, she saw the shadow shooting across, grabbing her companion by his shoulder, pressing hard. The boy, losing none of his fighting spirit, struggled fiercely, spluttering in the shallow water, digging in with all his limbs, it seemed, resisting his assailant's attempt to drag him out. It was a strange vision. Like in a dream, Chantli watched, stupefied for a moment. Yet, as the man cursed and his silhouetted arm came up, then descended with force, generating a muffled thud, then another, causing the boy to cry out, she pounced on this same hand with matching determination, more angered than frightened now. He was just a little boy!

Her fingers claws, slipping but holding on, she clung to the sinewy arm, revolted by its touch and smell but determined. Ahuitzotl couldn't be allowed into these people's hands, to follow Miztli's fate, maybe. Oh no!

The man whirled around, very put out, or so the loudness of his curses told her. A wild shake of the assaulted arm accompanied by a powerful push had her skidding into the water, to splatter there and spit in disgust, nauseated by the taste of the slimy mud, panicked again. Before she could straighten up on her own, a ferocious yank dragged her head upward, as though determined to make her entire scalp come off.

Crying out against her will, the pain so sudden and encompassing, she flailed her arms wildly, trying to free herself, or at least to find a grip. It didn't help. The same force that pulled her out was now dragging her along and onto the dry land, unconcerned with the multiple of obstacles her limbs hit along the way. Amidst the dread and confusion, she felt Ahuitzotl's hands closing somewhere around her ankles, hurting more than helping as he was pulled along too, achieving no worthwhile results.

When the ordeal stopped momentarily, she felt nothing but relief, curling on the sand helplessly, welcoming the respite, concerned with nothing but the receding pain. Had her hair come off for good? Instinctively, she reached for it, feeling out the agonized areas, afraid to think of anything else, a torch thrust too closely to her face, making her eyes water. As they focused, she could see the silhouettes, the one holding a torch leaning forward, studying her, the other holding the boy, struggling against his desperate kicks.

"They are nothing but children. Again!" exclaimed a voice that by now was familiar, the calmer of the two. "What is going on?" Even in the darkness, it was easy to see his squint. "Who *are* you?"

The light thrust yet closer. She squirmed to escape its heat, rewarded by a merciless kick for her efforts.

"Stop squirming and answer the question, you stupid fowl," demanded her interrogator, pushing her with the tip of his foot again, this time in a lighter way, forcing her to face the darkness of the star-studded sky. "What are you two doing here?"

"I…" She tried to make her voice work, too terrified to succeed. In her entire life, no one had kicked her or hurt her otherwise; her father too nice and her brothers too old, not interested in the lives of their younger half-siblings. "I… we…"

"Stop stammering." Grabbing her shoulder, the man yanked her back onto her feet with surprising ease, as though she had no weight at all, like a reed-woven doll. "Who sent you into this tunnel? Who?" The question was accompanied with a resounding slap that made her ears ring. Staggering, she would have fallen but for the firmness of the hurtful grip. "Who brought you here?"

She whimpered in response, unable to think clearer than that.

"Don't you dare hit her!" Ahuitzotl's smallish silhouette leaped toward them, squirming from his previous captor's grip, surprisingly agile. "Don't you dare –"

In response to this spirited chivalry, her assailant loosened his grasp, letting her go while grabbing her rescuer instead, landing him a generous blow in the process. The boy's smothered yelp brought Chantli back to her senses in force, sending her launching at their mutual enemy, only to be seized by his companion, again with a contemptible ease. Beside herself, she wriggled and kicked, held too firmly but berserk, not caring for her safety anymore. It was all just too much.

The man shook her hard, then tried to better his grip while dragging her closer to their meager source of illumination, now dancing wildly while its holder was busy with a struggle of his own, his prisoner yelling and punching, beyond any reasonable behavior as well. More sounds joined the turmoil, and as she shoved to break free again, her body suddenly took the weight of her assailant, leaning heavily against her, strangely limp, not clutching into her, or anything else anymore, for that matter.

Unable to keep her balance, she crashed down and into the sharp gravel, hurting all over, terrified beyond reason, taking his weight as he went after her, so listless and heavy, disgustingly soft. In a panic, she screamed, pushing and kicking, crawling from under the revolting pressure, seeing nothing but darting silhouettes, hearing the blows. Oh, but it was a nightmare!

In another heartbeat, one of the silhouettes dropped next to her, catching her shoulders between his palms, pulling her up uncompromisingly. She fought this new attempt at forcing her into something, sinking her scratched, aching elbow into his side, trying to kick. Then the familiar voice penetrated the raging tide of terror.

"Stop it, Chantli, stop it! What are you doing?"

Still, it took more squirming and pushing to make the words sink in. Upright already, she blinked, trying to understand. Necalli, unmistakable even in the meager illumination of a thin moon, was clutching her tight, staring at her, puzzled and worried, or maybe just dreadfully confused; she wasn't sure which.

"You... where did you come from?" she muttered, taking in the rest of the scenery, the narrow piece of the dry land adorned with two dark sprawling forms, with another standing above, as though at a loss. Ahuitzotl was hovering next to it, leaning forward but at a safe distance, not about to chance a closer look.

"I think... I think they are done for. Eh, Axolin?" There was a tone of uncertainty in Necalli's voice, so atypical for the boy she had grown to know through the last two days.

Axolin's silhouetted head moved faintly, in a vague, non-committal gesture. She could feel Necalli shuddering by her side, still pressed against her, holding her close, as though readying for another attack. Reassured, she didn't try to move away.

"What rotten pieces of stinking excrements!" exclaimed Ahuitzotl, apparently gathering his fighting spirit back.

"Did they hurt you?" asked Necalli, brisker this time, regaining his cheerfully bossy self as well. "Why didn't you two run after us?"

That was a good question. Chantli tried to shrug against the embarrassing trembling that was setting in, interfering with her ability to do simple things, like shrugging or talking. "Are th-they... are they... dead?"

She hoped Necalli wouldn't volunteer to go nearer and check, afraid that if he stopped supporting her, she might collapse onto the ground once again, unable to cope with this violent shaking. To accompany him those additional few steps was out of the question; she didn't intend to near any dead or even just merely unconscious bodies. Not of these dangerous, scary, terrible people!

"Maybe. I don't know and I'm not about to find out. Not this time." Shrugging, he began to turn away, propelling her alongside, not letting her shoulders go – thanks all the mighty deities for that! "Those training swords aren't that bad." He shook his head forcefully, as though trying to get rid of a bad memory. "Come, you two. Hurry. The *telpochcalli* boy will paddle away all by himself if we don't hurry. He is well capable of something like that."

"Paddle?" repeated Ahuitzotl, turning to follow with atypical obedience.

"Yes, paddle. There was this silly canoe right under the causeway. But for you two deciding to enjoy a dip in the reeds, we would have been in the middle of the lake by now." Another brief pause. She could feel that he was trembling too, lightly but unmistakably, in many little tremors. "Come, Axolin. Stop staring and come."

CHAPTER 13

The woman was strikingly beautiful and exceedingly well dressed. Even in the dim light of a pair of torches, it was easy to see the deep green of her blouse, the glitter of her jade necklace, an elegant row of thin polished pieces of turquoise chained to a single base of beautifully polished green stone. As she leaned closer, it swung prettily, slowly, and with much dignity, as though aware of its own preciousness. Miztli couldn't help staring.

"Why is the boy beaten and tied?" she demanded, her voice cool and melodious, not warming or promising safety, yet not scowling or menacing either. Indifferent, uninvolved. Better than the rest of them.

"He is wild and dangerous, Revered Princess." The elderly man stepped forward, as though eager to shield the woman from his, Miztli's, possible attack.

He wanted to roll his eyes or to tell them all go and dump themselves into the lake, the beautiful princess included. The elderly man's name was Tepecocatzin, he knew by now, as the brute that had kidnapped him from his own peers had addressed the elderly dignitary by this name enough times to catch the sound of it and to make him remember.

Not that he cared by this point. Since the last desperate attempt to escape, coming back to his senses in this, yet another dilapidated shed, retied for good measure, more tightly than before, his head resonating with clubs pounding inside it, his body so numb it didn't even hurt anymore, he discovered that he simply didn't care. Unconcerned, uninvolved, unresponsive. It was good to be this way; it made him feel safe. For what could they do to him now, except finish him off for good? Nothing else, absolutely nothing.

So he paid no attention to the threatening glares of his latest kidnapper and the growling quality of his words. Neither did he pay any respect to his new, more dignified interrogator, this same elderly man to whom his kidnapper addressed groveling comments and observations, taking with much deference, using the honorable 'tzin' every time he dared to speak the nobleman's name. Tepecocatzin – an impressive alias, as impressively cold and aloof as its owner, smelling of aristocracy.

Well, as haughty as this man was, he turned out to be a better company than the kidnappers from the warehouses, or their frighteningly soft-spoken master; certainly a more preferable presence than the man who had dragged him here, a treacherous piece of rotten fish that he was. A puzzling one as well. First advocating killing their prisoner, then kidnapping him from his fellow kidnappers, then turning all deferential and submissive before a haughty piece of work from this neighboring silly town. Disgusting. And boring too. He wished they would decide what to do with him once and for all, filthy pieces of dung that they were.

"You shouldn't have come here in person, Revered ChalchiuhNenetzin," went on the older man, his voice warm and tender, not remote anymore, brimming with worry. "At this time of the night... the spies of your husband... Oh, but what if someone had seen you leaving the Palace? There is no telling what this man might do to you. An allegation of unchastity; oh, this would be enough to give him an excuse..." The elderly voice trailed off, dying in the semi-darkness.

The woman looked up, her smile flashing suddenly, warming the night. She was a beautiful sight to look at, her face delightfully soft with no sharp angles to it, gleaming delicately, exquisitely. It made him think of a refined, subtly carved mask made of melted copper mixed with gold, annealed to perfection with those famous warm and cold hammering techniques afterwards.

"Oh Honorable Uncle! Your love and worry warms my heart. It

makes it up for the cold and indifferent treatment I received here in Tlatelolco Palace from the day of my arrival, from the dismal wedding ceremony I was subjected to." The smile was gone, replaced with pressed lips and a pair of knitted eyebrows, two perfect lines. A less pretty sight. "But for you, my life would have been so miserable, so worthless. My son sleeps in a drab cot, with not enough blankets and braziers to make his nights warmer, with a miserable nursemaid and barely enough servants to see to his needs." The pouting mask became more definite. "I'm not concerned with my private needs anymore, but only with those of my son, the lawful heir to the Tlatelolco throne but for the shameless manipulations of heartless people."

Fascinated, Miztli tried to wriggle into a better position without drawing their attention to him. Since being made to drink water and then that spicy beverage the people of the other warehouse promised but didn't have time to deliver to him, the pain and exhaustion had receded a little, yielding their place to this new sensation of eagerly welcomed indifference. Yet now he felt his curiosity arising anew, not a bad feeling.

"I know who these people are," muttered the elder man. "If only your revered husband was to bend his ear to my advice again, like he used to do before deceitful Teconal managed to ingratiate himself and his vile ways in your Palace, to ensconce his despicable person in the adviser's chair and his vile daughter in our ruler's bed!"

The woman's lips pressed tighter, taking much of her beauty away. He saw his kidnapper stirring beside the doorway, moving uneasily, shifting his weight from one foot to another. Didn't those two nobles have better things to do with their night besides huddling in this dilapidated shed, gossiping about politics and some palace's intrigues? He remembered Chantli boasting her knowledge of Tenochtitlan's Palace and from a royal source. Back then, all he wanted was to be able to sneak back into the workshop and forget about this whole thing, but now he wondered. Shouldn't he have listened more carefully, asked the girl questions? It certainly helped him to avoid being killed the previous night, her silly Palace's gossip, and it might still make his survival possible. The scary man in the warehouse wanted to know what he knew, and his name was, indeed, Teconal, wasn't it? Oh yes, Revered Teconal; that was how the smugglers back there addressed him, with plenty of humble floor-staring. And now these two nobles were talking about this same scary man and his ways of poisoning this other island's ruler's mind, or slipping vile daughters into people's beds. What was this man's name? Chantli used it too, while marveling at the prettiness of this Tenochtitlan's princess's name. Should have seen the princess herself.

He glanced at the doll-like face once again, all hidden by the nondescript hood of her cloak except the peek of the vivid green and the marvelous jade necklace, so fitting her name Noble Jade Doll. What did this woman want with him?

As though reading his thoughts, the exquisite eyes shifted back to him, measuring him with an unconcealed curiosity, clouded with contemplation, pondering. Forcing his body into stillness – not a difficult fit with his limbs being numb anyway – he didn't let his eyes drop or wander. If this woman wanted something, she would just have to tell it outright. He was not up to ceremonial games.

The perfectly plucked eyebrows knitted again. "Why is this commoner boy here?"

His other interrogators drew nearer, both of them. Involuntarily, he coiled, drawing his folded knees closer to his body, readying for the worst. The previous bout of careless bravery melted in the flickering darkness. The man from the tunnel and the boat was not a person to play games with. And neither was the elderly noble, another evidently stone-hard person, even if better mannered, judging by the previous questioning, which didn't progress far before the royal fowl burst upon them with her prettily spoken complaints. But was the other *calmecac* boy right about that one being a whiny thing!

"This man here." A light nod of the dignified head indicated Miztli's kidnapper, standing there tense and ill at ease. "He was with Teconal's men when this boy was caught sniffing around. They wanted to kill him, but Nexcoatl," another nod acknowledged curtly both the commoner's humble presence and his contribution, "heard the boy saying something about the Palace and weaponry, using your name, oh Revered Princess." A brief lift of the cloaked shoulders was followed by a slight grimace. "He thought that maybe the boy was sent by someone. Maybe by your revered brother himself, to deliver you a message."

The clearness of her forehead marred with creases aplenty. "My brother wouldn't send a barefoot beaten commoner." Then the displeased gaze focused on him. "Who sent you, boy? What did they ask you to tell me?"

He tried to think fast, knowing that his bluff would be exposed now, this time for certain. What to tell? The brother, who was her brother? The boy Chantli was talking about. Oh yes, she said that the boy was telling her about that noble fowl, claiming that this sister of his was no whiny doll. Or whiny genitalia, for that matter, a better fitting term in his private opinion. He said that her husband treated her badly and that it would end up in war, and then Axolin said that it wouldn't. Oh, but what was this boy's name? It was something… something…

"Tell the Revered Empress what she wants to know," growled his kidnapper, drawing yet closer, threatening. "Be quick about it!"

The elderly man frowned but stayed where he was.

"Don't be afraid, boy," added the woman coldly, not very convincing in her words. It was as though she was reciting a phrase with no meaning. "Hurry up and tell us."

He tried to slam his mind into working, which against his efforts went uncomfortably blank, the wave of helplessness spilling, threatening to drown the rest of his thoughts. If he didn't say something now, he would be done for. The royal woman would leave in anger, turning her back on the killing that would undoubtedly ensue, letting the smuggler drag him out and onto the lake, just like he intended to do in the first place, to feed the fish and those terrible spiny monsters, to let them tear his flesh with their terrible claws, to have his eyes and his teeth and his fingernails devoured, just like the priest in the temple told them while chastening them, scolding them for messing with mystical *ahuitzotls*... Ahuitzotl! But wasn't this the name Chantli bragged and Necalli grew angry with?

"He won't tell," observed the royal woman, pursing her lips while straightening up resolutely, drawing away a pace. Her face was pouting rather than angry. "Do something. Make him talk." Another petulant demand. It was as though she was asking for a meal to arrive warm and in time.

The man from the wharves gave the elderly dignitary a questioning look, as though asking for permission. The older man's eyes clouded with indecision.

"If you would like to be escorted back to the Palace, Revered Princess," he said slowly, deliberately, as though weighing his words, "I'll send you word the moment this boy tells us what he knows."

That did it. He felt the cold wave rising in his chest, threatening to drown him.

"Ahuitzotl," he said hoarsely, pleased to hear his voice ringing with enough clarity, with no coughing and choking accompanying it, not like during the previous interrogation. "Ahuitzotl, the boy. He sent me. He... he wanted me to find his sister..."

This time, their eyes pierced him, openly startled, even those of his abductor. Mere slits in the storminess of their faces, they now widened disproportionally, gaping. Miztli tried to stifle a hysterical giggle. But were they looking quite silly!

The royal woman came back to her senses first. "My brother Ahuitzotl," she repeated, as though not entirely sure of her hearing abilities. "The boy Ahuitzotl?"

Miztli just nodded, afraid to open his mouth in case the wild laughter would burst out, unrestrained. His stomach hurt from the necessity of holding it all in.

"Why would he do this?" demanded the elderly noble, somewhat indignantly, as though offended.

"It's just like the wild thing to do that," said the woman suddenly, a smile transforming her face back into a beautiful mask, warm and enticing. "He would think of just this sort of a messenger, the wild boy that he is." Coming closer, she knelt beside Miztli, the odor of her perfume powerful, penetrating even his clogged nostrils. Not a very pleasant smell, nauseatingly strong. "What did he ask you to tell me?"

This time, he didn't need to think hard. Under no immediate threat, he found it easier to search through his memory, which was always good, praised, even lauded. One of the reasons Father sent him to the Great Capital to learn the intricate craft of their family trade. He always remembered things.

"He is angry with your husband, who doesn't treat you well. He said you were sending messages." Another quick search produced more results. "He said it'll come to war if the Tlatelolco ruler doesn't start treating you well."

Her face lit like a torch wrapped in a too well-oiled piece of cloth. "He said all that? Oh!" The delicate palms shot up, pressed against the chiseled cheeks. "Was he repeating Axayacatl's words? Was he acting on his behalf?"

Who is Axayacatl? wondered Miztli, not curious in the least.

"Yes." He tried to nod reassuringly, his neck stiff and hurting.

"Oh, I knew it!" Her hands flew up again, this time to sway in the air like two elegant birds, sparkling jewelry. "My brother did not forsake me. He cares for my wellbeing and he will stand up for me." She looked up, beaming. "See, Honorable Uncle? He did pay heed. He did! Oh, what would have I done without you and your kindness?"

The recipient of the excited tirade was still frowning. "I don't understand," he said slowly, his eyes narrow, boring into Miztli, penetrating. "Why would Axayacatl act in such a twisted, intricate way?"

Miztli felt his back breaking in a cold sweat. But why should the perceptive old man be there at all? Why wasn't he enjoying a good night's sleep as of now?

"He must have his reasons to go about it in such a roundabout way," went on the woman excitedly, waving her hands in the air again. "He is a wise ruler. He wouldn't wish to cause a war between two sister-*altepetl*s, but he wouldn't leave his sister and his baby nephew in need, neglected, and alone. He is a good man!"

The smuggler at the doorway muttered something inaudible.

"What else did he ask you to tell me?" Her eyes were upon him again, bright with excitement.

Perturbed, Miztli tried to shift into a better position, wishing the other two men would scatter away for good. Didn't they have something better to do with their night? This woman was so gullible, so ready to believe anything he said! For the first time, he wondered what her true plight was. A spoiled royal fowl, according to the *calmecac* boy, or truly a woman in need?

"He was very concerned... concerned with your wellbeing." The exhaustion was creeping back in, enveloping him in its agonizing grip. But did his body hurt everywhere! He tried to make his eyes focus, her face dancing before his eyes, drawing away, then coming back, nauseating him.

"Untie this boy and have a healer see him." Apparently, she was standing again, straight-backed and imperial, her voice ringing with its initial coldness, uncompromising. "By the break of dawn, I'll send someone to fetch him, or maybe I'll pass through your house myself, Honorable Uncle, on my way to watch the contest." She paused momentarily. "It'll be held by the Great Plaza, when the sun is midway toward its highest."

"Teconal would have it this way," muttered the elder, as though transferring his anger to a more appropriate object. "I told your husband it wasn't wise to hold such a contest at such times. Certainly not as a large-scale event, with many hundreds of young warriors, the best of the Tlatelolco fighting force." Another pause. "Your revered brother won't be happy to hear about it. Let's hope he doesn't."

"Or maybe it's for the best that he does." The woman's face twisted in no prettily coy, petulant manner like before. "Maybe my brother should be made aware of what is happening, of the poor advice my husband is enjoying these days. Maybe Tenochtitlan should issue an advice of its own, make its closest of neighbors understand."

To shut his eyes against his growing nausea didn't help. It made the uneven swaying yet worse. He clasped his lips tight, not opposed to vomiting all over this place or these people, yet not in front of her.

"Do as I say about my little brother's strange choice of a messenger." Her voice was drawing away along with the blurring silhouette of her cloak, now just a shapeless shimmering form. "That Ahuitzotl bears watching, the fierce little thing. The most unyielding, stubborn child, but now I see that he does care about his family. I shall send him the nicest of presents. What shall it be?"

The darkness swallowed her words, along with the presence of the elderly man and the second most flaming torch. In the suddenly deepening dim, Miztli's sense of security evaporated all at once. Pressing against the wall, he watched his abductor nearing at a slow, deliberate pace, shaking his head, deep in thought. When he finally halted, his frown was meditative, not especially ominous.

"You are the luckiest thing I ever met," said the man finally. "Wonder what she intends to do with you." Another heartbeat of contemplative pondering and the massive shoulders lifted in a shrug. "I won't be untying you as yet. Not the wild thing that you are. But if I have to," the threatening scowl was back, thousand folds more menacing, "you better not do anything stupid, boy. If I cut you instead of your ties, it'll be your fault. And be sure that I won't be sorry for making any such mistake."

CHAPTER 14

The heavy odor of the lake was all around, splashing occasionally, murmuring in no calming way. Necalli clenched the side of the boat, careful not to upset the overloaded vessel. It was sitting so low! The tips of his fingers felt the touch of the muddy water, shrinking away from it, not welcoming the recollection – *the even hum, the rustling of the reeds*.

Well, at least no reeds surrounded them now, but who knew if the Spiny Monster favored the shallow vegetated parts or just happened to be passing through the marsh as they were invading its privacy with their stupid yelling and fighting. He shuddered at the mere memory, then pulled his palm back, away from the unwelcome touch. No, he didn't wish to find out what the favorite habitat of the water monsters was. If he could help it, he would not learn a thing about *ahuitzotl*s and their habits at all.

The girl by his side stirred, another heap of limbs, along with those of the others, all crammed in the smelly space of the leaking bark, except Patli, still in charge of the paddle and hence perching at the edge of the elevated plank, struggling with the crude piece of wood, trying to navigate the laughable shell, hopefully toward Tenochtitlan and not into the open waters of the Great Lake. It lurched mildly, bumping against yet another obstacle. Axolin cursed.

"Careful!"

Necalli made an effort to keep his mouth shut, not willing to contribute. The *telpochcalli* boy did his best, and he wasn't that bad, even though one wouldn't hesitate switching this one for his workshop peer. Was that Miztli boy still alive somewhere?

Chantli maintained that he was, but the stubborn girl's conviction was based on slim evidence, herself nearly being killed or at least beaten badly but for their timely interruption! His stomach constricted once again, with anger this time, so painfully he fought the urge to double over. That sensation of the training sword – just a club really, with no obsidian spikes to make it into a cutting weapon – making such a disgustingly wet, cracking sound when it landed upon the back of that man's head. He had swung it without thinking, running pell-mell and with not much care, anxious to reach Chantli and the royal boy, their whimpering and cries making his flesh crawl. No, he didn't stop to prepare or plan. And neither did Axolin, a good loyal friend that he was, ready with his knife, the best in their class concerning this weaponry. Still, the real thing was nothing like the tales and the lessons.

He shuddered, reliving the sensation, that dreadful recoil that his arms absorbed, and the sound of the wet thud as the inert body hit the ground, the realized connection between these two. It had made him nauseated and it had taken him a heartbeat or more to come out of the dazed stupor. Oh, but for Axolin attacking the second man, the one who tried to hit him with the torch he held, he would have been done for, maybe. An unwelcome realization. It took him another precious heartbeat to crush his would-be sword against yet another leaping form.

Fastening his grip on the greasy side of the boat, he struggled to straighten up without treading on too many limbs or causing them to overturn for good, remembering how they had run pell-mell, eager to reach their only means of escape, that smallish canoe Patli had spotted concealed between the reeds. Chantli had wanted to sniff around some more, claiming that Miztli might have been held somewhere there after all. Unimpressed with the beating she had just taken at the hands of the vile criminals, the insistent thing just wouldn't give up. The village boy was alive and kidnapped, she maintained stubbornly, oblivious of reason. If not here, then somewhere there in Tlatelolco, held by those who took part in the filthy politics and the game the vile Tlatelolco nobility was playing.

That much she understood while eavesdropping before getting

caught or while being interrogated, she claimed. These men complained of other spies sent by the elder called Tepecocatzin, the man Ahuitzotl hurried to identify as one of these same important Tlatelolcans, an adviser, a person bidden in Tlatelolco Palace and at home there and around its ruler. The same man who was bringing messages from the Tenochtitlan Emperor's sister, a spoiled crybaby fowl according to Axolin, but an innocent victim according to her youngest of siblings, if not her powerful emperor-brother. It was evident that Tenochtitlan's ruler wasn't impressed with persistent complaints his homesick, or just an overindulgent sister, was flooding him with, as no hostile action or any other problematic behavior toward the smaller island-city was reported. Nothing of the sort. Even though, upon reflection, Necalli remembered that about a market interval ago, some of Tenochtitlan's young hotheads were reported to harass Tlatelolcan noble fowls, or so the officially lodged complaint had it. There was some fuss about it and some agitation, with the youths being disciplined, and his *calmecac* fellow pupils occupied for some time with speculating on what kind of harassment it was and how far these youths got with those girls.

However, besides this incident, nothing changed in Tenochtitlan-Tlatelolco relations, and the imperial sister's nagging remained unnoticed, or rather, unaddressed. To the boy Ahuitzotl's chagrin, apparently. But did the little bugger keep grumbling about it! While Chantli kept carping on the whereabouts of her workshop family member or whatever, claiming that when the smugglers who caught them talked about little brats spying around, they were talking about no one else but him, the commoner with his spectacular name, and it was their duty to find and save him, no one's but theirs.

So much concluded from a few heartbeats of eavesdropping and a question or two while being slapped by the vile criminals. Necalli could do nothing but snort. A pity these chatty criminals didn't give out the exact description of the place where this same Miztli boy was being held, plus the best routes to get there. Over his initial shock and busy propelling their rescued back into the darkness and the more remote parts of the tiny island, he, Necalli, didn't hesitate to sound the most acid remarks. But wasn't she capable of thinking sensibly? They couldn't help the workshop boy but by informing the authorities maybe, asking for help. It was the stupidest thing she proposed, to cross the causeway on a wild rescue mission, knowing neither their destination nor their aim. The workshop boy might be alive somewhere, maybe – not a likely possibility judging by the swiftness and the ruthlessness of the tunnel's masters – but even if so, he would be guarded; otherwise, he would have managed to escape by now, and anyway, they simply didn't know where to look. Was she proposing to wander Tlatelolco warehouses or the wharves, asking the same people who had just beaten her in order to make her tell them what she knew before killing her?

At this point, Axolin was snorting loudly, struggling with the small fishing boat that they had run into while fleeing here before, a boat Patli was already sitting at, eager to paddle away and with no delays, a cowardly piece of dog meat that he was. Such an opposite to her and her reckless courage!

Piling into the crowded vessel, trying to make it remain stable despite its sides sinking almost to their edges, he found himself encircling her shoulders again, propelling her into the boat, making her settle there, protective. The leaking canoe was ripe for overturning straight away into the claws of the water monster, maybe. Still, her warmth and her scent, something faint but sweetish, something belonging to her, kept distracting, making him feel lightheaded, inappropriately cheerful. Let useless Patli struggle with rowing, navigating their overloaded vessel in the clumsiest of ways. He could feel Axolin's sandaled foot pressing against his side, another limb, probably that of the boy Ahuitzotl, sticking into his ribs. Impatiently, he shoved them away, careful not to upset their only means of escape.

"Why didn't you run after us?" he asked the girl, her limbs as pointy but softer, welcome against his various parts.

He could feel her shrugging lightly, as though not uncomfortable in his semi embrace.

"In the reeds, it was safer." As expected, Ahuitzotl was the one to jump into defending their stand.

"Safer, oh yes. And that's why we had to run back, rescuing you two."

Axolin's snicker wafted in the darkness.

"We just didn't think those men would find us," ventured Chantli, her breath warm against his cheek. For a wild moment, he imagined pulling her closer, finding her lips with his. An insane thought. "And they wouldn't, if you didn't start arguing," she went on, turning in the general direction of their youngest and most spirited company, a wet tendril of her hair striking Necalli's face, irritating for some reason. Abruptly, he moved his head away, bumping it painfully against Axolin's shoulder.

"I didn't start arguing," cried the boy out hotly. "I –"

"Shut up and stop screaming." Necalli rolled his eyes once again, then listened to the hesitant splashing of the paddle. "Can you see where we are going?"

Patli muttered something, not comprehensible in the least.

"It is taking us too long. We should have –"

An ear-splitting screech accompanied by a powerful shove made him lurch forward, knocking his head against the rough wood of their boat's side. It swerved wildly and for a moment looked as though about to overturn. His panic back, he threw his body backwards, dragging the girl along, hitting too many flailing limbs in his wake. For a moment, Patli's paddle's desperate splashing seemed to be the only sound. Then the boat lurched again, spraying them with a generous amount of muddy water, wavering for several more heartbeats, creaking in a pitiful way. A darker shade towered above, blocking the last of the moonlight.

"We are under the causeway somewhere," breathed Axolin, scrambling back into a sitting position, stepping on Necalli's thigh in the process.

"Watch it!" Careful not to upset their boat again or make his friend fall out of it, he pushed the intruding foot away, straightening into a sitting position himself. The girl was scurrying by his side, picking herself up as well. He steadied her before pushing himself past.

"Give me that paddle."

The *telpochcalli* boy, nothing but a faint silhouette, recognizable by his drooping shoulders, gave up his tool without resistance.

"We need a light! At least a little bit of it."

"Tell us something we don't know." Axolin sounded satisfyingly spirited, back to his spicy sharp-tongue self, unlike down there in the tunnel. Necalli grinned, reassured. Together they'd find a way to bring them back safely.

"Shut up." Narrowing his eyes, he surveyed the dark mass spreading above their heads and to their sides, distinct even in the pitch black of the night. "If we follow it, we'll get either back home or to Tlatelolco, won't we?"

"And then we just cross back to Tenochtitlan using the causeway," cried out Chantli, sounding excited and unconcerned. "The easiest thing."

"Not that easy," drawled Axolin, clearly rolling his eyes, maybe in amusement. "But yes, having no better ideas…"

"That's better than sleeping in *calmecac*," declared Ahuitzotl all of a sudden, his voice atypically perky, ringing with a surprising ease. "Better and more fun."

Necalli pursed his lips, putting it all into the attempt to push the boat away from the slippery earthwork. The thought of *calmecac* was not an encouraging one. But they would be punished most severely this time, with no halfhearted scolding and a few direful promises. A bother!

"That's what you think," he muttered, shaking his head while struggling to make their overloaded vessel move. "But I bet even royal *pillis* get disciplined for doing wild things."

The little brat chuckled smugly. "Not like the city boys, that's for sure."

"City boys? I bet your royal back will absorb some rough treatment for this night."

"It won't." An annoying little bugger!

The boat lurched again, bumping against the slippery surface of the earthwork's wide base. A new rush of marshy water washed over them.

"You can start by rowing better than that." Axolin staggered to the side, rocking the boat once again. "Give me that paddle."

"Go away." He shoved his friend with none of the force he

wished to apply, fighting to maintain the boat's balance, pushing yet another darker mass, so slippery and unsteady against the splintered wood of the oar, just a crudely carved stick, really. But for a flicker of light, only a tiny little spark. They were so hopelessly lost, and what if they got carried away, away from this causeway and both islands and into the depths of the Great Lake. In this overloaded nutshell, they would go down faster than it'd take one to say 'Tlatelolco.' He cursed through his clenched teeth.

"If we only had another paddle or stick." The girl's voice wafted in the darkness, calm and pleasantly soft, with no hysterical or incensed tones to it. He felt a surge of warmth rushing through his stomach, making it tighter but in a good way.

"We'll manage. Just watch for it from your side. Push anything harder than air away if you can."

Again, the thought of *ahuitzotl*s made the good feeling disperse. But were the Spiny Ones feeling their staggering? Were they gathering around, swimming closer, licking their whiskers – did they have such things? – whipping their palm-fingered tails, readying for a satisfying meal? So many eyes and fingernails! Ah, and teeth, plenty of those to offer. He shuddered again, feeling his bandaged arm cramping, straining more than the other one, aching dully. Oh mighty deities!

For a while, they proceeded uninterrupted, with no darker shapes lurking, lying in wait, determined to see them sputtering in the water. No more foul-smelling obstacles pounced on their staggering vessel, and while enjoying the benefit of a smoother sail, he could not but start to wonder. Where were they?

"We should have reached Tenochtitlan by now." Patli's miserable whisper tore the silence. It was so eerily quiet. No murmuring of the reeds, no twittering of the night insects. Just the splash of the paddle, the uneven pitifully hesitant sound.

"We must be close to it." As always, the girl had nothing but positive things to say, still even her voice lacked the previous cheerful firmness. "Aren't we?"

"Yes, we are!" stated Necalli stubbornly, refusing to think of other possibilities. "Close to this or that shore. Not the other side of the causeway, but maybe the wharves, or any other shore."

"Yes, that's what I thought," confirmed Chantli when no one else ventured a word. Even the boy Ahuitzotl had sunk into gloomy silence and just as they needed his spicy presence and brazen remarks.

"What do you think, Axolin?" he asked in desperation, hating the almost imploring tone to his voice.

"Nothing good." What a talker. Necalli cursed through his clenched teeth.

More drifting in the pitch black. But it was like a journey through the Underworld, a helpless wandering. He put it all into the strikes of his paddle, uncomfortable and cramped as he was, with his arm hurting with every strike, but his spirit soaring. He would get them somewhere, anywhere!

"Did you hear it?" Ahuitzotl's cry made him jump, interrupting his rowing, causing his paddle to lose its tempo. The boat wavered precariously, splashing them with a new surge of warm flow. "There, to the left."

He spat the muddy taste from his mouth, the warmth of the water revolting. "Where? What?" The others were stirring nervously, rocking the boat even worse.

"Stop jumping around!" He struggled with the stupid stick, shifting it left and right, aware of the increasing wavering and the helpless spin their only means of survival was getting into. "What did you hear?"

"Reeds; there are reeds out there!" The boy was shouting shrilly now, panicked as they all were, trying to overcome the tumult. He could feel Chantli scurrying about and Axolin throwing himself toward what he hoped would be the opposite side as their canoe was careening helplessly, with his, Necalli's, limbs partly under the water, his elbow and side, still flapping his paddle but with no notable results. Patli was moaning somewhere at the bottom of the leaking wreck, whimpering in an annoying voice.

"Stop it! Someone make him shut up!" He felt the crude stick slipping from his slick grip and didn't manage to even attempt recapturing it as by then his entire body was sliding out along with the toppling-over vessel, and there was nothing he could do about it but to remember to hold his breath.

The water was colder than the ripples that reached them while still in the boat, as revoltingly muddy, making him gag. He kicked back for the surface, his hands flailing wildly, desperate to grab something steady, anything, acting on their own accord. When his elbow hit something greasy and splintered, he clutched it and didn't let it go.

It was the bottom of their overturned boat, his senses told him, calming gradually now that there was something to cling to, something steadier than the blackness and the merciless water, eager to swallow them all.

Clawing his way up the greasy bark, he listened to the wild splashing, then, still clinging to it with his good arm, reached out, grabbing a handful of clothing. A desperate pull had his precarious perch wavering, about to topple again maybe, but the struggling form was still beside him, coughing and spitting.

"Where is Chantli?" he sputtered, himself retching as viciously, his nose clogged with mud, his mouth lined with it, or so it seemed.

"Th-there," heaved the boy, coughing between wild gasps. "Th-there. Other side. O-other side of the boat."

"Wait here!"

To let go of his slippery perch was an effort, not coming easily, shaming him. Holding his breath, he slid toward the worst of the clamor, the gagging and the sputtering coming indeed from what seemed to be the other side of their floating obstacle. It was reassuring to have it around, even if slimy and precariously unsteady. One hand on the slippery slickness, he tried to reach into the spluttering scuffle without being hit by too many thrashing limbs.

"Chantli!"

Catching something, a handful of hair, he pulled as forcefully as he could, his grip on the boat slipping. He could hear someone gasping, choking in no promising way. It wasn't hard to recognize Patli's angular limbs. Didn't the stupid commoner know how to swim?

"Hold on to the boat!" he yelled, crushing the thin body against its slimy roughness, kicking the grip of the persistent fingers away. But this one was a pest! Charging into the agitated water again, Necalli held his breath, worried now. She surely didn't know how to swim. Why would she?

The soundlessness enveloped him again, the murky depths. Fighting the urge to kick back to surface and the relative safety it offered, he dove under the wavering bark, feeling plenty of movement, probably that of the kicking feet belonging to the clinging survivors. Still, he charged toward the most desperate churn, his senses informing him that it was too deep, under the boat and not beside it, to belong to any of those attached to its sides. There was a little air to be had here, under the vessel's insides, and as his hand caught something, a handful of wet material, then the pleasant roundness of the familiar shoulder, his spirit soared. Oh yes, no mistakes this time.

Pulling her firmly, paying no attention to the desperation of her struggle, he made them dive back and away from this trap, careful not to get hit by her pummeling limbs. By the time they surfaced, she was clutching to him in the most hurtful of ways and with much strength, arresting his movements, interfering with his ability to swim.

Swallowing more and more water, he struggled back toward the drifting boat, near panic again, not sure of its whereabouts. If only the terrible darkness would disperse. The temptation to push her away grew. Why was she clinging to him so? Why wouldn't she let him hold her in a comfortable way instead of trying to make them both drown? But for the rippling all around his face, he would have yelled at her. As it was, he didn't even dare to open his mouth, the water splashing everywhere, covering them again, claiming them to be its victims, a worthy sacrifice to mighty Tlaloc. Or maybe a good meal for the monsters inhabiting its depths. The thought of *ahuitzotls* gave his panicked mind strength to kick for the surface again, forcefully enough to have them both popping out like dry pieces of bark.

Letting his instincts guide him, he charged toward what looked like a thicker darkness, his ears informing him that it must be the correct direction, with all its choking and spluttering. And when

Axolin's unmistakable palm wrapped around his elbow, pulling with great force, he knew they were temporarily safe.

CHAPTER 15

The girl was thin and painfully angular, her face nothing but sharp angles, surprisingly pleasant to look at but unsettling. One would expect at least some roundness watching a human face.

Meeting her curiosity-filled gaze once again, Miztli took his eyes away, embarrassed. She had been sneaking those glances aplenty, all fidgety upon her perch at the edge of the wooden dais, among the colorfully dressed noble crowd. His own position at the base of this same towering podium was not nearly as comfortable, enjoying no benefits of the additional height, able to see only the nearest warriors and contestants. Still, the crowds that filled the spacious plaza under the shadow of the Great Pyramid were in a worse situation, most of them seeing nothing unless climbing on something elevated, even the nearest smaller pyramids' stairs.

Acutely aware of his abductor's nearness, the man's palm locked around his elbow uncompromisingly, crushing it in its firm grip, relaying a message, Miztli tried to concentrate on the magnificent show of colors in front of his eyes, grimly amused. Compared to his previous day and two nights, he wasn't so badly off, come to think of it, standing among these well-to-do people, dressed in clean loincloth, his feet encased in the unfamiliar sensation of sandals' straps, awkward but strangely comfortable at the same time, his shoulders covered with another pleasantly soft cloth, like the cloaks sported all around here as in Tenochtitlan, a wonder. This beat not only the ghastly time of captivity, but the days of sweating next to the braziers of the melting room or working the fields of his home village. He tried not to snort. But for the dull pain in the back of his head and in other various beaten parts, and most of all, his kidnapper's uncompromising grip and his grim tension-filled presence, he might have enjoyed himself like never before. What fascinating, beautiful, lively clamor!

Another covert glance up that same lower dais informed him that the beautiful Tenochtitlan princess, his current benefactress, or rather, an eager user, was already there, sitting straight-backed, magnificent and aloof, decidedly above her surroundings. Other lavishly dressed women flanked her, some waving their prettily feathered fans, as haughty as the princess, unattainable and remote, some chatting happily, beaming with excitement, exchanging lively comments, their colorfulness and the sparkling of their jewelry hurting the eye.

The girl on the lower tier was still staring at him, wide-eyed. This time, he returned her gaze, somewhat incensed. Why was she gawking at him so? Her eyes were large and widely spaced, tilted at their edges quite sharply, pleasing the eye but in a strange fashion. They remained fixed on him, filling with what looked like a challenge, not about to be stared down. He made a face at her, then looked back at the warming-up warriors when the rock-hard fingers yanked at his elbow, pressing as though trying to crush it.

"Don't gawk, you stupid cub," hissed the man angrily, not easing the intensity of his squeeze. "Do what you are told."

Clenching his teeth, Miztli made it a point not to squirm or show his discomfort otherwise. Deliberately slow, he transferred his gaze from the crowds splashing on the other side of the podiums with the dais, two in their number, towering loftily, enjoying the shadow of the nearby pyramid. Warriors armed with long, dangerous-looking spears kept the rest of the crowds at bay, not letting anyone near.

The competitors, different from the guarding warriors by their prettier-looking attire of loincloths and cloaks alone, were the ones he was supposed to watch, he remembered. To watch and to report to the boy Ahuitzotl, whose name he had used to such telling effect. The results of the impending contest and the local ruler's speech about it, whatever was his name. He didn't remember. Moqui-something. The neglected princess of Tenochtitlan's royal house did not come to elaborate as she promised to do at night. Neither did she send to him anything but a maid with instructions, which left his abductor to elaborate and enlighten on his own.

Not in a hurry to take Miztli's ties off despite the clear orders, not trusting him to behave reasonably, as his kidnapper was willing to inform his prisoner again and again, the man did bring him food and drink, and even sent for a skinny foreign-looking slave loaded with smelly ointments and balms, all the while talking about what he, Miztli, was expected to do if they decided to trust him and what would happen to him if concluded otherwise. In the end, he felt like promising anything, mainly in order to have the man stop talking and let him rest. And maybe release his ties. His hands had no feeling in them anymore, and his back felt like a wooden plank, stiff to the point of being ready to crack. But didn't the woman tell them to treat him well?

Only when the dawn was about to break and people came to talk to his unrelenting watchdog, the man did cut his ties, breaking into more dire promises as he did. Yet all he cared about was the possibility of stretching his limbs, then curling around himself, drifting into a dreamless slumber against the incessant shaking and some kicking around, as his captor kept elaborating on the important mission of watching contesting warriors while listening to Tlatelolco's mighty ruler making mighty speeches and memorizing every word of those – as though he could do something like that – or else. Then it was again a long colorful description of the various slow torturous possibilities included in 'or else,' but by that time, he truly didn't care. The sleep was more alluring.

Yet the food brought to him afterwards, when the sun was relatively strong already, penetrating every crack in the cane-and-reed shack, refreshed him, and he found himself more attentive, even nodding halfheartedly when commanded to conform to his expected new duties, to repeat what had been required of him in general terms. Topped with the offer of water to clean himself and a neatly folded pile of pretty clothes of a sort he had never seen up close before, let alone was offered to wear, made him feel elated, nearly grateful, full of strength. Yes, he could watch some contest of would-be young warriors, to listen to the ruler of this other island preaching to his subjects bad things about Tenochtitlan, then repeat it all after being delivered back across the causeway. He would make Chantli help, he decided. She'd know how to reach her newly found friend, the spoiled snotty princess's little brother, or if not, then she might be able to ask for the *calmecac* boys' aid. After all, they were the ones to drag him into all this. There was no reason they should not wish to help at least by delivering clandestine messages. And if they didn't, Chantli would make them, of that he was sure.

Trying to shake off his captor's hand, not to succeed – a possibility too good to be true – but to make his point, he concentrated on the young men nearest to their vantage point, all impressive, spectacularly decorated individuals in their loincloths and short cloaks, their jewelry sparkling. Some were striding back and forth, restless and impatient, dangerously excited. Others exchanged exclamations, waving their weaponry, commenting on it, complimenting each other.

Fascinated, Miztli watched the nearest group of men comparing their slings, impressively long, tightly woven affairs, connected to wide pieces of leather to host their missiles comfortably, he presumed, having never seen such shooting devices before. People of his village used slings aplenty, simple maguey-woven strings with a widening base to hold the stone in, to help it remain still through the spinning until the desired speed was achieved. He remembered himself rotating anything that could hold in even the tiniest of rocks since being a small child, loving the sensation, proud of the accurate hits that he came to achieve aplenty with the passing of time. He was the best among the rest of the village boys, unarguable winner of every challenge. Even the older people commented on his shooting skills. Father, while preferring his good sturdy bow and meaty deer it might get, took his youngest on plenty of hunting missions, trusting him to shoot enough rabbits or birds for the rest of the family to enjoy.

Craning his neck, he tried to see better, the nearest man's sling so long and prettily made, with such a sturdy base of decorated leather. And the missiles! Forgetting himself, he stared at the perfectly round ball one of the warriors was bouncing on his open palm, talking to his neighbor, shrugging in pretended indifference. Was it a stone polished to perfection?

"What are you staring at there?" demanded his guard, his grip tightening once again.

Clenching his teeth, Miztli shrugged and tried to shake off the persistent grip, to no avail.

"If you try to do something silly…"

"I won't!" He was so tired of all this! "I promised to do all this stupid listening and I'll do it. Stop trying to break my arm!"

It came out in quite a shout, causing more than a few heads to turn at them.

"Shut up!" hissed the man, his grip not relaxing but squeezing harder, indeed set on checking his bones' endurance. "One more word…"

"I'll scream all I like if you won't stop hurting me," he answered in the matching hiss, this time careful to keep his voice low, as reluctant to draw attention as his captor was. What would he say to this well-to-do crowd if questioned? The spearmen, those who were pushing the more common crowds away, would be the first to beat him down with their spears, if not to impale him on them.

Standing the fury of the murderous glare, he forced his own not to waver, struggling to stay upright despite the hurtful pressure and the awkwardness of his own stance. People around them moved uneasily, bestowing reproachful glances of their own. The man next to them lifted his shoulders.

"Take your quarrels elsewhere," he tossed, pursing his lips in an open disdain. "What manners!"

Miztli's guard tensed dangerously but said nothing, turning his face away, his grip not relaxing. On the higher dais, people were stirring as well, the seated nobles and their entourage. In spite of himself, his eyes followed the tall figure in a long glittering cloak and a magnificent headdress strolling toward the edge of the high platform, as though about to address the crowded Plaza. This same Moquihuixtli, the questionable ruler of this other island, the one he was supposed to listen to carefully, remembering his words? Well, this time the name popped into his head, when less needed.

Two more imposingly clad figures moved forward, following their ruler, halting a pace behind. Miztli's heart stopped all of a sudden. Frozen in dread, he watched the unmistakably stout form, standing with his bejeweled arms crossed and the massive legs wide apart, in such familiar fashion, towering above the crowds in the way he had towered above him, Miztli, only the night before, eyeing the crowding people as he had eyed the dubious prisoner, with a mix of an open suspicion and a healthy dose of a gauging calculation. From such a close range, it was easy to decipher this particular expression.

Aware of the cold ring tightening around his chest, Miztli fought for breath, struggling against the overpowering urge to dive into the crowds and be gone, in a headless run if need be, the hurtful grip of his current abductor and his dire promises or not.

"What?" the man was whispering, tugging at his arm violently. "What happened?"

Swallowing hard, Miztli forced his eyes off the dais, his mind numb and still in a panic but noting the details – the roaring of the crowds greeting their leader, the sparkling of the contestants' weaponry, mainly spears and arrows, their chipped polished obsidian reflecting the rays of the sun fiercely, dangerously, swaying in the air; the way the strange girl on the lower dais watched not the gesturing ruler but the terrible man behind him, her eyes narrow, brimming with concentration.

"My brave people of Tlatelolco," the ruler on the higher podium was thundering, his voice strong and high-pitched, resonating through the packed plaza, his hands spread wide. "Today we gather to watch our daring young men display their bravery and skill, our invincible men who, if called upon to wage war or defend their beloved city, would do so with their hearts and bodies strong and unyielding, and their spirits like that of godlike jaguars and pumas, unstoppable and mighty."

The crowds and the competitors roared again, as though

having one throat instead of many hundreds. How many people were packed on the pavement of this vast square? His eyes drifted beyond the gesturing ruler again, unable to listen. The man from the warehouse was frowning now, observing his surroundings with his arm shielding his eyes, as though looking for something. Miztli's heart missed a beat once again. Could the man see him here, in such dangerous proximity, at the base of the podium upon which the dais was situated? Would he recognize him? What would he do then?

The human lake shifted, the wave of their movement reaching even this sheltered space, causing the spearmen to struggle not to let the crowds overrun the base of the podiums and the dais. He could hear people yelling, barking orders, clearing their way somewhere further ahead. The noblemen and women upon their elevated seats were sitting straighter now, craning their necks, trying to see better. Even the mighty ruler stopped orating, motioning with his right arm, indicating the direction of the growing commotion, smiling proudly, well satisfied. Both his followers reinforced the broad gesturing, the face of the man from the warehouse clearing momentarily, turning as satisfied as that of his sovereign.

Miztli found his own gaze drifting in the indicated direction, balancing on his tiptoes, curious in spite of himself. Where the shadow of the Great Pyramid did not reach, another podium now hosted a form, a statue that hadn't been there before. Everyone was looking this way, it seemed, the warriors busy clearing a space around it.

"Brave Tlatelolcan warriors," cried out the ruler upon the dais. "You have come here to practice the arts of war, to show your aim and your skill, to display your endurance and strength." The man encircled the packed plaza with his gaze, arms spread once again, benevolent and encouraging like a proud father inviting his children to show their skill, sure of their success and achievements ahead of time. "This stone statue was made especially for you. It will test your skill with your slingshots, your aim, your prowess with your deadly weaponry."

Another roar of approval, this time dominated by the

contestants, those who were armed with the slings, assumed Miztli, watching the shooting devices that impressed him earlier. The proud owners were waving those in the air, well above the heads of the crowds.

"He whose aim proves the best and the deadliest will be declared the most outstanding warrior among you all," cried out the man from the warehouse, his voice low but powerful, sending a new surge of panic up Miztli's spine. But did he recognize *this* voice!

The Tenochtitlan beauty upon the lower dais shielded her eyes, scanning the plaza and the base of their podium with her gaze in her turn, her prettily full lips pursed with displeasure. When her eyes rested on him, she relaxed visibly, her proud head crowned with a glittering diadem, nodding imperceptibly, with grudging satisfaction. But this woman was as annoying as she was beautiful!

The angular girl, he noticed, was frowning, staring at the royal woman as well, her face twisting with distaste. When her eyes darted back to him, they were still frowning, but he was too busy to get incensed once again, distracted by the sensation of the crushing grip upon his elbow relaxing. A glimpse of his guard's face showed him that this one was observing the dais of the ruler and the men upon it as well, the standing dignitaries. Seizing upon a chance, Miztli pulled his arm away, moving it to return the feeling.

The ruler was speaking again, gesticulating vigorously. But this man liked using his hands! He reminded Miztli of that boy from their village, the one who could not say a single word without outlining it in the air. To mimic this one was always fun, the surest way of getting hearty laughs from everyone around.

"The best shooter among you will be rewarded by your Emperor in person."

In what way? wondered Miztli, feeling better by the moment, out of his captor's clutches, even if temporarily. Was there a way to slip away, to disappear in this lake of people, everyone busy and gaping, not caring about foreign boys or their belonging in this Tlatelolcan crowd? Why should he care about their contests, even if spectacularly large, or their rulers' speeches, to be eager to run and report it to some royal boys of Tenochtitlan Palace?

The orating ruler stopped waving and turned around, strolling back toward his lavishly decorated seat. His followers seemed to be doing the same, yet the scary man from the warehouse seemed not to be in a hurry, hovering near the edge, scanning the crowds below his feet, his gaze sliding up toward the lower dais, lingering upon none other than the displeased beauty, measuring her thoughtfully as though trying to find an answer. Then, as though stimulated, the penetrating gaze slid downwards and straight toward them, sparkling with triumph. At the same moment, Miztli felt himself yanked once again, pulled backwards, stumbling into a man standing next to him, treading on someone's sandaled feet.

"Come, quick!"

Fighting to keep his balance, even though it was difficult to fall flat in such a melee, he followed for some time, finding it easier to escape the new grip, not as firm or as uncompromising as before, not in this more densely packed part of the crowd. Here the smell was stronger, an odor of sweating bodies clad in plain maguey cloaks or even without any such adornment at all. Thrilled with the possibility of simply bolting away, he fought his watchdog's repeated attempts to recapture him fiercely, not about to be dragged anywhere now, not after being so close to his freedom as he was.

The man cursed venomously, but so did the crowding people, pushing them with their elbows, cussing with much spirit, eager to see the happenings upon the plaza, from where deafening sounds of shattering stones and crushing rocks came in a powerful surge.

"You stupid half wit," his former abductor was hissing, grabbing the side of Miztli's cloak after a less successful attempt at capturing his elbow, which Miztli made sure to land into his attacker's ribs instead. It was a good blow that resonated through his own battered body, but it made his pursuer waver and his attempt to seize any more of his parts became more careful.

"Stop it, you stinking frog-eaters." A mountain of a man

shoved them away with enough force to have them crashing into the packed bodies to their left, cramming some of them into roughly laid stones of a crumbling wall. Curses erupted everywhere, colorful in their ferociousness and venom.

Struggling against a possible fall now, elbowed and pressed from all around, Miztli tried to push his way toward the dusty stones, momentarily frightened. If he fell in such a melee, he would be done for, trampled or worse.

Clawing his way up the half-crumbled wall, he somehow managed to gain a foothold, perching along with other improvising observers, momentarily relieved. In the immediate proximity of his awkwardly sandaled feet, a gushing lake of heads was splashing forcefully, the brawl they had caused progressing at full speed, with much spirit, heedless of its original reason. From his elevated position, he could see people further away watching the competition, like him climbing upon every possible obstacle to see better. Yet some were clearing their way in this direction, very determined. A group of men, maybe three or more, their eyes focused and their faces grim.

Someone screamed, and Miztli's eyes leapt toward the portly form of his former captor, crashing his fist against someone's jaw, shoving his way toward his wall, swearing venomously. About to leap toward the safety of the other side, whatever might wait for him there, he glimpsed the pushing newcomers reaching the tussle, diving in with single-minded determination, like a canoe spreading lake's waters, relentless and implacable. In less than a heartbeat, they were upon his pursuer, colliding with the bulky man in force, his scowling face registering a childlike surprise, reflecting in the unnaturally round eyes and a gaping mouth to match. In another heartbeat, the unseemly stunned face disappeared, plummeting between the agitated people and their feet, putting up no fight whatsoever.

For another fraction of a heartbeat, Miztli just stared, aghast, before his body threw itself over the wall, following his instincts rather any thoughtful reaction, landing on the vacancy of the polished stones, pell-mell, with his hands and feet, terrified beyond reason. *Who were these people?* Scrambling up frantically, he didn't pause to look behind, racing along the wall and in the direction of the deafening noise. Back toward the noble parts of the plaza, his petrified senses urged him, back where people behaved more reasonably.

He could hear the shouts, the heaviness of their footsteps resonating against the cracked stones – or was it just his imagination? The low wall ended abruptly, with the clamor rising, the deafening bedlam of roaring shouts and explosions of smashing stones and shattering pieces. To his left, the royal podium with both daises could be seen clearly, still an island of relative tranquility as opposed to the rest of the spacious square, towering above the pushing crowds.

His heart pounding, he paused, less dismayed than back among the brawling riffraff. People were pressing here and jumping to see better, but not as wildly or as violently as back by the wall. Was his former abductor still searching for him? Was he alive to do so? He shuddered. Who were those people, the ones who had barreled in to confront this man specifically, clearly going after him? And maybe him, Miztli, too. Were they connected to the nobleman upon the royal dais?

Think, he ordered himself, *think*. The causeway, he needed to find the way back to the causeway. To cross it and find Chantli, ask for her help at finding that *calmecac* boy, the reasonable one of the two. He might be able to think of something.

The thought of coming back to the workshop he preferred to ignore entirely. There was no way to pacify old Tlaquitoc, to try to explain or reason. What would the old metalworker do? Nothing pleasant, one could be sure of that. Would he throw his absent apprentice out? That would be not such a bad development, but Father's disappointment might be too great. Oh mighty deities, but how to make it all right again?

The warriors guarding the royal dais were pushing the pressing crowd away, using their spears as though they were poles. He turned back toward the low wall, then his blood froze once again. One of the men who had accosted his kidnapper was posing at the top of his previous perch, looking straight at him, gesturing vigorously.

His mind went numb all at once. The noises receded. As if in a dream, he whirled forcefully, barreling his way into the packed wall of people, oblivious of reason. The spears blocked him, pushing him roughly with their wooden parts, shoving him aside. He resisted their force, his mind running amok. *These people, they were coming! They were after him, and not to kidnap,* his panicked senses told him. *They wanted to knife him just like they did to that other man!*

The spearman was yelling at him, threatening. He could not understand his words, but the meaning was clear, related through the furiously twisted mouth and eyes. Behind his back, he could feel people pushing. His pursuers already? Did they move through the crowds as though there was no one there, so forcefully and with such ease?

He tried to sneak past the guarding warrior by faking a movement toward the other side. It worked to a degree, as the man lurched at the same direction, but as he charged past, another warrior's javelin shoved into his side, sending him crashing ahead and into the space they were trying to protect from his intrusion.

Gasping for air, he scrambled onto his feet, charging ahead and toward the dais, hearing the shouts, glimpsing nothing but the dark spark of obsidian behind his back, pointed at him, its message clear. No more simple shoving away, not for him. Still, he dove into the well-to-do crowds, his previous vantage point, afraid of the people who were after him more than of the guarding spearmen. The warriors wanted him away; the other ones wanted him dead!

The murmur around went up, but it was the thin palm clutching his arm that made his berserk progress slow down. Small and surprisingly cold, it signaled no danger; still, his heart tripled its racing.

"Over here! Quick!"

As in a dream, he stared at the slightly familiar face, all bones and sharp angles, strangely defined, like a stone mask carved with very bold lines, adorned with a wide mouth and a pair of large, well-spaced eyes, their edges slanting sharply, again too decisively. Those peered at him with a measure of urgency, not reassuring but not threatening either. Just insistent, displeased with his slowness.

Come, she motioned again, her head tilting pointedly, eyes urging, hand tugging at his arm with more spirit. Dazed, he hesitated, then let her pull him into a small opening, maneuver their way along the wavering lake of people, diving under the stone of the podium's base, sneaking alongside it with the nimbleness of a tiny lizard, slender and sure of her step. In another few steps, the brilliance of the sunlight disappeared, replaced by the dimness of twilight and a slightly damp smell. Blinking, he tried to look around, but she kept pulling him on, along the unpolished stones and toward what looked like the next source of light streaming in through a rectangular opening, a crudely made hole.

"Here!"

Releasing his arm, she turned around, eyeing him with an open satisfaction, beaming now. He stared back at her, numb.

"They won't find you here," she went on, not taken aback by his lack of response, as it seemed. Her voice was husky and not unpleasant to the ear.

The roaring of the crowds just outside their stony protection soared.

"I suppose the statue finally went to pieces," she commented, leaning to look out through the dented hole. "At long last. I thought that their rain of missiles would overturn it right away." Her mouth twisted into the semblance of an inverted grin. "You should have seen it. It was quite a show. One doesn't see something like that ever. Unless on a battlefield, I suppose." Her slender shoulders lifted in a shrug. Even though covered by an intricately decorated blouse and a collar made out of interlaced beads and turquoise, it was easy to guess that her shoulders were as bony as her face was. The slenderness of her arms, covered up to their elbows, told him that, their bracelets looking too heavy, out of place.

"Why were you running like a mad turkey instead of watching the slingers?" she asked, peeking out again, not perturbed by his lack of response in the least. "Were you trying to get away from that man who was holding you back in the beginning? I thought it was strange that he held you like that, even before that whimpering spoiled crybaby princess started making faces at you." Her eyes sparkled proudly. "I noticed you before she began staring at you. Before my father too. I knew there was something wrong with you. What is it?" The flow of words stopped momentarily, arrested by a returned frown. Not a grim frown but a thoughtful one. The strangely tilted eyes were appraising him inquisitively, reflecting an obvious thought process. "Tell me what that man wanted from you, and what the crybaby whiner did?"

He blinked, overwhelmed by so many demands in one outburst of a rapid speech. "Who is the crybaby whiner?"

Her beam was back. "That fat fowl, the Emperor's former Chief Wife. Tenochtitlan moaner."

"Your emperor?" he asked blankly. "That man who spoke from the dais? Moqui-something?"

Her frown returned as suddenly as it disappeared. "Yes, Moquihuixtli. Our lawful ruler. Don't you know who he is?" Now her eyes were mere slits, taking some of her strangeness away, disappointingly so.

He wanted to curse himself for opening his mouth at the first place. Who was this girl? What did she want from him?

The crowds were calming down, their ear splitting thundering receding. He wished to peek out but didn't dare to move past her in case she got scared and started to scream or something; or maybe ask him many more questions. It was so calm in their extraordinary hideaway, an island of tranquility.

"It's only temporary," she volunteered as though reading his thoughts, leaning toward the opening once again, her turquoise necklace ringing, weighing on her slender neck. "They'll be getting excited once again soon."

"What were they screaming about?" he asked, curious against his will.

"Before now?" She made a face. "I told you already. They put up this huge stone statue, in the form of a man. A tall and a broad fellow, I must say." She snickered. "It held a pretty shield and an obsidian sword of a size one doesn't see around often." Another smirk. "Like a truly huge thing, with twenty blades on each side. I counted them!" The unreserved wideness of her grin was contagious. He couldn't help but chuckle himself. "Our Revered Moquihuixtli must have paid so much for that statue. It was made out of stone, you see. Not a simple wooden carving or something."

"And what did he do with it?" he prompted when she began frowning again, as though calculating the possible cost of such undertaking.

"Oh, he invited all those warriors, the ones you must have seen out there even though you were too busy with your silly running around to pay attention." The pronounced reproach in her words made him wish to snicker as well. But she was something else, this girl, a thing out of storytellers' tales. "Anyway, their first test was to take that statue down, make it fall, or maybe even break it. They were to shoot their slings and not to miss one single throw." Her dancing eyebrows related what she thought of such an ambitious undertaking. Nothing good. "The one who shot the best was to be rewarded by the Emperor himself and with great pomp."

He remembered the words of the orating ruler. "So he is rewarding someone right now?"

Her shrug was brief, disinterested. "I suppose. But for you, I would have known that."

"You... you helped me out there. I'm grateful. Very much so." He hesitated, not knowing what to say. "I will repay you, somehow."

She grinned with one side of her mouth. "That would be nice." Then the smile widened, evened out. "You can repay me now. Tell me what your story is. Why were you running all over as though all the worst spirits of the Underworld were after you?"

"It's a long story," he said, feeling surprisingly at ease, not threatened or even troubled for a moment. But it was good to be here in this hideaway, to relax for a little while, not to think of all the terrible things, from the games of Tenochtitlan or Tlatelolco nobility to the kidnappers who were after him to the troubles that awaited him back in the workshop. His mood began to plummet once again. "What are they going to do now, these people out there on the plaza?" he asked, thinking about his possibilities. "Go home?"

She made a face at him, opening her huge eyes too widely, her eyebrows arching in different ways. A funny mask. "You wish!" Her thin arms flew up, outlining wild pictures. "I told you it was just the beginning. Now as we speak, or so I'd say, they are cleaning the pieces of the stone statue, rewarding the best shooters and all that." Pursing her lips, she fell silent, leaning toward the opening once again, the image of attentive listening, an exaggerated one. "Yes," she confirmed, nodding to her own words. "He is speaking now. Can't you hear? Rewarding the winner or winners, I bet."

"And then?" he prompted. "What will he do afterwards?"

"Oh, then they'll put up a wooden statue to replace the stone one. And they'll make the other young warriors, those who brought along spears and bows and *atlatls*, to show their skills, against a wooden enemy this time. But it'll be as huge and as heavily armed, I can promise you that. To represent all sorts of enemies, you know." Her grin again turned uneven, one corner of her mouth climbing up, the other down. "Like presumptuous Tenochtitlan brutes, eh?"

"Tenochtitlan?" he asked, frowning. "But your islands are not at war!"

Her eyebrows lifted high again. "Maybe not now, but that may change. They do presume to tell us what to do. All the time they do that. And they are violating our rights, and sometimes even our citizens. Think about it." One of the narrow palms came up, extending a long slender finger. "They violated those girls on the marketplace not so long ago. Then, only a market interval later, they filled up our canal one night." Another finger thrust forward. "And they have been full of all sorts of demands, all because our ruler put that fat whiny fowl aside, preferring my sister in her stead." She nodded sagely. "And my sister is so much prettier than the complaining turkey, so much more fitting to be the Emperor's Chief Wife."

His head reeled from so much information, delivered again in a breathless rush. But what was she talking about, this strange, curiously chatty girl?

"Also, our city is not a tributary of Tenochtitlan. They can't lord it over us as though we were nothing but a tiny village. They can't tell us what to do!"

He watched her eyebrows knitting, creating a single line below her high forehead, her expressions changing as rapidly as her spilling words, too rapid to follow.

"Will you slow down?" he asked when she paused for a heartbeat, probably in order to draw a quick breath. If she dove under water, she would be able to stay there for a long time, he decided, longer than many boys he knew. It would be funny to see her taking part in such a competition. Would she stay down after everyone surfaced, defeating them all with her ability not to breath for a long time? "Tell me how to get away from this plaza without drawing all these thousands of warriors' and onlookers' attention. There must be a way to do that."

She wrinkled her nose, contemplating him thoughtfully. "After they'll be heading out there, to the lake shores, to watch the rest of the competition. I suppose then you'll be able to sneak away easily." Her eyes lit again. "The last part of the competition will be the most thrilling. The slingers will be at it again, but not assaulting a helpless statue this time." Her gaze was boring at him, glowing with excitement. "They will be shooting waterfowl in flight. Imagine that. Hundreds of missiles flying all over, hitting those birds! No one will be allowed upon these shores, naturally, no one but the commoners who will be spooking the birds from the reeds. Imagine that!"

He didn't bother with any of it, perturbed. "Won't it be possible to sneak away before that?"

Her glow dimmed. "Wouldn't you want to see it, this huge hunt and all? It won't be something you'll see every day, you know." Even the bracelets adorning her thin arms seemed to lose some of their spark along with the rest of her, so unduly disappointed.

"Yes, it would be nice to see it, yes," he muttered, curiously unsettled, wishing to see her return to her previous enthusiastic state. "But I don't think I –"

"It won't take them long to get over with this other statue," she pleaded, her eyes clinging to him, full of anticipation. "They took that stone statue down quickly enough. The sun has not even reached its zenith and it began when it was already high enough."

"Oh well, yes." He felt as though a whole day had passed since being dragged to this plaza, pushed at the base of the dais, forced to wait for all eternity, until the warriors and the nobility and the onlookers filled every corner of the spacious square. And then the fight, and the flight, and these people probably killing his abductor, but for what purpose? Were they connected to the scary man from the imperial dais? After all, his people were the ones to kidnap him in the first place for sniffing around their tunnel filled with weaponry. Why weaponry? Was all this connected to the warlike intentions of those same Tlatelolcans the girl was talking about?

Oh mighty deities, but it might be just that! And the imperial sister from the Tenochtitlan royal house, a fat whiny fowl, according to this girl, having one of the kidnappers to snatch him from the original ones, eager to have him deliver messages to her little brother back in Tenochtitlan, repeating what the ruler of this other island had said, or what he made his warriors do. But after this girl's words, it was clearer what the haughty noblewoman wanted. A fat whiny fowl? He snickered against his will. She was complaining aplenty, indeed, that spoiled royal princess, but her beauty was not something one would doubt or argue against.

"Don't you want to see them taking the wooden statue down with their spears?" the girl was pressing, all expectancy now, her eyes open wide again. "I don't want to miss them, and they might start doing it any moment. Hear the crowds?"

Indeed, the commotion outside was growing again. He dared to near the opening, rewarded with nothing but a view of brightly decorated cloaks and densely packed backs.

"You go back there," he told her helplessly. "Just don't tell anyone about me being here. Will you? Please?"

She frowned once again, pondering. "Yes, I can't bring you up there and into our dais, I suppose. Too many prettily plucked eyebrows would go up in indignant surprise. Not to mention my father. He will be the most indignant of them all." One of her own eyebrows was climbing up fast. "Why was he looking at you, do you know? And why were you staring at him the way you did?"

"I was staring?" he repeated, baffled. "At whom?"

"My father. You were staring at him. Plenty of times. And you looked frightened too. Really terrified."

He felt the air escaping his lungs all at once. "Your father is not... not the man... the one from the... the..." For the life of him, he could not finish that phrase.

"The one from... where?" She was eyeing him, openly amused, as though pleased with making him frightened again. "My father is the Emperor's Head Adviser, Revered Teconal. You know, the man closest to the Emperor, the father of the Emperor's Chief Wife." She rethought her words, then snickered. "Which isn't me, obviously. My sister is dreadfully pretty, and she is well educated and the best mannered girl in the entire world. Much better mannered and educated than the fat Tenochtitlan's fowl. My sister draws beautiful pictures and she can draw plenty of glyphs and she weaves beautifully too. She is so accomplished!"

He didn't listen. Teconal? The man from the warehouse, the name the princess and the nobleman from the shed used with so much loathing and resentment. Oh mighty gods! He fought the urge to turn around and run.

"We can try to peek from under this podium if we go up a little, try to see from under the dais," she was musing, unaware of his agitation or indifferent to it. "Wouldn't you want to look from there? It's high enough and we could see nicely far."

"I need to get out of here," he mumbled, eyeing the corridor they had slipped through while coming here in the first place. If he chanced going out the way they had come, would he manage to do so without drawing attention, mostly that of his pursuers? Were they still prowling out there, looking for him?

"Well, you can't." Her lips pursed again with decisive practicality. "So why not make the most out of it while you are waiting for your chance to get away? It would be most sensible, wouldn't it? You can help me up there and climb after me."

Narrowing her eyes, she measured him with a businesslike gaze. "Yes, you look strong and able, like commoners do. Are you a commoner?"

He shrugged, still too perturbed to feel angered or offended. After the *calmecac* boys, he knew well enough what the word 'commoner' meant. Nothing complimentary. And a fitting description too. Even Patli was considered a commoner by those snotty noble boys' judgment.

"Come, we'll do it quickly," she went on, imploring. "It won't be difficult and we'll keep so quiet no one will ever notice. Come!" Catching his hand once again, she pulled, her smile urging, curiously appealing in its mischievous pleading, difficult to resist. "Come! I promise nothing will happen to you. Please! And then, when they are done killing that other wooden enemy of theirs, when they'll be still busy rewarding warriors or making speeches, I'll show you the best way to escape this plaza. It'll be the easiest thing, I promise you!"

CHAPTER 16

"You all wait here while I go and sniff around and get help."

Shutting her eyes against the fierce glow of the strong midmorning sun, Chantli tried to make her headache go away. It was daunting, those clubs pounding inside her skull, trying to squash it and make her eyes wish to pop out of their sockets. It felt as though they had popped out already.

Pressing her palms to her face in a helpless attempt to ease the pain, she glanced at her companions from between her fingers, too spent to participate in their disagreements. It was just too much, all of it. Their adventures, or rather misadventures, back in the temple and the tunnel, and under the causeway, none of which coming even close to the dread of the open lake. Oh, but what a horrifying experience it was! Even now, in the softness of the high morning sun, she still couldn't bring herself to think about it without her back breaking out in a bout of cold sweat, the ghastly sliminess of the overturned boat and its suffocating dampness as she had flung around, trying to break from its clutches, finding no way out, crazed with fear, the dreadfulness of the water everywhere, so cruel and eager to swallow her, the darkness so hopeless, closing indifferently, as though they had all already been dead.

After Necalli had dragged her out and away from the trap that apparently was their overturned boat – she had been too terrified to realize that before, the problem and the easiness of the solution, she who could swim like a fish – it became better, of course, with the mere possibility to breathe freely. Clinging to the overturned vessel helped, but Patli kept slipping off of it, murmuring something incoherent every time he was pulled back by either of the *calmecac* boys, themselves as battered and spent but still acting like heroes, like true warriors, true men.

Oh, but did she wish to tell them all of it and more, especially Necalli, who was now pacing back and forth, so well built and so handsome, still full of forcefulness and decision, but haggard-looking now, with his shoulders sagging, if imperceptibly, and his arm held awkwardly against his body, the old bandage gone and the wounds underneath it looking painfully inflamed, glaring red, oozing liquids. Not a good sight. He certainly needed to visit a healer and with no delays. Still, he was the one they looked up to now as before, and not because he seemed to be less harmed than the rest of them.

"Wait for me here," he repeated firmly, stopping his pacing and turning to face them.

His eyes narrowed dubiously against the picture they must have been presenting, crouching there on the gravel in various poses, spent or hurt to various degrees, with Patli being in the worst condition, sprawling in the dust, his hair sticky with blood where the boat's side had evidently cracked his head open, probably while overturning – which explained his delirious state back in the water as well – his eyes moving rapidly under his shut eyelids, darting back and forth, wandering the worlds of the spirits, conversing with them. It was hair-raising in the beginning, his rapid unintelligible murmuring. Now it irritated her to no end.

"Take Ahuitzotl with you," called out Axolin, curled on the gravel as well, unable to walk. She remembered this boy's slight limp through their previous adventures, yet now, after the night in the lake and probably having it hit or twisted again, he could barely step on his hideously swollen ankle.

Necalli pursed his lips tight. "If he promises not to argue or nag." He squashed the boy with a threatening glance. "Do you?"

"I don't need your permission to go anywhere," muttered his younger adversary, yet with less fighting spirit than of yore, his own lips pressed into an invisible line. "I can go and bring us help all by myself."

"See?" growled Necalli, the nostrils of his prominent nose

widening in no promising manner. "He is not coming with me!"

"Oh, you two!" Rolling his eyes, Axolin emitted a sound somewhere between a groan and a grunt. "Hopeless boneheads, both of you!"

She drew a deep breath, trying to disregard her headache. "I'll come with you." They all turned to stare and she fought the urge to close her eyes again, the piercing pain somewhere behind them annoying and persistent. "What? Why are you staring at me? I got hurt less than all of you put together. I have no wounds or broken limbs."

"Mine isn't broken," muttered Axolin, dropping his gaze. "It's just twisted."

"And I didn't hurt anything at all," contributed Ahuitzotl, making Necalli roll his eyes in his turn.

"We'll go out there and get help," she said hastily before a new heated argument broke. "Beg the first fisherman we meet to take us back to Tenochtitlan, or at least to take Axolin and Patli, to sail them in a canoe."

"And pay this nice helpful man how?" Axolin was still staring at the ground he crouched upon, glaring at it.

"We'll find a way." Decisive as always, Necalli didn't hesitate any longer. "Will you hold on here on your own?" His eyes narrowed, assessing his friend.

"Of course. I'm not the problem here." Axolin's eyes brushed past Patli's lethargic form. "Hope he is not hurt that badly as to just die on us."

Chantli shuddered at the very thought. Oh, but Father would be so furious, with everything by now – her disappearance, and that of Miztli probably, and now Patli. And what if her cousin died because of this stupid adventure? Father cherished a soft spot for this particular nephew, the mysterious family member out of the northern mainland, with his Toltec accent and gifts for the written word worthy of *calmecac* training.

"Chantli is pretty. No one will say 'no' to her, even if we don't have slaves to pay any cocoa beans right away." Ahuitzotl's voice broke into her unhappy reverie, severing the unwelcomed thread of her thoughts. "No commoner will tell us to go and jump into the lake if she is with us."

"Smart aleck," muttered Necalli, an amused half smile twisting his lips. His gaze leapt at her, lingering for a heartbeat, making her stomach tighten. There was a question in his eyes, a wondering inquiry. It made her expectant and relieved at the same time, expectant that he would look at her again and relieved when he took his eyes away. An unfamiliar feeling, strangely pleasing. From the moment of the first light, it had been like that, since the dawn-break found them here, sprawled on this neglected piece of shore, surrounded by marshy dirt and the crisply rustling reeds, clearly a place even Tlatelolco commoners didn't favor, as any such coastline should be swarming with canoes at this time of the morning, brimming with fishermen engaging in their trade.

"Well, let us hope it is still part of Tlatelolco, this place, and not just a stupid side of a deserted island with nothing on it." Motioning with his head, the *calmecac* boy froze for a moment, listening intently. The new surge of a distant hum that sounded like hundreds of people shouting all at once erupted once again, impossible to miss. Somewhere far away, people were shouting, a serious crowd. "Judging by this noise, it is connected somewhere big and mighty. Tlatelolco, most surely. The stupid provincials don't even bother to make use of their entire island!"

Ahuitzotl snickered, charging up the shoreline already, heading for the bushes adorning it. "They'll be taught a lesson and soon!" Impatiently, he waved at them. "Are you coming?"

Shooting an uncomfortable glance at both tiredly crouching Axolin and helplessly sprawling Patli, she got to her feet, welcoming the chance to get away from the gloom of this place, consumed with guilt on this same account.

"Are you sure you will be well?"

The wounded boy shrugged indifferently, but as their eyes met, his lips twisted in a surprisingly open, mischievous grin. "Make sure that our hothead Necalli doesn't land into trouble, will you? Keep a close eye on that boy."

"Shut up," was the other *calmecac* pupil's parting words, already drawing away in the direction Ahuitzotl was hurrying to, springy and sure of himself, as though no recent hardships had them in more trouble than they were able to cope with. "Look who is talking about *landing* badly." His chuckle trailed after him like the edge of his mangled cloak, in no better condition than a stepped-on rag by now, grayish and wrinkled, stinking of rotten fish. "The boy who could not put his ankle right, not even when thrashing in the water."

This time, it was the other youth's turn to demand shutting up action and with much gusto. Chantli felt her mood improving by leaps and bounds. Oh yes, they'd manage to get home in one piece. Somehow. Those boys would make it happen yet.

The briskness of their pace served to lighten her mood even more, signaling that not only her previous despondency was lifting. Necalli had clearly welcomed the proposed change of activity, or rather inactivity, the opportunity to do something. As battered and exhausted as he looked, he was a doer, that boy.

Shyly, she side-glanced him, taking in the broadness of his shoulders and the muscled chest, clearly visible under the remnants of his torn muddied cloak that he still wore as though it was the expensive neat cotton garment it used to be, proudly and with a certain amount of chic. Not as tall as his friend, but so much better looking, with his cheekbones so prominent and his eyes so large and nicely spaced. Blushing, she took her gaze away. What was she thinking? Oh mighty Coatlicue, mother of all gods, but what silly thoughts those were!

Hastening her step, she waved at Ahuitzotl, motioning him to keep close. Another true rascal and a tough little thing. After the night in the lake, lost and terrified to death, all of them, a ten summers old should be downcast now, or at least frightened, huddling on the shore, asking for his mother; not seeking additional adventures that very well might hamper their rescue efforts, putting them in more trouble, maybe.

"Would you listen to this?" Necalli was shaking his head, frowning against the new outburst of shouting that erupted now much louder, with true zeal. "What are they doing out there?"

From behind the rustling bushes that grew sparser as they progressed, they could glimpse the shape of the towering pyramid, distant but impossible to miss. A smaller replica of Tenochtitlan's Great Pyramid, two temples and all. Tlatelolco's island was of about the same size, tracing it roots back to the same beginning the Mexica Aztecs of Tenochtitlan brandished, so close that it was sometimes considered to be just an extension of Tenochtitlan's main island. Yet there, the similarities ended. Tlatelolco did not participate in the war against the Tepanecs and it had not flourished ever since. It tried very hard to keep up, but in Tenochtitlan's shadow, nothing could thrive, or so Father would say. Tenochtitlan was the capital of the world, with provinces aplenty, ruling huge parts of the mainland, building lavishly, conquering wide. Still, the neighboring island tried to emulate whatever they could, like replicating the shape of the main pyramid or making the local ruler behave as though he wasn't accountable to anyone but the gods.

"There are plenty of canoes massed out there in the water," reported Ahuitzotl excitedly, coming back on the run, spilling down the mild incline they were ascending, having rushed back and forth, unable to just walk. "And I mean *plenty*. Twenties by twenties!"

Necalli hastened his step, forcing them to break into a near run. But was it hard to keep up with him! And he didn't even turn his head to make sure she was still near and hadn't fallen behind. Chantli pressed her lips tight. Why should she care about something like that? At this point, all she needed was to return home, in one piece and unharmed, punished not too badly preferably. But what would Father or Mother do to her? She had never absented herself from home for longer than an occasional evening, plenty of unauthorized running around but always in small amounts, not very noticeable. Yet this time, oh mighty deities, this time, she would be done for, that much was certain. And she must have looked dreadful too after all they had been through, not pretty and not attractive, despite the boy Ahuitzotl's claim. Involuntarily, her hands strayed to her hair, trying to smooth down the tousled braids.

"What's wrong?" The smaller boy was peering at her, his wide forehead puckered with too many creases.

"Nothing!" Now she felt her cheeks washing with a hot wave as well. Bother this! But why didn't the little rascal do something useful, like running ahead again?

"Are there people in those boats?" Necalli was asking. "How many?"

The boy shook his head vigorously, his yet uncut hair jumping high. "No people. They are empty, those boats." His eyes sparkled. "We can take one."

Necalli's teeth were out again, chewing his lower lip, making a mess out of it. "With all the commotion out there in the city, and the shores being abandoned like that..." he muttered, shaking his head with an obvious doubt. "Something is wrong here."

As though eager to reinforce his suspicion, the distant noises erupted anew, the clamor of too many throats shouting at once.

"There are no ceremonies to be held until the end of this moon. Are there?"

The boy Ahuitzotl shrugged, unperturbed. "Maybe they are celebrating something."

"Like what?" Necalli made a face. "It has to be something royal to have people of this city to gather on the Central Plaza and scream like the World of the Fifth Sun is about to end." He wrinkled his nose. "Not to mention this multitude of boats of yours."

"We can sneak to their Plaza and see what it is all about."

"Start with sneaking back to these boats and see what's with those."

Ahuitzotl's face began molding into a familiar expression of utter stubbornness, eyes narrowing into slits, lips a thin line to match.

"We need to get one of these boats and fast," interrupted Chantli hurriedly, anxious to stop yet another verbally violent exchange. "Patli needs help and so does Axolin. And you too." She glanced at the arm Necalli was once again holding awkwardly, wrapped in the supportive grip of his good hand. "If we can take one of the boats..."

"Yes, that's what I've been saying." The *calmecac* boy snorted impatiently. "Why do you argue all the time?"

She gasped at this unexpected attack. "I'm not arguing with you. I'm saying what needs to be done." But what an annoying thing this boy was! "You are the one angry all the time."

Ahuitzotl snickered, then hastened his step, eager to reach the top of the incline before they did. Against her will, Chantli chuckled. The little rascal was not about to let them take the credit for his discovery. Which, indeed, was impressive, she saw, hastening her step in her turn, determined to bypass both of her companions and not to just follow. That would be giving too much honor to their dominant would-be leader. Fancy flaring at her like that!

"See? I told you!" Ahuitzotl's voice trailed behind him as the boy broke into a run again, down the incline this time, waiting for no followers or reinforcements.

"Wait!" Shielding his eyes with his hand, Necalli scanned the view of the twisting marshland, looking perturbed. The boats, indeed, seemed to be amassed in twenties upon twenties, tucked in an artificially made inlet most of them, but some adorning the shallow shoreline, splashing in the thick reeds, surrounded by waterfowl wandering all around, the rest of the marsh teeming with heron and ducks. "There are people there. One can see that most clearly."

"Where?" She shielded her eyes in her turn. The boats closer to the marshes seemed to be swaying lazily, with no one to supervise or make use of them. "Why aren't they out there fishing?"

He shrugged. "Has to do with all the yelling and screaming in the city, I bet. We picked a bad day to flounder all over these shores." Another shrug. "Or maybe not. If we can pinch one of these vessels without being caught doing this... and if we managed to navigate it back where we left the others..." His frown flickered with helplessness, relating the depth of his exhaustion. "But we won't be piling there in a stupid heap. I'll be taking you back by the way of the causeway, when we manage to find it."

Her stomach squeezed painfully, constricting as though she had eaten something bad. "I've yet to thank you for what you did back there in the lake," she muttered, hardly recognizing her own voice, so low and throaty it sounded. "I... you saved me, and I –"

She could feel him tensing by her side. "It was nothing," he murmured, eyes firmly upon the view of the spreading shore but not shielded anymore, not trying to focus.

"No, it wasn't." She paid his gallant protests no attention, suddenly needing to talk about it, to say it, the memories vivid, overwhelming, threatening. "I would have drowned. I know I would have. It was so scary! That darkness and nowhere to go. Not even sounds... just water. I was so terrified, and I couldn't even breathe and that boat, it was everywhere. It *wanted* to have me drown!" Pressing her arms around herself didn't help. The tremors were bad, and the trembling of her voice, climbing to shrill heights. "I didn't... I was so scared!"

When his palm touched her arm, warily, unsure of itself, she shuddered but didn't move until it slid up to rest on her shoulder, squeezing it lightly, hesitantly. It banished some of the desperate fright, just the edge of it, but enough to make her feel better, capable of dealing with the terrible memory.

Afraid that the good feeling would disperse, she shifted involuntarily, leaning against his warmth, needing it. For a heartbeat, nothing happened. He didn't move away, but she could feel him freezing, holding his breath. Then, hesitantly, his arm wrapped around her with surprising assertiveness, pressing strongly, with firm resolution. Heartened, she let it pull her closer, guide her toward the safety of his chest, to snuggle there and feel safe, at long last. The most glorious feeling. Oh, but now she could cope with it all, the memory of the darkness and the muddy water and the terrible bottomless fear, and the ordeals that were still ahead; the need to steal a new boat, the necessity to enter it as, despite his promises to take her across the causeway, she could not let them take the responsibility of rescuing her cousin all by themselves, the prospect of facing her father and the depth of his rage – but what would Father do? – all these weren't so scary, possible to deal with as long as he was there, next to her and ready to help. Inside his warmth, it felt as though she could deal with those challenges.

His heart was beating strangely, very strong, very fast.

Listening to its tempo, she felt the calmness dispersing once again. But what were they doing, snuggling here like that, on the top of the incline and at the mercy of every wandering gaze, at the place they weren't supposed to be in the first place? And above it all, what did it mean, this incredibly good feeling and the wish to stay in his arms, or even to sneak her own around his torso, to press closer, to do... what? His body was tense against hers, not cozy or relaxed, not like before.

"We must... we..." His struggle with words made her senses come back to order and she slipped away hastily, embarrassed to no end.

"Yes, we must..."

To their left, a commotion was growing, drawing their attention from their private embarrassment, welcomed in its timing. Down the incline, many of the boats were moving now, sliding between the reeds, rowing around but in a strange fashion, as though not eager to leave the shoreline but rather to wander about, with no aim and no purpose. Fascinated, she followed the agitated fluttering of the spooked waterfowl with her gaze, a multitude of ducks, wild geese, heron, and other winged hunters of fish scattering frantically, frightened into a hasty flight.

"What are they doing?"

"Fishing, I suppose." Her companion was studying the unfolding show with his eyes narrowed, fitting well in the broadness of his face, above the sharpness of his well-defined cheekbones. So handsome! She felt her own cheeks beginning to burn.

To concentrate on the silliness of his words helped. "Fishing? One doesn't fish in the reeds. What would they pull from this marsh besides frogs and *axolotl*-salamanders? And one doesn't need a canoe to do that."

He shrugged, not impressed. "You don't want to wander in those reeds with no special reason, believe me on that. Frogs and *axolotls* or not. I have this arm to prove the inadvisability of such roaming around those marshes." As though succumbing to a weakness, his eyes slid toward the angry mess of his limb, lingering there for a heartbeat, his face contorting momentarily, the wide lips pressing grimly, determine to dominate… what? His fear? Exhaustion? Both?

Without thinking, she reached out, touching his bare upper arm with the tips of her fingers, caressing it lightly, giving off her warmth. It was unsettling to see him like this, always so dominant and decisive, spilling instructions and orders, making it all work. Unsettling yes, yet pleasing too, making her feel powerful in some unknown, indecipherable way. A thrilling sensation.

"It's all going to be well, you know? Your arm will heal and we all will return home, and everything will go back to what it was." She pressed her fingers lightly, enjoying the new sensation. "You'll see."

He nodded stiffly, still staring at his wounded arm, but with less desperation than before, deep in thought.

"What are you thinking?"

His grin flashed briefly, accompanied with a flicker of amusement. Not nearly enough but more than she counted on to achieve. "I think that you are not like the other girls."

Her stomach squeezed. "Why?"

He shrugged again, his grin spreading, one side of his mouth climbing up faster than the other. "I don't know. You tell me. Are all commoner girls like that?"

"Like what?" That 'commoners' bit was annoying, taking the edge off her excitement.

His grin widened. "Brave. Argumentative. Giving measure for measure." A light frown appeared, shadowing his grin, but only a little; not a grim frown but a mischievous one, playfully mocking. It made him look impossibly boyish, no better than Ahuitzotl. "Running around like boys, speaking out, doing what they like…" The mocking spark intensified. "Knowing things about fishing…"

She pulled her hand away. "I'm not like that at all!"

"Yes you are." His beam was one of the widest, shadowed by no more misgivings or fears. Was it worthwhile pulling him out of his previous despondency? Suddenly, she wasn't so sure. "Even now, I don't know what you will do. Scream or hit or curse or just sulk and make faces."

She was pondering all those possibilities and worse, and his seeing through her so easily didn't help. "I'll do none of that," she said with as much dignity as she could muster. "I'll go and look for Ahuitzotl and I will not run around with you anymore, ever. Find yourself a noble girl for your next adventure."

He made a face, his grin retreating, disappearing rapidly. "We did well enough with no girls in our adventures, I and Axolin. We'll be all right." A curt shrug had an offended quality to it. "You can enjoy your precious royal *pilli*'s company all you like, as far as I'm concerned."

"Fine!" She tossed her head high.

Turning away and beginning to storm down the grass-covered incline, made her feel better. What an annoyingly arrogant piece of rotten fish this boy was, talking about her like that, and to her face, of all things! Just who did he think he was to imply that she was behaving like boys and not like respectable girls from his noble parts of the city? As though a girl couldn't come along if she wanted to. Admittedly, Mother had carried on and on about this same thing, for days on end recently, carping on feminine duties and responsibilities and appropriate behavior, but it wasn't as though she behaved inappropriately, did she? Or at least, not too inappropriately. She did her duties, spun maguey threads and weaved enough material to keep Mother happy, and helped with cooking and cleaning when their only servant was busy at the market or on various other errands, or when Father needed to clean the workshop.

A longing for home twisted her heart. Oh, but they must be truly furious now. Or maybe terribly worried. She had worried all day when Miztli didn't come home, and now she had been missing for the same amount of time, if not worse? And Patli too. Oh mighty deities, but they must be worried sick!

"Oh no! What's that little brat up to now?"

Necalli's exclamation jerked her from her unhappy reverie. Coming from some distance – but was he anxious to make his point by going separately, even if heading in the same direction! – it drew her attention against her will, his eyes wide open and incredulous, his hand up and pointing, indicating a smallish figure that was making its way among the nearest cluster of reeds, creeping in an unmistakable fashion.

"He is going to try and snatch one of the canoes! Stupid rodent. He'll never make it."

The cluster of boats he pointed at looked, indeed, somewhat removed, seemingly unattended, just a few vessels tied together, swaying in the shallow ripples. Yet from their elevated position, it was easy to see that some fishermen were heading their way, following the twisted shoreline or wading through the reeds, waving their hands agitatedly, spooking more of the waterfowl, plenty of those. Why?

From the other side of the incline and their previous vantage point that they had abandoned without much thinking, the clamor was growing by the moment, turning into a roaring wave. A large body of people, unmistakable now. Interweaving with the wild flapping of too many wings and their owners' agitated outcries, it created such tumult as though the entire world had gone mad or was shattering. Was this how the previous four worlds ended? The question did cross Chantli's mind as she stopped dead in her tracks, her heart beating fast, threatening to jump out of her chest. *What was happening?*

Closing the distance in one powerful leap, Necalli was already hovering next to her, looking like a spooked animal himself, all ears and senses, ready to pounce or flee, or do both. It made her taut nerves relax, if only a little. This boy would know what to do. For good measure, she pressed closer.

The first wave of running people appeared at the top of the incline opposite to the one they had just left, coloring the brightness of the skyline in too vivid a celebration of colors. Their cloaks swaying, oiled buns of hair glittering, faces red and glistening with sweat and maybe remnants of the paint, the men, clearly warriors, spilled toward the shore, partly charging, partly rolling down the incline, a lethal radiant wave.

Eyes glued to the terrible wave, she watched in a numb stupor, noting that not everyone was surging down the incline, eager to storm the lake. Some halted on the top of the incline, clearly about to use its good vantage point. To do what? The long pieces of woven material looked dangerous in their hands, twirling like vicious snakes. The rest kept running, their spears and other menacing-looking devices balanced easily in their hands, swaying deftly, ready to attack.

In another heartbeat, Necalli's hand was locked around her elbow, pulling her firmly, making her sway. "There! Run down there!" he yelled. "Back... back where we came from!"

Struggling to break free, uncomfortable with him half dragging, half pulling her along, she tried to make her mind work. What was happening? His idea of getting out of the lethal wave's reach was good, oh yes. But why were these people charging? The warriors, oh mighty deities, but what did this mean? Above their heads and to their left, the air was swishing, buzzing with flying objects, hissing dangerously.

"Here!"

Again Necalli's hand was yanking her sideways, pulling behind a small bluff, nothing but a cluster of rocks laid there by someone, for whatever purpose, where some of the canoes were still wavering, still unattended. Where was Ahuitzotl? Behind their backs, the lake churned with the desperate flapping and screeching of the falling birds, twenties upon twenties of those, tumbling into the water, making it froth.

"What is happening?"

He was already back on his feet, bent but ready to lunge. "Stay here!"

"No! I'll come with you!" Relatively safe or not, she wasn't about to remain alone in a world that made no sense anymore. Whatever was happening here in this neighboring island city, it was wild and...

In another heartbeat, an additional commotion erupted from behind the reeds, where they had spotted their royal companion slinking away in the fashion of a marketplace thief. Furious plopping of several feet or paddles, accompanied by shouts and the already familiar flapping of wings and crowing and cackling of the spooked birds made them dive behind their meager means of cover, their hearts thumping.

Flying missiles filled the sky again, like a flock of pouncing birds of prey, plunging into the lake or raining around them in a lethal outpour, a terrible rain. Covering her head, out of an instinct rather than as a thoughtful reaction, Chantli whimpered, frightened for real. But it was a nightmare! The yowling of the hurt fowl, another thing to rain on them now, made her blood freeze. Such a terrible sound.

When it seemed to lessen, she didn't want to uncoil, but Necalli was already back on his feet, dragging her up, his forehead scratched, eyes wild.

"Did, did y-you…" She tried to make her lips work, her tongue as heavy as a slab of stone, refusing to be moved. "Wh-what…"

People were running toward them, quite a large group, their loincloths soaked, their feet covered with mud.

"What are you doing here, you stupid halfwits?" someone yelled. "Go away from here, go!"

Their hands clutched sticks, or maybe those were paddles, she noticed, again too numb to react. Or maybe clubs. She couldn't tell for certain, unable to see properly, Necalli's wide shoulders blocking some of her view, getting between her and the approaching fishermen, comforting. Heartened, she peeked out carefully just as another wave of running feet began to reach them from the opposite direction. Sandaled feet this time, her instincts told her, not barefoot commoners like the fishermen who were very close now, clearly visible, sweat-covered and upset.

"What is going on?" Necalli shouted, cupping his hands around his mouth to be heard better. "What are you doing here?"

"Go away!" was the shouted response.

From another part of the twisting shore, a new bout of shooting could be heard most clearly, this same dangerous droning. Her eyes swept along the bumpy earth, taking in the round objects that dotted it, smooth glittering balls the size of a bird's egg, glassy and inviting to touch. Quickly, she picked one up. It felt good in her hand, fitting.

"What is it?"

Necalli was looking in the direction of the shooting, shielding his eyes. "Those are clay missiles," he muttered, not taking his gaze away. "From their slings. They are shooting waterfowl with it, hunting it." His face twisted in a familiar half-mocking grimace.

"Don't ask me why they do that. This Tlatelolcan stupidity is beyond me."

The fishermen were already busy picking up the fallen birds, collecting the warm, dripping, sometimes still-fluttering corpses and the clay missiles that took them, tugging at an occasional arrow or even a spear. But what was this strange event all about? Why were Tlatelolco warriors hunting the local birds and why in such quantities?

Quite a few warriors were descending the incline as well, some arrogant and high-bearing, strolling ahead, others in an obvious hurry. She could feel Necalli muttering to himself, again tense and ill at ease but unable not to comment. Were those warriors anxious to retrieve their weaponry or were they eager to inspect their catch, to make sure no one claimed their achievements? Somehow, she knew the answer to that.

"Come." Necalli's hand pulled her back toward the shore and away from the nearing warriors, obviously preferring the fisherman to the unasked-for encounter with authorities of the city they weren't supposed to be touring as of now.

At this very moment, another commotion, this time in the lake itself, erupted in an outburst of indignant shouts and some frantically vigorous plopping that sounded like paddling. A faltering canoe was zigzagging its way, trying to break clear of the encasing reeds and the dead and wounded poultry fluttering among those, crowing and cackling. So much noise!

The knot in her stomach tightened anew. No, there could be no mistake of the cloaked figure perching in its midst, wielding the longish pole awkwardly, with notable lack of skill. She knew who it was before her dismayed eyes confirmed the assumption.

The fishermen were clearly yelling, three of them wallowing in the shallow water, aiming to reach the floundering vessel while still on foot. Not a difficult feat, she reflected, breaking into a run herself, not thinking any of it through.

All around and further up the incline and along the shore, people were wandering, simple crowds and warriors mixed in an atypical fashion, talking excitedly, picking their missiles and sometimes their catch, comparing or maybe arguing about it – it was easy to recognize *that* body language. Further up, on the clearer and comfortably elevated ground, with the distant silhouette of the Great Pyramid disclosing the presence of the city not very far away, clusters of litters huddled together, with cloaked figures strolling around those, keeping the crowds away. The watching nobility? But what *was* this event?

She paid those questions little heed, concerned with the slippery ground under her feet and the only important question looming above it all – what to do? How to help Ahuitzotl to get away with the stolen property, or at least not to end up dragged to a court, accused of as grave a charge as a proven theft. She had seen enough marketplace courts in session to know how hard the judges would go on thieves in particular, the most abominable crime of them all.

Sliding down the slippery pebbles, she saw one of the chasers reaching the faltering boat, himself chest-deep in the water but not giving up, attempting to grab its wavering side. The next thing she saw was the cumbersomely long paddle striking out, colliding against the man's chest, pushing him away deftly, with surprising skill. The act not only put the stolen canoe out of the grabbing hand's reach but also gave it a push into a desirable direction. She felt like cheering the wild rascal. But that boy was good!

"Don't shoot!" The shouting broke behind her back, not very far, jerking her off her temporary cloud of triumphant glowing. Yelled in a familiar voice, it made her heart lose its tempo. "Wait, wait! Don't shoot!"

Necalli's disheveled silhouette, outlined clearly against the blinding midday sun, was jumping up and down, his hands waving wildly, desperately, as though trying to attract the attention of the warriors further up the incline, a few of whom strolled toward their part of the shore and the minor commotion upsetting it. One of the warriors slowed his pace and was messing with the wide leather strap he held expertly in one hand, the other busy fitting a familiar-looking round ball into it, working with thorough competence. Another of his peers was scanning the ground, his strap of leather as ready and as eager, but missing a missile probably, something the earth offered in great quantities in this particular place.

"Don't shoot!"

She watched Necalli break into a run, looking grotesque in his torn, wrinkled cloak, his hair sticking everywhere, one arm swollen, his other hand holding it awkwardly, pressing to his chest, his gait the only self-assured trait but even this not perfectly even, having a panicked quality to it, indecently hurried. Not a vision of a proud, good-naturedly arrogant *calmecac* pupil – anything but.

The man searching the ground straightened up, triumphant. A quick exchange and the other warrior, who had already stood very upright, legs wide apart, narrowed his eyes against the occurrence in the water, in the direction of the stolen canoe, his sling up and ready, relaxed a little. Another quick exchange, a new outburst of laughter, a wandering glance at the running Necalli.

Then it dawned upon her and she broke into as wild a run as that of her companion, oblivious of the slippery ground and the way the nearby bushes flogged her legs, as though trying to stop her. Now she knew why Necalli was so upset, what was so important about two warriors with their lethal slings out and ready, about to engage in one more competition, not on the flying fowl this time. Ahuitzotl! They were going to shoot the thief down!

By the time she could hear their words, Necalli was already in front of them, blocking their view, breathing heavily, talking in a rush.

"Move away, boy!" One of the warriors pushed the intruder rudely, not attempting to be polite. But of course! They were warriors, above everyone but the royal family and the Palace's dwellers. What was Necalli thinking?

Apparently, nothing good. Caught by surprise, it seemed, he wavered, struggling not to lose his balance, waving his bad arm clumsily in order to make it happen. By the time she halted beside them, he was still in their way, glowing worse than a brazier in the melting room.

"You are asking for a good beating, boy, aren't you?" The

second slinger, a squat heavyset man of not such a young age, raised his leather strap with clear meaning. Necalli didn't stir, staring at his assailant, only his eyes alive and blazing out of the stony mask.

She didn't wait for him to continue. "Wait, please!"

To say that and not to take a step back, or quite a few steps, actually, took almost all of her courage, but she didn't move either when the incredulous gazes leapt at her, both men turning to stare, their expression wavering between an open amusement and a direful indignation, undecided. It was easy to see how upset one of them was as he moved into her view promptly, curiosity-consumed.

"What's with the stupid cubs popping up on us like pieces of wood in the lake?" The laughter of the first warrior did not reflect the fury of his companion. "Go away, you wild things. Go back to the crowds up there."

"You can't shoot that boy in the boat," repeated Necalli firmly, sweat glittering upon his forehead, accumulating in his pointy eyebrows. He blinked it away forcefully. "He is an important *pilli* of the royal family. If you shoot him, you will be executed." His chin jutted firmly. "And so will your families."

The second man regarded him grimly. "Stop talking nonsense and go away. The royal family is out there, crowding the dais and the litters."

But the first man shielded his eyes against the fierceness of the sun, his words nothing but a menacing growl. "They caught him already. But for the stupid cubs!" His hand raised again, swift and decisively heavy, but this time, she saw Necalli ducking and the slap that might have pushed him off his feet with the power of it brushed against the side of his disheveled topknot, harmless. "You filthy cub!"

As Necalli's assailant groped for his shoulder, with the clear intention of doing better with his fists this time, Chantli felt her heart coming to a halt.

"No, please wait! You don't understand. He speaks the truth, he does! That boy out there, you should let him go. He is very important. You can't harm him. It will harm you if you do. Please,

you must listen to him, please! Necalli is the best student in his
calmecac; he isn't lying."

The second man still looked as though not about to give up on
violence as a means of venting his frustrations, knowing what his
rights were, yet his companion frowned soberly, his narrowed
gaze sliding down the *calmecac* boy's battered body, clearly taking
in the patterns of the torn cotton cloak. His eyebrows knitted into
nearly a single line.

"What are you doing here and why in such state, boy?"

Necalli's face turned stonier, even though it was anything but
relaxed before. "We... we got lost in the lake waters, under the old
causeway." His tongue came out briefly, licking the cracked lips.
"I... I know it's not something we should have been doing. In
calmecac, we'll receive the deserved punishment and," another lick
of the colorless lips, "and we won't seek adventures again."

"Who are these 'we'?"

"I and that boy out there in the boat," he said readily, too
readily. She saw the eyes of their interrogators narrowing again,
the other warriors nearing, dragging the resisting Ahuitzotl along.
"He was trying, trying to help us return back to school."

"There are no lessons in schools today!" exclaimed the second
man, grabbing Necalli by his upper arm, squeezing hard. She saw
the boy's lips pressing tighter, losing the last of their coloring.
"You are lying to us, you filthy piece of human excrement. And
what's with the girl?" The furious eyes leaped to her, piercing.
"What are you not telling us?"

"He tells the truth, all of it!" she cried out, pressing her hands
to her chest, her stomach twisting. "Please. You must believe us.
We just want to... to go back home, and we won't, won't come
here again, won't cross the old causeway –"

"You what?" The first man's eyes grew so wide they turned
almost round. "You came from Tenochtitlan? You... you are
Tenochtitlan *pillis*?"

She tried to think of something to say, her heart making
strange leaps inside her chest, informing her that something went
wrong, terribly wrong. She had said something that shouldn't
have been said. But what?

Necalli thrust his chin yet higher. "Yes, we are," he said proudly, his haughty *calmecac* self again, this time welcomed most eagerly. "We are of noble families, and to be treated as such."

The warriors exchanged openly contemplative glances. "Tenochtitlan noble cubs, eh? Running around the right place at the right time..."

"Have been to the Plaza and the morning competition as well, I bet. Have you?" The second man thrust his face closer, threatening again.

"No, we haven't been to the Plaza," she heard Necalli saying, his voice surprisingly calm but strident, having a lower tone to it. "As I said, we came upon this shore by mistake. We have –"

"Save your breath, boy." The heavyset man shook his prisoner hard. "Tell your tales to the noble persons who'll be asking you questions. Then you'll have plenty of opportunities to talk, more than you might wish to." The wide lips pressed tighter. "The Head Adviser will wish to see them, won't he?"

His companion just shrugged, then turned his head in the direction of the heated protests that exuded from the group of the ascending warriors, heralding the reappearance of their royal company in the worst timing ever. Numb again, Chantli turned to stare.

Pressed between two sturdy-looking men, partly dragged, partly carried, Ahuitzotl was kicking viciously whichever way, his red-hot harangue spilling twenty words for a heartbeat, each expletive more colorful than the previous one.

"A high-spirited beast." The leading man among the newcomers frowned. "What to do with him? Take him to the judge of the nearest district?"

Their captors exchanged quick glances, their eyes narrowing against Ahuitzotl's wrinkled but still perfectly whole cloak, the richness of its embroidery peeking from behind the generous cover of mud, the turquoise of his sandals' straps glittering, undamaged by their nighttime adventures.

"Who are you, boy?" After another exchange of glances, Chantli's captor released his grip on her arm, letting it drop with pronounced contempt, unimpressed with her maguey garments, barely there by now, her best *huipil* a dirty rag from under which the edges of her skirt hung in torn, muddied shreds. A sight, but the one that clearly put her off the suspected list, at least for the moment.

"I'm the Emperor's brother and when Axayacatl hears what transpired here, he will level this entire city and make a huge marketplace out of it!"

The newcomers rolled their eyes, having probably heard worse promises while dragging their prey out of the lake, but Necalli's captor's eyes widened again, with much apprehension.

"Which brother are you, boy? What is your name?"

"Ahuitzotl!" spat the boy with such fury, even Chantli felt like stepping aside and away. His eyes glowed like a pair of coals. "And if you don't let us all go now, I promise you that Tenochtitlan will make your pitiful island sink under the water and he will never let you as much as take your own lives when you beg us to let you do that."

More spirited harangue flowed like a river of fire, like a melted copper when it has been kept in an impossibly hot brazier for longer than half a day. People were heading their way, groups of younger warriors and other well-dressed folk, while the rest just spilled all around, raising the commotion to impossible heights.

Among all this, she felt a palm brushing by her side, drawing her attention back to Necalli.

"Run," he breathed into her ear, leaning as close as the grip of his captor allowed him. "Run for the shore and hide there. Find Axolin. Do it now, before they remember." His eyes glimmered steadily, relaying no fear, giving her power. "Now!" Another fraction of a heartbeat and he motioned with his head, a light imperceptible movement. *Go*, his eyes told her, *go and get help*.

She didn't think it all through. An opening to her left beckoned, the warriors' attention on the combative royal boy undivided. As though all lowlifes of the Underworld were after her, she bolted toward the trampled-on grass, its brown and green glowing in the strong high noon sun, slippery and full of pits.

Putting it all into this concentrated attempt, she skirted around the multitude of obstacles, people standing or strolling, waving their hands, talking agitatedly. So many warriors! Difficult to clear one's way in such a commotion, difficult to tell if she was being chased.

Not looking around, she pressed on, panicked, not knowing where she was heading. Away from their captors. To get help! What help? Who would help them? Limping Axolin or barely conscious Patli with his bleeding head? But maybe they'd know what to do. She had to find them and tell them.

An upward tilt in the ground sweeping under her feet and a quick glance around told her that she had been heading in the wrong direction. No more damp grass made her feet struggle against the slippery surface. Now it was the dusty pavement, the cracking stones, warm and pleasant to the touch on her partly bare skin, her sandals flopping, threatening to fall off. People were crowding all around even worse than down there by the shore, staring at her; well dressed, good-looking people, no marketplace scum. She tried to make her mind work, her breath coming in gasps, head reeling. But she needed to get away from these crowds! Then she'd manage to find her way back to the shore, the one where Axolin and Patli were loitering. Why couldn't they sense her predicament and come out and help?

Just as she felt that her heart was going to burst if she didn't stop, bouncing off yet another blurry form, the passerby's exclamations loud and full of indignation, a low wall loomed ahead, blocking her way. Blinking, she tried to see her way past it, unable to go, doubling over to catch her breath, not worried about her possible chasers, not anymore. Let them catch her and drag her wherever they wanted. It was hopeless anyway. No one would help them, no one would come to their rescue. Unless she managed to find the causeway, to cross to Tenochtitlan maybe, run to her father and brothers and beg them to help. Would they agree?

The tears were near now, not tears of exhaustion but of sadness and fear. She wouldn't be in time to help Necalli or Ahuitzotl. They would die like the village boy, that nice closemouthed Miztli, such a welcome addition to their household, and such a short one. She wasn't in time to bring help, and his blood sprinkled that old temple's floor back in Tenochtitlan, and she would be as late for the others. Useless and late and of no help, and…

"Chantli?"

The loudness of the outcry made her look up, not encouraged and not curious but just startled. From behind the polished stones of the wall, a face peeked out, peering at her with intensity.

Recognizing the familiar wide, well-pronounced features – did she bring the village boy back here with the mere power of her thinking? – she gasped, blinking to make her vision clear. He didn't look like an apparition, a ghost from the Underworld, dead for more than a day now. Ghosts didn't sport cuts and bruises, and his face was dotted with them, colorful and pale at the same time. Also, his eyes were wild and too widely opened, as though in shock. But was it possible to surprise a ghost in this way?

Before she could say something, try to reason or ask questions, he grabbed her upper arm forcefully, pulling her into the dimness behind the wall's opening, again unseemly determined and sure of his actions. Disoriented, she tried to make sense out of it, still out of breath and reeling.

"Chantli, what are you doing here?" he gasped, barely visible now in the dimness of the strange low-roofed building, nothing but a shadow, but there.

Yet as her eyes grew accustomed to the meagerness of this new illumination, she could see that they weren't alone. A girl of about her age, or probably younger, judging by the angularity of her limbs, was staring at her, her scowl well pronounced.

"Who is this?" the strange fowl was asking, a grudge in her voice, like that of a petulant child, impossible to miss. "Who is this girl and how do you know her?"

He was frowning painfully, blinking as though trying to make his mind work.

"This is Chantli," he said slowly, chewing his lower lip. "She… she is the best girl in the World of the Fifth Sun."

And that made it all right again.

CHAPTER 17

To see Chantli racing up that narrow side alley made Miztli's head reel, even though, in some way, it fit the bizarreness of this entire day. Combined with the previous night, it should have left him immune to surprises. Still, when he had seen her dashing up the dusty cobblestones, out of breath and clearly in a panic, he wanted to pinch himself in order to make sure he wasn't dreaming.

Even now, with her calming gradually, looking less like a cornered animal in the tranquility of yet another cozily hidden hideaway his forceful Tlatelolcan new companion called Tlemilli – or just Milli, as she was quick to inform him in her decisive hurriedly chatty way – had found despite her claim that she had never been so far out in the city before, he still felt as though he might have imagined her, having finally gone mad on account of the wild happenings.

"What... what is going on?" he asked her again, deciding to treat this new puzzlement in the same vein of placidness no matter how wild or unreasonable – the lasting lesson of the previous night and the day. "Whom were you running from?"

Her gaze flickered with a renewed bout of panic. "Oh, the warriors... out there on the shore... oh, you wouldn't believe, they were so, so scary!" Wide open, her eyes clung to him, imploring. "You must help them! Necalli and Ahuitzotl. You must help them. You must... Now that you are here and alive, and in good shape, and not wounded... Are you?" Her gaze darted wildly, scrutinizing him, widening upon reaching his feet, turning astounded.

His sandals, he knew, that most uncomfortable piece of

clothing, something he would have gotten rid of but for the girl Tlemilli. She would be shocked, wouldn't she? But for her, he would have kicked off the stupid pieces of leather readily, their maguey strings wrapped around his ankles, rubbing his skin into sores, trying to slip off for good, the layered soles flapping uncomfortably, hindering his step.

However, as long as she had hurried beside him, trying to show him the way to the shore ahead of the rest of the crowds, herself clad in glaringly expensive garments, colorful and crisp, as though never worn before, all the splendor of softest cotton and expensive embroidery, it felt wrong to get rid of the uncomfortable but necessary wear, something that set him apart from the worst of the commoners apparently. Her own sandals' straps sparkled with green stones and their leather soles reached over her heel, he had noticed with envy, covering it up to her ankle and higher, supporting well, as it seemed, making the walk easier, more convenient. Was that why she displayed no signs of discomfort, hopping beside him with such obvious enjoyment, radiant and more glowing and chatty even than back under the dais of the plaza.

"Why are you dressed like this? What happened to you?" Chantli's wrinkled forehead brought him back to the present, to this strange half crumbled construction that Tlemilli claimed would give them shelter for the time being, until they stopped shooting or made speeches about it. She did bring him to the shore, as she promised, but it was not the shore with the causeway attached to it. Apparently, she didn't know her way around her island town any better than he did, having never visited here before, a realization that had her fuming for some time. She clearly hoped to be more successful.

"Why don't you start by answering his questions?" she tossed at their new company now, her forehead creased, pointed eyebrows creating almost a single line above her angrily sparkling eyes. "He asked you first, you know. Why don't you answer him before bursting out with strange comments about his clothing and things?" A stormy gaze leaped at him, appraising him momentarily, returning to glower at Chantli. "He is dressed well enough. You are the one looking like a kitchen slave, all disheveled and smeared. You have no right to deride *his* clothing!"

Used to his Tlatelolcan companion's outspokenness by now, as much as to her way of saying whatever came to her mind, in quantities of half twenty words per heartbeat, Miztli fought his grin from showing. But she was something out of this world, and was she actually getting offended on his behalf? Amused, he watched the wideness of her forehead, now creased like a wrinkled blanket, a scowl sitting well with the sharpness of her features, enhancing the abrupt angles, making her face look like a mask chiseled out of stone, here in the semi-darkness of their shelter as much as back under the dais. In the brilliance of the daylight, the strangeness of her features was more prominent, unsettling rather than pleasing.

Chantli looked like a person who came down to draw water out of an innocent spring only to be confronted by a huge talking serpent, at the very least. Another unseemly sight. The fight against a nervous giggle became more difficult.

"What... what are you talking about?" she muttered in the end, blinking. "What... who are you?"

"I'm the person who saved him back there on the Plaza and I will not tolerate you talking to him nastily –" began Tlemilli hotly, but by this time, he managed to find his tongue, at long last.

"Wait, both of you. Chantli, tell me what happened! Why are you here and looking like that?" Her disheveled appearance was appalling, so unlike her, her *huipil* wrinkled and torn in places, muddied beyond recognition, her hair sticking out, face covered with streaks of mud, usually so fresh and tidy, the prettiest sight every morning and noon. "Tell me what happened! Who was after you?"

Her gaze leapt at him, eyes still wide but filling with an obvious relief. "I... I don't know. These people, the warriors, they got Necalli. Ahuitzotl tried to steal a boat and they were about to shoot him, so Necalli and I, we tried to stop them, and then, somehow, somehow they were grabbing him and when they heard that we came from Tenochtitlan, oh, they turned yet more unsettled and furious, and then," her voice was climbing to unpleasantly high tones, trembling badly, "then they got Ahuitzotl too, and I ran to get help." The huge eyes clung to him, unblinking. "You must help them to get away from these men. You must!"

"Who? Who are those men?" he mumbled, his mind unable to cope with this flood of information. Necalli, the *calmecac* boy? Was he here with her? Why? And Ahuitzotl! Wasn't this the royal family *pilli*, the boy whose name he produced on a spur of a moment, a most convenient memory, while being interrogated by Tenochtitlan's princess with a pretty name? He knew this *pilli*'s name thanks to Chantli, yes; she had been boasting her acquaintance with the royal offspring, relaying some of the Palace's gossip, hadn't she? "Who got them? Who are these men?"

She wrung her hands with an obvious desperation. "I don't know. They said this town's nobility would want to question them. The Head Adviser, they said."

This time, his involuntary gasp was backed by another. He glanced at Tlemilli briefly, surprised by her widening eyes but having no time to process it as well. What Chantli said was more unsettling. The Head Adviser? Teconal? The terrible man from the warehouse, the bejeweled noble upon the dais, the dignitary who sent the people who had knifed his abductor and were still after him? But for Tlemilli's timely interruption! The man who was obviously meddling in some intricate politics, angering Tenochtitlan's princess and the friendly nobles like that older man in the shed, talking about this same Teconal's daughter replacing... Another gasp came out on its own, and this time, his eyes darted toward the Tlatelolcan girl, his gaping mouth matching hers, of that he was sure. This same intimidating Teconal was her father as well!

"I... I don't understand," he mumbled, but Chantli was grabbing his hand with both of hers, pressing it urgently, with much desperation.

"You must help me find them and free them. You must!"

"Stop yelling!" This time, it was Tlemilli again, over her initial startle, apparently, and as furious with their intruder as in the beginning. "You'll bring this entire *altepetl* here. There is a reason why your savior is huddling here with me. But for me, the people who were after him would have gotten him long ago." The angry girl shook her head, talking as loudly as Chantli before, oblivious of her own demand. "Also, my father is not after you or your stupid friends. He has no interest in Tenochtitlan and its unruly youths running around, getting in trouble. So leave him alone and stop talking nonsense. He has enough troubles without you!"

But this time, Chantli turned to face her adversary with matching spirit and spitefulness. "You won't tell me how to talk to him, you slimy fowl. I will ask him whatever I like, and I will talk to him in any way I want, and you can go and jump into the lake if you don't like it." The enraged girl drew a deep breath. "I've known him for long enough, longer than you surely, to be allowed to talk to him when I want to, and I don't care how richly you dress and how important your father may be. You can stick your sparkling bracelets you know where! And your pretty sandals as well!"

At this point, Tlemilli was drawing such a long breath, Miztli was afraid she would faint from a mere lack of air. Her chiseled cheeks were definitely changing their coloring to something glaring and fiery.

He pushed himself between both furious girls. "Stop it, both of you. It's not the time, and anyway, you don't have to argue because of me. Those boys..." He turned to the panting Tlemilli, liking the sight of her smoldering eyes and the glowing face, like the braziers in the melting room, like the beautifully dangerous liquid of flaming copper mixed with gold. "Those boys, they are my friends and I will help them. We were in it together." The thought occurred to him, and he turned to Chantli, his stomach contorting in an uncompromising knot. "Did you come here because of that tunnel? You and Necalli. Did you find something there?"

Her eyes were still wild, darting from him to his extra-spirited company. "Yes," she said finally, nodding with atypical stiffness. "We went there looking for you when you didn't come back and, well, one thing led to another..." Her eyes narrowed toward

Tlemilli. "We thought you were in trouble, hurt, or killed, maybe. Not running around with Tlatelolcan would-be nobility."

The royal girl snorted loudly. "He chooses his company well, obviously."

"You came here looking for me?" he repeated, incredulous.

"Well, yes." Chantli's gaze softened reluctantly. "We were worried. You didn't come back and there was blood in that temple. Patli said all sorts of marks said that it might be yours, and Necalli argued. But then Ahuitzotl found your talisman. And then –"

This time, he gasped outright. "You found…" Again, his mind struggled with the incredibility of it all. "You found the obsidian… the obsidian…" The words refused to formulate. "You found… but how… how did you know? Where is it?"

She frowned, then dropped her gaze. "The obsidian puma, yes. Patli said it was your talisman. He said you carried it with you all the time." Her shrug was brief, full of uncertainty. "Ahuitzotl kept it. I hope he didn't lose it back in the lake or even now, when the warriors were fishing him out…" Her eyes lost their spark, filled with tears once again. "You have to help them! You have to do something!"

He pushed away the thoughts of the sacred figurine with much effort. "Where are they? Where did the warriors take them?"

She shrugged miserably.

"Where did you see them last? Where did it all happen?"

"Back on the shore, down there, behind that incline, where the reeds and the water birds are." She sniffed through her nose. "They killed plenty of birds, shot them with slings for some reason. It was scary. Those clay balls they shot, they were everywhere, falling from the sky. Necalli shielded us both and he was bleeding, his forehead…" Again, the convulsive breath turned her words into an incomprehensible flow. "He was… he was… brave…" Another loud snuffle. "Why would warriors shoot flying birds?"

"Because this is what they were supposed to do." Tlemilli's voice tore the dimness of the air, ringing tersely, reminding them of her presence. Poised next to the opening, half turned toward the outside, she regarded them with her eyes narrow and her head tossed very high. "Our warriors are the best warriors around the entire Great Lake and beyond it. They have shown their valor and skill today, taking off the stone statue with their slings, the wooden statue with their spears, and the soaring birds in their flight." Her shoulders jerked lightly, in open resentment, her eyes glancing at him, their reproach on display. "We would have seen it too but for your troubles and your need to hide." Another offended shrug. "As it was, I missed it all." Her chin thrust forward again in a familiar gesture. "I wish you well in your flight wherever you are heading and wherever you came from."

"Tlemilli!" Without thinking, he darted toward her, covering the crammed space with one leap, catching her thin wrist before she could bolt away. No, she wasn't bluffing, lingering there to be persuaded to return. Not her. Somehow, he knew it for certain. "Wait. Don't go."

She struggled to break free, yet not as fiercely as he expected, pulling her hand away, her nostrils widening with each taken breath.

"Listen!"

But what did he want to tell her? He searched through his mind frantically. Why did he want her to stay? To help them along? She was very helpful until now, there could be no argument about it. Overwhelmingly chatty and bubbling, unpredictable and as impulsive as no human being that he had known so far. She was something different; challenging but refreshing, reliable in her own wild way, solid and trustworthy, and somehow, he just didn't want her to leave and be gone.

"What do you want me to stay here for?" she pouted, turning her face away, studying the cracked wooden floor. "You don't need me. You have her now." A grudging half a nod indicated Chantli, gaping from her far corner, another unseemly sight.

He had no time to puzzle over this statement. What did Chantli have to do with any of it?

"Stay here, at least for a little while. Please." Curiously comfortable with doing this, he reached for her chin, pushing it up with his fingers, gently but firmly, making her face him, not about to take 'no' for an answer. "Stay!"

Her pointed eyebrows were nothing but a solid line, her high forehead creased like a wrinkled blanket; still, her eyes, which peered at him now, held nothing but expectation, a childlike anticipation, a touching hope. It made him feel strange.

His stomach hollow and quivering, he took his hand away, the sensation of her skin lingering upon his fingertips, not helping the confusion. She was so smooth to the touch, so pleasantly cool, like a mask made out of jade, slick and perfectly polished, not soft or tender but glossy and sharp-edged, yet more pleasing because of it. He fought the urge to touch her face again, if for no other reason than to verify the sensation. It was the strangest thing, wasn't it?

"Come with us and help us find those boys, will you?" he repeated more briskly than intended, his embarrassment difficult to hide. It came out as an outright demand. "You know places around here. You can find them faster than either of us."

"Oh well..."

One of her slim shoulders jerked, indicating the indefinite 'maybe,' so childish it made him wish to laugh in a hysterical manner. For a good measure, he moved away a pace, the wish to touch her face still strong, interfering with his ability to think reasonably.

"Yes, without me, you won't find anyone here, not in a hurry," she went on, the smug chattiness itself once again, speaking too many words in a heartbeat. "Those boys, your friends, who are they? What did they look like? Why did she say my father wanted to question them? It doesn't make any sense. My father has nothing to do with Tenochtitlan troublemaking boys. He has important matters to take care of." A dark glance shot at Chantli, who was still standing where she was, watching them through her eyes narrowed into slits, glimmering with professed defiance, challenging. "I don't believe my father would want to question those boys. But maybe the Emperor. They are from Tenochtitlan, you said?"

He paid the flooding of her words no attention. "Chantli, come. We'll sneak back to the shore and start looking from there. We'll be careful. Come."

She neared them warily, bestowing mistrustful glances on them both. Tlemilli answered that with her fiercest of glares. He pushed his way past them, too busy thinking to roll his eyes. But wouldn't he be better off trying to find the *calmecac* boy all by himself, without quarrelling girls to hinder his progress? He knew the answer to that.

"Where to?" he asked when the brilliance of the sunlight poured on them unrestrained, hot but so very welcome despite the possibility of exposure it brought along. The semi-darkness of the abandoned construction was depressing.

"The shore. Where else?" Tlemilli took the lead firmly, over her previous bout of uncertainty and back to her impulsively bossy self. "They must have stopped shooting by now. Or we would have heard and seen much of it." Excitedly, she pointed toward the cloudless sky. "Like back on the Plaza, eh? The sky went black from all those flying missiles."

"Yes." He remembered the orating ruler and the various noblemen and noblewomen upon the dais, the spearmen keeping the crowds away, the crushing grip of his captor's rock-hard fingers upon his arm. Shivering, he put the thought of that terrible nobleman Teconal away, the ruthless politician, the Head Adviser of the local ruler, involved in plenty of dubious enterprises no matter what the girl claimed. Oh, but did he remember the smugglers from the wharves, ruthless killers but groveling before this man, so very afraid of him! This head adviser must have readily available killers everywhere, prepared to do his bidding, on the wharves or among the crowds, where his kidnapper was knifed, or even in Tenochtitlan. But didn't they track him back there so easily and so fast?

He clenched his teeth tight, suppressing an involuntary shiver, suddenly cold in the fierce midday sun. One thing at a time. No one was chasing him as of now, but Chantli and the *calmecac* boy needed his help.

"There are different shores here," whispered Chantli, looking haunted, her furtive glances making him wish to bolt back toward their previous hiding place.

"Take us toward the one where you were caught."

People rushed past them, talking excitedly, crowding the alleys adjacent to the pebbled incline, waving baskets and bags. A few carried dripping corpses of water birds in their bare hands, swinging their catch or, rather, plunder proudly, happy with their prospective meals. Miztli could relate to that. But wouldn't it be nice to snatch one such thing for oneself? His stomach churned in reply.

"If they recognize me, I'm done for," declared Tlemilli all of a sudden, peering at the crowd next to the clearly improvised dais, the familiar gesticulating figure already posed upon its edge, waving its hands. The orating ruler! Shielding his eyes, he watched the warriors crowding the spacious square, the guarding spearmen mixed with the victorious contestants, easy to recognize by their shorter cloaks and spark of their jewelry.

"Are there more competitions expected to be held? More shooting or fighting?" His stomach turned once again at the mere thought.

"No, this shooting was the last thing." The wideness of her lips twisted in a mocking grimace. "Do you expect them to run back to the Plaza now, all smeared in mud and what-not, to crowd the pyramids and shoot at more statues?"

"I don't know what to expect from your people," he replied tersely, suddenly out of patience. "So far, I learned to expect anything unexpected."

Surprisingly, she took it well enough to giggle in response. "Yes, they can be that way. I keep expecting the unexpected too sometimes. Even from myself."

He could hear Chantli snorting softly, muttering to herself.

"We must go there and sniff around," he said, shrugging. "Blend with the crowds."

"Not her surely," offered Chantli, nodding toward their noble company quite reluctantly.

"Yes, I can! I can blend all I like." As expected, Tlemilli reared like a cloud snake from his home village, the ground-colored, striped, dangerous thing, raising its upper body high when surprised into attacking. "You will be the one sticking out like a torch in your stupid torn commoner clothes."

"And you will be sticking out with your stupid yelling and all the rest," retorted Chantli, as spirited and as venomous as her rival. "Why do we have drag around with her?" she demanded. "Why can't we go looking for Necalli and Ahuitzotl by ourselves?"

He had no answer to that, yet before he could say something non-committal, hoping that both girls did not plunge into a new row full of mutual insults and accusations, a roaring of the crowds they were heading toward caught their attention, making them lower their tones. The Emperor was still speaking, leaning forward, stretching his arms. Praising the warriors and their achievements, certainly. About to reward the best shooters again, like Tlemilli said he had promised. Well, he himself heard the orating ruler declare that.

Miztli made a face, then tried to see the elevated platform better. Who was behind the speaking noble? His regular entourage? He hoped this would be the case. Less dangerous to have that ominous Teconal up there and busy than sniffing around, interrogating Tenochtitlan intruders or sending killers to get rid of the ones he didn't manage to interrogate the night before.

"My brave warriors of Tlatelolco," thundered the gesturing ruler, so loudly he could be heard even on the edge of the crowds, his words muffled by the agitated whispers and talks but still there, vibrating quite clearly. "You have shown your valor and I have been pleased to see the skill and the spirit you possess in abundance. The best warriors of the entire valley of the Great Lake, even though our neighbors do not know it as yet. But they will." The arms spread once again, encompassing the listeners, making them shift alongside with the motion. Somehow, they were again surrounded by pressing people, and he had a hard time trying to shield both girls with his own arms and body, not to let them be crushed or jostled too badly.

"If one day, you find yourself waging a war to defend our beloved *altepetl*, you will know that the enemy's flesh is no stone, no wood to resist the strength of your spears. Even so, your intrepid arms broke the stone, tore the wood into splinters, your weapons superior, your strength and your determination more so."

The crowds were going wild with excitement, yelling and shoving, veering whichever way. Tlemilli cried out as a wide-shouldered fisherman, judging by the stench of his hair and his clothes, pushed himself past them, barreling his way in, shoving her aside as though she was nothing but a reed-woven doll, with no weight and no width whatsoever.

He caught her before she could crush into the packed figures to their right, then pressed her closer to his body, shielding. All angles and sharp edges, he still found himself enjoying the contact greatly, relishing the unfamiliar feeling, embarrassed by it. Even her elbow, jutting against his hurting ribs, was not something he would push away given a choice. Which wasn't offered them anyway. He tried to make sure Chantli did not disappear from the corner of his eye. Tlaquitoc's daughter seemed to be at ease and not afraid, elbowing her way in and out with no additional thought; still, he felt responsible for her wellbeing as well. She had come all the way from Tenochtitlan, trying to find and save him. She and the *calmecac* boy. Oh, but they were so good to him, so incredibly kind, so trustworthy!

"My brave people of Tlatelolco," went on the man on the dais, well in his stride and oblivious to the passing of time. "How much easier it will be on the battlefield, fighting against a flesh-and-blood enemy. No stone giants or wooden monsters, no soaring birds. On the battlefield, you will be like ferocious jaguars and pumas. You will know that our enemies are not birds to soar in order to escape your missiles, even though very few nimble flyers managed to escape your *atlatls* and slings today. Have courage and soon our people will be more important than Tenochtitlan Mexicas and our city will be revered as theirs never has been before."

Perturbed by yet another wave of agitation all around, Miztli put it all into the attempt to propel both his charges into a momentary gap that was opening to their left. An easy fit with Tlemilli pressed tightly against his body, snug under the crook of his arm. Chantli presented a more difficult challenge with her independent movements. For a heartbeat, he saw her head diving inside, disappearing in the vacillating crowd. Worried, he prepared to throw himself in, in order to catch hold of her, yet before he could figure out what to do about his frightened noble charge in the meanwhile, her face popped out again, flushed and out of breath, glaringly red but beaming.

"See this?" she yelled, struggling to pull her hand up, unsuccessful on this score.

"Let's get out of here," he shouted, exasperated. "Grab my hand."

A glimpse of greener ground gave him hope and he pushed with renewed vigor, welcoming the light breeze that managed to reach them on the outskirts of the agitating hordes, refreshing, promising relief. The Tlatelolcan girl was pressing into him with too much force, frightened now, volunteering no comments and no independent reactions, following his lead. It pleased him, made him struggle to clear their way with renewed vigor and force.

By the pebbled incline, the wind was stronger, bringing along an unpleasantly heavy odor that made him remember his village and the hunting parties Father would bring him and his brothers along. Sometimes the men were lucky to shoot quite a few deer, and then the heavy aroma of meat juices would haunt one's nostrils, penetrating and sticking around, in one's hair and clothes, and even the skin itself, it seemed.

"Come, let's get down there," he breathed, relieved to glimpse Chantli surfacing close by. But this girl was a survivor! How could one guess that from the mere look of her, so sweet and demure, running between the house and the workshop, exuding niceness? Three moons of working in her father's workshop, seeing her every day, peeking in to greet him with a cheerful *niltze* or sneak him an occasional tasty treat, a still warm tamale or a bowl of maize gruel, and he hadn't known her at all, either the outspoken argumentative fowl of two nights before, meddling in royal affairs, arguing with *calmecac* nobles, running all over the nighttime Tenochtitlan, or feeling at home in the aggressive crowds of Tlatelolco, coming after him on a rescue mission, a foreigner no one cared for or worried about. But he still needed time to think it all through.

"We are still alive," muttered Tlemilli wonderingly, stirring under his arm, forgotten there for a brief moment so comfortably she snuggled there, very fitting. "Aren't we?"

He smiled at her from above, suddenly terribly uncomfortable hugging her like that, and in front of so many possibly staring eyes.

As though sensing his thoughts, she pulled away quickly. "But it was scary in there! So many people. I got hurt all over!" Hastily, she turned away, inspecting her limbs in question. Too hastily. He saw Chantli grinning briefly, with puzzling superiority and even some condescension thrown in.

"Look what I got!" She cried out before he could start wondering about that puzzling look of hers, beaming with happiness, her previous distressed lack of confidence forgotten. A decorated strap of leather connected with sturdily woven maguey on each side looked impressive and unmistakable, clutched tightly in her raised hand.

"A sling? But where..." He found himself stammering. "Where did you get this?"

"I found it." She pulled her arm away, as though afraid he might try to snatch it. "Down there, under everyone's feet." Victoriously, she waved it again, spinning the flexible strap above her head, her excitement spilling. Yet just as he pondered her newly found treasure, wishing to ask to hold it but daring not, Tlemilli came back to life with a strangled cry.

"Father," she squeaked. "There, by the shore. Over there! Can't you see him? He is coming this way!" Her palm clutched his arm forcefully, squeezing hard. He paid it no attention, his eyes leaping toward her pointing finger, his heart thumping.

The greenish incline she indicated spread to their left, away from the commotion upon the main shore, sliding down and toward the water, it seemed, impossible to see from their vantage point. The men that hurried alongside it were just turning away, disappearing behind the slanting side, the cloak of the leading one swaying in the strengthening breeze, its design colorful, catching the eye.

"Was that your father?" He tried to disregard the shivers, the urge to turn and run in the opposite direction welling, overwhelming. "Are you sure?"

"Yes." She was staring at him, wide-eyed, blinking in confusion. "His cloak, you know, the insignia of the Head Adviser. It's him!" Her slender eyebrows were flying high above the round helplessness of her eyes, so atypical to her vigorous fiery self – her name TleMilli meant Field of Fire, so very fitting. "But why would he leave the Emperor like that? In the middle of the speech and the ceremony of rewarding the best shooters and all. It doesn't, it doesn't make much sense. Why?"

"Who is her father?" Chantli was asking, tugging at his arm in her turn. "Why is he important to us now?"

But he paid both girls no attention, thinking fast. That same frightening Teconal, scampering away and in the middle of a relatively important ceremony. The head adviser or whatever this man's title was; it didn't make sense, unless…

"He went to interrogate the *calmecac* boy." The words, even though his own, coming out of his own mouth, made his heart lurch in fright. Abruptly, he turned around. "Come!"

They stared at him, stunned, but as he broke into a run toward the incline that the ominous men disappeared behind, he could hear their footsteps, following, trying to keep up. Both of them! But shouldn't he have left at least Tlemilli out of it?

The breeze coming from the waterside refreshed him, made his thoughts organize. With the local ruler making the most out of his dubious competition, enjoying himself and his flowery speeches, his closest adviser and right arm could surely not absent himself for a long period of time. Not enough to extract information, make prisoners talk by scary ways and hurtful means. There was simply not enough time for this and not enough privacy anywhere around. And if so, they'd follow the man now, find out where the *calmecac* boy and the other one were held, stay until the hasty interrogation ended, and then either try to free them immediately, if possible, or track their new whereabouts and free them then.

A simple plan, but Father said that plans, no matter which or what, should be always kept as simple and as uncomplicated as they came, because there would be enough factors to complicate matters later on. The thought of Father encouraged him. They would manage, somehow. There was no reason they wouldn't.

"Where are we going?" demanded Chantli, catching up with him at long last. "Do you think these men will bring us to where Necalli and Ahuitzotl might be held?"

He nodded briefly, sneaking a quick glance behind his shoulder. Tlemilli was panting quite a few paces away, running cumbersomely, waving her thin arms in a funny manner. No runner, this one. He slowed his step.

"Who is her father?"

"This same Head Adviser, the man you said the warriors dragged the *calmecac* boy to for interrogation."

Her gasp tore the air and her palm locked around his arm, slowing his progress even further. "Then why did you let her come with us?"

He shrugged. "She is not her father."

Tlemilli was gasping for breath, her usually pale face glowing red, glistening with sweat, making her look less like an intricately carved mask and more of a human being.

"Stay here until we come back," he told her, anxious to go on. But what if they lost sight of these people, what if they weren't about to stay down there on the shore, easy to spot? They disappeared from their sight quite a few heartbeats ago, didn't they? "Wait here."

She shook her head violently, too out of breath to articulate her protests in words. He felt a brief smile sneaking out on its own. If she obeyed, it would be disappointing. Motioning her to keep up, he broke into a renewed run, only to trip on the loose sandal's strap, the stupid thongs trailing after him since leaving the plaza, trying to fail his step ever since. Cursing, he kicked the annoying garb away, liberated, relishing the familiar touch of the earth upon his bare soles.

A hard round ball rolled away along with the discarded shoe. Without thinking, he picked it up, then rushed on, feeling better by the moment. But was it good to move without the stupid leather flopping around, challenging his every step!

The top of the incline offered nothing outstanding, reinforcing his fears. Shielding his eyes, his heart fluttering at the awareness of the exposed nature of their new vantage point, both girls panting beside him, catching their breaths, he surveyed the view of the spreading tracks of grass and gravel, trampled on and soiled badly, dotted with people and crumbled gruesome fowl remnants. So many carcasses! Some of the fallen birds were still fluttering, picked up by the determined seekers, bands of barefoot people wandering in the reeds.

The group of cloaked figures was still there, hurrying along the vegetated shoreline now, following its twists. The reeds would be helpful in this matter, he reflected, charging down the trampled incline. Both girls kept close behind, volunteering no comments. What bliss!

By the pebbled strip of land, shielded from the clamor of the shoreline by thick vegetation, his eyes picked out several figures crowding the reed-covered inlet, some gesturing, others just standing. Six or maybe eight all in all, his eyes informed him, relishing the advantages of his elevated position but knowing that he could do nothing from such a distance, nothing at all.

"Keep down!" he whispered, pulling the Tlatelolcan girl behind the coverage of unsatisfactorily low bushes along with himself, counting on Chantli to follow the example. She did so promptly and it pleased him. But what a fighter this one was! "You two stay here," he added in a louder whisper. "I'll go take a closer look."

Both started to protest, but he shot them a warning glance, then dove into the thicker reeds, hating the memories of the monster from the other side of the causeway their rustling brought or the sense of helplessness the thoughts of his next step induced. What was he to do upon reaching these people? What could he do? Hesitating, he listened to the uneven murmuring of the dry twigs.

"Go back," he hissed without turning his head, indifferent to the question of which one of the girls was ignoring his instructions. He knew the answer to that. Both!

"Take this!" Chantli's whisper was equally loud, sure of itself. "You might need it."

The woven slingshot with its quality leather base was thrust into his hand, pleasing to touch. He glanced at it briefly.

"Just in case," she whispered again, crawling along awkwardly, thrusting her knee into his hurting ribs as she did. "Sorry!"

He wanted to tell her to go and jump into the lake, but the sling felt good, fitting in his palm perfectly, and his appreciation of her courage and her gesture was greater than the pain her clumsiness brought along.

"Yes. You are right. Thank you! I... it can be handy, this thing. Especially with this one." Absently, he glanced at the smooth round ball still clutched in his other sweating palm. Oh, but now he knew what it was. A missile! A real quality perfect stone, or maybe a clay ball, exact replica of the things the slingers were hurling back upon the plaza while competing for the best shot. How hadn't he realized that before?

Feeling better by the moment, he grinned at her, then, unable to fight the temptation, peeked out again. The men upon the tiny strip of land were moving about, talking with agitation. One of them rushed away and up their incline. He heard the Tlatelolcan girl gasping, atypically quiet since escaping the crowds, curiously subdued. Afraid to take his eyes off the happenings upon the shore, he reached out with his free hand, pressing her upper arm briefly, trying to reassure.

The figure in the colorful cloak moved, gesturing in the direction opposite to the waterline, clearly talking, revealing another silhouette, that one pressed between two others uncompromisingly. Their prisoner? He thought he recognized the familiar broadness of the shoulders, not cloaked or covered otherwise anymore, the disheveled topknot. The wide sweep of the cloaked man's arm was also unmistakable, landing against the prisoner's side of the head, making him sway in the grip of his captors. A nearby smaller figure was struggling to break free from yet another warrior, the fury of its screams reaching even their hideaway.

This time, it was Chantli's turn to gasp. "It's them, it's them," she repeated again and again in an annoyingly strident whisper. "We must get to them somehow. We must!"

He enjoyed the pleasant roundness of the missile as his fingers closed against it, feeling it out, measuring its weight and its merits, calculating. Not close enough to achieve a good throw. He would have to come closer, much closer, lose the advantage of the elevated ground, risk the surprise. But now he had the sling. Oh, this one would reach that other shore easily, taking down its target. Which one? The evil nobleman or any of his cronies? Those who held the *calmecac* boy or the other spirited *pilli*? And would he manage to shoot accurately enough, without harming the boys he was trying to rescue? Too many questions. He studied the decorated sling for another fraction of a heartbeat.

"See if there are more of those rounded things, or even just simple stones." Both girls were staring at him, wide-eyed. "I'd better do as much shooting as I can before they manage to reach us here."

The faint shouting intensified, joined by more loud voices. He let the clay missile roll into the comfortable leather base.

"Wait!" This time, it was Tlemilli, her strangely husky voice pleasing his ear, encouraging. But was she quiet since escaping the crowds! "Wait!" Her fingers were closing around his arm in a familiar fashion. "I'll go there, take my father away. I can do this."

"You what?" He found himself staring, beyond comprehension, feeling Chantli freezing as well, not daring to breathe.

Her eyes were again brimming with mischief, excited and confident, dominating the gentle sharpness of her face. A familiar sight, pleasing and unsettling at the same time. The girl from the Tlatelolco plaza was back. "I'll manage to take him away. And the others too. I can do it easily." Her grip on his arm tightened, relating that typical enthusiasm. "I'll tell them that there is trouble out there at the contest. I'll tell him that the Emperor needs him. I won't leave until he comes with me. I will be very insistent. I promise!" The way she beamed at him tore at his heart. Oh yes, the girl from under the podium, sure of herself and trustful, full of silly ideas, but oh so reassuring, so encouraging in her innocent confidence. "When they leave, you can go there and free your friends. It won't be hard once my father isn't there. You'll see."

He still stared at her, his heart beating fast. "Will you do this for us?" The need to clear his throat became urgent. "I mean…"

"Yes, I just told you so. Aren't you listening? Is it back to the Plaza and all, with you acting strange?" Her giggle warmed the air, uncomfortably loud. He fought the urge to tell her to lower her voice. "I liked you better now, around here, leader-like and all that."

He shook his head, fighting his smile no longer. "If you do this for us, I will… I'll find a way to repay you. You'll see."

Her entire face lit like a brazier at which twenty straw pipes blew all at once. "You will? You will find me later on? You promise?"

He just nodded, bereft of words.

"Then I'll be off." Springing to her feet with her typical bouncy vigor, she shot down the incline with no additional glance. One moment there, the other gone. Blinking, he stared at the place her face was peering at him from such close proximity only a heartbeat or two before. His mind refused to process any of it.

"He is not hitting him anymore." Chantli's voice tore him from the stupefied staring, ringing with urgency. Half crouching half squatting, she was leaning forward and away from the protective screen of the bushes, as far as she dared, looking like a forest fox, ready to bolt for cover at the slightest sight of danger. "Think she'll manage to do something?"

He just shrugged, busy with observations of his own. The cloaked man was strolling back and forth now, gesticulating, addressing the younger boy, judging by that one's wary pose and the pause in the furious yelling. Tlemilli's flying garments bounced down the grassy incline, not far enough yet, progressing in a funny gait. Oh yes, a runner she was not. The warmth in his chest spread along with his worry. What if she got punished for this diversion? And would she be successful? While facing her oblique, widely open, sparkling eyes and the boundless enthusiasm her entire being exuded, it was easy to believe her that her father would turn around and go away, swallowing her hastily concocted lies, leaving his prisoners behind, carelessly unwatched. What silliness!

He shook his head forcefully, furious with himself. What a stupid assumption. The ruthless, violent, evidently highly experienced in all sorts of shady dealings man, the noble dignitary, the Emperor's Head Adviser and all, furious with one escaping prisoner by now surely, why, such a man would not leave his new prisoners unattended, with no adequate guard and whatnot.

Narrowing his eyes, he let his gaze wander, scanning the ground nearest to their hideaway, satisfied with the amount of midsize rocks and pebbles it offered. More than enough for one desperate attempt. He clenched his clay treasure tighter in his sweaty palm. This would be the first one, the most important, the shot that would seal their fate. Hastily, he dropped to his knees, crawling as far as he dared without leaving the safety of their cover, picking up the best-looking rocks.

"She is running really fast now." Another observation from Chantli, this time in a calmer voice. She seemed to be amused. Why would she be? "Where did you find that bizarre-looking fowl?"

"She is not bizarre-looking," he muttered, curiously incensed. Tlemilli looked or behaved anything but ordinary, didn't she? But bizarre? No. Just different, nicely at that.

"Oh well." There was a peculiar note to the girl's voice and he glanced at her briefly, puzzled. What troubled that one? Besides their current troubles, that is. "She is strange and bizarre, and if you don't see it, then maybe we shouldn't have trusted your judgment and got her involved at the first place. How do you know she won't be telling about us the moment she reaches that dear father of hers?"

"She won't," he grunted, his stomach twisting violently. Not with warmth this time. And what if Chantli was right? How did he know that he could trust the girl he had just met and under the oddest circumstances? "Stop talking and let me think."

To concentrate on sorting out his improvised ammunition

helped. He did so with an exaggerated care, picking up the best fitting rocks, five in all, enough for the first concentrated attack. He wouldn't be able to shoot any more than this before all those warriors broke into a wild run, trying to catch them here, or wherever.

"When I tell you, try to sneak away and toward the shore if you can," he said, eyes still on his unimpressive arsenal, not daring to face her, not yet. Not until Tlemilli had proven her worth. "When I start hurling those stones, they'll be coming here fast enough. In the meanwhile, if you are anywhere closer to where they are now held, you may be able to sneak in and free them somehow. It may be possible. Maybe they'll all run here. Let's hope they do." He sighed. "We can't do any better anyway."

"And you?" she asked, peering at him from above. He could feel her eyes boring at him, drilling holes in his skin.

"I'll deal with them. It won't be difficult." He forced his shoulders into a breezy shrug. "There are too many people still wandering all over, up there and down the main shore. You saw them too. It'll be difficult to chase me out there, not like in nighttime Tenochtitlan."

Another heartbeat of strained silence. "Did they get you back there at night? When you were on your way home?" Her voice dropped to a mere whisper.

He shrugged again, shifting to get a better look at their prospective target, his stomach as tight as a wooden ball. The cloaked man wasn't pacing anymore. Standing with his legs wide apart and his hand shielding his eyes, he was peering in their direction in a pose like that of a predator, ready to pounce. Miztli's heart missed a beat, then threw itself wildly against his ribs. Did the man see them somehow? Did he guess?

The answer presented itself readily, not calming but letting him breathe again. Tlemilli's prettily bright garment was fluttering not far away from the shore, her arms flailing as though greeting, or maybe just enhancing her run. She must be badly out of breath now, he reflected randomly. Would she manage?

"He saw her," observed Chantli, herself looking like an animal, hovering on all fours, leaning as far out as she dared, supported by her arms, ready to spring into action. "He is looking this way!"

I can see that, he thought, keeping his peace, not wishing to snap at her. She was a good girl and a true friend, even though she was so foul-mouthed about Tlemilli.

"I think you should go now. Crawl around those bushes and then down the slope." A brief glance to his right reassured him, enough vegetation in their immediate proximity and further down. "The moment she takes him away, I better start shooting. Then it will all go very fast, I suppose."

She nodded readily. "Promise that you won't stay to face them all here."

The corner of his mouth quivered almost against his will. "I won't. I promise." It was difficult to hold the snicker in. "If I don't hit your *calmecac* boy instead of his attackers, I'll join you down there, somehow. But you need to hurry now. The moment she leaves, I'd better start swinging that sling."

Down by the shore, Tlemilli seemed to be talking rapidly, waving her hands as profusely as their orating Emperor did before, not sparing on broad gesturing. The cloaked man looked up and toward the crowded incline, and so did the rest of them, even the prisoners.

"You don't believe she'll manage to take them all away." Chantli's whisper trailed after her, disappearing behind the next cluster of bushes, as nimble and as matter-of-fact as she was.

"What she'll manage will be more than enough," he grunted louder than he wished, incensed once again. But why did she have to pick on the Tlatelolcan girl all the time?

By the shore, the agitation was increasing, with the cloaked man talking now, gesturing curtly. Unlike his emperor or his lively daughter, that one seemed to be sure enough of his words without reinforcing those with gesticulation. Tlemilli was hopping nearby, exuding nervous impatience, still talking, or trying to, judging by the movements of her thin arms. He willed her to shut up and run away. What if they wouldn't leave at all, not even her and her father?

Chantli's rustling somewhere further down the incline frayed his nerves. But maybe he shouldn't have sent her to approach that shore all alone. What if they caught her sniffing around?

As though anxious to either allay or increase his fears, the cloaked man began walking, turning his head as though scanning his surroundings. It was easy to imagine his eagle-like frown and the squinted eyes. As opposed to her father, Tlemilli was bouncing like a spirited *itzcuintli* on a leash, indeed resembling those slick hairless dogs the people of his village kept for various uses and people of Tenochtitlan grew mainly for food, bred or herded not far away from the troublesome causeway, making much noise. He felt his palm going rigid around the first perfect missile. But what if…

The cloaked man turned abruptly, breaking into a swift walk up the incline, storming it with much forcefulness. Miztli's heart stopped once again. One heartbeat, then another. Nothing happened in his chest, while he struggled to drag himself onto his feet, knowing that he had to do something, anything. To try shooting his sling? Oh yes, he must have enough time for that. It would be easier, maybe, if he managed to hit this man, the main enemy, with this one closing the distance, making it easier… Easier to do what? He didn't know. As though in a dream, he began to get up, twenty heartbeats spent on each movement, so unbearably slow.

Up at long last, he adjusted the sling, then blinked. The group was ascending the hill, drifting away and far to his left, walking briskly, not interested in his side of it in the least. Except the girl. She was sneaking covert glances, of that he was sure. Against his will, his eyes lingered, enjoying the sight of her, so breezy and bouncy, so out of place and not in accordance with the forceful firmness of her escorts. He could bet she was looking his way.

Before his instincts made him dive back behind the protection of the bushes, he glanced at the shore, then went numb all over again. Eerily empty, the place that until now was full of pacing or angry or violent people was gleaming peacefully, abandoned in the light of the afternoon sun. Blinking, he tried to understand, his eyes darting around, picking another group, this one drawing away along the shoreline, six in all, walking briskly, or forced to do so, an obvious case with the smaller boy. His *calmecac* fellow was walking on his own, proudly but with obvious difficulty, pushed by one of the men, roughly at that. Of Chantli there was no sight.

Slipping behind the following bushes in the direction the girl disappeared earlier, Miztli tried to think reasonably, the urge to break into a wild run overwhelming. What if they disappeared from his view for good? What if he didn't manage to catch up with them crawling like that? If it took him too long, that scary Teconal would be back, with her attempt to take him away coming to nothing, resulting in no action, a futile thing.

Daring to straighten up again, he sighted the entire group not far away, progressing slower than his crawling apparently. And with good reason. The *calmecac* boy wasn't cooperating anymore, struggling to break free, fighting with desperation, kicking viciously, overwhelmed but not giving up even when pressed to the ground by the weight of two of his captors. The third man was kneeling nearby, leaning forward like a priest preparing for a ritual, deliberate and slow. The thrust of his right arm could not be mistaken.

Miztli fought his misgivings no more. The cherished clay ball slipped easily into the leather base of his slingshot, his right arm already shooting upwards, enjoying the motion. A familiar feeling but better than he remembered, with this real warriors' weapon being sturdier but easier to handle, to push into a strong spin, nothing like the homemade woven straps he used to hunt with.

His mind went perfectly clear and his hand enjoyed every round, knowing that it was its decision when to let the missile go, nothing to do with his mind but only his instincts. When it finally flew, it did so in a viciously powerful swish, crashing into its intended target – no running rabbits or flying birds this one – sending the kneeling warrior down and away to slam onto the ground and lie there still in a heap of limbs.

The others froze in surprise. Even their struggling victim stopped his mad wriggling. Still in control, relishing the sensation, Miztli groped for another stone, his previously assembled arsenal forgotten back in the bushes. His next shot wasn't as good, crashing against the second man's shoulder, making him merely sway, in the process of springing to his feet, leaving his perch upon his victim's chest readily, too readily. In less than a heartbeat, he was already charging uphill, determined like a whirlwind, not about to be stopped. There was no point in searching for a new missile. Still, Miztli darted toward another temptingly round stone.

By the time he pushed it into its leather bed, the man was almost upon him, charging recklessly, blind with fury. The ragged obsidian of his knife glowed dully, reflecting the sun. For a moment, he followed it with his gaze, fascinated. Then the sling was twirling again, not to hurl but to hit. He didn't realize this was his intention himself until it happened. And so did his attacker. The spinning leather caught the man in mid-leap, crushing against his temple as though planted there at leisure, with perfect accuracy.

Swaying from the impact of the recoil his arms had absorbed, Miztli fought for his balance, his mind exceedingly clear, noting the details – the brownish slough of the damp earth, the remnants of the trampled grass, the crimson splashing upon it, coming from the half open mouth, the rest of the crumbled limbs inert, indifferent, just sprawling there, a part of the scenery.

The next thing he knew, he was racing madly, down the slope and toward the shore and the sounds of struggle coming from there, skidding on the slippery ground, all amok. Oh, but he needed to reach them, Chantli and the *calmecac* boy, if for no other reason than to have them by his side, to not feel alone anymore, pitted against terrible people, deserted and forgotten.

CHAPTER 18

Necalli tried to make sense out of it all, his head reeling, mouth full of bile, the side of his face where the knife slashed at it on fire, his wounded arm pumping with pain. The entire world was whirling, with footsteps running and Ahuitzotl's shouting, cursing in his typical flowery manner. The other men's swearing shook the air too, at least one more voice. Where were the others?

With no crushing weight upon his chest and no rock-hard arms pinning his limbs to the ground, he sprang back into an upright position as fast as his aching body allowed him, his head spinning but not too badly. Supported by his good arm, he blinked, taking in the bedlam, one of his captors still nearby, whirling back at him, wild-eyed. To roll away from the renewed charge was the best thing he could think of for the moment. Accompanied by a desperate kick, it gained him another precious heartbeat to try and regroup. Not enough but better than nothing. His sandal connected with some flesh, pleasing him greatly, but the weight was back upon him, this time worse than before, and the coarse palms wrapping around his neck did not help the disoriented sensation.

In a panic, he wriggled madly, pushing and kicking, not sparing his wounded arm an effort, not anymore. Just like before, when those people had held him while the knife was plunging toward his eye, determined to take it out because he wouldn't tell what they wanted to know, some questions important, like the whereabouts of his friends, or accomplices, as they put it, some just silly and irrelevant, like the question of what were they doing here in Tlatelolco in the first place. It was the strangest thing of all, the way their mere presence here was considered an affront. As though Tenochtitlan citizens did not swarm Tlatelolco markets, or the other way around. The marketplace of this other island was huge, the largest and the richest among the Great Lake cities and towns. Thousands who traveled would arrive here for the market days. The stupid city was used to visitors aplenty, so what was their problem?

In desperation, he pummeled the assaulting body as hard as he could, kicking with enough force to feel the smothering hands slipping, relaxing their grip but not enough to let him breathe freely, not about to disappear for good like that knife before, when the ragged obsidian slid away at the last moment, not piercing his eye but slipping downward, leaving a burning sensation. Somehow, that made the people pinning him to the ground back away too, yet now it didn't seem as though about to happen again.

Clenching his teeth, he slammed his knee into what felt like the softness of a belly before the hands were back, groping their way toward his throat, annoyingly persistent. The world spun again, then shook with a fuzzy thud. The fingers stopped pressing, but it took him another heartbeat to push the face that slammed into his away. For some reason, it annoyed rather than stunned him, making his head clear. Shoving the weakly straggling limbs aside, surprised with the ease with which it came to him this time, he blinked to make his vision clear.

The next thing he knew, Chantli's unmistakably oval face was swimming before his eyes, her hair loose and fluttering, tickling his nose, her hands tugging at his shoulders, pulling him up, not very successful.

"Oh mighty deities, are you all right? You don't look good!" She was sobbing, stumbling over her words, sniffing loudly, pulling the air through an obviously clogged nose.

It made him want to snicker. *Just don't sneeze on me,* he wanted to tell her, but the brief moment of hilarity was over before he could comment on it, banished by the sounds of struggle. Ahuitzotl, he knew; the wild beast. Who else could curse so lavishly, with so many insults put together in neatest of strings?

Pushing himself up along with her helpful efforts, her hands not strong enough but efficient, giving him power with their mere presence, her warmth encouraging, promising nothing but good, he blinked the persistent mist away, forcing his eyes to concentrate, tracing the sight of the yelling and screaming. The man was staggering up the incline, heading in the direction the scary leader had disappeared earlier, summoned by a skinny interesting-looking fowl. Burdened with the boy who was thrown over his shoulder, kicking and screaming, twisting wildly, writhing like a snake, pounding with the aid of his every limb, the would-be abductor had evidently had a hard time, making slow progress.

Clenching his teeth, Necalli tried to will away his dizziness, knowing that he needed to reach them and fast. It might be enough to catch up with the kidnapper, to make him drop his cargo. The fierce cub would help him from there. Briefly, he wondered why the man didn't knock his charge off for good, or at least make him behave with a punch or two. The royal *pilli*s always had it easy, hadn't they?

"We must catch him somehow," Chantli was murmuring, still supporting him, taking some of his weight.

"Yes." He pulled away firmly, clenching his teeth against the nauseating sway of the shore. There was no choice but to chase them, spinning head or not. He had to…

As though in a dream, he watched another figure running down the incline, heading in their direction, racing along the wet grass in a frenzied hurry, as though all the spirits of the Underworld were after it. Not on the path of the kidnapper, the runner still halted with the abruptness matching his previous dash.

Necalli narrowed his eyes, recognizing the broad figure. Could it be? He tried to make sense of the scene, watching the workshop boy spreading his legs wider, stabilizing himself, concentrating visibly, his right arm shooting up, the rotation of its sling monotonous, just an extension of the spinning wrist.

Sensing the danger, the man carrying the boy slowed his step, wavering under his difficult cargo, but the stone was already cutting through the air, flying with a graceful ease, crashing against the turning nape, sending its owner collapsing, headfirst, in a helpless heap.

"Miztli!" yelled Chantli, breaking into a wild run of her own.

Blinking, Necalli just stared. Upon the incline, Ahuitzotl, seemingly unhurt, was busy wriggling away from the inert body he was momentarily trapped under, scrambling to his feet with the agility of a non-aquatic creature. No real *ahuitzotl*, this one, reflected Necalli for the thousandth time, beginning to tread his way toward them. Oh yes, it was getting wilder and wilder – the previous night, the tunnel and the criminals in it, killing one with a training sword or at least knocking him out, then the ordeal at the lake, a terrifying experience, and now this, the mad, unfamiliar, violent Tlatelolco, not the neighboring *altepetl* he had visited plenty of times, sneaking along the old causeway with other boys or riding his mother's litter when smaller, the ladies loving to visit its marketplace on the market days, such a huge happening, always. Well, now it felt as though they had wandered into the wild eastern highlands by mistake, a place full of hostile people and warriors. Not logical in the least.

By the time he reached them, they were crowding their fallen enemy, all three of them, agitated to various degrees and wild-eyed. Ahuitzotl was kicking at the inanimate heap of limbs repeatedly, spitting colorful curses. Chantli and the workshop boy just stared.

"He is dead, isn't he?" muttered the girl, giving Necalli a look full of frightened expectation.

He glanced at the motionless figure, then shrugged. "Ask your friend. He was the one to shoot him." Then the full realization dawned. "You are alive, workshop boy! I can't believe it. We thought you were dead all over."

The badly bruised face flickered with a sort of an inverted smile, decidedly crooked. "Not all over, no."

He felt his own lips twisting as crookedly. But it was good to see this one, looking wild and thoroughly drubbed but alive and in good enough spirits. "You came back to life just in time, I say." A glance at Ahuitzotl reassured him that the wild *pilli* wasn't harmed or even humbled. "A nice shot. Where did you learn to shoot like that?"

As expected, a shrug was his answer.

"He took down these other people," burst out Chantli, eyes shining. "The ones who were beating you."

This time, he found himself staring. "You did?"

Another shrug. The man upon the ground shuddered ever so slightly.

"We need to get out of here."

"Yes." The urgency of their situation dawned on him again. "Come. We get down that shore, get into the reeds, *ahuitzotls* or not. Wade all the way back to that other shore, back to Axolin and Patli. We —"

"But we didn't get a boat!" cried out Ahuitzotl. "We have nothing to take them back with."

The familiar resentment with the presumptuous *pilli* surfaced. "You stay here and search for that boat if you like. Your last attempt at stealing one was a brilliant affair, to say the least."

"And you…" began the royal boy hotly, but the raising clamor beyond the incline, many throats shouting at once, cut their argument short. Whatever was happening in this filthy town, it moved closer to the lakeshores, and they didn't need any of that. Their presence here wasn't welcome. Of that they had been informed in too many ways by now.

"There, down the shore!"

They didn't wait for another invitation; still, he made sure they all broke into a run before doing the same, his dizziness there but less tormenting now, just a slightly woozy sensation, a bit of a flickering fog in the corner of his eyes. He paid it little attention, bending to snatch a temptingly unattended dagger, glittering in the grass, not far away from its fallen owner, a prettily carved affair of decorated handle attached to the ragged obsidian, a treasure.

Down by the reeds, their assailants were still sprawled, one motionless, the other stirring, groaning in a low croaking voice. Necalli clutched his newly acquired dagger, his heart pounding. Another, simpler looking knife glinted next to the motionless man. Shuddering, he pushed the memory of this particular blade away, the way it had neared his eye, so slowly and deliberately, enjoying his terror, the softly spoken words flowing ahead of it, describing what is going to happen next.

His nausea returned twice as strong as before. Pressing his lips against its intensity, he raced on, noticing the workshop boy bending to pick up something round and bright, barely slowing his step to do that, chancing a good roll straight into the worst of the reeds. Chantli and her royal company were already charging behind those, oblivious of the angry rustling.

"What is it?" he asked, pausing to catch his breath before plunging into the slough of mire and water vegetation, his heart pumping insanely, his burning arm reminding him that it wasn't much safer in the reeds than back up the incline and in the city full of nastily violent nobles and warriors.

"A missile. From their slings." His companion paused as well, his coarse palm shooing forward, offering a view of a ball, perfectly round and slick save a few cracks running alongside its surface. "A neat thing."

"It is." Necalli tried to make his mind work. "You shot that man with it, didn't you?"

The commoner nodded, non-committal.

To take a deep breath became a necessity. "You saved my life."

The pursed lips twitched in embarrassment. "It's nothing. I didn't do anything. You came here to help me out. We were in it together."

He could see Chantli waving at them from further down the mire, over her knees in the muddy water, jumping up and down with impatience. Of Ahuitzotl there was no sight. The unruly *pilli*! But they needed to keep an eye on that one. Was he the only one to realize the implications of the royal boy's presence and the need to keep him safe? Incensed by the realization that he was, he hastened his step, wishing to avoid entering the swamp and its gleefully murmuring reeds, because this time, the spiny monsters would have even an easier time. There would be not much of an effort on the slick creature's part.

He pressed his bad arm with the good one, trying to disregard the exploding headache and the fire that kept burning his cheek where the vile man's knife managed to slide against it. Oh mighty deities, let them come out of this terrible adventure alive. Of the punishment that was waiting for them back at school, he preferred not to think. There were more pressing matters to attend to.

The workshop boy kept close by, a jumpy but reliable presence, surprisingly reassuring. Necalli side-glanced him once again, taking in the wide, well-defined features, haggard but strong; and unyielding. "You are a warrior, copper-melting boy. Too good to be spent in your stinking workshop."

An indefinite grunt was his answer.

"Look at this thing!" Again, young Ahuitzotl was the one to forge far ahead, coming back with new findings. But this boy was a force of nature!

Necalli made a face at him, glad to take his thoughts off more worrisome topics. "Don't scream."

The sounds of the shore and the town behind it were still strong enough here, louder than one would feel comfortable with. Plenty of feathers and sometimes the mangled corpse of a bird floated in the muddied shoals, suggesting the possible intrusion of sniffing-around commoners, anyone who cared to add a good chunk of meat to their maize meals, all those gruels and stews. The workshop boy, he noticed, was glancing toward the shore every time the uproar grew in volume, his gaze yearning somehow, as though sorry for not being able to join the festivities.

Puzzled, Necalli concentrated on the agitated *pilli*. "What?"

"There is a strange thing floating out there, behind those reeds. Not a boat."

"What is it?"

"I don't know. But it isn't guarded. Not like that stinking canoe back there."

He tried not to snicker. "For a royal offspring, you know way too much about creeping around and stealing things."

The boy made a face at him, curiously not offended, not this time. "I know many things."

"That you do." Uneasily, he eyed the thick cluster of reeds.

Those weren't as dense or as deserted as the ones beneath the causeway; still, possible predators in it made him wish to bolt away and up the slanting shore. "Where is this thing?"

"Out there." Again, a noncommittal wave indicated the general direction of the marshes he didn't wish to enter. He rolled his eyes, glancing at Chantli, who trod close by, keeping very little distance, trusting him to keep her safe, a most pleasant realization.

The warm wave was spreading again, making it difficult to fight a smile. She was so pretty and wild. Unruly, yes, but trustworthy, someone to rely upon, a true survivor. Not like girls from old stories, like in the legend of the two smoking mountains from the eastern highlands, the beauty who waited for her warrior to return, dying upon hearing the false message of his death, both of them turning into two massive peaks, lying side by side. A boring business. Well, on Chantli one could count not to die just like that, waiting and waiting. This one would go out and look for him, proving the false message wrong, helping along if he needed help. Not what one would expect from a good, well-mannered girl. Not to mention her looks.

He glanced at her again; it helped to battle the exhaustion and pain. All those scratches and bruises, and with her hair sticking out in a wild way, how was it that she pleased the eye so, looking more enticing than ever? He tried not to let his gaze wander, her skirt torn badly, hanging in shreds. The most tempting of sights. Embarrassed, he looked away.

"What?" She was peering at him, frowning comically. "Why are you –"

"Here!" Ahuitzotl's cry came in time, before his face started to blaze with the fire that had nothing to do with its injuries and wounds.

Minding his step, the slippery mud making it difficult to keep one's balance, he hurried after the muddied cloak, its decorations missing or mangled badly. But what would they do to them for drawing a royal *pilli* into this trouble? Nothing good!

The construction of a few planks tied together in an oblique way looked strange, lolling among the reeds, brushing against the stacks, bending them.

"We can't sail in this!"

The boy's lips pursed in a familiar manner. "It's better than nothing."

"Yes, we can put Patli on it, and Axolin too," contributed Chantli, bursting with lovely vitality again, her reflective mood forgotten.

"And do what with them?"

"Drag along the shore until we reach the causeway." This came from the workshop boy, still at some distance, as though unwilling to leave the safety of the shoreline, or maybe its temptations, glancing back toward the roaring city again. What had he been doing here in Tlatelolco for a whole day and two nights? wondered Necalli, suddenly perturbed. The strange boy had better make sense with his story when questioned. How, for all mighty deities' sake, did Chantli manage to unearth him here, being in the right place and the right time, in a fairly battered state, yes, but waving a warrior's sling, volunteering nothing, no excuse, no explanation?

He pushed the questions and the dilemmas away, aware of his bottomless exhaustion and his head, which was trying to explode from within, his throat hurting, arm on fire. But he wouldn't mind stretching on this same improvised raft himself, letting them drag him along the shore and toward the causeway. Not such a bad idea, come to think of it. That commoner was too good for his stinking workshop.

"We'll take this thing," he said tiredly, craving to find something to lean against. "Drag it toward the boys, then decide what to do." Even a shrug came with difficulty, a somewhat painful business with that stupid arm hurting like the Underworld. "Just make sure to draw no attention from that wild gathering up there."

CHAPTER 19

Chantli shifted her shoulders, then stretched, staring at the colorful variety of strings spreading before her eyes, hating every single one of them. It was a difficult design, too many threads of too many colors, each pattern demanding the entirety of her concentration, challenging. Usually, she didn't mind weaving, the work on her loom not as boring as parting or spinning maguey threads, yet today, she hated every moment of it.

Oh, but how frightfully enraged Father was, how he fumed. He, who had always a good encouraging word for her, finding excuses, curbing Mother's punishments sometimes, when she, Chantli, had been caught in various small transgressions. Mother was the one who tried to be stern, with her and her youngest brother. The oldest were too old, and not her sons anyway, their mother being Father's Chief Wife, now dead for almost ten summers. Which made Chantli's mother into a chief spouse, and the only one too, a nice thing. It wasn't as though Father couldn't afford another wife in his household. It was more that he didn't want one. Too many women, too many troubles, he would say, grinning, making Mother giggle. Well, since last night, no one was grinning in this household, not even the maid.

Forgetting her loom and the threads stretched alongside it and across, she pressed her palms tight, shivering, wishing to groan aloud. But how loudly Father had yelled, how frightfully, so harsh and uncaring; how terrible his threats were. She had never suspected that a calm, deliberate, exceptionally understanding man could turn into someone so frighteningly unreasonable. Even Mother had quailed and did not contribute a word, even Acatlo.

Oh yes, both her elder brothers, so outspoken and quick to criticize or complain, to talk to Father freely and with respect but no fear, beat a hasty retreat, taking themselves off and away, along with her scampering-off younger sibling and the slave. Even Mother retreated into another room, to tend to Patli and the local healer woman who came to check on his bleeding head, and with Miztli locked in the workshop to await his own judgment, it left Chantli all alone to face that atrocious rage and ear-splitting harangue about disobedient children and the punishments reserved in the law for such ungratefulness and lack of manners. Oh, but how frightening it all was!

Even now, after a night spent in this backroom, charged with a ridiculously large amount of weaving she couldn't possibly complete in a moon, forbidden to communicate with anyone, not even Mother, ordered to think of her crimes and think well, she still wasn't sure that the worst was over. Father never hit her. Even his sons he had rarely punished by physical means; however, by law, he could do this. She was of an age to receive physical punishment, parents allowed to whip disobedient children with a stick after the age of twelve, and she was already fourteen. Oh mighty deities! To inhale hurtful smoke coming out of a pot boiling with chili peppers was a bad thing, but the possibility of whipping scared her for real.

Forcing her concentration back to the loom and the material it was supposed to produce – but she had better make as much of it as she could, show her regret in this way – she thought about the others. Were they facing as terrible ordeals? About Miztli she didn't even dare to muse. But what Father would do to him? What could he? That boy was standing not much higher than a cheaply bought slave in their household, but slaves did have rights too, and judges to appeal to. One couldn't just punish a slave without stating one's case before the local district's court, explaining the gravity of the transgression, but Miztli wasn't even a slave. He had no status, come to think of it, and Father was clearly beyond any reasonable type of behavior.

Shutting her eyes, she whispered a prayer, asking Coatlicue, mother of all gods, to keep them all safe, the village boy included.

He didn't deserve punishments, not with his bravery and loyalty and dependable ways. Even Necalli told him that he was worthy of all the rest of the *calmecac* boys put together. He had said so in these very words while climbing the sloping planks of the wharves on other side of the causeway, pushing their improvised raft back into the lake, breathing with relief, all of them. Almost home!

Easing her aching back, the loom's strap wrapped around it, pressing with comfortably familiar ease but the rest of her pose awkward, the little backroom not equipped for a long term weaving, having no available beam to tie the loom's other end to, she remembered Necalli, battered and exhausted, barely able to stand straight but beaming, glowing with a triumphant grin, proud of their achievements, besting the odds in such a way.

"This Tlatelolcan scum is nothing," he had declared, standing on the edge of their side of the causeway, *the right side*, balancing there with the ease of a mighty conqueror. "All their plotting and scheming and their stupid birds shooting and kidnapping people, but here we are, alive and away. The easiest thing." His beam was one of the widest, making her chest tighten. So handsome!

"Oh yes, the easiest. No sweat at all." Miztli's badly bruised face reflected the wideness of the *calmecac* boy's grin, as beaming and uninhibited. But she had never seen the village boy smiling with such openness, such lack of reserve. Well, those two days were a revelation.

And then Axolin was snickering, and Ahuitzotl – another radiant, atypically light, bouncy being, not hurrying to take offense or argue or prove his worth. And then they were all roaring with laughter, doubling over, unable to get enough air. Even Patli, swaying while leaning heavily against the nearest plank, his face pasty, hair caked with a mixture of mud and blood, contributed to the wild guffawing. It was truly too funny, this entire thing, and the way they all looked, so badly bashed and trounced. It was impossible to take it all seriously, not anymore.

"Now let us go back and get all the punishments over with," declared Necalli, catching his breath in the end. "After surviving those, we can get together again, eh?" His gaze lingered on her, gauging in a way, making her insides jelly. "To discuss it all." His eyes left her reluctantly, moving to Ahuitzotl. "There are some nasty things going on in this Tlatelolco, something your brother may wish to hear about. If they don't kill you up there in the Palace for what we've done, try to let them know. It may be important, all those things, especially that filthy Teconal's eagerness to keep you in his custody."

"I know that!" cried out the royal boy, nodding too vigorously, making his matted hair jump. "I was going to."

"Good!" Necalli didn't make any faces, not this time. "Axolin, lean on me." A curt motion of his head was accompanied with a needling grin. "Let's take your limping carcass back to school, for their sticks and maguey thorns to get to work, eh? I bet they are waiting for us with all of it and more."

"Beyond doubt," was the other *calmecac* boy's nonchalant response.

"Will you two manage with your cargo?"

She remembered nodding readily, and so did Miztli, already propping up her cousin, offering the broadness of his shoulder to lean against. A conscious Patli was easier to deal with than the unconscious one. It was such a relief to find him alive and responsive back on that abandoned shore earlier. Running around the more inhabited parts of the island, dealing with their mounting troubles, she had forgotten all about her wounded cousin and it still made her ashamed, this particular feeling.

"Come near our school the moment you can," were Necalli's parting words. "Try to send us word somehow."

She felt the tears beginning again, insistent, making the threads upon her loom blur. It sounded so easy back then, funny, hilarious. Get over with punishments, then to the new adventures. But now... Oh, now she was a prisoner for an indefinite period of time, unable to go out freely, if ever, not allowed to leave this small storage room, not allowed to converse with her own family. With Miztli probably faring even worse. And Necalli and Axolin? What were the school's punishments for pupils being absent for more than an entire day and with no permission and not a word as to their whereabouts? What were the authorities allowed do with them? She remembered his mangled arm, and the rest of his cuts and bruises. Did they go easier on him back in school or at his own family house because of his injuries? She hoped they did. He did not deserve punishments. He was so strong and reliable, taking care of them all, making sure she was well, even after their frequent arguments. Why had she argued with him so much?

Fitting a new thread between the stretched fibers, she blinked her tears away, wondering about Ahuitzotl. Well, the royal *pilli* would probably get away lightly, but the rest of them, oh mighty Coatlicue, but they were done for, their lives ruined, forever, maybe. At fifteen, girls were liable to be offered in marriage and what if Father locked her up until that happened?

The tears were back, flowing unrestrained. Through the small opening in the wall, the light surged softly, caressing, offering comfort. The house was so terribly quiet, no voices, no sounds of running feet, all the regular clamor of midday. Father must be in the workshop now – poor Miztli! – and her brothers too, but Mother and the rest, weren't they going about their business? The maid must be back from the marketplace long since, grinding maize, cooking or cleaning, and her little brother would be all around the house, getting in everyone's way. She swallowed a new bout of tears.

From the outside, somewhere beyond the patio or the adjacent alley, the thundering of quite a few sandaled footsteps were nearing, loudly determined, accompanied by voices of several people talking at once. Not a regular occurrence between the quiet dwellings of their neighborhood. What now?

Tensing despite herself, she listened, her senses telling her that the newcomers were progressing purposefully, sure of themselves and their destination, their thick-soled sandals resounding against the cracked cobblestones, firm and unwavering. Warriors? But why here? On the marketplace, upon hearing such sounds, one was wise to move away, as the warriors would usually escort a litter carrying nobility or accompany an official, a judge or a tribute collector on duty, expecting the crowds to clear off on their own. However, no nobility or officials frequented regular neighborhoods, having nothing to seek there, no goods to purchase and no tribute to collect. The head of the district, a noble person in himself, and his council of elected officials was taking care of any such business on behalf of the citizens entrusted to their care.

Her heart pounding, she listened to the voices, now rolling down the patio, talking loudly and curtly, distributing orders. She could hear Father's words, his hurried footsteps coming from the direction of the workshop, followed by the frantic echoing of more sandals, belonging to her brothers surely. It was difficult to decipher their words in this clamor.

Father sounded atypically agitated again, and it seemed that he was asking questions, arguing, maybe. With warriors? It didn't make any sense. Her fingers twisted the stretched maguey strings, messing up the entire frame. But she would have to redo it all in the end, to unravel the work of half a day. Numbly, she stared at the scrambled fabric.

The voices and the footsteps began drawing away. She could hear them pouring from beyond the patio now, the opposite direction they had come from. Father's too. He was still talking rapidly, with clear agitation.

Another sound, this time of the drawn screen of the doorway, made her jump, overturning the inadequately secured loom, ruining her work for good now. She didn't care, staring at Mother's lithe figure, bereft of words. After the semidarkness of her room, her eyes found it difficult to adjust; still, it was easy to see how upset Mother was, how flustered, even more than on the evening before, upon her, Chantli's, return. Back then, the poor woman looked terrible, gazing out of her swollen ringed eyes as though dazed, her face puffy and red, stained with tears. The memory made her heart twist despite her own ghastly feeling. It was all because of her, she had known immediately, a dreadful worry and not a simple anger at the displayed disobedience, but with Father thundering fiercely, shooting his direful promises and threats, forbidding her contact with anyone until deciding her fate, she couldn't throw herself into Mother's arms, to cry and ask for forgiveness. Yet now...

The loom still strapped to her back dragged awkwardly across the floor, screeching, forgotten. Oblivious of it all, she hurled herself into her mother's arms, heedless of reason, or that she had been forbidden to do so, sobbing her heart out. It was so good to feel this wonderfully familiar warmth and comfort, something she needed oh so very badly, she realized, through the last two days.

"*Nantli*," she sobbed, pressing into the crispiness of the familiar *huipil*, its patterns friendly and cheerful, its touch intimate, smell cozy. "Oh, *nantli!*"

The loving arms were pressing her tenderly, trembling too. "Hush, little one. Don't cry."

"But, *nantli!*" She felt her words about to burst out in an unstoppable gush. It made her head dizzy. "It's so unfair. Father is so angry and won't let me explain. And he won't let me be with you. And I... I... I'm so miserable. I'm sorry about everything. I didn't mean to do any of it. I, I was just worried, worried about Miztli, and I went to see the *calmecac* boys, to ask for their help. Because Patli, you see, Patli showed them that place, that temple with the tunnel, and they got in trouble and Miztli didn't come home, and we just wanted, wanted to find out what happened to him..." The hysterical sobbing was taking over again, making her struggle for breath. "And I didn't, didn't mean to get into all this trouble, or to make you worry so. Or to make Father that angry. I didn't..."

The familiar comforting warmth was all there, enveloping, rocking her back and forth, calming. "Come now, little one. Don't cry. Not so loudly," Mother was chanting, whispering into her hair. "Calm down, little one. Calm down. It's important that you do." The embracing hands were pushing her away gently, still holding, giving her strength, but now at arm's length. "You must tell me what happened, little one. You must calm down and tell me. It's important that you do and we don't have much time."

Something in the older woman's tone made Chantli concentrate. She tried to see through the veil of tears. "Wh-what, what d-do you mean?" But this stammering was annoying! She swallowed hard. "What do you mean, Mother?"

The woman sighed. "You must tell me where have you been and what exactly happened."

"Why?" Somehow, it felt important to know that. Mother wasn't being just comforting or invoking her right to know where her daughter had spent a night and half a day. She was after something. "Why do you ask?" To sniff with her clogged nose felt silly. She glanced around, hunting after a discarded piece of cloth.

"The warriors came here just now. They had been sent to collect the apprentice, to take him to the Imperial Court."

She felt her heart tumbling down to her stomach, to lie there like a dead weight. To bring her hands to her face didn't help. They were trembling too badly, doing a silly dance.

"Why?" she whispered, marveling at her ability to say anything at all. "Why would they do that?"

Mother's eyes didn't shift, boring into her, stern and unwavering, reading her thoughts. Now it was the interrogator asking, the stern parent that she always was. Father could scold and admonish, but it was always Mother who made sure she and her sibling behaved on a daily basis.

"It has to do with your adventures out there, Chantli. Tell me what you did and where. And why."

She drew herself together, ashamed of the tears. "I was trying to tell you, Mother. Since coming back here, I was trying to tell you what happened, where we were. Father was the one who told me not to talk but to listen. He locked me in this room and he didn't let me out for the entire night!" It felt childish to raise her voice, surely with the warriors still around, maybe wishing to drag her to the Imperial Court as well. But why would they want to judge Miztli? For what offense? Did Tlatelolco authorities lodge a complaint of a sort? She shivered, her newly gained confidence trickling out fast. "I don't know what we did wrong," she went on, hating the pleading tone, so obvious, impossible to miss. "I don't mind telling it all, all of it. But the village boy doesn't deserve to be dragged into the courts. He didn't do anything wrong. None of us did!"

"Tell me about it, Chantli, and do it quickly," was the unsympathetic response.

She struggled to keep her gaze level and her back straight. "Miztli was kidnapped. I don't know exactly who did it. You should ask Patli about it. He was the one to drag them all into it, Miztli and some other boys. I don't know who they were. Patli could tell you." It was wiser to pretend that she didn't know who Necalli was, to what school he belonged, or what his name was. Maybe he and his friend would manage to stay out of it somehow. She drew another deep breath. "Anyway, Miztli was kidnapped and Patli and I and those other boys went looking for him, and, well, we got stuck under the causeway and there was this canoe..." But wasn't she telling too much? Mother's eyes were mere slits in the gentleness of her face, their suspicion well on display. "In the beginning, we drifted to Tlatelolco, and then it took so long to find our way back. And, well, in the end, we managed to return."

"With the village boy miraculously recovered?"

That came out slightly mocking. Chantli pressed her lips tight.

"Yes, we did find him. And in the strangest of companies." She remembered the Tlatelolcan girl, so bad-tempered and haughty, so foul-mouthed. So obviously taken with Miztli too, the most transparent thing, stupid fowl. As though such obviously high nobility could be allowed to run around with barefoot villagers from across the causeway. Ridiculous! Even though he did wear sandals back then. Where did he get something so costly? He didn't explain, neither his sudden change in appearance nor his unlikely company, and she had been too busy to stop and ask questions. Their predicament was too direful back then.

"Tell me what you did in Tlatelolco, Chantli. And what that boy did."

To gain some time, she bent to pick up the fallen loom, its unfinished fabric hopelessly messed up, beyond repair. "I don't..."

The voices were pouring in again, reaching them through the wall opening and the gaping doorway, such loud talking. They were crowding the patio, now unmistakably. Chantli stopped breathing again. Father's voice was not among the commotion of curt words and shuffling of thick-soled sandals, but she knew he was there, watching silently, his fury well hidden, and when his shadowed silhouette blocked the light seeping through the narrow doorway, she knew that her troubles were far from being over.

"Tell me everything you know about that boy and what he did through the last two days here and in Tlatelolco, and do it quickly, Daughter!" His tone left no doubts in her dread-frozen chest.

CHAPTER 20

The dusty stones of the road behind the marketplace were surprisingly smooth, pleasant to step on. Even though scorching hot, they provided a welcome change to the unevenness of the gravel alleys. So much easier to walk on, a real pleasure, despite his battered, disoriented state.

To keep his back straight and his step satisfactorily steady was a challenge in itself, not helped by the briskness of his guards' walk. However, the paved surface helped. Having never set his foot in this luxurious part of the city, glimpsing its towering pyramids and their glittering temples from afar, he now found his interest genuinely piqued, eyes comparing. That crowded plaza of Tlatelolco, with one towering pyramid and a few smaller ones, filled with people and warriors to the brim, sporting two podiums and two lavishly decorated daises; would Tenochtitlan's Great Plaza be that imposing? It was easy to guess the answer. Judging by the several plazas they had passed until now, after leaving the marketplace and the simple yet well-to-do neighborhoods behind, he didn't even try to imagine what the Great Plaza and the Royal Enclosure would look like. Tlatelolco might as well declare itself as a village. But would Tlemilli get mad hearing him thinking something like that!

The thought made him chuckle inside, too spent and dizzy to try and do it for real, even without the presence of his grave, close-mouthed escorts. He didn't dare to glance at them, concentrating on the dusty stones sweeping below his feet, trying not to trip, his stomach tightening in a hundred painful knots. No, he wouldn't be able to tell her any of that. He wouldn't be able to see her again, ever! Even if he survived that court ordeal, something old Tlaquitoc threatened him with for the entire evening before locking him in the melting room, too frightened and exhausted to protest or even feel bad about it; even then he wouldn't enjoy any freedom for many moons to come, if ever. Oh mighty gods!

Even now, half a day later, after that troubled sleep on the bare floor and the whole morning of working with no meal in sight – not even a moldy tortilla, although he was too exhausted to feel pangs of hunger by now – he could not bring himself to think about it all, the direful consequences of his deed. But how did it come to this? Yes, he went to wander around with Patli, succumbing to his boredom and the need of company. Yes, he got in trouble down there in that tunnel and in the reeds of the lake. Still, how had it come to something that hopeless and terrible?

The dreadful adventures, yes, hurtful and scary, resulting in plenty of beating and running around, facing scheming nobility, lying to them, trying to survive. Then her, that fiery Tlatelolcan girl, a noble of the Palace of all things but so trustworthy and down-to-earth, demanding, impulsive, talking with no pause, pleasing with her bubbling, enthusiastic presence, making him feel curiously important, strong, in control. Until Chantli had fallen on them, angering his companion greatly, causing a strange outburst of nastiness, lashing out like a slender, furious serpent. Not TleMilli – Field of Fire, but TleCoatl – Fire Snake; they should have called her that.

Still, he didn't want her to leave, not minding the complications her presence might have brought, with her connection to that dreadful Teconal, her father of all things, not only after him, Miztli, but after the *calmecac* boy as well. And yet, from that moment on, it all went downhill, he reflected now, clenching his teeth against the smothering wave that was rising again high in his chest, threatening to choke him.

Although back then, it didn't look so bad. They had managed to free themselves, escape with their lives and even some of their dignity, laughing about it in the end, feeling good, victorious. But was it good to be a part of this group, the cheerful leader-like

Necalli so sure of himself, so reliable and a friend, not a snotty violent noble-school pupil, not anymore, full of needling jokes but not meaning to hurt, a lighthearted fellow. Even Patli was not that unbearable, contributing a little to their talks, wavering and swaying, his head bleeding but not too badly. They said it was a relief, as in the morning he was out cold, conversing with the spirits. Chantli kept worrying about that.

So all reeling and tottering, hurt to different degrees but in the best of spirits, they had waded their way to the causeway, climbing the slippery earthwork, choking with laughter at each other's clumsiness. The wild pell-mell run across had them doubling over yet again, spilling into Tenochtitlan's wharves, unable to breathe from the wildness of their laughter. The dangerous adventure was over and they had come out of it in not such bad shape.

Or so he thought. Until they staggered into the narrow yard of old Tlaquitoc's house. Then the illusion broke into twenty little pieces, like a clay form under the annealing hammer.

Crazed with anger in a way he couldn't even imagine the dignified, well-spoken, solemn craftsman succumbing to, he listened to the blistering screams, the man's face glowing with unhealthy red, his huge fists clenched and shaking, dangerous looking, promising no good. Even half-conscious Patli drew himself up, daring not to slide along the doorway beam he had pressed against as though trying to disappear there, or faint, for that matter, his face a grotesque mask of dry blood, mud, and pastiness.

Chantli didn't look much better at this point, so openly shocked and frightened it made his own dread multiply by leaps and bounds. For all eternity, it seemed, twenty upon twenty direful promises were heaped upon their heads, then Chantli and Patli were hastened inside the house, while he had been grabbed by his shoulder with rock-hard, crushing fingers – but this man should have been a stone worker! – and dragged into the workshop, frightened for real and resisting to no avail, hurled into the melting room as though he had been a reed-woven mat with no weight, a disobedient mat at that. But he never suspected the old man as being so terribly strong.

Anticipating a savage beating at the very least, he sprang back to his feet almost against his will, his heart pumping insanely. Yet what came next made him regret the lack of physical punishment. Suddenly calm, ominously in control, the old man stood there, studying his victim, his massive head shaking, lips twisting unpleasantly. He, Miztli, was the most ungrateful human being that ever trod the earth of their World of the Fifth Sun, his employer had informed him, most ungrateful and worthless, thinking nothing of people who were good to him, repaying kindness with nastiness and self-serving indulgence, harming his benefactors and even his own family, the poor farmers of his home village, those who put their trust in him, going to great lengths in order to obtain him a place in the Great Capital to learn and evolve. The punishment for his vile ways would harm his family, oh yes, he had been informed, his stomach nothing but jelly, quivering, his limbs refusing to support him. Such crimes as his were dealt harshly by the courts of the Great Capital, laziness and theft being two of the seven most abominable transgressions in youths and adults alike.

As the man went on, speaking in his old deliberate way, tranquil and almost compassionate, he kept wondering how it had come to him being accused of all those things, but his mind refused to concentrate, unable to cope, and it left his ears alone to absorb the assaulting phrases, telling him how he would be strangled or maybe stoned, depending on the judge and his mood, and how his family would have to be sold into slavery in order to repay the debt his absence of three full days had created. Oh mighty deities, but what did his family have to do with all this?

Pressing against the inner wall, fighting the suffocating fear with no success, he remembered being informed that the courts were convened in the first part of the day and so the next day would seal his fate – his and his family's. But did the man keep harping on that, *his family, his father*. It was all too bad that it had come to this, his tormenter would sigh several times. What an unfortunate ending.

In the end, he remembered himself finding his tongue at long last, breaking into a frantic begging. No, not the court, please, anything but that. He would work for days and nights, wouldn't even move from the braziers, would do anything and everything, but please not to have his father involved, not to have the courts selling his father or anyone else of the family into slavery, anything but this!

It took some time and many frantic promises to have the old craftsman relenting, letting himself to be persuaded, albeit reluctantly, to have him, Miztli, sold into this workshop's slavery instead, until his debt was paid in its entirety however many moons it took. A hard, dedicated work with no payments and no meals, but by this point, he would have agreed to let the man cut off his right arm and his left one in the bargain. Even when locked in the melting room, to think it all through as the old man informed him, he still didn't dare to believe the lucky outcome, still feared that the man would drag him to the court first thing in the morning, demanding his execution and his father's slavery to make it all right again. Oh mighty deities!

Clenching his teeth against the terrible memory, he lifted his eyes, watching the colorful walls that were now slanting all around, the stairs of some of the lower pyramids glimmering in the strong sun, so perfectly polished, they shone. Beautifully dressed crowds surrounded them now, less pushing and loudmouthed than the multitudes swarming the alleys behind the marketplace or even back in Tlatelolco, upon that plaza that could not be compared with Tenochtitlan's spacious vastness or the richness of its coloring and adornments.

The warriors slowed their step and he breathed with relief, welcoming the respite, not sure he would be able to keep up with them for much longer. The air kept swimming before his eyes, flickering with a light mist, and his legs felt as though made out of maguey, not firm enough to support him for real. But he was so tired! Since before dawn-break, it had been like that, pushing the dizziness and exhaustion away, tormented with hunger but paying it no attention, not counting on any food offering, not thinking how he would go on working without it. To keep himself away from courts and his family away from slavery was the first priority. He would manage somehow. He had to!

Grateful for the pile of firewood that had been left near the shut doorway, he had stocked both braziers, having them blazing with red-hot fire by the time his master came in, nodding in grim approval. Then it was blowing the first load of powdered copper, a simple melt in a few smallish clay pots, something he was grateful for, as when the metal liquid had been ready, he managed to lift both loads and even pour their contents into their designated containers without faltering, breathless with the effort but successful. Had those been the usual midsized pots, he would have been in trouble. With the annoying dizziness and those wobbly limbs of his, he couldn't possibly lift any of those.

"Keep it up, boy. It's not such a long walk now." One of the warriors pushed him lightly, urging him to go on. Briefly, he wondered at their amiable ways. Wherever they were taking him – please not the courts, anything but that! – these people were surprisingly considerate, even polite. A wonder!

The wideness of the glittering canal and the bridge stretching over it made him gap again, but it faded into complete insignificance at the sight of the Great Pyramid and the vibrancy of its colors. So impossibly high! He watched it towering behind another imposing building and the vastness of the walled square, with more pyramids surrounding it. The alley they turned into brought them toward another wall, this one plastered in brilliant shades, gilded at its upper parts, hurting one's eye with the glitter of it. The opening they approached was guarded but unbarred. A few words and he had been pushed in, not violently but firmly. He wondered about it once again.

"Where to?" puzzled one of his escorts in a low voice. "Not the main entrance, surely."

"Yes, the main entrance," was the laconic response. "The Palace's servants will take it from there. Leave it to their administration to deal with." There was a chuckle to the speaker's voice.

The dazzling green of the trees all around made Miztli miss the rest of the exchange, the radiant vividness of the flowerbeds, the perfection of the ornamented pathways. Dazzled, he stared, not watching his step anymore. The loftily soaring walls, the glistening stairs, so wide and polished they shone, the delicately illuminated hall adorned with gilded statues of a man's height and more, paneled with glassy wood, the people who stared at him, the obvious discomfort of the richly dressed person who had been approached by his guards, a small army of equally meticulously clad aides hovering behind – all those were wasted on him, blending into a vibrant flow, too vivid and rich in detail to comprehend or try to process.

"He'll need to be cleaned," was someone's lofty conclusion, but he didn't catch this person's expression or looks. The blur of colors all around made him dizzy. "Get him to the redwood room and get the maids with the cloths to clean him thoroughly and dress in an appropriate way." A pause. "Tell the kitchen maids to feed them. This one especially. He can't be brought before the Revered One looking like that."

Then it was back to the moving, another bright room, this one cozily narrow, with a breeze coming in through the open shutters. Prettily dressed women, wet cloths, and bowls of splashing liquid, stripped but not caring, beyond embarrassment, the feel of the new clothing good, again unwarranted softness covering his shoulders, his feet rubbed vigorously, then ensconced in crude leather, this time even his heel. Like Tlemilli's sandals, he reflected numbly, the dreamy sensation fading, banished by the tightening in his stomach. She counted on him to come back and find her. She risked so much, confronted her father, tricked the frightening man into leaving in order to help, trusting his promise, believing in him.

Hands tugged at his shoulder, urging him back to his feet. He complied listlessly, aware of his surroundings now, indifferent to the incomparable beauty and luxury.

"Please follow." A good-looking middle-aged woman motioned him with her hand. But were they so impossibly polite here, from warriors to servants. Obediently, he followed. What else was there to do?

Back in the statues-filled hall, a group of imposingly clad men was progressing toward the stairs and the brilliance of the outside, the headdress of one of them towering above the entire group, radiantly green. He followed it with his gaze. But were their high-soled sandals making a loud noise! Again, he wondered about his own surprisingly comfortable wear. Was he sticking around less than before? The lingering glance of another passerby, a man with a wide tray balanced neatly in his hand, informed him that he still did. Good for them. His guide pushed him hastily into another opening.

"The workshop boy?"

The exclamation made him forget his dazed musings. Blinking, he found himself staring, facing none other than the *calmecac* boys, both of them, squatting on two opposite mats, snatching greedily at the plate of tortillas that separated their seats.

"I knew it had to do with our high-spirited royal *pilli!*" A careless wave of an oily palm invited him to join the feast. "Still didn't expect to see your commoner face in the Palace, copper-melting boy. And dressed like a person this time. Nice work."

"What are you doing here?" mumbled Miztli, feeling called upon to say something, to respond to so much friendly chattering. The woman who brought him here dissolved in the dimness of the hall outside the opening.

"Same as you, brother. Waiting for our fate to be decided upon. A rescue from more punishments or a deeper hole full of excrements to fall into? You name it and they may have it in store for us. We've been waiting here in this side-room forever, but before you showed up, they didn't even think to offer us refreshments." The well-defined eyes sparkled with mischief. "Bad hospitality."

"Would you shut up?" demanded the other one, Axolin, squatting with less comfort than his friend, his bandaged ankle folded awkwardly. "At least lower your voice!"

Necalli made a face. "Help yourself to the mats and the food, working boy. You look like you need it." The glittering eyes narrowed, turned serious. "That old craftsman went hard on you, didn't he?"

Nearing their cozily arranged corner, Miztli just shrugged. "And you?"

"Did they?" His companions rolled their eyes in perfect unison, exchanging glances. "You must have fared easier than we did, working boy. There are no laws to govern your workshop, no one to flaunt your punishments before and make an example out of you."

"No noble father to disappoint either," added Axolin bitterly, "to send messengers informing of his precious son's unworthiness."

"They didn't do that yet!" exclaimed Necalli, losing some of his good humor. "Maybe they won't go so far if we behave. Old Yaotzin and even Revered Teohuatzin himself said nothing about that. "

"I bet they informed our fathers while we've been missing. You just don't know it yet. When you are allowed to leave the school, you'll have that stick waiting at home. Or plenty of boiling chili peppers," he added after a thought, his grin crooked.

Necalli was staring at the plate of tortillas, not amused anymore. "They didn't," he muttered in the end, pursing his lips stubbornly. "They wouldn't be so silly as not to have yet another threat left hanging above our heads, to be used at their will." His eyes flashed with dark anger, then cleared once again. "Sit down, workshop boy. Don't hover there like a pretty maid not sure of her welcome."

That and Axolin's snicker made Miztli drop onto the vacant mat and fast. But it was good to be in this company again. Reviving, even. He reached for the nearest tortilla, still warm and oily, spilling between his fingers, dripping greenish stuffing, avocado for sure. His hunger exploded in force.

"So what did this metal-worker of yours do to you all?" Necalli snatched another pastry greedily, yet his gaze lingered, searching in a way. "He had three culprits to deal with, more than our *calmecac* authorities, come to think of it. Poor man." The twisting of the generous lips was impossible not to snicker at.

"I don't know what he did to the others." He forced his shoulders into as casual lifting as he could manage, his insides again squashed by a stony fist, the devoured tortilla lying in there like a dead weight, revolting. "There was much yelling coming from the house." He marveled at the sound of his own voice, so level. "Chantli must have had it the worst. He was yelling mainly at her when still out near the patio."

The *calmecac* boy's back stiffened. "He has no right to punish her harshly. She did nothing wrong!"

"He has every right, you know." Again, Axolin, the voice of reason. Miztli felt like demanding from that one to shut up as well. "She spent a day and a night away from home. Think what your father would have done to your sisters if they did something like that. Mine would invoke every parental right there is in the law. In the best of cases, that non-existent sister of mine would be married off to the most meager villager with no fields to work." His grin flickered grimly, not brightening the atmosphere. "It's good that my father has only sons."

Necalli was staring at the diminishing plate. "She didn't do anything wrong. We got carried by that stupid canoe and she was the bravest. Certainly the bravest out of her family representation," he added with a snort.

"Her father wouldn't care about that."

"Didn't you manage to see her today?" The scowling eyes were upon him again, demanding. "You must have seen her sometime during the morning. It's high noon now!"

"No, I didn't," tossed Miztli, incensed. He had his own troubles to deal with. He wasn't Chantli's keeper. "She wasn't allowed to run around outside, obviously."

"But in the house…"

"I'm not allowed in there."

The pointed eyebrows climbed up in surprise. "Why not?"

To just shrug felt safer.

"It doesn't make sense," insisted Necalli. "You can't *not* be allowed in the house at all. You must eat and sleep somewhere, don't you? Even slaves sleep inside houses and you are not a slave."

He clenched his teeth tight. "I am now." It came out strangled, a gruff, muffled sound.

Both boys were gaping at him, wide-eyed. He stood the incredulousness of their stares for another heartbeat, then dropped his own. It was disheartening, the depth of their surprise.

"How? Why?"

He studied the ornate doorway, wishing to spring to his feet and run out.

"It doesn't make sense," insisted Necalli, forceful as always, not about to let go. "One doesn't become a slave just like that. What did you do?"

"Ran away with you all, absented myself for three days, didn't do my work, caused damage." The words spilled out monotonously, even dully.

"What damage?" Axolin's eyes were as narrow as cut on a tree bark.

"The damage my absence has caused." It pleased him how detachedly he was talking, with so little feeling. "It's equal to a theft, a taking of goods, all this time that I was out and not working. In court, it counts as theft."

"A theft?" cried out Necalli, incredulous. "What nonsense!"

"Who told you all that?" Axolin was squinting dubiously, one corner of his mouth tugging with a skeptical grin. "That craftsman of yours, I bet."

This time, Miztli felt like dissolving in the thin air. Staring at the prettily ornamented tiles, he said nothing.

"If your absence from the workshop could be considered as a theft, half of Tenochtitlan would be strangled or sold into slavery by now," cried out Necalli. "No, two-thirds. Most of the city, everyone who didn't feel like getting up with sunrise, took their time returning from a journey, got lost, or any other plentitude of reasons. It's pure nonsense what you told us just now. Think about it!"

He tried to do that, his mind buzzing, thoughts rushing around in silly circles, refusing to organize. There was much sense in what they said. Theft was a serious crime, punishable by death even back in his village, but how could one's going away from his duties be considered a theft?

"So he told you that you stole from him by going away for a few days without permission." Axolin was arriving at his conclusions and fast, his eyes still narrow, lips twitching with the satisfaction of a hunter following a clear trail of footprints. "And to make it up to him, you will have to sell yourself into his slavery until the debt is paid. Did he tell you that?" There was a triumphant glitter to the boy's eyes.

Miztli found it safer to just shrug, taking his own eyes away again.

"Well, it won't work in your district's court, I can tell you that," contributed Necalli. "No judge in his right mind would agree to that claim."

"But were you paying attention to the old Axactzin's class back when the man tried to drum some laws into our heads, brother." Axolin's laughter was healthy, his elbow making its way toward his friend's ribs. "And here I was thinking you were busy snoring with your eyes open."

Necalli laughed as heartily. "It was boring, yes, but I remember some things." His forehead furrowed. "Twenty ears of maize, no? Twenty ears of maize as the maximum cost of the stolen property to be sold into slavery until it's paid. Or the culprit is strangled."

"Yes, I think it was that. Or maybe more. Maybe two twenties. Or maybe two baskets full of maize up to twenty ears each." The taller boy waved his hands in the air. "Who can remember all this? We are to be warriors and leaders, not filthy scribes. When it's my time to be an emperor's most important adviser and a judge in this or that court, I'll refresh my memory." A snicker. "Then I'll look up old Axactzin and ask him."

Necalli was guffawing as well, supporting his bandaged arm with his good one in a familiar gesture. "So don't worry, brother." The crinkling eyes focused on Miztli again, their wink unmistakable. "No judge would sentence you to that much-coveted slavery of yours. Not until you actually steal something. His hammer or whatever other tool your craftsman is fond of."

Miztli's head reeled. "But it's too late. I already agreed. I am his slave now. There is no way back from it." He felt silly talking like that, in a breathless rush. They were staring at him again, their eyebrows arching in a ridiculously similar manner. "I agreed beforehand, so he won't take me to the court. You don't understand. He'll do it, he meant what he said. This is the law.

And then my family… my father… I can't let it happen!"

Necalli's forehead was again wrinkling like an old blanket. "You are afraid to go to the court? But that's silly. The judges know their work. They are good judges, usually. And you can't agree to anything without their involvement anyway. You can't just start slaving on your or his say-so. It's not lawful. How would you know when your debt is already paid? How would you determine the amount of what you owe? How would he?"

"Yes, man. That's what judges do. No smelly craftsmen, or traders, or anyone else, for that matter, can make or implement laws. That's just ridiculous."

He tried to take it all in, his head hurting. "But I agreed already," he muttered helplessly. "I can't go back on my word."

"You can't agree to anything on his say-so, you stubborn, thick-headed villager," cried out Necalli, exasperated; yet his grin crinkled, taking the edge off of the offensive title. "What you agreed on wasn't lawful. It doesn't work like that in Tenochtitlan, even if in your village, you all may be selling yourself left and right if you feel like it, not stepping outside your houses to do that. Here, it is different, and that annoying would-be owner of yours is a liar and a thief himself, stealing your freedom and making you agree to unlawful things. He promised you the judges would find you guilty, didn't he? That they would strangle you right away?"

He shrugged again, feeling incredibly stupid, wishing to break something on account of it.

"What else did he promise?" demanded Axolin shrewdly. "You wouldn't be cringing so fast if it was only about that strangulation. You are no cowardly Patli."

"He said my family would be sold into slavery to pay my debt after I'm strangled," he muttered, the tiles of the floor gaining the entirety of his attention again, such pretty patterns.

"What a lowly piece of excrement!" Necalli flailed his good arm in the air, its fist clenched. "After this Palace's interrogation – if we survive it, that is – I'm off to visit that workshop of yours. Eh, Axolin? How about we talk to that brother of yours, the brood of that other mealy-mouthed fowl that is preceding your mother, eh? He knows his way around laws and rules, that one. He'll intimidate that craftsman into paying Miztli half of his workshop in order to forget this whole thing."

Axolin was beaming. "Not a bad idea. Chichimitl might agree. He is the best of my brothers and this visit promises to be fun. He won't miss something like that."

Miztli's heart was making strange leaps inside his chest, beating too fast, threatening to jump out. "I... you don't have to... it's too kind of you two." He licked his lips hastily, needing a gulp of water desperately. "I... I'll manage, somehow. I didn't know. I thought that he meant what he said. I thought it was lawful. I... I don't know why I didn't think straight..." For the life of him, he could not admit to the bottomless fear of the last night, the choking quality of it, drowning in his own terror, helpless like a broken canoe in the rapids of the highland streams. Oh, but how vivid this memory was, how real, even now, half a day later and in the safety of the bright beautiful room, in the company of these boys, so light with their banter, so sure of themselves, set on helping him, eager to do this. But he didn't deserve that, did he? "I just didn't think. It was stupid of me. I... I thank you for telling me all this, for wishing to help..."

"No need to get all flustered like that, man." Necalli was snickering again, over his previous rage in this typical fast fashion of his. "You'll faint or puke on the Palace's floor. Calm down. Whoever wants to interrogate us here will not appreciate the stammering mess that you are now. He'll sell you into slavery for offending royal ears and eyes."

Axolin was guffawing too loudly again.

"Go and jump into the lake," muttered Miztli, his face burning so badly he was afraid it would make the beautiful floor ignite. "I'm not stammering."

"Eat tortillas and relax," was the nonchalant response. "It might get scary soon enough. Who do you think wants to ask us questions, eh?" he added, addressing his *calmecac* friend again, sobering gradually. "I hope the royal *pilli*'s tales didn't put us in a bad light, eh? That one is capable of wild embellishment to make himself look like the bravest of heroes."

"He didn't come out cowardly as it is," protested Axolin. "If anything, he behaved like not many half twenty summers old would."

"I didn't say he was cowardly. Just that he can lie to make himself look even better."

Relieved to be away from the center of their attention, helpfully friendly or not, Miztli reached for another roll, then froze. The men who had poured in through the doorway were meticulously dressed and stern, greatly foreboding. Four all in all, they halted at the doorway, studying the three of them with open doubt – measuring, deliberating. The *calmecac* boys straightened up but did not jump to their feet. Conscious of his crawling skin, Miztli did the same.

"Send a maid to bring in bowls to wash their hands," tossed the leading man curtly, his gaze narrowed, penetrating. "Afterwards, bring them to the paneled hall. I'll take it from there." Another scrutinizing inspection. "Be quick about it. The Revered One may wish to see them soon."

At least this time, he was allowed to wash himself, reflected Miztli, grimly amused, dipping his hands in the bowl of water in his turn, washing his mouth and chin quickly, concentrating on irrelevant things. The soft cotton of the cloth he was offered to wipe the water off, the *calmecac* boys' atypical quietness – no more needling banter and no elbowing either – the way one of the maids was sneaking glances at him, openly curious. The extent of his true troubles he would consider later, he decided, much later, after the Palace's interrogation was over. Oh, but what to do? How to face old Tlaquitoc now? How to talk to him? Was this man truly nothing but a deceitful snake, the shameless unscrupulous liar out to use his, Miztli's, naivety and lack of knowledge, eager to exploit it, to work him into death and with no remorse? No, he couldn't be that bad. He was anything but scrupulous and just until now. Or wasn't he? What else had the man lied about? To Father too, maybe. Oh mighty deities!

The walk along the bright halls refreshed him, made his racing heart slow. One thing at the time, Father always said. Each trouble in its turn. No need to agonize over something you can't confront and try to solve right away. Put it aside, deal with the more pressing issues. Not all at once, never this.

The thought of Father made his stomach constrict. What would he think about all this? Would he consider his son a failure now, the boy who couldn't even stick to simple work in the workshop for more than a few moons, the place Father went to such great lengths obtaining for him? And what if his family still could be made involved, somehow, sold into slavery or at least harassed about it all? The ice in his stomach kept piling, interfering with his ability to think.

"Take off your shoes."

The *calmecac* boys were already kicking off their prettily decorated sandals. Miztli stared at their bared feet for another heartbeat.

"Do it quickly." Another order, less cordial than before. He struggled with the intricate cobweb of straps, aware of the impatience surrounding him. But it wasn't he who had tied those things at the first place!

"Now remember," went on their escort, his lips pursing in open displeasure, "you prostrate yourselves when you near the Revered Emperor's seat, at the edge of the mats you'll be conducted through. Do not step any closer. After you've been conducted to the place designated for you, stay there and do not step forward or aside." Another piercing glare focused on them; Miztli in particular. He felt his cheeks beginning to glow anew. "Do not look the Emperor in his eye unless he addresses you. Do not look at the revered person at all unless being spoken to."

The hushed up harangue went on, laying out more rules, or rather restrictions, plenty of forbidden gestures or motions. His concentration vanished together with the recently gained semblance of confidence. It was impossible to remember it all, let alone to implement. And what would the all-powerful ruler do then?

"You may enter now."

This came from another imposing figure, majestic in wittily patterned garment and glittering jewelry. The *calmecac* boys followed this celebration of colors, quiet for a change. Then he felt

Necalli's whisper, just a brush of a breath by his ear. "He forgot to tell us not to break wind. So we can, can't we?"

The rest of the walk he barely managed to complete, the splendor of yet another great hall lost on him amidst the worst stomach cramps, his facial muscles going rigid with the attempt not to let it dissolve into the wildest guffawing and worse. The prohibition to look up helped. It left his eyes free to concentrate on the softly carved tiles, then the intricately woven mats placed one after another. At the edge of those, he even managed to prostrate himself in the way his companions did, or at least close enough to it, bowing his head to the embroidered straw but not touching it, freezing in such a pose.

"You may rise to your feet." The deep voice rang clearly in the vast chamber, not rising to make itself heard better. It was a voice used to talking to vast crowds, realized Miztli, remembering the orating ruler of Tlatelolco. But did he encounter nobility aplenty through these last two days, he who had never seen even a tribute collector up close before.

"Come stand on those mats next to the podium," went on the man on the elevated chair, brisk and efficient, matter-of-fact. "Here." A wave of an outstretched hand indicated a long podium and two lower chairs, occupied as well. The bracelets adorning the well-muscled arm sparkled green, ringing lightly, bumping against each other. "Make yourself comfortable here, where you can answer not only my questions but the inquiries of Honorable Tizoc and Lady Atotztli." A brief twist of the royal lips. "And of course our high-spirited adventurer Ahuitzotl, who will not be asking questions but probably answering those alongside with you."

The regal head inclined toward the boy who was poised between the two chairs, not honored with seating arrangements, standing as straight as an arrow, his head held high. The sight of the familiar eyes and the jutting chin made Miztli feel better, bringing the memory of the wild laughter at the edge of the causeway. Even though dressed in a vibrantly embroidered cloak, his arms sparkling jewelry, and his head sporting an intricate topknot of warriors, his hair oiled and glistening, the boy didn't look changed, his expression familiar, not haughty or indifferent, holding recognition.

"Do not be afraid or bashful." The measured voice upon the elevated chair was speaking again, deliberate and calm, reassuring. "Your adventures in Tlatelolco are of an interest to me. Answer truthfully and with no fear. Do not omit any detail, even if it puts you in a bad light. If you do so, you will be punished." A brief pause. "As on the contrary, your truthful answers will save you plenty of trouble."

Against all instructions, Miztli found his eyes drifting to the imposing figure, impressed. Like Father, the man knew to relay sternness without raising his voice or using threats and intimidation. Sitting with ease, not leaning on the tempting softness of the intricately embroidered and cushioned upholstery, Tenochtitlan's ruler presented an impressive picture indeed, broad-shouldered and straight-backed, without a headdress to shadow the strong face, wide in its lower parts as much as in its cheekbones, with the forcefully jutting chin like that of Ahuitzotl. There was much likeness between the two, besides the expression. The Mexica ruler did not look like someone challenging the world perpetually. He looked like someone who had already challenged it and come out victorious. Shuddering, Miztli took his eyes away.

"You." The ringed finger singled out Necalli. "Tell us your name and your family status."

The *calmecac* boy cleared his throat. "I... my name is YoloNecalli, Revered Emperor. My father, Tlilocelotl, has the honor of serving your illustrious grandfathers, both Revered Itzcoatl and Moctezuma Ilhuicamina, distinguishing himself and receiving many honors."

The Emperor nodded calmly, neither impressed nor repulsed. It was as though he knew it all beforehand. Did he?

"You are attending the noble *calmecac* school along with my brother." It was a statement.

He could see Necalli nodding, swallowing once again

"Tell me what makes a good student, an ambitious pupil as you must be, with such a father and an example to live up to, sneak around the Tlatelolco causeway, exploring deserted temples and dubious activities inside those."

This made Necalli swallow yet harder. "I... I shouldn't have done it, yes," he muttered, licking his lips with an obvious desperation. "It was wrong, not an admirable thing to do, Revered Emperor."

The Emperor's mouth pursed. "As I said, you are not here to be reprimanded. It will be up to your school authorities to discipline you along with your friends and accomplices. Neither will my brother escape retribution. Do not mistake me. It will be done." The generous lips pressed tighter. "While I appreciate your illegally acquired knowledge, I do not condone your breaking your school rules. A good warrior and leader does not break the rules his superiors laid out with great care and much forethought. If you wish to grow into worthwhile warriors, you will keep to the resolution of breaking no more laws. As the students of the best school in our capital, you can't be expected to behave with less decorum than this."

Now even young Ahuitzotl flinched.

The Emperor's eyes softened. "For now I wish to hear your side of this story. What weaponry has been stashed in this tunnel under the temple and how much of it?"

As the *calmecac* boy went on recalling their first evening's adventures, Miztli stopped listening, his eyes drifting toward the occupiers of the other chairs, a thickset man in his early twenties, pale and undistinguished, and a woman, not young but strikingly good-looking, her face oval and soft, delicate, pleasing the eye, even if her expression did not. Such a cold, indifferent gaze. But where had he seen such an expression before?

A light nudge in his ribs made him concentrate on the flow of words that had stopped for some time, his gaze leaping back toward the presiding ruler. Appalled, he watched the narrow eyes focusing on him, the thick eyebrows arching with a silent question, not threatening but not reassuring either.

"Tell me what it was that you had seen in this tunnel on your way back, boy."

Now it was his turn to lick his lips, his tongue too dry to be of help, bringing no relief, the eaten tortilla lying heavily in his stomach. But what had he seen in the tunnel that the other *calmecac* boy didn't? He should have listened to Necalli's words, shouldn't he?

"I... there were weapons, all over this tunnel. In the room that we had reached first, many weapons, clubs and spear-throwers, whole crates of those. Plenty of weaponry. And in the other corridor... tunnel..." He paused to catch a breath.

"Revered Emperor," offered the ruler softly, his lips tugging in one corner, whether with a smile or displeasure, it was difficult to tell.

"Revered Emperor," he repeated, aghast.

The smile won, an amused twist of lips, not reflecting in the watchful eyes, or maybe yes, just a little. "Go on, young commoner. Your knowledge is more important than your lack of manners for now. Tell us what you had found under the earth of this temple."

He swallowed hard, wishing to disappear, to tumble down into the Underworld if necessary, if that was the price of leaving the Palace at this very moment. The smile disappeared, replaced by thinly pressed lips. No more amusement reflected in the strong face. He felt like fainting for good.

"While looking for his way out, he had found more tunnels, besides the one we were walking at first, Revered Emperor." Necalli's voice was music to his ears, the most welcome sound. "There, Miztli happened to overhear the smugglers. They were talking about additional weaponry and Tlatelolco nobility. Weren't they?"

The fleeting glance made him snap back to life, encouraging, giving him strength. "Yes," he said hurriedly, surprised that the words managed to come out at all. "Yes, there was this other tunnel, Revered Emperor. The people who carried crates with more weaponry were talking about it. About Tlatelolco nobility not being happy with the damaged goods."

He saw the ruler straightening up, his eyes narrowing with attention. The heavyset man upon the lower chair leaned forward, making his reed-woven seat creak. Only the haughty woman didn't move, her feathered fan swaying slowly, as though on its own.

"What else?"

Miztli forced his thoughts to focus. "These men, they were talking about Tlatelolco nobility and how unhappy they would be with the damaged goods." But didn't he say that already? The pursing lips told him that he did. He fought to draw another breath. "The men who kidnapped me talked about it too. Back in the boat. They said that the nobleman named Teconal would wish to know all about my spying on this Tlatelolcan hiding weaponry place and that the chief wife of their emperor would wish to know about it too."

Now even the woman straightened with unseemly abruptness. "How is my daughter connected to this?" Her voice was unpleasantly harsh, ringing stridently, intimidating.

He swallowed his tongue once again, not sure how to proceed. It was what they said back in the boat, wasn't it? Or maybe it was he who had brought the Tenochtitlan princess's name up, desperate not to let them throw him overboard, struggling to survive. Well, it didn't matter at this point.

"Go on," said the Emperor calmly, still unperturbed, his voice encouragingly temperate. "What you say is enlightening and of importance. Do not omit anything. Try to remember every word of what has been said."

He nodded eagerly, grateful. "Yes, Revered Emperor." But was he lucky to remember to use the title this time! "In the boat, they didn't talk much, but in the warehouse on the next day, this same nobleman Teconal came to question me. He thought I would know something. Because I had been in the tunnel, I suppose, sniffing around, as they said. They –"

"Teconal is the most abominable human being that ever treaded our World of the Fifth Sun," declared the woman, breaking into his speech. It made him grateful, the opportunity to draw a deep breath while organizing his thoughts, what bliss.

"Please, let us hear the boy out, Mother," said the Emperor sternly, a clear edge to his voice.

The woman pursed her lips and said nothing, her eyes mere slits, taking much of her beauty away.

"What did this nobleman Teconal wish to know?" prompted the Emperor.

"I... well, I suppose he wanted to know who sent me to that tunnel to spy, as they kept assuming that I had been sent to spy. And well..." He licked his lips once again, getting no relief. But he was so thirsty! "I don't know exactly what he wished to know, as before he could come back, that other man, one of the kidnappers, he crept in and dragged me away." To clench his teeth helped but only a little, the mere memory of that warehouse and the occurrences there making his back break out in a bout of cold sweat. "And well, it occurred that he was spying too, on... on the princess's behalf. He took me to another place, where one nobleman questioned me and he sent for the princess to come and question me too."

"What was the nobleman's name?"

"I..." He racked his brains, desperate to remember – the memory wasn't coming, making him cold with fear. Instead, his kidnapper's alias kept surfacing. NexCoatl, Gray Serpent, an interesting name. "I don't, don't remember. Revered Emperor."

"Leave the titles alone for now." The contemplative eyes shifted, staring past him, very absorbed. "The name Tepecocatzin tells you something?"

He gasped. "Yes, yes! That was the name of the old man!"

The Emperor shook his head. "Thought so."

"And you've been disregarding this noble person's repeated messages," said the Emperor's mother reproachfully. "He has sent you plenty of warnings, taking the plight of your sister closer to his heart than you, her full brother, did."

The suddenly fierce glare of the ruler cut the rest of the tirade short, making even the cold noblewoman subdue, leaning back on the upholstery of her chair, the nostrils of her delicate nose widening with the strongly drawn breath.

"Go on."

This time, it was a curt order with no encouraging softness to it. Miztli clenched his palms tight. "Yes, Revered Emperor." At least the title came out in time now. He collected his thoughts hastily. "Well, this nobleman Tepecocatzin, he sent word to the princess, I suppose, as later, she came as well."

"You talked to my daughter?" Again, the Emperor's mother had a hard time keeping her peace despite her illustrious son's repeated demands. "You actually *talked* to her?" Her eyes bored at him, wide open, round with astonishment. "What did Noble Jade Doll tell you?"

He fought down a hysterical snicker, remembering the alternative nickname the people in the boat used, interpreting the word *nenetl* – "doll" – with its different second meaning. No doll, this one.

"She told me... she asked me to send word to Ahuitzotl. I mean, she wanted to send word through me."

"Revered Lady!" This time, the correction was spoken in a cutting ice-cold tone.

He quailed once again. "Revered Lady."

"No titles for now, I said." The Emperor's voice rang with matching coldness, its fury unconcealed. "I will be asking this boy questions, and no one besides me. I will not be repeating myself." The recipient of this curt reprimand tossed her head high and leaned back in her chair once again, her own eyes ablaze. "Go on, boy. What else did the Lady Noble Jade Doll tell you?"

"She told me to watch... to watch the contest held on the Central Plaza, and then report it all to Ahuitzotl, so he would able to... to pass the word."

A decisive nod. "Go on."

He could feel his fellow *calmecac* companions holding their breaths, staring at him as incredulously as the royal family did.

"And well, there was a competition, Revered Emperor." Oh, but did this man say not to use the titles now? He bit his lower lip hard. "There were many hundreds of warriors and their emperor, he talked to them, encouraged them to show their valor and spirit. He said they were invincible, that even Tenochtitlan warriors can't defeat them." He remembered the gesticulating ruler upon the edge of the dais. "They shot their slings at the stone statue that was made especially for this occasion, in the likeness of a warrior, with obsidian sword and a shield."

Tlemilli's lovely, animated, bubbling-with-excitement face

swam into his view, giving him strength. Using her words, it was easier to describe the event. He hadn't seen much of it, anyway, trapped, frightened, eager to escape. Until she came. Oh, but from the moment she had grabbed his arm, pulling him under that podium, into its dusky, slightly damp, chilling safety, everything became right again, somehow – right and worthwhile. And so, now it was her words coming out of his mouth and the warmth was spreading, banishing the fright once again.

"The Emperor promised to reward the best shooter, slinger, or spear-thrower, but not before another competition was held. When the stone statue was shattered by the missiles of the slingers, it was replaced with a wooden statue, another replica of a man with a shield, wielding its sword. This time, it was to be taken down using mainly spears, hurled or shot from *atlatls*, but some warriors shot their bows as well."

He was listening to himself, fascinated like the rest of them. Where were those words coming from, pouring out with such eloquence, such confident skill? It didn't seem possible. He wasn't good with making speeches, not even back home, ensconced by familiar people and surroundings, liked and accepted, and equal to everyone, not a naked commoner to be looked down upon and manipulated into filthy lies. Still, even back home, he never felt like talking at length, not like some others who could describe even the most trivial happenings with plenty of flowery words, making people listen. Still, the memory of him and this lively girl running down the slanting alley, heading toward the shore where the rest of the competition was to be held, anxious to keep ahead of the crowds, lingered, rendering him with words he didn't know he could use.

"The closing part of the competition was to be held at the lake's shore, where the contestants were to shoot the water birds in the flight. Hundreds of winged creatures were spooked out of the reeds, and the warriors again took them down using their slings and their spears. The sky went dark from hundreds of flying missiles."

"Do I remember that!" breathed Necalli, his whisper barely there, brushing against Miztli's ear. He tried not to smile.

"In the end, their emperor gave another long speech, again talking about the might of Tlatelolcan warriors and how the real enemy will be easier to take down, their flesh softer than stone, easier to split than hard wood with one's spear, simpler to hit than a bird in flight."

But how did he remember all that? He couldn't have possibly listened while being jostled by the excited crowds, worrying about both girls and his need to take them out and away, anxious for the *calmecac* boy's safety, fearing the worst, knowing how ruthless these people were, how cold-hearted. Was he listening to the orating ruler's speech in spite of himself? Or was it again Tlemilli's magic? She felt so snug under his arm back then, so fitting.

"Did he mention Tenochtitlan openly?" The Emperor's face was not a mask anymore, his eyes alive, blazing with undivided attention.

"He did, yes." The magic was gone, dissolving together with the readily weaving words. "I... I had to get away by then. That man Teconal, he kidnapped Ahuitzotl and the calmec– Necalli, and I couldn't... couldn't stay and listen..."

"He shot the sling, like I told you," interrupted Ahuitzotl, more relaxed now, not as straight as an arrow, leaning forward with his entire body. "He took down the man who was kidnapping me, and he knocked out the one who was threatening to take Necalli's eye out. He did it with two mere shots – only two! – each one hitting its target." A snort. "That's why he couldn't stay and listen to that good-for-nothing would-be-a-great-emperor scum!"

All eyes were upon him again. He felt like running out and away.

"What district's school you are attending, boy?" This came from the stocky man, the one who didn't utter a word until now. He didn't even move in his chair, only inclined his head royally.

Miztli swallowed hard once again. "I... I don't... I..." For the life of him, he couldn't find something worthwhile to say. He couldn't even understand the question. What district? What school?

"He is not attending his local *telpochcalli*, Revered Emperor."

Necalli's voice rang clearly, with no misgivings. "The craftsman in whose workshop he is working wouldn't let him."

The Emperor's face reflected no reaction. He felt the contemplative gaze lingering, assessing him calmly.

"Where did you come from?"

"T-Teteltzinco," he stammered, wishing to disappear yet more ardently. But why were they asking him so many questions?

The Emperor frowned, then shifted his eyes toward the man in the other chair. "What is this place, Brother? Where is it?"

For the first time, the unperturbed man moved. Only so slightly, an imperceptible straightening of the back. "I'll inquire with the advisers."

"It's a village, somewhere out there," volunteered Ahuitzotl, looking unconcerned. His eyes rested on Miztli. "Where is it exactly? Near what?"

"Oaxtepec." This time, he managed not to stammer, the boy's friendly eyes giving him strength. "Where the tribute collectors are coming from."

Now the Emperor's eyes flickered. "Oh, Oaxtepec! I see. This area's tribute collectors certainly made sure to establish themselves among those warm springs and beautiful gardens." Another nod indicated the man in the chair. "Our grandfather built there lavishly, water construction to irrigate and plenty of country houses. Our nobles do favor this area."

"Yes, they do," grunted the man, sinking back into his previous state of impartial staring. "Maybe they should be watched for their activity. The tribute collectors certainly. This area is known for occasional troublemaking."

"With the locals shooting as accurately as this one without attending warriors' school…" The Emperor laughed for the first time, a clear, uninhibited sound. "Oh yes, we would do better watching these areas." The crinkling eyes rested on Miztli. "What else can you do besides spinning a sling?"

"I… I can shoot a bow."

An appreciative nod was his answer. "A shooter, eh? Well, we'll have to examine your skills, village boy; see how good you are with all sorts of relevant weaponry. I can certainly use more shooters among my warriors." Again, the heavyset man was the recipient of the curt nod. "Supervise this affair, Brother, will you? Let Noble Yaotzin and the others examine this boy, see if he is worthy of certain investment, trained either by them or in one of the districts' *telpochcalli*."

"As long as he is in our *calmecac*, I'll put an eye on him," volunteered Ahuitzotl, puffing with importance. "I'll make sure he does well."

"Isn't this a high order for a boy of your age, Little Brother?" This time, the Emperor grinned quite widely. "You are the one who is needed to be put an eye on. After your last escapade, you certainly earned not a little supervision."

"I don't need any of that," cried out the boy hotly, rearing like a snake before striking. "I didn't run away or make trouble. I spied on Tlatelolco and brought important information back. You can't treat me like a child! I'm not little anymore."

Through this spirited protest that made even the reticent man of the second chair grin with the side of his mouth, the royal woman sat uninvolved, tight-lipped, and aloof, not partaking in her sons' mirthful exchange.

"I wish to hear more about my daughter," she said when the boy Ahuitzotl paused clearly in order to draw enough breath to plunge into more speeches concerning his privileges and rights. "And I wish to hear what you intend to do about your sister and her unworthy husband, Son."

That put a stop to the mirthful commotion, with the Emperor sobering at once, disappearing behind his previous stony mask. His hands clapped only once, bringing in servants or maybe advisers and aides. It was difficult to tell with quite a few men flooding in. Miztli felt his own rigid muscles relaxing, his lungs beginning to breathe again freely. Was it over for good?

"Take these boys back to *calmecac*, then return to escort my brother," the Emperor was saying. "Send Noble Yaotzin here and ask Revered Teohuatzin to attend my evening meal." The pensive eyes rested on Miztli. "Place this one along with the other two for now. Until Noble Yaotzin makes a judgment. Do not decide anything concerning this boy without consulting me first." The decorated shoulders lifted in a shrug. "Have all three of them ready to be brought back for more questioning. They are not to be allowed outside the school's grounds for any reason, not until word from me or my brother comes."

His legs still not perfectly steady, Miztli followed the boys as they prostrated themselves once again, murmuring customary greetings of parting, ushered away by the groveling servants, a whole bunch of those. His mind was blank again, refusing to think it all through.

Then, as his legs carried him along the embroidered mats and past the lower chairs, the grinning face of Ahuitzotl sprang into his view, drawing closer, then stepping away again, slipping something into his hand in the perfect fashion of a smuggler. His fingers locked around the familiar edges, so smooth and glassy, so lustrously sleek. His heart made a somersault, then threw itself wildly against his ribs. The obsidian puma, gloriously slick and powerful, warm from the hand that had clutched it before, fitting in his palm perfectly, giving off its magic, *keeping him safe*. He didn't remember passing the outer hall or even putting his new sandals back on.

"Now you are in, workshop boy."

Necalli's voice penetrated the haze as the softly illuminated chambers remained behind and the sun greeted them with its midday fierceness. From the top of the stairs, the view of the gardens behind the mosaic-covered patio was magnificent, a celebration of colors, with richly dressed people hurrying alongside it or just strolling casually, blending with the vibrancy of the carefully trimmed trees and beautifully laid flowerbeds, such intricate patterns.

"I bet the school authorities will go easer on us now, brought back by the Emperor's personal servants and all." Axolin hesitated on the top of the stairs, observing the spreading view, clearly preparing for the feat of descending, his limp one of the worst.

"Yes, let them show the prettier side of their faces now that the workshop boy is gracing this establishment with his skillfully-shooting presence." Beaming, Necalli skipped a few stairs at once in a happy leap, his smile one of the widest. "It can be such a bore, this school business, but it beats the sweaty workshop for sure. No more slaving for the smelly craftsman, eh, Miztli-boy? Let the old liar go to the Emperor now, complain about your absence of more days and more damage. Maybe he'll threaten to take the Emperor himself to the courts." The crookedness of his grin made Miztli wish to chuckle aloud. "That would be a sight worth seeing."

"They won't necessarily let him stay in *calmecac*, you know." Axolin was limping behind, challenged by the descent. Miztli side-glanced him, puzzled. But was this one so very quiet back at the imperial audience. "All his shooting notwithstanding, if he doesn't do outstandingly on the other counts, he'll be shipped away to this or that *telpochcalli*. They teach people to shoot slings and *atlatls* in commoner schools as well."

Necalli waved his hand in dismissal, hastening his step to catch up with their escorts who had been lingering at the bottom of the stairs, shooting impatient glances. "He'll do outstandingly. Won't you, ItzMiztli?" A wink. "They won't be throwing you out of that school in a hurry."

"They never received real commoners in there," insisted Axolin. "He will be the first foreigner ever."

"More honor for them."

He concentrated on his steps, watching the intricately ornamented stones sweeping below his feet, too busy thinking to get incensed with the way that snobbish Axolin was talking about him, as though he wasn't there. It didn't matter now. The reality of what happened kept sinking in, making his head reel, his hand clutching the wonderful talisman, relishing the feeling. Was he truly out of old Tlaquitoc's clutches, not sold into slavery, and not even forced to work in the workshop anymore? It didn't seem possible, and yet Necalli kept talking about it as though it had been an accomplished fact. A school? What would he do in that place besides learning all sorts of crafts he didn't know a thing about? Axolin was right. He would never make it. And yet...

The sun was blazing strongly, warming his skin and his spirit. The Emperor, not such a terribly foreboding presence in itself, appreciated his Tlatelolco tales, it seemed, his saving the imperial brother from falling into the manipulative Teconal's hands. Oh, but was it a lucky thing, to have this sling, in time and handy. He'd have to thank Chantli for that.

The thought of her made him worried, still held in her nasty father's hands. But shouldn't they have tried to talk to the Emperor about that? Even though mighty rulers surely didn't concern themselves with troubles of commoner girls from the wharves. But maybe through Ahuitzotl. The fierce royal *pilli* seemed to like Chantli. And Necalli too. Oh yes, the *calmecac* boy kept worrying about her, plying him, Miztli, with too many questions, anxious to hear that she had not been punished too harshly. Maybe together, somehow, they would manage to help her in some way.

"What are you dreaming about? The glory of your future campaigns, oh mighty warrior with a sling?" Necalli's elbow was again pushing its way into his ribs. He twisted away from it, his grin impossible to stifle.

"Hurry up, boys. Pick up your step!" Their escorts seemed as though about to lose their patience.

They hastened their step obediently, still grinning.

AUTHOR'S AFTERWORD

In the mid-15th century, Tenochtitlan was already a fairly dominant regional power, with many provinces and dependent entities, towns, and villages to manage. Their influence spread far and wide, even though it was still nowhere near what it would be only a few decades later, under the rule of the vigorous eighth ruler Ahuitzotl, who would conquer lavishly, stretching Tenochtitlan's influence almost from coast to coast. Axayacatl, the elder of the three ruling brothers, was a renowned warrior and leader, but it was the youngest, Ahuitzotl, who would spread the Mexica domination truly far and wide.

However, this story deals with somewhat earlier times. While our young ten-summers-old Ahuitzotl was busy sneaking out of school, getting bored, and looking for adventures, and maybe also gathering his future followers along the way, minor nobility and exotic commoners alike, his brother the Emperor, Axayacatl, was busy with the most known conquest of his rule, the conquest of neighboring Tlatelolco.

Unlike other cities, towns, and villages spread around the great Texcoco Lake and deeper inland, Tlatelolco, located on the adjacent island or even the same island, as some claim, were true kin, a sister-nation, the same Mexica-Aztec people as Tenochtitlan citizens were. Tenochtitlan's partners in the Triple Alliance, *altepetls* of Texcoco and Tlacopan, were no Mexica. The first, Texcoco, were Acolhua, ruling eight other Acolhua provinces; the second, Tlacopan, was the remainder of the Tepanec Empire, ruling a few provinces of their own, the Tepanec ones. Tenochtitlan, as mentioned before, ruled farther and wider than its partners, and their Mexica nationality was exceptional. Besides them and this same troublesome Tlatelolco, no one else claimed to belong to the Mexica roots.

According to the most widely accepted narrative, both *altepetl*s were founded not so far apart from each other, in the first part of the 14th century, both suffering a fair share of contempt and oppression from the surrounding cities and regional powers. Some say they had been sharing the opposite sides of the same island; others claim that they had been two separate islands that had been united by artificial means later on, after Tenochtitlan had conquered Tlatelolco.

However, before it happened, both sister-cities got along fairly well despite their rapidly changing circumstances. In 1428 Tenochtitlan was the one to participate in the revolt against the mighty Tepanec Empire alongside other subjected or just threatened nations, such as Acolhua of Texcoco or the dwellers of the Eastern Highlands. While the radical politics and the subsequent great wars rocked the entire Mexican Valley, Tlatelolco kept quiet and carefully neutral and out of the way, thus sealing its future history. Left out of the postwar dealings and invited to partake in no rich pickings off the fallen Tepanec Empire, Tlatelolco remained what it was, a fairly large independent *altepetl* that could not complete with the expanding giants of the Triple Alliance, especially the one in their backyard, the most ambitious, industrious entity out to grow and expand.

Still, it had taken nearly half a century for the real trouble to erupt, and what exactly happened there we might never know for certain, as the most detailed accounts of those few market intervals in the middle of the dry season of 1473 came to us via two different historians living two centuries later, after the entire Mexico had been destroyed by the Spanish invasion. One was Diego Duran, a Spanish monk (Dominican friar) enamored by the local Nahua culture, language, and history to the extent of displeasing his superiors and the church. The other, Domingo Chimalpahin, the 16th century Nahua annalist from Chalco – both post-conquest historians, both clearly relaying Tenochtitlan's point of view. However, they give us the most detailed accounts of this period, aside from the Codex Mendoza, which doesn't go into as many juicy details but supports the above-mentioned historians on the main developments.

In 1469, Axayacatl, Tenochtitlan's sixth ruler, came to occupy his grandfather's throne. A vigorous young man of reportedly great valor and outstanding leadership skill, he had waged a few successful and less so campaigns, gaining respect of the capital despite his young age.

At the same time, the neighboring Tlatelolco had also seen a change in rulers. Moquihuix or Moquihuixtli was also a relatively young man of presentable appearance and good orating skills. No tension between the two neighboring cities seemed to accompany those changes. On the contrary, to strengthen their ties, a customary exchange of a marital nature had taken place. Axayacatl's elder sister, ChalchiuhNenetzin, Noble Jade Doll, was offered to the Tlatelolco ruler and promptly accepted as his chief wife, bearing him a son upon the very first year of their marriage.

The lives of both island-cities went on as usual until, according to both Chimalpahin and Duran, a certain nobleman Teconal came to occupy the reed-woven chair and the office of the head adviser to the Tlatelolco ruler. Suddenly, Moquihuixtli became less enamored of the neighboring island's capital, the rich influential giant growing by leaps and bounds, a somewhat threatening presence. According to both Duran and Chimalpahin, his royal wife of Tenochtitlan origins did not please him greatly, not anymore. A void that Teconal's daughter had managed to fill, added to the collection of imperial wives, and probably promoted to the highest rank among those. Polygamy was a way of life for the Mesoamerican nobility, so what must have been angering Tenochtitlan royal house or, rather, its female representative in the Tlatelolco Palace, was the advancement of the new wife above the other.

Chimalpahin and Duran both report various different complaints Axayacatl's sister was flooding her powerful brother with through the old nobleman Tepecocatzin, a Tlatelolcan high aristocrat with apparently certain sentiment for Tenochtitlan. And yet, the busy young emperor did not interfere. Not until several other incidents made him start glancing at the neighboring island with suspicion.

One day a newly dug canal across Tlatelolco was found partly filled with rubbish (according to Duran). The suspicious Tlatelolcans accused their powerful neighbors of ill will. Sometime later, again according to Duran, a group of young Tenochtitlan nobles were reported to harass, or even molest, Tlatelolcan noble girls. A complaint was lodged with the Tenochtitlan authorities, but it is unclear what came out of it.

The storm clouds kept gathering, and it was in this uneasy atmosphere that Moquihuixtli decided to hold a competition of young Tlatelolcan warriors described by Duran in great detail. More than two thousand men came, summoned to the central plaza in order to *'practice arts of war,'* or so their ruler had put it. A stone statue in the image of a fully armed warrior was erected upon a podium, to be taken down by slingshots aimed from a close range. *"... He who aims best at the statue will receive the honor and glory as the most outstanding warrior..."* were Moquihuixtli's alleged words, accompanied with the promise of a personal reward for the best shooter (Duran). The statue was shattered in no time, to be replaced by another warlike likeness, this time made out of wood. The warriors were required to take down the new target using their spears and bows, which they did, with *'great skill and valor.'* The Tlatelolcan ruler was impressed, telling his warriors that he could not judge the winner, as no warrior outshone his peers.

The eventful day was finished with an improvised hunt upon the shores of the Great Lake, where plenty of waterfowl was spooked, with the warriors required to use their shooting devices but only on the birds in *'full flight.'* Again, the Tlatelolcans had reportedly outdone themselves, receiving much praise and flowery speeches but no promised rewards, which seemed to satisfy everyone nevertheless. The warriors went home puzzled but happy. Moquihuixtli and Teconal remained less puzzled but full of ideas. The emperor's closing speech, reported by Duran, gave a clear indication. *'...Tlatelolcas, I have been well pleased to see your ability... if some day you must wage war against the enemy, you will know that their flesh is not stone, that it is not wood, and that since your intrepid arms break through wood and stone, how much easier will it be to destroy flesh. You will be like ferocious jaguars and pumas. I also want you to know that our enemies are not birds that can fly and can slip between one's fingers. Today few flying birds slipped between your fingers. Therefore, have courage, for soon you will you have need of your hands, and Mexica-Tlatelolco will be honored and all the nations will be subjected to us. Tlatelolco will rejoice in all those things that had been Mexica-Tenochtitlan's prerogative up to now...'*

So has spoken Moquihuixtli through the dry moons of 1473, counting on the Tenochtitlan emperor's youth and lack of experience, edged by Teconal, a reportedly wise man but a very ambitious, ruthless, and single-minded individual of great willpower. Not relying on his emperor's pretty speeches or the valor of their young warriors alone, he had sent envoys to the Eastern Highlands, the towns that were not a part of the Triple Alliance's vastly diverse relationships. However, the Highlanders answered with suspicious reserve and no commitments. They did not see the difference between the two Mexica-Aztec towns and did not wish to be involved in what might turn out to be nothing but a fishy plot.

Yet, at this point, the Tlatelolcans would not be budged.

In this first novel of the series, I outlined the beginning of the Tlatelolcan revolt. A few liberties were taken, but mainly with the fictional characters of the story, placing them at crucial points and important historical happenings, letting them rub their shoulders with historical characters, helping to push the story, and the history, along.

However, as with the case of young Ahuitzotl – a future remarkably famous eighth ruler of Tenochtitlan – I have taken the liberty of placing him alongside the fictional characters of his newfound friends, as of course no ancient historians would bother mentioning any possible antics of a ten-year-old youngest brother of an emperor. He must have been at school at this time, as imperial children were admitted to *calmecac* at such young ages as opposed to the rest of the nobility youth. Yet, judging by his future role in Tenochtitlan's history and various sources describing his character's traits – short-tempered and warlike, lavish, boisterous, courageous, loyal to his friends, and so on – he might have been as fierce and restless while back in school, up to no good in the way most leader-like boys can be, especially in a city faced with a crisis of nearly a civil war with its neighboring sister-nation. Ten years old or not, a person like Ahuitzotl would not likely allow himself to be left out of the activities.

His namesake water monster *ahuitzotl* is based on various accounts of local legends involving this particular beast. Many are guesses surrounding this legendary creature that dotted Nahua lore aplenty. The Spanish accounts used translate its name as a Water Dog, but this translation is far from being linguistically accurate. The first letter '*a*' here is indeed standing for *atl*-water, but there end the similarities. No word meaning dog – *chichi* or *itzcuintli* – seems to be present in the word *ahuitzotl*, not even remotely. The closest interpretation I found plausible is the Water Spiny/Thorny One – again *a* for *atl*-water, *huiz* for *huiztli*-thorny/spiny (also south, relating to the spiny cactuses of the region probably), and *otl* for *yotl*-to be like.

So with the canine 'accusations' safely out of the way, it still leaves us with many guesses as to who was this lethal creature with spiky fur, pointy ears, slick body, and black long tail upon which a '*...hand like this of a person sprouts...*' (Florentine Codex). With this disproportionally long tail and the hand crowning it, the creature reportedly would grab its victims in order to pull them under the water until they drowned. Only then, it would feast on its prey's eyes, teeth, and nails, and then let the body float again. In cases of such discoveries, only *tlatoque*, priests belonging to the worship of Tlaloc, the deity responsible for watery deaths, among his other vast responsibilities, were authorized to deal with the burials, special rites, and ceremonies of purification. *Ahuitzotls* were feared but rarely encountered to describe them in more detail.

The speculations as to the possible source of the legend are varied and contradicting. From opossums to dogs to otters to something completely legendary – the guesswork is lively and not convincing. For this novel, I picked the explanation that looked most plausible to me, namely an otter. Quick research on this relatively small water predator showed a violent streak, readiness to attack humans under certain circumstances, usually to protect their litter, disproportionally long and wide tails, even if those are not crowned with a human-like hand at its edge, and nicely fitting eating habits of the occasional scavenging of drowned bodies, with eyes, gums and fingertips being some of the temptingly softer parts. In addition to slick, oily fur, sharp teeth, and only the pointy ears not fitting the description, an average river otter certainly answers the criteria, even if roughly. So this animal was the one to give inspiration to certain scenes in this story.

Metallurgy was another interesting factor to explore. People of Central Mexico, while interested in creating copper and golden jewelry, ornaments and occasional tools, did not invest in their metalworking in the way people of Western Mexico or Yucatan did. Tenochtitlan dwellers seemed to prefer to import any such trinkets. Still toward the later years, the actual metalworking began to gain momentum, and workshops like that of Miztli's employer started to dot the city until a guild of copper and gold smiths was organized, alongside traders and stone or feather workers' organizations. A divine patron of metalworkers was Xipe Totec, a Flayed God that normally dealt with agricultural cycles, yet accepted offerings from its urban copper-melting subjects as well.

By the time of the Spanish arrival, about half a century later, production of metal objects and tools in Tenochtitlan and its provinces was greatly organized and vast. However, Miztli himself seemed to be destined to take another path.

What happened next can be read in the second book of The Aztec Chronicles, **"Field of Fire"**.

The story continues with

FIELD OF FIRE

The Aztec Chronicles, Book 2

CHAPTER 1

Tlatelolco,
1473 AD

Tlemilli had a hard time restraining herself from breaking something. That prettily painted vase with annoying patterns; it stood upon the narrow reed podium, tempting her. She had actually left the cushioned mat in order to snatch it, then stopped herself, admiring her own self-restraint. It wasn't wise to antagonize them further by breaking more pottery. She had been driving them all mad as it was, Father's wives and their various serving maids, even the slaves.

Grinding her teeth, she stomped back toward the padded alcove, all colorful covers and embroidery. To administer a kick to one of the cushions helped. Planting another before risking admonishment by a farsighted maid, she watched it slip away and onto the tiles of the floor. But was it annoying, this prohibition to leave the women quarters. She couldn't even wander the Palace's gardens anymore. What a bore!

It had been more than a market interval. No, two by now. Well, one and a half. It was no market day. Still, she felt as though a whole lifetime had passed, many dry and rainy seasons since the day of the contest, the wonderful freedom of it, the most exciting of adventures. She had rarely left the Palace's grounds before, knowing every knoll and shrub in it, every single marble of every mosaic, every corner and every bench – oh, but did she know all those by heart.

When younger and just having moved to the Palace upon Father becoming the Emperor's adviser, she had been expectant and thrilled. What possibilities there were to sniff around forbidden grounds! She would wander those beautiful gardens for days, pretending that it was a forest, straight away from Tlaco's stories – her old personal maid had those in abundance – hunting insects and small animals, imagining that those were mystical creatures, with her being a powerful goddess, or a courageous huntress, half human, half jaguar, maybe, or any other entity she cared to admire on a given day. It was thrilling to think of herself in the middle of this or that wonderful legend, the stories Tlaco had in many twenties, telling her tales since Tlemilli could remember, the ones she demanded every morning and every evening, even now that she wasn't little anymore.

These days, Tlaco was old and ailing, unable to perform her duties properly. However, Tlemilli had adamantly refused every new personal maid that they attempted to press on her, even at the price of making them angry. Two of the stupid fowls, Father's second wife and his favorite concubine, went as far as complaining to him in person, nagging about the intractability of his daughter, but she had stood up even to this formidable man, claiming that Tlaco still did her job perfectly. They all knew she didn't, even Father himself, but luckily, he had been too busy, waving his nagging spouses and their petty complaints away. He had more important matters to attend to, as back then, two summers earlier, he had already became the new Emperor's Head Adviser. A more important job than keeping track of his numerous wives and daughters, and the commoners who served them. There were too many female offspring in Father's family and too few sons. He had enough frustration to face on that score alone, without being involved in the petty squabbling between those same shrilling females.

The only daughter who had brought satisfaction to him, earning her keep, was Citlalli, the sweet, beautiful, good-natured Emperor's wife – Chief Wife these days. The nicest person of them all, in Tlemilli's private estimation. Citlalli did not visit their side of the Palace anymore, but Tlaco's stories made up for this lack.

As long as those were forthcoming, she didn't mind imperfectly laundered clothes or badly served meals. Tlaco was part of her life ever since she could remember, Tlaco and Citlalli. But now both were away, one in the kitchen area, taking care of the midmorning meal, and the other in the Emperor's bed, taking care of their father's ambition.

Was Citlalli more of a tool to Father than a favorite daughter? The question kept nagging ever since that thrilling afternoon with that boy. He and his dubious Tenochtitlan friends and their troubles were all to do with Father and his work against the neighboring island's scum. She knew it before too, in the habit of sneaking around and eavesdropping on everyone, out of boredom rather than true curiosity. But now it all made her wonder. That boy had such fear of Father and with good reason, apparently. It was a terrible sight, when Father was hitting that other boy, held from both sides and helpless; it haunted her ever since. It was a bad thing to do, and why would Father do this?

Unable to stay still, she sprang to her feet, rushing toward the opening in the wall, the view it offered painfully boring, the same colorful mess of flowerbeds and carefully trimmed trees, with birds chirping in the treetops, unable to shut up. She wished she had something to throw at them. Like that sling he had clutched in his hand, the sling and the glistening round missile, so perfectly smooth, inviting to touch. Had he used it in the end? she wondered. And to what effect?

Back then, while talking her way up the incline, anxious to keep Father's attention, she didn't dare to glance toward his hiding place, of course. But now she regretted it. The chance to see him shooting his sling was worthy of a fleeting peek, wasn't it? That and the possibility of finding out if he managed to free his friends in the end. She didn't know even that. Father was too angry with her to answer her questions, had she dared to venture even one. Not on the same afternoon, when he didn't manage to make sense of her jumbled explanation and protests of misunderstanding. He didn't expect anything worthwhile from her anyway; no one did. However, later on, the next day, someone had told on her, Tlemilli, let the Head Adviser know that his daughter had been barely present at the Great Plaza, sneaking away from the royal dais, spending her time gods-know-where, such unladylike behavior. Then she was in for real trouble as, suddenly, for the first time since she had been born, Father paid attention to her, clearing his busy day for a private conversation; interrogation, really. But did he get angry, barking those questions! Where had she been and with whom? How had she found herself running around the shores of the Great Lake, unsupervised, interfering with his activities?

Frightened to a degree, she bore his barking demands with enough aplomb, but when he lost his temper and started to scream, summoning his servants in order to demand the execution of her favorite maid to begin with, she had lost her spirit altogether, bursting into the most shameful tears, begging to spare Tlaco, telling it all to him, every tiny detail. Which sent his rage straight to the skies, but by this point, she didn't care. To save the woman who had raised and taken care of her since she could remember, telling her amazing tales and listening to her charge's silly ones, was more important than anything. That boy was nowhere near the Palace or the Plaza to get hurt, or hunted down, or so she hoped.

And now, five – no, six! – days later, here she was, a prisoner in these same women's quarters, not allowed to go anywhere, not even the Palace's gardens, not even the relevant classes in *calmecac*, something she hated with all her heart but now found herself missing. Oh benevolent Coatlicue, mother of all gods!

Outside the opening in the wall, the sun was blazing happily, unrestrained. Like in the tale of the Smoking Mountain from the Eastern Highlands, whose peak was easy to spot on a bright cloudless day even from the Palace's gardens. Both mountains were towering out there on the mainland, telling their tale of two lovers separated by jealousy and lies, to be reunited only in death, in the shape of two white-topped peaks, after the desperate girl had killed herself in order not to be given to another and her lover, finding her dead, doing the same to himself. A sad story, but a beautiful one. Tlaco told it differently from time to time, but they always ended the same. Well, of course they would. The mountains were there for everyone to see and behold. She always envied the warriors who were sailing toward the eastern shore, usually on behalf of annoying Tenochtitlan and its projected expeditions of conquest, and as much as she disliked the obligation of her city to obey the wishes of their pushy neighbors, she knew that she would hop into one of the sailing canoes given half a chance, if only for the opportunity to see both legendary mountains from close up. The tale had a ring of finality to it; still, for her, it had a different ending. The girl didn't have to give up and kill herself before her lover found her. She might have put up a fight or something.

By the distant cluster of trees, her eyes spotted a movement. At this time of the high morning, not many people were out strolling the gardens. The noblemen were busy with politics, courts, and meetings, and the noblewomen with their looms and their gossip. Some of her half-sisters and cousins of a relevant age would be escorted for their daily lessons in *calmecac*, some for the classes or services in the adjacent temple. If only she could have sneaked out together with them! Typically, she hated both the school and the temple training; however, now she needed a pretext. Somehow, in some way, she needed to get out and try to find that boy, to leave him a message. Maybe through the annoying filthy-mouthed commoner that kept clinging to him, if she managed to find this one. It was dangerous for him to be near the Palace, trying to keep his promise. Maybe later, but not now, not when Father knew all about him.

The man she had spotted, a short heavyset individual clad in a bright non-descript cloak, was pacing back and forth, exuding impatience. There was something about his pose, the furtiveness of his movements. Her instincts of an experienced eavesdropper told her that he might rather wish to be elsewhere, eager to have his meeting – what else could it be? – done and be over with. She contemplated going out through the wall opening whatever the consequences. It didn't look like a high jump.

"What are you doing?"

The annoyingly melodious voice made her almost topple over, perching on the windowsill, balancing there with an effort. She clutched the wooden plank tighter.

"Are you out of your mind? Look what she is doing!"

"Nothing out of the ordinary," was the first girl's showily loud reply. She didn't need to see the speakers, two stupid half-sisters of hers, empty-headed, coy, deceptively demure, giggly things, the contestants for the title of the best-behaved fowls in the world. A bore.

"What are you up to now, Tlemilli?" asked the older one, all sensibility and prudence, her tone that of a responsible adult tired of another child's antics.

Tlemilli rolled her eyes. "Nothing!"

"Why are you perched up there like a bird on the branch of a tree?" piped up the younger one, barely eleven summers old, an annoying thing, playing at being grown-up like her perfection of a sister.

"Because that's what I want to do." This time, she snorted loudly, incensed, yet at the same time grateful for their interruption. It wasn't a wise thing to do, to go out of the window and after being forbidden to leave the girls' quarters unless escorted by someone who wasn't a servant. Even Tlaco wasn't trusted anymore. Poor Tlaco.

"Whom are you spying after now?"

"None of your business."

The older girl snorted in her turn. "Leave her alone, Sister. She is the strangest thing in our world of the Fifth Sun. I wish the Adviser decided to remove her from our quarters."

The Adviser? To call one's father a father was apparently not in the line of grown-up behavior. This one was nearing her fifteenth summer, over the temple and *calmecac* training, and lording it over everyone, fluttering her eyelashes, hinting that the real grown-up matters were waiting for her now, beckoning out there.

"He will be removing you faster than me, you empty-headed heap of fat," said Tlemilli calmly, used to their confrontations, not opposed to those. Father's brood of shrill female snakes was exceptional, with his collection of wives being no better. Citlalli was the only worthy person, her only full sister too, but it had been close to three moons since she had left their quarters, moving to occupy the main wing of the Palace instead. A great honor on one score, a glaring disappointment on another. It was nice to have a readily spoken word of protection or encouragement. Citlalli was one of the oldest and greatly respected on all counts. "He will marry you off the moment he finds a stupid enough person to ask for you."

The delicately plucked eyebrows arched. "He will never be so lucky as to get rid of you in the same way. Not even the most meaningless of the Emperor's advisers would be prevailed upon into taking such an ugly heap of bones with the filthiest temper ever. Not even a tradesman from the marketplace with ten illiterate wives. Not even the filthiest slave from the kitchen houses!"

The younger girl was doubling over, all agog with delight. "Yes, yes. Not even the slaves who clean our rooms!"

Tlemilli felt like throwing something at them. "Shut up, you stinking, ugly snakes, both of you. Shut up!"

"See? She is even speaking like commoners. Shut up and all that. They say you were running around the Plaza among the commoners on the day of the contest." The older girl's face glowed with unconcealed satisfaction. "One hears that you did all sorts of things unworthy of noblewomen or even their personal maids. Which wouldn't surprise any of us, those who are forced to tolerate you all our lives. But maybe this time, you did take it too far. Father locked you up now. Maybe next time, he will prove even sterner. I hope he gets rid of you and not through a hastily arranged marriage." A fleeting glance beckoned the younger girl. "Come, Little Sister. Let us find worthy company to spend our time with, before a young thing like you gets corrupted in here."

Tlemilli searched her mind frantically. "You are nothing but a stupid, ugly, mean-tempered turkey," she shouted toward their disappearing backs. "And you smell of excrements straight away from the chamber pot."

"And you..." began the younger girl, turning back gleefully, ready to return measure for measure, but her sister's palm closed around the embroidered sleeve, pulling with force.

"Come, little one. Don't answer this commoners' slime."

The sound of their sandaled feet echoed down the hallway while she struggled to keep her balance on her narrow perch, refusing to come down out of sheer protest. Commoners' slime! Just who did they think they were, these two stupid turkeys? And what did they know about what happened there on the Plaza, or worse yet, on the lakeshore? Were they the ones to tell on her in the first place, the moment she succumbed to the temptation of sneaking down the dais upon seeing that boy anew? He looked so frightened, so desperate back then, running pell-mell, with no clear direction, with no one to pull him and yank like the man he had stood with before. What was he involved with? And where were his friends at that time, the pushy commoner girl and the other two? Back by the lakeshore already? What were they searching for, what were they seeking?

The room was quiet once again, a blessing. She peered at the trees where the suspicious man was pacing before. There was no one there now, but further down another pathway, she could see Father's unmistakable cloak, his regalia of the Head Adviser on full display, such a beautiful headdress, radiant green, rustling with the slightest breeze.

Quailing inside, she slipped over the windowsill, giving her actions not much thought. Father was up to something, that much was obvious, and she needed to know what it was. Maybe it had to do with this boy. Since that scary scene and the vicious dressing down, she kept trying to spy after Father in particular every time she managed to spot him, a few times through the last three days. He never talked about what happened on the day of the contest, but she still hoped he would. Maybe this way, she'd know who this boy was and where he came from. Or why he didn't come as promised. Couldn't he sneak into the Palace for at least a very short time? He promised! And it wasn't that difficult to sneak around here, was it?

The touch of the damp grass and the soggy ground on her bare feet made her wince, freeze for a heartbeat. Such a strange sensation. Not entirely unpleasant but not the most comfortable as well. Oh, but she should have paused to put on her sandals. Fond of walking around the inside rooms barefoot, liking the sleekness of the floor's chilly flagstones, she never stepped outside without appropriate shoes wrapped around her feet and her ankles. The servants could do it so quickly, so efficiently, to tie the multitude of straps and make the wear fit comfortably. Unlike the sandals of that boy! Grinning, she remembered how loudly his crude maguey soles flopped on the cobblestones, how they hampered his step every now and then. He seemed to be having a hard time with it, and at one point, he looked as though about to kick off the stupid rags for good. To do what? To go around barefoot? A wild idea! And yet, somehow, it looked as though he could manage that particular feat.

Stepping carefully, her senses on the new sensation, she slipped toward the line of the thicker trees and their relative protection. The moving figure wasn't where she had spotted it earlier anymore, but she knew where the newcomer would be heading if wishing to whisper something into someone's ear. The mosaic pond behind the main wing, where the artificially planted trees were denser, allowing a freer movement. She had listened to many private conversations in this corner of the Palace's gardens.

Revived by the pleasure of moving around unwatched and unhindered, she slunk into the dimly lit pathway, smiling to herself, careful of jutting stones and other hurtful pieces that made it their business to stab her unprotected toes. The clamor of another relatively secluded area brushed past her ears, making her roll her eyes in disgust. The Palace's noblewomen's favorite place of gathering when wishing to spend their time outside, all those chatty females, her various cousins, half-sisters, or just fellow unmarried noble girls, with the same dreary weaving and embroidery threads, glued to their looms, gossiping – a bore! However, it could give her a perfect excuse. She was allowed in the women's hall, wasn't she? That overly decorated chamber padded with cushioned mats and alcoves, podiums and even reed chairs, spinning tools and stashes of *amate*-paper, sharpened coals, colors and brushes, even columns to tie one's loom to comfortably. Everything to make the female heart flutter in delight. Disgusted, she used to avoid passing anywhere near this place unless forced – an often enough occurrence. Yet now it was her only possible shelter.

Pausing, she listened to the usual quarreling sounds pouring out, marring the clarity of the high morning air. The filthy-tempered Tenochtitlan's whiner, for sure, lashing at her maids, or her fellow wives, or other hapless victims. She was such a moaner! Even though, since the great competition, the displaced would-be empress had been remarkably quieter, more self-contained, judging by the lack of the usual morning noises. Did the event on the Plaza change her life in a way too? She remembered the annoying fowl sneaking plenty of glances from her royal dais, staring at *him*, that battered, haunted boy, seeking him out. What was her thing with him? She should have asked him that. Oh, but she had to find the way to return to this grass-covered incline or the alleys they had run together, or at least the Central Plaza. What if he was trying to keep his promise, but she wasn't there to help him along?

The voices broke upon her unexpectedly, with the pond still nowhere in sight. She stopped dead in her tracks, her heart pounding. Father's voice was impossible not to recognize, his way of twisting certain words, as though not in a hurry to let them out of his mouth, as though tasting them. Her limbs tingled with familiar excitement, their trembling threatening to give her presence away. If caught eavesdropping on Father now, she would be done for, this time for certain.

"Moquihuixtli sent the previous envoys without my agreement." Father seemed to be enraged already, raising his voice before remembering the clearly clandestine nature of this meeting. "But was he trying to send more delegations without consulting me?"

"No, no, Honorable Adviser." The other voice sounded more frightened than agitated, stumbling over his words. "No, the Emperor wouldn't do anything of the sort."

"Then why has this last envoy gone out without my knowledge?" Another stern accusation. She could imagine Father's converser quailing. "Why wasn't I informed of the futile attempt to approach both partners of their so-called Triple Alliance? How could this have happened?"

Something was tickling her heel, crawling beside it. Tlemilli clenched her teeth in an attempt to remain still. Father's wrath was scarier than silly creatures unless a snake or a spider. She slanted her gaze, worried.

"I don't think it was done on purpose, Honorable Adviser," the man was muttering, anxious to convince. "The Emperor trusts you with his life and his *altepetl*. He wouldn't wish to act without consulting you."

"But he did!" exclaimed Father, again forgetting to talk quietly. "Tell me about this delegation. Who was leading it? Who was instructed to do the talking?"

She tried to shake off the spider without moving, flexing whatever muscle made her ankle work, getting nowhere. It had such a round, fat body, and so many small, disgustingly hairy legs. But to have her sandals back on! The man kept talking for a long time, without Father interrupting; a novelty.

"So Tlacopan was stern in its refusal, the junior partner in the Triple Alliance, yet Texcoco did not commit itself firmly for either side. Interesting." Oh yes, he did sound interested. But what were they talking about, and why couldn't they move on and reach the damn pond, allowing her to retrace her steps safely, to run back into the security of the inner rooms. From spiders to enraged fathers, she didn't want to face any of that. "The death of Nezahualcoyotl, their famous *cultured* ruler, did change things, didn't it? And not for the worst."

"Yes," agreed the other man, clearly placating. "His heir is young and timid. With him, Tenochtitlan will have less stern of an ally."

Another pause full of agreement. She breathed with relief as the hairy legs stopped tickling her heel. Instead of those, now ants were having their go at her toes. There must be a reason people weren't going around barefoot.

"Tenochtitlan's emperor is as young and more impatient, even if he isn't timid. Not that one! And yet that would-be great ruler might be unbalanced easily, maybe even removed. Without the advice of old foxes like Noble Tlacaelel or the old Texcoco ruler, he is vulnerable, prone to making mistakes." Father was orating now, forgetful of his lack of proper audience or an appropriate podium to stand on. Tlemilli fought her grin down. "Still, it wasn't wise to approach his official allies, the members of the Triple Alliance. Moquihuixtli made a grave mistake." The air hissed loudly, clearly drawn through clenched teeth. "He should have waited patiently, should have consulted me. His meekness and lack of confidence will be the end of us, all those erratic decisions – one moment the great ruler with no need of an advice, the other imploring and needing help like a little boy." Again, the raising voice. She tried to focus on her muddied toes and the ants running there busily, greatly content. "We can't best Tenochtitlan on the battlefield, not yet. We need committed, strong allies. And time. And good strategy." A brief pause ensued that made Tlemilli sick with impatience. "I sent envoys to Toltitlan and the neighboring towns. Unlike the Eastern Highlands, they will receive our swords and shields with open hearts. But Moquihuixtli will ruin it all with his impulsive moves, approaching Tenochtitlan's formal allies, of all towns and *altepetl*s of our Great Lake. What silliness!" Another dour pause. "I bet it's his former Chief Wife making him do stupid things. Maybe she puts something in his food. I wouldn't put it past her. She is well capable of such treachery. The despicable over-indulgent rat should be executed for infidelity or any other appropriate accusation. He isn't man enough to do even that!"

Tlemilli felt like nodding this time. Oh yes, Father had been right about that. And wouldn't it be great fun to see the execution of the fat fowl, to hear her complaining about the unworthiness of the process by which her slimy neck was snapped, commenting on the lack of cleanliness of the strangling cord or its lack of refinement. The fight against a wild fit of laughter turned harder.

"I bet Tenochtitlan knows everything about those stupid delegations to Texcoco and Tlacopan by now. And about their outcomes as well. Such a futile action! And the one that puts Axayacatl on guard." Something swished, bouncing off the nearest tree trunk. A thrown stone? "While my envoys in the north and the east did bring us allies, without Tenochtitlan's awareness at that." Another brief pause ensued. "Come to think of it, we should not neglect the southern shores as well. The Lake Chalco dwellers are proud people, and they must still remember their glorious past, not so far removed from now, eh? They might wish to avenge themselves against the grandson of the emperor who has crushed them so soundly."

"Oh yes, Revered Adviser!" The man's excited exclamation made Tlemilli almost jump, forgetting Father's audience for a moment, with him orating for so long and with no interruptions. "The Chalcoans might wish to join our case with true zeal."

"Organize that delegation at once." Father again sounded calmer, deep in thought. "Do not involve our Emperor. He'll know in due time. His Tenochtitlan love has spies all over the Palace and the city, and still he refuses to get rid of her properly. Or at least to send her back to her brother. Claims it would be tantamount to a declaration of war. As though sending envoys to this same annoying *altepetl*'s allies, asking to rally with us and against it is not tantamount to the same thing!" Now he was almost spitting with rage. "From stinking commoners to even high born *pillis* – mere children, imagine that! – sniffing around our plazas and shores, spying on us, eager to report our activities and competitions. Oh, but this woman has no shame! And when I lay my hands on her filthy spies again, they won't be sneaking away from me, not this time. They'll be begging to be put to death after I'm through with them!"

Forgetting the ants, Tlemilli fought for breath, her heart fluttering, refusing to organize into a proper beating. It was a struggle to get enough air. Oh, but Father didn't forget. He was still angry about it all, and should that boy try to find her, like he promised he would...

"The fact that Tenochtitlan might hear about our competing warriors was taken into account, Honorable Adviser. You said so yourself."

"Yes," grunted Father, quieter again but refusing to be pacified. "Wandering commoners who didn't bother to return home from the previous day's markets, yes. There was nothing unlawful in what we did, nothing inappropriate. No declaration of warlike intentions, even though Moquihuixtli did get carried away with his speech. That man is not subtle enough and his lack of patience is appalling." A loud snort shook the afternoon air. "But to plant outright spies, sniffing around with no shame or disguise, little *pillis* of her own family? Oh, she'll pay for this. She and her entire *altepetl*, from the young hothead of their emperor to their unrestrained noble youths, untamed beasts every one of them."

Oh mighty Coatlicue! Tlemilli sucked in her breath, desperate to get away from where she was and fast. If she dared to move, she would have leaned against the supportive bark of a tree, her limbs jelly.

"That little beast Ahuitzotl! No wonder the boy carrying such a name turned out to be so obnoxious, so loathsome, a perfect member of this entire brood. But how this royal fowl Atotoztli keeps giving birth to son after son, like a commoner or a village peasant and not Tenochtitlan's noblewoman, the daughter of the previous Emperor. Disgusting!" The angry flow stopped momentarily, for a lack of air, Tlemilli suspected. The royal fowl Atotoztli was Tenochtitlan's current Emperor's mother, wasn't she? But who was this obnoxious Ahuitzotl?

"And his cronies," Father went on, apparently needing to talk, to vent his frustrations. Well, she didn't mind that as long as she was hidden and away from it all. And if he kept talking about spying boys, then he might tell what she wanted to hear, in case he knew more than she did. Her three days of stalking him might have paid off in the end. She held her breath. "Mere *pillis* that should be in school, not spying around, sticking their noses where they shouldn't." Another heavy pause ensued. "The first one knew more than anyone, the beaten commoner that he was. But for the outright betrayal!"

More direful cursing. So many colorful words. She tried to will away her trembling. She wasn't in danger, even if caught. He wouldn't hurt his own daughter. Or would he? He looked as though he might back then after the competition. And he certainly meant to execute Tlaco! She held her breath again, this time more scared than curious.

"Keep your ears open, and spread more people around the marketplace and the wharves."

"Oh yes, Honorable Adviser. I've already done that, but I'll double the amount of our men here and next to the causeway."

"In Tenochtitlan too. Send people there, to wander around the markets and wharves, even the plazas. Hear what they are saying, have them reporting on the locals' mood."

There was a brief pause.

"What about the tunnel?" asked the man quietly.

"Leave it as it is. The dirty commoner is the only one who knows about it. If only they remembered his looks! The useless pieces of rotten fish kept him for an entire day and now they can't even remember what he looked like. All beaten and dirty, they claimed. Well, mud and blood in moderate amounts don't cancel people's looks!" A longer pause ensued through which Tlemilli didn't dare even to blink. "Oh, but I know who might remember! Why didn't I think of it before?"

And then her heart was making wild leaps inside her chest, while her instincts told her what it was before her panicked mind did.

ABOUT THE AUTHOR

Zoe Saadia is the author of several novels on pre-Columbian Americas. From the architects of the Aztec Empire to the founders of the Iroquois Great League, from the towering pyramids of Tenochtitlan to the longhouses of the Great Lakes, her novels bring long-forgotten history, cultures and people to life, tracing pivotal events that brought about the greatness of North and Mesoamerica.

To learn more about Zoe Saadia and her work, visit
www.zoesaadia.com

Made in the USA
Lexington, KY
02 November 2019